WRONG PLACE

Michelle Davies has been writing professionally for twenty years as a journalist on magazines, including on the production desk at *Elle*, and as Features Editor of *Heat*. Her last staff position before going freelance was Editor-at-Large at *Grazia* magazine and she currently writes for a number of women's magazines and newspaper supplements. Michelle is also crime fiction reviewer for the *Sunday Express*'s Books section. She lives in London and juggles writing crime fiction with her freelance journalism and motherhood. *Wrong Place* is the second novel featuring DC Maggie Neville, following *Gone Astray*.

Also by Michelle Davies

Gone Astray

WRONG PLACE

Michelle Davies

PAN BOOKS

First published 2017 by Macmillan

This paperback edition first published 2017 by Pan Books
an imprint of Pan Macmillan
20 New Wharf Road, London N1 9RR
Associated companies throughout the world
www.panmacmillan.com

ISBN 978-1-4472-8422-2

1 3 5 7 9 8 6 4 2

A CIP catalogue record for this book is available from the British Library.

Typeset by Ellipsis, Glasgow
Printed and bound by CPI Group (UK) Ltd, Croydon, CR0 4YY

Visit **www.panmacmillan.com** to read more about all our books
and to buy them. You will also find features, author interviews and
news of any author events, and you can sign up for e-newsletters
so that you're always first to hear about our new releases.

To Mum and Dad, for everything

Prologue

21 August 1999

'Please stop, you're taking this too far. We can't just leave.'

As the rest of them ignore her again and traipse on ahead, she wonders if she's making sense. She knows her speech is slurred, the effect of a drinking session that began at three in the afternoon and lasted until just ten minutes ago, when the clock chimed midnight. The amount of alcohol she's consumed has numbed her lips and thickened her tongue and it's like she's trying to talk under water. She inhales deeply in a futile attempt to sober up and when she exhales all she can smell is cheap white wine on her breath.

'Niall, we have to go back,' she says, more clearly this time.

Niall does not react. He strides ahead, his back rigid and his pace brisk, leaving the rest of them stumbling in his wake, her trailing last. She calls to Ross and Kelvin to make them stop but neither does. It's as though Niall is pulling them along by invisible thread, like puppets.

'Why won't anyone bloody well listen to me? We need to go back and unlock the . . . Ouch!'

Her feet are bare and her right foot has landed on a thistle. She wants to stop, to bend down and rub away the sharp pain, but she is worried about being left behind. Staggering forward along the mossy path, braced for the next sting, she wishes she'd worn flat shoes instead of the platform sandals she's now forced to carry in her right hand, the purple suede ankle straps curled round her fingers like maypole ribbons. In her left hand she grasps a black satin clutch bag.

The moon is a sliver away from being full and patches of light are pushing through the branches bowing across the woodland path. The light expands and grows brighter as the canopy starts to thin and she realizes they are nearing the edge of the woods. Panic catches in her chest.

'Stop!' she screams.

But Niall's pace remains constant, his long, muscular legs propelling him forward. She forces herself into a run to catch up with him, barging past Ross and the others. She has to make Niall see sense. He is the orchestrator of this nightmare.

Almost level with him, she forcibly jabs the heels of her shoes into his back. He spins round in fury.

'We have to go back,' she yells in his face, even though part of her is scared of what he might do to her for shouting at him, because she's already seen how far he will go when provoked. Ross and Kelvin look apprehensive too, but they remain mute, happy for her to put herself in the firing line. For a second she hates them both.

'No we fucking don't,' Niall hisses, spittle flying off his tongue and landing on her chin. His face is twisted in anger and she can't believe she ever found him attractive. The sculpted cheekbones and thickly lashed brown eyes she had secretly lusted over earlier now make her stomach turn.

'Niall. Please. I want to go back.'

She's crying now, she can't help it. Unmoved, Niall grabs her hair at the crown and its coarse, mousse-enhanced volume affords him a generous handful. He yanks her along the path and she shrieks in pain, begging Kelvin and Ross to stop him, but they just trot behind like a pair of obedient dogs following their master.

'Get in the van,' Niall snarls as he finally lets go of her hair.

She sees they're back where they started, in the lay-by. Niall's is still the only vehicle parked there and he wrenches open the rear door and orders her to get in. Her mind reverses to the journey there: there had been nowhere to sit but on the floor and they had laughed hysterically every time the van went round a corner and they were sent flying into each other. It already seems a lifetime ago.

'No, I'm not leaving,' she says, shaking her head. 'Don't you care what you've done?'

Before he can answer, she feels the whisper of warm breath on the back of her neck and hears Ross's voice in her ear.

'Do as he says,' he mutters. 'Don't get yourself hurt.'

Ross had boasted earlier that he knew Niall better than anyone, and his warning is enough to make her clamber into the back of the van. She's wearing cut-off denim shorts and the metal floor is freezing against her bare legs as she sits down. Niall gestures for Ross and Kelvin to climb in beside her, then slams the door shut on them. The noise makes her flinch.

As Niall starts the engine, she tries to catch Ross's eye but he won't look at her.

3

'We've got to stop him—'

'Just shut the fuck up,' he whispers, casting a fearful glance towards the front of the van, where Niall is revving the engine. 'Give him a minute and he'll calm down. Then we'll go back.'

The speed at which the van pulls away sends her flying sideways and her right temple catches on the wheel arch. She tries to pull herself upright but they swing first to the left, then to the right, accelerating with every turn, tossing them around like buoys at sea.

'Slow down!' she screams, certain she'll throw up. Ross pitches across the van and lands heavily on her legs; he too yells at Niall to slow down but the response from the driver's seat is to go even faster.

She's crying uncontrollably now. She wants to go home. They should never have accepted Niall's invitation to meet for drinks, much less agreed to go for the drive with him once they were all tanked up. But he had been so persuasive and charming . . . right up until the point he snapped.

They hit a straight bit of road, giving Ross the chance to climb off her and help her sit up. There is no partition between the front and back so she reaches forward and grabs Niall's shoulder over the top of his seat, clawing at his black T-shirt with her fingernails.

'Stop the van!' she shouts hoarsely.

As he shrugs her hand off, Niall yanks the steering wheel to the right. The van veers across the road and blinding yellow light suddenly illuminates the windscreen. She falls backwards, dazzled. A second later the high-pitched squeal of tyres burning against tarmac fills the van, immediately followed by an almighty bang.

The impact is violent and crushing and the next thing she knows their vehicle is rolling over and over. Pain slams through her body as she bounces off the ceiling and off the sides and within seconds she loses track of which way is up. Her face crunches into metal and she screams in agony as she's blinded by blood pouring down her forehead. Somewhere nearby Kelvin is screaming too.

Then, just as suddenly, the rolling stops. She lands awkwardly and heavily, the bones in her lower legs splintering as easily as glass. She tries to cry out but shock has robbed her of speech. The pain is unlike anything she has ever experienced – her body feels like it's been ripped in two. She shakily wipes the blood from her eyes and tries to stay calm but it hurts so much to breathe and her vision is blurring around the edges. As the blackness claims her sight, she manages to find her voice one last time. It is small, pitiful, barely a whisper. It doesn't sound like her any more.

'We have to go back.'

1

November, present day

The carpet in the sitting room was a mishmash of brown, red, orange and purple swirls, a relic from a decade when taste was dubious at best. Years of footfall had worn it away in places and even though her ankle boots were shod in protective blue plastic and she was keeping to the metal plates of the common approach path laid down by forensics, Detective Constable Maggie Neville was still mindful to avoid the frayed white patches as she crossed the room.

The rustle of her temporary footwear alerted the two men already there to her arrival. One of them, Paul, was from the Crime Scene Investigation Unit and he was crouched on all fours, peering into the gap between the bottom of the high-legged sofa and the carpet. The other man, whose name Maggie didn't know, was from the Imaging Unit, the camera in his hands a giveaway. He was taking photographs of whatever it was Paul was pointing to. Both men looked up and nodded a greeting.

'Is that where she was found?' Maggie asked.

Paul's white coverall crackled as he shifted his sizeable bulk to standing. He pulled down the mask that covered the lower half of his face.

'Yep. There are no blood traces anywhere else in the room, so she fell where she was hit.'

'She's the first victim to be attacked from behind,' said Maggie. 'The others were approached head on and pushed to the floor.'

'Lucky for her she didn't see it coming.'

'Is there anything that does match the other break-ins?'

'It looks like they got in the same way,' Paul replied. 'There's a glass pane broken in the back door: presumably the girl knocked at the front again to distract the victim while the bloke smashed his way in the back. Did the little shits get much this time?'

'We don't know yet. The victim's obviously not in a position to talk and the granddaughter who found her went to hospital with her. We'll interview her as soon as we can to find out what's missing.'

'When you do, ask her about this.'

Paul reached beneath the sofa with his gloved hand and pulled out an empty bottle of Bombay Sapphire gin. The bright blue glass glinted in the light being cast from the fringed brown lampshade in the centre of the ceiling. The overhead illumination was necessary, despite it being three in the afternoon, because a dense hedge growing outside the front-room window blocked natural light from getting in.

'Judging by the blood on it I'd say it's what was used to knock her granny out,' said Paul, holding the bottle up so Maggie could inspect the dark stain smeared on the base.

'Why didn't the glass break?'

'If it was full it might've done, as liquid puts pressure on glass at the point of impact,' Paul explained. 'But as there's no trace of gin on the carpet I think we can safely assume it was empty. We'll test it for prints and DNA – if they're stupid enough, they might've drunk straight from the bottle.'

'What makes you so sure they brought it with them when they broke in? It could be the victim's,' said Maggie.

'I've had a scout around in here and in the kitchen and dining room and I haven't found any other booze, not even a bottle of cooking sherry,' said Paul. 'If the victim didn't keep any alcohol in the house, isn't it less likely to be hers?'

'I guess. How soon until we get the lab results back?'

Paul shrugged. 'How long's a piece of string?'

His nonchalance riled Maggie. She wished his boss Mal Matheson, the Chief Crime Scene Examiner for their force, was there instead, but he'd been called out to a more serious case in the north of Buckinghamshire. Matheson always grasped the need for urgency and Maggie knew he would've expedited the bottle for testing. This was the fifth distraction burglary in Mansell in three months and the most violent yet.

'Is DS Renshaw out there?' said Paul as he carefully placed the gin bottle in an evidence bag. 'I should show her this.'

'She's taking a statement from the neighbour. I'll see if she's finished.'

Maggie picked her way back across the carpet then stepped into the narrow hallway. It was dingy and cold – the hedge outside the front also buffered daylight coming through the two glass panels set in the front door. The asymmetric rows of framed photographs, decorative plates and brass hangings jostling for space on the walls again added to the sense of being closed in.

Having to squint to see didn't help the headache she was nursing. She wasn't in the habit of coming to work with a hangover but the celebration last night that had precipitated it was worth the pain, as it had marked the end of the trial involving one of her previous cases, the abduction of a teenager called Rosie Kinnock. Easing her way down the hall towards the kitchen, she pondered Paul's assessment that today's attack was by the same young couple believed to have already robbed four elderly women in their homes in Mansell. Based on the accounts provided by those victims, the couple were in their late teens/early twenties and on each occasion had been dressed head to toe in black. The female, said to be well-spoken, used the same sob story each time about being mugged for her mobile phone and would ask to use the victim's landline. Meanwhile, her partner broke in through the rear of the house. The descriptions became vague after that, as none of the victims had got a good look at the pair's faces. The girl's would be partly covered in what the police suspected was fake blood, presumably to make the mugging story seem more convincing, and the male accomplice always wore a baseball hat pulled down low so his face was half hidden.

The previous victims were all in their eighties and lived alone on quiet streets. Another commonality was the appearance of their homes: the front doors of all were shielded by dense bushes, gifting the 'Con Couple' – as the local paper was now calling them – privacy in which to carry out the distraction break-ins. The raids took place in the daytime, before schools finished for the day, when fewer residents were around to take any notice. Maggie and her colleagues at Mansell Force CID were certain the girl wasn't applying the fake blood to her face until she was partially hidden on each victim's doorstep, as there had been no witness sightings of an injured young woman beforehand.

Today's victim was called Sadie Cardle. At seventy-one she had the distinction of being the youngest victim so far and Maggie wondered if her relative youth meant her attackers had overpowered her by more drastic means because she'd put up a fight. She'd sustained a severe blow to the back of the head and the paramedics who took her to hospital were concerned she might not survive the journey. The last word they'd received was that she was hanging in there – just.

2

Sadie Cardle's home was on Frobisher Road, in the hilliest part of Mansell. As towns went there was little to distinguish Mansell from countless others in the south of England: it was an aesthetically mundane mix of former council estates and tightly packed new-builds with a struggling high street and far more supermarkets than were necessary for a population of 110,000. Although it was in a county renowned for its wealth – Buckinghamshire was also famed for being home to Pinewood Film Studios as well as the prime minister's country residence, Chequers – there were pockets of deprivation spread across Mansell, niche areas notorious for the crimes and anti-social behaviour played out there. Frobisher Road was in one such pocket on the north side of the town.

To reach it, visitors had to drive through an industrial estate full of empty units, the businesses that once filled them either departed for a better location or consigned to the scrapheap of failure. There wasn't much in the way of manufacturing to be found in Mansell these days: the furniture industry for which the town was once acclaimed was now a rose-tinted reminiscence. The furniture giants had long moved out and their factories razed to make way for more estates; now the town was mostly lauded for its proximity to London – thirty miles as the crow flew – and those priced out of the capital found its abundance of housing a handily commutable alternative.

The twenty-four homes that made up Frobisher Road were once council-owned but tenants had been encouraged to buy them decades earlier under the Thatcher government's right-to-buy scheme. The police had already established that Sadie was one of only two householders in the street still renting, her landlord no longer the council but a housing association named Quadrant Homes.

In the kitchen Maggie found Detective Sergeant Anna Renshaw talking to Sadie's neighbour, Audrey Allen. Even though Mrs Allen had come only the short distance from next door, the biting November chill warranted the thick navy anorak that swaddled her down to her knees. As she spoke, she used a scrunched-up tissue to dab away the tears pooling in the deep creases beneath her eyes.

'Sadie would never let in anyone she didn't know,' Mrs Allen was telling Renshaw, who was taking notes. 'She's very careful about that kind of thing.'

Clocking Maggie in the doorway, Renshaw shot her a stern look and mouthed, 'Wait outside.'

Maggie's face mottled as she backtracked into the hallway. She wasn't adapting well to becoming Renshaw's subordinate since her colleague's promotion to DS two months ago. Perhaps if Maggie actually liked her she wouldn't mind, but they'd never gelled in the three years they'd worked together and that barely concealed enmity had intensified since Renshaw had been put in charge of the team investigating the burglaries. She took every opportunity to make sure Maggie knew that she was the boss.

Maggie distracted herself by studying the photographs on the walls. A visual timeline of family life, they included a monochrome wedding-day portrait of a couple wearing of-an-era attire that made her presume they were Sadie and her late husband. There was also a series of school photographs of a dark-haired girl and another one of the same child aged about nine or ten, perched on the arm of a chair next to the man from the wedding photograph, the lights of the Christmas tree behind them flaring like fireflies in the camera's flash.

Her gaze was then drawn to a small framed photograph of a young woman with long brunette hair sitting on a beach in a vest and shorts, hand raised to shield her eyes against the sun. A quick check confirmed it was the only image of her anywhere on the walls, whoever she was.

'Neville, in here.'

Renshaw beckoned her into the kitchen. Still weeping, Audrey Allen flashed Maggie a sad smile as she squeezed past on her way out.

'Don't ever interrupt me when I'm taking a statement,' said Renshaw coldly, when Audrey was out of earshot.

'I didn't say a word,' Maggie protested.

'You didn't have to. The way you barged in was enough.'

Renshaw was standing in the middle of the tiny kitchen with her arms crossed. She was dressed in one of the new black trouser suits she'd been favouring since her promotion, her long auburn hair pulled tightly off her scrubbed face and secured in a low ponytail. That Renshaw felt compelled to underplay her femininity now she was elevated a rank baffled Maggie, who did not consider herself particularly girlish but liked to think she wouldn't suppress the part of her that enjoyed wearing make-up just to be taken seriously in her job.

'You made me lose my thread,' said Renshaw. 'Now, what did you want?'

Maggie fought to keep her voice steady. Anger wasn't an emotion she succumbed to that often but now it simmered constantly in the pit of her stomach, stoked by Renshaw's affronts. One of these days the new DS would poke too hard.

'Paul's found something he wants you to see,' she said.

'Fine. In the meantime I want you to go to the hospital and talk to the granddaughter. Uniform took an initial statement but it needs doing properly. Call me when you're done. Oh, and if the victim dies I've decided you can be the Family Liaison.'

That decision wasn't Renshaw's to make, as they both well knew. Maggie's deployment would be up to DI Tony Gant, the Family Liaison Coordinator for their force – her other boss.

For the past four years Maggie had specialized as a Family Liaison Officer for Major Crime investigations in addition to her detective constable duties with Force CID. DI Gant worked with the Senior Investigating Officer (SIO) at the onset of each case to ensure he dispatched the most suitable officer and had to clear each FLO's deployment with their line manager, as it often meant them being away from their day job for weeks at a time. In Maggie's case that would be the Detective Chief Inspector at Mansell Force CID, *not* Renshaw.

'We should be hoping she doesn't die,' said Maggie pointedly.

'Of course,' said Renshaw.

She didn't sound like she meant it. But then her focus was not dealing with the victim's family but running a potential murder investigation, a coup for any new DS. Renshaw had a limited view of how a family's grief manifested, whereas Maggie knew from being up close how raw, visceral and bewildering it could be. Stepping into that environment was not easy.

But although being a FLO was at times harrowing and wearing, Maggie loved the role. She knew how crucial it was for the victims' relatives to feel like they had someone from the police acting in their interests during the investigation. At the same time she collated and fed back information to the SIO about the victim – and about the relatives themselves if she suspected the guilty party was among them.

'Right, you need to get going while I talk to Paul,' said Renshaw.

As Maggie nodded, she glanced at the back door. The top half was made up of six equally spaced glass panels but the one in the lower right-hand corner, nearest to the handle, was broken. The key was still in the lock, covered in fingerprint powder from Paul's earlier examination.

'Did the neighbour hear the glass being smashed?' she asked.

'I'll brief everyone back at the station later,' said Renshaw haughtily.

Maggie stalked out of the kitchen before she said something regrettable. Her question about the broken glass was perfectly reasonable, unlike Renshaw's reaction to it. The new DS's habit of sharing only the minimum of information outside of the briefing room frustrated the hell out of Maggie and she imagined Renshaw had been the kind of pupil at school who shielded her work with her arm so the kid sitting next to her couldn't copy it.

Maggie was almost at the front door when something caught her eye and she stopped. There were more framed photographs on the wall at the foot of the stairs but there was a gap in the middle where one was missing, the wallpaper bordering the empty space noticeably darker.

She snapped an image of the wall on her iPhone for reference then stuck her head round the sitting-room door.

'Paul, I think a frame's been taken off the wall out here. Can you have a look?'

'Just the one?' he said as he followed her into the hallway carrying a small jar of fingerprint powder and a brush.

'Yes. Look, it's just over here.'

'Perhaps Mrs Cardle removed it to clean it,' said Renshaw, who'd joined them in the hallway. She clearly didn't want to acknowledge Maggie might have found something of significance. 'You could ask her granddaughter, Della, if she knows where it is when you *finally* get to the hospital,' she added, her voice dripping with sarcasm.

Maggie didn't rise to the bait and kept her expression neutral as Paul, seemingly oblivious to the tension, painstakingly dusted the inky black powder onto the wallpaper until a partial handprint emerged. He stood for a moment, head cocked to the side as he contemplated the finding.

'I bet it's the victim's,' said Renshaw airily.

'Not based on what I've found so far. This,' said Paul, pointing at the wall, 'is a bit smaller. I wouldn't assume it's hers if I were you.'

Renshaw looked so furious that Maggie had to turn away so she couldn't see her smile.

3

Della Cardle had never been one to stand out in a crowd, but right now she felt invisible in the same way a homeless person begging for the price of a cup of tea must feel, looking up at the sea of faces dashing past and praying just one kind soul would slow down long enough to catch their eye. Ten minutes she had been waiting outside the room where her nan was being treated but not one of the nurses or doctors who'd bustled past her had stopped to ask if she was okay and needed help.

She wished her boyfriend, Alex, was with her. He'd have made sure someone stopped, would've found out the name of the consultant treating Sadie and he'd have got an update on her condition. But when she'd rung to tell him what had happened, his boss said he couldn't leave work. Not for someone else's grandmother.

A young nurse with hair dyed the colour of a ripe plum bowled past her into Sadie's room, eyes fixed straight ahead and mind clearly focused on whatever task she needed to execute next. Della raised her hand to get her attention but dropped it just as swiftly as the nurse shut the door firmly behind her.

Della had been timid for as long as she could remember. While other children excelled at sport or topped the class in maths, shyness had been her chief attainment. Isolating her in the playground back then, now as an adult it thwarted her from applying for jobs she'd be good at given half the chance and stopped her pursuing friendships with people she had enjoyed meeting. The only reason she was with Alex was because he wouldn't take no for an answer. She'd initially rebuffed his request for her phone number the night they met, in a pub, baffled as to why someone as confident as him would be interested in someone like her. Ten months down the line, although happy and in love, she still wasn't sure what he saw in her.

You're being silly, she scolded herself as another nurse, this one older and with blonde hair tied back in a ponytail, scurried past. *Just stop someone and ask. You need to know how Nan is.*

As the same nurse made her way back, a quaking Della blocked her path.

'Excuse me, can you help me?' she said.

The nurse's expression immediately softened. 'Are you okay?'

Della's eyes brimmed with tears as she shook her head.

'My nan's in that room and I don't know how she is. Her name is Sadie Cardle. I didn't think I could just go in . . .'

'Let me see what I can find out,' said the nurse, touching Della lightly on the arm. The gesture, though fleeting and infinitesimal through the sleeve of her thick Puffa jacket, made Della want to weep with gratitude.

The nurse returned in less than a minute.

'Your grandmother is about to be transferred upstairs to HDU. The consultant up there will be able tell you more.'

'What's HDU?'

'It's the High Dependency Unit.'

That didn't sound good.

'Will you come with me?' said Della anxiously. 'I don't know who the consultant is.'

The nurse touched her arm again. 'I'm afraid I'm needed down here,' she said. 'But the staff up there are lovely and they'll look after you.'

Overcome, Della began to sob. She scrabbled in her pocket for something she could use to wipe her eyes with but all she found was a torn receipt. Embarrassed, she stuffed it back in.

'Your nan is in good hands,' said the nurse kindly.

The door to the treatment room flew open and suddenly Sadie was in front of her, laid out on a trolley, a blanket tucked firmly around her stout body and tubes snaking out of her exposed arms. Her face was half covered by a clear, plastic mask.

'Oh, Nan,' Della whispered, brushing the veins on the back of Sadie's hand with her fingertips. Her skin was clammy but reassuringly warm.

'We need to get her upstairs,' said the grim-faced porter at the head of the gurney. 'Now.'

With him was the young nurse with the plum-coloured hair. She flashed Della a dimpled smile.

'Hi, I'm Zoe. Do you want to come with us?'

Della did as she was told, bringing up the rear of the sad little procession as it reached the lifts. Inside, as they headed up to the fourth floor, she caught Zoe's eye.

'Do you think she'll be okay?' Della asked. 'She's not going to die, is she?'

'The consultant on HDU will talk to you about your nan's prognosis.'

Zoe spoke in an accent that Della recognized as being the local dialect for their part of Buckinghamshire, a lilting hark back to the area's farming origins. It wasn't commonly heard any more, not since Mansell's population had swelled with out-of-towners blending Estuary English with immigrant patois from far-flung continents. But it was how Sadie spoke and in a panic Della wondered if she'd ever hear her nan's voice again.

'Is she going to die?' she repeated.

'Let's get her upstairs and then you can talk to the doctors there.'

'Of course, I'm sorry,' said Della humbly. The last thing she wanted to be was annoying.

'Don't be. I'd be asking the same in your shoes. It's understandable.'

Della looked down at her grandmother's inert form and her insides clenched with fear. Zoe was wrong: there was nothing at all understandable about this. Sadie shouldn't be here, not looking like this. Her grey curls, set every fortnight in her kitchen at Frobisher Road by a mobile hairdresser called Jackie, were hidden from view, swaddled in a tightly wound bandage. Della stared down at her nan's slackened face and willed her to wake up. Give me a sign, Nan, she prayed, anything to let me know you're going to be okay. Tell me you're not going to leave me on my own.

Sadie was Della's maternal grandmother and her sole guardian. She and her late husband Eric had raised Della from the age of three; Della had no relationship with her mum and her knowledge of her dad was limited to just his first name. Della was an only child too, as her mother had been, and any extended family on the Cardle side had been snuffed out decades previously: Sadie's brother was killed during the Korean war of 1950 and Eric's sister passed away in her twenties before she too could start a family of her own. It was just the three of them, alone.

Della was eleven when Eric died and the loss of the only father figure she'd known still affected her keenly. The prospect of losing Sadie as well was more than she could bear and she bit down hard on her bottom lip to stop the wail that was building inside her from escaping.

The lift shuddered to a halt and the doors slowly slid open. Della waited for the porter to push her grandmother out then followed Zoe. Two nurses were waiting for them, poised to spirit Sadie into HDU.

'They need to get her settled, so it's best you wait in the relatives' room for now,' Zoe said as they watched Sadie disappear from view with her new carers. 'Is there anyone else we can call for you?'

Della quickly shook her head.

'Are you sure? I don't mind giving them a ring.'

'Really, it's fine.'

'What about your parents? Is your nan on your mum's side or your dad's?'

'I don't have any parents,' said Della quietly.

Zoe appeared confused for a moment then, with a fleeting look of contrition, gathered herself. 'Well, let me show you where to wait then,' she said. 'It's along here.'

She steered Della into a room furnished with two sofas

covered in a murky green fabric and the means to make tea and coffee laid out on a table in the corner. The room already had occupants: a middle-aged woman and two teen-aged boys talking quietly amongst themselves on the sofa farthest from the door. They had an ease about them that suggested they were regular visitors and made Della wonder about the plight of the patient they'd come to see.

'I'd best get back downstairs,' said Zoe.

Della was overcome with anxiety. She'd only met Zoe five minutes previously and already she felt like someone she couldn't manage without.

'But who do I speak to now? What do I do?'

Before Zoe could answer, the woman, who'd been eyeing them from the sofa, got up and came across the room.

'Don't worry, everyone feels a bit lost at first,' she said. 'I know I did.'

She smiled companionably at Della, but she had an air of sadness about her.

'Would you like a cup of tea? Liam will make it, won't you, Liam?' she said, nodding to the two teenagers on the sofa, who Della presumed were her sons. The one who looked to be the eldest unwound his lanky frame and lolloped over to the table bearing cups and saucers and two huge urns.

'It looks like I'm leaving you in good hands,' said Zoe with a smile, and she shot back into the hallway.

'There's a toilet through there if you need it,' said the woman, pointing to a door on the other side of the room. 'I'm Trish, and this is Liam and Leo. Their dad, Tony, my husband, is just down the corridor.'

Della wasn't sure how to respond to that but Trish was the chatty type and ploughed on regardless.

'He was in an accident at work. He's a warehouse manager at the Falkland Depot and he got hit on the head when a pallet fell on him. The silly bugger wasn't wearing his hard hat.' Trish sounded like she was trying to be matter-of-fact but her voice caught as she explained that while her husband was badly injured, he was conscious. 'This is our seventeenth day here,' she said with a grimace. 'I think we're here for the long haul.'

Della was still at a loss for what to say. It was difficult to find the words to react to someone else's bad news when her mind was filled with her own.

'At least he's awake, even if he can't remember my name,' said Trish resignedly. 'Right, I won't ask you why you're here; there's plenty of time for that later. You drink your tea and we'll leave you in peace for a bit. I could do with stretching my legs.'

'You don't have to go on my account.'

Trish shook her head knowingly. 'The day Tony was brought in, another family was already in here, "old timers" like we are now. They left us to it as well because they knew the last thing you want or need is a bunch of strangers fussing around you when you're still in shock. So you have a bit of time to yourself and have a think about what you want to ask the doctors. It's worth writing down the questions so you don't forget when they blind you with jargon.' Trish beckoned to her sons. 'Right, come on boys, let's leave – sorry, what's your name, love?'

'Della.'

'Right, let's leave Della alone.'

The room felt huge once they'd gone. Della thought about ringing Alex again but decided it wasn't fair to badger him and he would get there as soon as he could. He was busy preparing for a presentation later in the week and had been stressing about it. She hadn't seen him all weekend because he said he'd had to work.

Alex was the sales manager for an independent car dealership in Mansell. Four years older than Della, who was a month from turning twenty-one, he was ambitious and determined and had his sights set on running the company one day. Della wasn't anywhere near as motivated and had been happy ticking along as a backroom administrator at a hotel on the fringes of town until Alex decided she should aim her sights higher. Now, under his direction, she was studying for a degree in event management in her spare time through the Open University, even though the thought of hosting events made her sick with nerves. It was bad enough when one of the receptionists was off and she had to fill in on the front desk.

The cup of tea Liam made was on the table but Della left it where it was. She settled herself on the other sofa but kept her coat on because she couldn't stop shivering as the shock of the past few hours took hold. In her mind's eye all she could see was her nan sprawled out on the carpet in a halo of blood. What if it had been any day other than Tuesday? It was the only lunchtime Della popped round to see Sadie during the week, to drop off her favourite magazine, *My Weekly*. If it had been any other day – how long would she have lain there before someone found her?

Della had been expecting to find her watching *Loose Women* like she always did. At first she hadn't noticed the blood, only Sadie's slippered feet poking out from behind the coffee table. Her immediate thought was a heart attack, the same thing that had killed her grandfather, Eric. He'd got up from a chair to fetch something one Sunday afternoon then fell backwards seconds later, already dead. There wasn't even time for him to clutch his chest the way heart-attack victims supposedly do.

It was only as she drew closer that Della had seen the blood pooling around Sadie's head. But even then she still believed it to be an accident – her grandmother had fallen and somehow struck her head. To be told by the police that the wound appeared to have been inflicted deliberately was more than Della could comprehend. Who would do that to her? Sadie was the gentlest, kindest person she knew, adored by everyone who came into contact with her. She was diminutive in stature, barely five feet two tall, but she had the presence of a giant, filling every room she walked into with her unending cheerfulness. 'No point worrying about it,' was the motto Sadie lived by. Only Della knew that to scratch below the surface would reveal a mother who never stopped wondering about the adult daughter who upped and left one day, leaving her three-year-old child behind.

Della frowned as an image of Helen intruded on her thoughts. She had long ago stopped thinking of Helen as her mum and she wasn't about to start now – Helen lost that right when she abandoned her into the care of Sadie and Eric like an unwanted puppy. To push her from her mind, Della began reciting the Lord's Prayer over and over to herself – the only prayer she knew – until at last the door opened and another nurse appeared, this one male. His hair was almost entirely grey but he had the relatively youthful face of someone still in his thirties.

'Are you Sadie Cardle's next of kin?' he asked.

Della's throat went dry as she stood up.

'Yes,' she rasped. 'I'm her granddaughter. How is she?'

'You'd better come with me.'

4

Despite the seriousness of its function, Maggie found HDU to be a tranquil place to visit. The majority of its patients were bed-bound and unconscious, meaning a more peaceful environment prevailed compared to the general wards.

Today was different though. Peering through the glass-panelled double doors at the entrance to the department, Maggie watched as two nurses in light blue pinstripe tunics and navy trousers sprinted down the corridor in the direction away from her. Their sense of urgency was palpable even from behind the glass and moments later a doctor with unruly brown hair, shirtsleeves rolled up and a stethoscope slung round his neck, sprang from a side room and raced after them.

Maggie didn't know the door security code required to gain access to the ward and was reluctant to ring the bell next to the keypad to summon assistance when an emergency was clearly taking place inside. But as she hovered outside the doors a male nurse on the ward side spotted her and opened them. His expression was set like stone and when Maggie showed him her warrant card and told him why she was there he blanched.

'Mrs Cardle just went into respiratory arrest. My colleagues are working on her now.'

'Is her granddaughter with her?'

'Not right now, but she was when it started. I've taken her back to the relatives' room.'

'Can I check on her?' asked Maggie.

'She's too upset to be questioned right now,' he retorted.

Maggie kept her tone level. 'If her grandmother dies as the result of her injury, this becomes a murder inquiry. So while I take on board your concerns, I do need to speak to her. I promise I'll go easy on her though.'

The nurse pursed his lips and Maggie could see he was trying to weigh up whether she was the type of person who kept her word. She'd been told she looked trustworthy enough; her face was soft and round – she would forever lament her lack of cheekbones – and she had unusual blue-green eyes that combined to make her seem approachable and friendly. She flashed the nurse a smile for reassurance and it seemed to do the trick.

'Okay, I'll show you where she is but make sure you do take it gently,' he said sternly. 'I don't want you causing an upset on the unit. We're got enough on our plate today, what with that stabbing victim on her way in too.'

'There's been a stabbing in Mansell?' Maggie exclaimed, surprised none of her CID colleagues had let her know. Bad news usually travelled fast.

'You'll never guess what happened,' said the nurse, his voice dropping to a hush and his face taking on the look of someone who enjoyed imparting gossip. 'Attempted murder-suicide. Husband stabbed his wife then took an overdose but by some miracle they've both survived. It happened in

Trenton this morning. The wife is being brought down here to HDU while the husband stays up there under police guard. It's nothing for you and your lot to worry about though,' he said, misinterpreting the look on Maggie's face. 'From what I've been told the police in Trenton are dealing with it.'

That wasn't what concerned her. Trenton was only half an hour's drive away from Mansell, towards the north of Buckinghamshire, and Maggie knew the town well. It had a quaintly rural charm that Mansell lacked, emphasized by its pedestrianized town square and the imposing twelfth-century church flanking it, which was often used as a location by film and TV production companies.

Trenton was also where Detective Chief Inspector Will Umpire lived.

Umpire was the SIO on two of the last three cases Maggie had been assigned as Family Liaison and while their roles at work were easy to define, outside of it their relationship was not so easily pigeonholed. When she was injured making an arrest during the Rosie Kinnock abduction – six months previously – and put on enforced sick leave for a fortnight, Umpire had visited her at home to see how she was. Once she was back at work he then suggested they meet for a drink one evening – ostensibly to discuss the court case that would follow – so a few times they'd met in a pub halfway between Mansell and Trenton. Then, three months ago, dinner had been mooted for the first time and the two of them travelled into London to eat at a restaurant Umpire had been raving about. Further dinners followed, but still very much on a platonic footing; mostly they talked about work and the forthcoming trial.

Maggie liked having Umpire as a sounding board and had initially refused to consider there could be anything else between them other than friendship. He was a senior officer, after all, and he was also in the final stages of his divorce: the welfare of his two children, a boy of nine and girl of eleven, was his overriding concern, not a new relationship. Maggie also had a self-imposed rule never to fall for someone already in a relationship and in her mind Umpire was technically still married. The rule stemmed back to when she was eighteen and had fallen in love with a man who was engaged to another woman; although the affair had remained a secret, the ramifications of it could still be felt.

Yet the more they socialized, the more attracted she was to him and at their last dinner two weeks ago she'd suspected the feeling was mutual: there was a flirty edge to their conversation that hadn't been there before and the air had crackled with possibility. Maggie was certain that if she'd made a move Umpire would have happily reciprocated, so when he let slip that his decree absolute was only weeks from being signed she had started to tell herself he was as good as single anyway.

Until she blew it.

5

The nurse said he would update Maggie on Sadie's condition when he could.

'The granddaughter's in there,' he added, coming to a halt and gesturing towards a door.

Maggie thanked him and rapped softly on the pale wood. She heard a faint 'Hello?' from the other side and let herself in.

A young woman was sat hunched over on one of the sofas. Her face was bright red, possibly because she was crying, but just as likely because she was sweltering in the oversized black Puffa jacket she had on. It looked as though it was made for Arctic conditions, with a huge, stiff collar that sat up past her ears like an Elizabethan ruff. Although the coat's inflated folds swamped her, Maggie could see she was petite.

'Are you Della Cardle?' she asked.

The woman nodded nervously, tucking her hair behind her ears. Dark brown, in no discernible style, it had the same fluffy, flyaway texture as candyfloss.

'Yes, I'm Della,' she replied in a voice so small and faint it was as though the volume on it had been turned down to almost nothing.

Maggie introduced herself and explained she was part of the CID team investigating the attack on Sadie.

'I know this is a difficult time but I have a few questions I need to ask you,' she said. 'It would help us if you could answer them now.'

'Do you know how my nan is? I was sat there and the machine started beeping and she just, just . . . The noise she made—' Della faltered and bit down hard on her bottom lip as her eyes shone with unshed tears.

'The doctors are still with her,' said Maggie. 'Mind if I sit down?'

Della shook her head and shuffled across on the sofa to make room, even though her tiny frame barely took up any space as it was.

'What if she dies?' she cried. 'What will I do?'

Maggie decided to employ the same approach to questioning she used in Family Liaison, even though she wasn't acting in that capacity – at least not yet: go in gently.

'I know you're not in the right frame of mind to answer lots of questions right now, but I do need to ask you a couple of things about your nan that would help move our investigation along. Are you okay with that?' she said.

Della puffed out her next breath and the exhalation seemed to calm her down. Her face was as bird-like as the rest of her: she had the sharp, angular chin of someone who carried little or no excess body fat and the hands and wrists poking out of the thick sleeves of her coat were similarly waifish. Although close up she looked to be in her twenties, at a distance she would easily pass for a teenager still.

'What do you want to ask me?'

'You don't live with your grandmother, do you?' said Maggie lightly.

'No, I moved out around a year ago, to a flat about five minutes away. There was no row or anything that made me leave,' Della added hastily. 'I just wanted my own space. I pop in to check on Nan all the time.'

'I understand you don't have any other family we can call for you?'

'It's just been Nan and me since my granddad died. They raised me.'

'Your parents aren't in contact at all?'

Della couldn't find the words to answer and her eyes filled with fresh tears as she gave a brief shake of the head. Realizing there was a story to be learned, Maggie mentally filed away the question to mention again later.

'I'm sorry, Della; I didn't mean to upset you. It just helps us if we know a bit more about your nan – what she's like, who her friends are, any other relatives. We need to draw up a list of witnesses to talk to, to find out if anyone knows anything.'

'But aren't the people who attacked her the same ones who broke into those other old people's houses?' asked Della, looking confused. 'I read about them in the *Echo*. Why would you think it was someone else?'

'While the crimes do appear similar, we have a duty to consider other possibilities too,' said Maggie. 'Can you think of anyone else who might have had reason to confront your nan like that?'

Della recoiled and as she did the sleeves of her Puffa jacket rubbed against her sides, making a scraping sound that set Maggie's teeth on edge.

'Why would anyone she knows want to hurt her?' said Della.

'There could be lots of reasons.'

'No, it can't have been someone she knew. Everyone loves Nan and I've never known her to fall out with anyone about anything—' Della let out a long, tremulous sigh and rubbed her temples with her slim fingers, averting her gaze.

Maggie waited for her to continue but Della would not look up. It was time to break her promise about not badgering her for answers.

'Are you holding something back, Della? If there's something or someone we need to know about, you must tell us.'

'There's nothing to tell,' Della insisted.

'Are you sure?'

'I promise you I would say if there was.'

For the first time in their conversation, Della's voice reached a normal pitch and Maggie was forced to change tack.

'I know you were probably too upset because you'd just found your grandmother, but I don't suppose you happened to notice if anything obvious was missing from the house?'

Della thought for a moment. 'Her rings. I noticed they were gone.'

'From her jewellery box?'

'No, her wedding band and engagement ring were gone from her finger. She never takes them off, not even to have a bath.' Della began to cry again. 'She will be so upset when she finds out they've been taken. See, that's why it can't be anyone she knows – who would be so cruel?'

Maggie frowned. In the previous raids the 'Con Couple'

had stolen cash from the victims' purses and taken easily transportable valuables from around the house but nothing from their persons. Had their greed escalated along with their thirst for violence?

'Do you have a picture of your nan wearing her rings? We could circulate the image in case they turn up in one of the local pawn shops.'

'I can find one for you. I'm sure there will be one in Nan's photo albums.'

Maggie made a note to have the photograph collected.

'Actually, talking of pictures, I noticed one was missing when I was at the house earlier.' Maggie pulled out her phone and found the image she'd taken. 'Here, can you see the gap on the wall?'

Della let out a short gasp as she took Maggie's phone and studied the image.

'That's the only one that's missing?' she said, her voice back to a whisper.

'It looks that way. Can you remember what the frame's like? If it's worth a bit, that may be why they took it.'

Della seemed paralysed for a moment as she gripped Maggie's phone. 'I . . . I can't remember.'

'Who's in the photograph?'

'Um . . . I'm not sure. Nan has so many.'

Della threw the phone back at Maggie as if it was scalding hot.

'Are you sure?'

'Stop asking me, I don't know!' Della flared up angrily.

The sudden spark of aggression surprised Maggie.

'Well, if you do remember, let me know. If we have a

description of the frame, we might be able to track it down if they try to sell it on.'

'It's a silly old photograph, it doesn't matter,' Della snapped. 'We don't need it back.'

'If you don't remember it, how can you be so sure you don't want it returned?'

6

Della tried to keep her breathing normal but she could feel her lungs constricting as her body spiralled into panic mode. It took every ounce of self-control not to start gulping in mouthfuls of air and when she swallowed it felt like her throat had been sandpapered.

'I'm sorry, I didn't mean to snap,' she managed to say. 'It's just that with Nan in such a bad way, it seems silly to be worrying about a missing picture.'

The detective nodded but didn't seem convinced.

'I am sorry,' Della repeated. 'I can't think straight until I know she's going to be okay.'

'Of course,' said Maggie, tucking her notebook into her handbag. 'I'm sorry if I upset you.'

'You really didn't,' said Della, mortified she might have annoyed the officer. 'Let me have a proper think about it. Maybe I'll remember later.'

She didn't need time to remember though. In a heartbeat she could describe every inch of the picture – she simply didn't want to have to explain to the police why nothing would make her happier than to never have to clap eyes on it again.

The photograph was of her and Helen, taken in the post-natal ward at Mansell General Hospital on the day Della was born. To anyone else it was a touching picture of a mum and her newborn, but when Della looked at it all she saw was Helen's dispirited emotional state reflected in her expression and her body language. Dead eyes, downturned mouth, arms stiff and unyielding as she awkwardly cradled her tiny daughter's sleeping form. Della felt a stab of hurt every time she looked at it.

Helen had never wanted her, a fact Della discovered around her ninth birthday. Until then she'd grown up believing her grandparents' explanation that Helen had been forced to leave her in their care because she was unwell. There was never any elaboration on what kind of illness would cause a woman to have no contact with her child for almost six years, but the way Sadie said 'unwell' in a pained, hushed voice as she pointed to her temple convinced Della of its seriousness.

It was Eric who finally told her the truth, after tiring of her incessantly questioning why Helen wasn't any better after years of supposed treatment. Surely she wouldn't mind a visit wherever she was, Della would ask him over and over. Patience stretched to breaking point, Eric decided he could no longer acquiesce with his wife's view that Della should be protected from knowing what had really happened. So he sat his granddaughter down and told her, while outside the rain pelted so hard against the window his voice was almost drowned out.

Mindfully using words he hoped a nine-year-old would understand and not be too upset by, Eric had revealed that Helen's pregnancy was unplanned. She was eighteen and felt far too young to be a mum – she wanted to go to college and have a career, make something of herself. As Della grew up, she came to understand what this actually meant, what her mother would have wanted to do. But she also knew that, due to her grandmother's Christian beliefs, Sadie would have been strongly opposed to an abortion. Helen's baby deserved to be born and would be.

Sadie was even willing to overlook the fact the baby was the result of a one-night stand between Helen and a lad she didn't know. In fact his name was Andy and he came from somewhere in the north of England; Eric told Della that Helen had met him in a pub in Mansell one weekend when he was visiting friends but he'd left town without giving her his surname, let alone an address or phone number, and had consequently continued his life unaware he'd fathered a child.

Eric also revealed that Helen had tried her best to be a good mum but it was hard when all her friends were out clubbing every night and she was stuck indoors with a baby. By the time Della was three and a half, Helen was rarely home, disappearing for days on end with no word of her whereabouts. As the rows between Helen and her parents over her neglect of Della worsened, it was almost a relief when, after a week of particularly vicious arguments and shouting, she left again. At first they supposed she'd just gone off with her friends for a few days like she had before, and would turn up when she was ready. But when four weeks passed with no word at all, they contacted the police and a missing person's investigation began. The police interviewed everyone from Helen's best friend, Gillian, to the man she bought milk from at the corner shop, and concluded she'd disappeared of her own volition – she had threatened to so many times, after all – and the case was swiftly closed.

The truth had overwhelmed Della. So many lies had been told, so much deceit spun, that it was hard for her to make sense of it. But she understood, even that young, the impact Sadie's intervention had had. Was it any wonder Helen didn't want to stick around to see her grow up? She must've hated Della for ruining her life.

As Della approached her teens, a sense of abandonment attached to her psyche like her shadow to her feet. Even though Sadie and Eric loved her without question, it wasn't the same. She'd watch her friends being embraced by their mums and would feel physically sick with longing. Once, when she was twelve, she'd gone to a friend's house after school and had hurt herself jumping off the top of bunk beds. The mum had given Della a hug to comfort her and she'd held on to her with all her might, breathing in her perfume until she felt dizzy, her body barnacled against the woman's motherly form. She hated having to let go.

Maggie interrupted her thoughts. She handed Della a business card with a police logo on it.

'If you remember anything else you think is important, let me know. My number's on here.'

'Thank you,' Della stammered.

She didn't know what else to say. She fell silent and shifted awkwardly in her seat until salvation came in the form of Sadie's consultant, who stuck his head round the door and asked if he could interrupt them.

Della rose unsteadily to her feet, not taking her eyes off the doctor's worn face as he stepped into the room and pulled the door shut behind him.

'Is she . . . ?'

'Your grandmother is stable for now,' he said. 'She's suffered acute respiratory failure and we had to perform an
emergency tracheotomy.' He caught Della's terrified expression. 'It means we've inserted a tube into her throat to create
an airway and put her on a ventilator to help her breathe. In
a little while we'll take her for a CT scan so we can see the
extent of the damage caused by the blow to the back of her
head.'

'Is she going to get better though?'

The doctor looked grim. 'It's too early to say. We'll need
to see how she fares in the next twenty-four hours.'

'Can I see her?'

'Yes. It's fine for you to sit with her now.'

Della expressed her gratitude and the consultant left. She
turned to Maggie, who looked like she already knew what
she was about to say.

'I should be with her.'

'Of course. We can pick this up again later.'

Della felt so guilty at lying to a police officer that a con-
fession formed in the back of her throat, ready to gush forth.
She swallowed hard to quash it. Telling Maggie about the
photograph meant having to say out loud that she'd been
abandoned by her own mum as a child and she'd never
admitted that to anyone, not even to Alex. Like her friends,
he thought Helen was dead, because that was what she'd
told him. Better to let people believe Helen had died than
to have them think Della wasn't loveable enough to make
her stick around.

Hardly anyone knew the truth about Della's past – and
that's the way she wanted it to stay.

7

Sitting cross-legged on the single bed, Bea Dennison gnawed at the hangnail on the side of her thumb until, with a final, painful tug, it came away from its fleshy anchor. A tiny spot of blood appeared in its place so she stuck her thumb in her mouth and sucked.

'You look like a baby,' Sean admonished from across the bedroom. He was on the carpet, legs splayed open as he counted out ten-pound notes into a pile.

Bea made an exaggerated sucking noise, drawing her thumb into her mouth right up to where the knuckle joined it to her hand. She immediately stopped when she saw Sean's jaw clench, wiped her thumb on her skirt and drew her legs in until her chin rested on her knees. She felt safest like that, her back pressed against the headboard, legs hugged to her.

'Right, that's £120 from what we've taken so far,' said Sean. 'Not bad.' He rolled the notes up into a tube and secured it with a thin elastic band, snapping it loudly with obvious satisfaction.

Bea didn't agree. It was hardly worth what they'd done to get it. It worked out at £30 a house, less than the monthly allowance her parents gave her. But she wouldn't tell Sean that. If he knew she had her own money he'd want that too.

Silently she watched him open the flimsy pine door to his wardrobe and stuff the roll of notes inside a trainer at the rear, presumably so his dad didn't find it. Another waste of time in her opinion: Gary Morris never looked up from the television when they came in the flat, let alone ventured anywhere near his son's room to go searching through his belongings. Bea wasn't sure he had even registered she was there. If he had, he certainly didn't care enough to question why Sean was taking a girl obviously below the age of consent into his bedroom for hours at a time.

Her own parents would go ballistic if they knew where she was and what she'd been doing. They thought she'd gone to a friend's house after school, but the note that Sean had forged for Bea to give to her teacher, saying she had another hospital appointment that day, meant she'd been at his flat since shortly after 9 a.m. She'd had so many hospital appointments over the past two years that none of the school staff bothered to check it was genuine, and because her younger sister's classroom was in a different building to hers, she never noticed Bea wasn't around all day either.

Bea hugged her legs tighter and shivered. The flat was so cold it was making her fingers and toes ache but she knew it was pointless asking Sean to put the heating on. He and his dad would rather spend what money they had on takeaways than topping the meter up. They could have insulated the walls with the number of empty pizza boxes stacked up in the kitchen and there was a lingering scent of stale, rotten food throughout the flat.

She steeled herself to tell Sean she had to go home. She

could never predict his reaction: sometimes he'd be lovely and would send her off with a hug, reminding her of why she'd liked him in the first place. Typically, though, he sulked and slammed his bedroom door shut as she let herself out the front. Gary, still in the same position he'd been when they'd arrived, ignored the noise.

It was four months since Sean had come into Bea's life. The first week of the school holidays, she and some friends had gone into Mansell to hang around the shopping centre. At lunchtime they ventured into Subway and that was where she'd clapped eyes on Sean for the first time as he took their order. It was his eyes she'd noticed first: they were a startlingly bright blue, offset by his dark hair and olive skin. Bea thought he was the most gorgeous boy she'd ever seen.

She returned to Subway every day for a week after that. Eventually, with some giggly prompting from his colleagues, Sean twigged that Bea's repeated visits signalled a crush on him rather than a craving for sandwiches and he asked her to meet him when he finished work the next day.

Bea told her mum she was going to the cinema with a friend. Instead she ended up in a cafe on a back street she'd never been down before – her first proper date. Sean ordered her a coffee at the counter – she didn't have the courage to say she hated the taste of it – and as they sat down in a booth at the rear of the cafe, Bea fretted about what to say to him without sounding like a silly kid. He was seventeen, only three years older, but he seemed way more mature.

But before she could say a word Sean shocked her by kissing her. It wasn't the best first kiss – his lips landed only half on hers because she turned her head away in surprise

– but it didn't matter. It was still her first kiss and her insides fizzed as he followed it up with a second that lasted far longer.

It didn't take long before their differences became apparent though. Sean lived with his dad – his mum had died from cancer two years previously – in a flat they rented in a part of town her parents would be horrified to live in and he'd been in trouble with the police. Her family lived in a four-bedroom semi on a road where all the lawns were landscaped and most of the cars were four-wheel drives.

But when Sean referred to her as his girlfriend within days of their first date, any concerns Bea had melted away. More firsts swiftly followed, some more fun than others. Her first taste of alcohol boosted her confidence and made her feel grown-up around Sean's mates, who'd dismissed her as a silly little posh girl. When she was drunk she made them laugh. But the first time she and Sean had been alone together in his bedroom she hadn't enjoyed at all.

'We need to think about when and where we do the next one,' Sean said, closing the wardrobe. 'There's some sheltered housing near Arnold Avenue, we could give that a go.'

Bea was horrified.

'You said we were stopping after the last time.'

'I've been thinking about that and it wasn't that bad. We'll just have to be more careful.'

'Careful? You could've really hurt her.'

'I only gave her a slap,' Sean protested.

He sat on the bed next to Bea and tucked a strand of her blue-black hair behind her ear. Naturally fair, she'd dyed it using a home-colouring kit because Sean thought it would be a good disguise. Her parents went berserk when they saw what she'd done: her mum, Caroline, cried and said she didn't want to have 'one of those Emo kids for a daughter', while her dad, Chris, grounded her for a week. Bea initially railed against the punishment but was then surprised to discover she didn't miss Sean as much as she thought she would. If anything it was a relief not to have to see him every day and she almost didn't reply when he texted her demanding to meet when the week was up. The trouble was they'd done two houses by then and she felt she had no choice.

'Don't look at me like that, babe,' said Sean as he caressed her cheek with his thumb pad. Bea fought the urge to pull away. 'This was your idea, don't forget.'

Shame flooded through her because she knew he was right. It *had* been her idea. They'd been watching television in his bedroom one afternoon and Sean was complaining about not earning enough. Flicking through the channels they came across a repeat of an old Nineties police drama and the episode featured some kids carrying out distraction burglaries on old people. Bea made an off-the-cuff, jokey comment – 'maybe you should turn to crime' – and that was all it took to set the wheels in motion, spinning so fast she had no idea how to stop them. Before she knew it Sean had bought them both black jeans and black T-shirts from Primark, figuring the less identifiable clothing they wore the better, and after settling on the mugging story as a means of convincing the old people to let them in, began experimenting to see which made the more convincing blood: tomato ketchup or that strawberry syrup you pour over ice cream. The syrup won.

Two days later, a Wednesday afternoon in late August when school was still out and her parents believed she was at her friend Clara's house for the afternoon, Bea found herself committing an offence that – according to the Internet, because she looked it up – could result in her being locked in juvenile detention for six years. Afterwards she had cried for hours remembering the old woman's horrified expression when she realized Bea had tricked her way in and that she wasn't horribly hurt like she'd pretended to be.

But they got away with it and their success – if you could call thirty pounds' worth of valuables that, which Bea didn't – convinced Sean they should target someone else. She knew she was an idiot for going along with it, because now she was as guilty as he was. She should have said no. She should have said no to everything.

'If we do it again, the police will catch us for sure,' she said, finally pulling away. Her skin where his thumb had touched it itched like mad.

'I'm not worried about that. Not a single one of those old dears has been able to ID us properly. I'm either really tall or really short with blond hair or black hair and you've been either white or Asian. They haven't got a fucking clue.'

'That doesn't mean we should do it again.'

Bea was terrified when she saw reports about the break-ins in the local newspaper, the *Mansell Echo*. The paper had nicknamed them the 'Con Couple', with the police describing them as 'dangerous individuals'. To keep tabs on the story, Sean had signed up for an email alert from the *Echo*'s website every time there was a mention.

'Are you going soft on me?' he said quietly.

His tone was menacingly calm and Bea shivered, this time from fear.

'No, I just think it's too soon. Let's wait a bit.'

'You want social services to find out, is that it?'

Bea flinched. It was Sean's favourite threat – play nicely or I'll tip off social services about what we've been doing and you'll be taken into care. The first time he'd said it she thought it was a joke. Wouldn't he get into trouble too, because she was under age? But Sean said he'd tell them she'd lied about how old she was to trick him into sleeping with her and just like that they went from being boyfriend and girlfriend to something horrible and frightening from which Bea could see no escape.

'No, of course I don't want that,' she said in a hollow voice.

'So it's settled. We'll pick a house, then keep an eye on it for a few days before we go in.'

'I've got to go home now,' said Bea. 'My mum will be expecting me back from school.'

'We've got time, haven't we?' he said, a smile spreading across his face. Bea tensed as he reached for the hem of her shirt, but then she noticed the notification light flashing on his phone, which was on the upturned orange plastic crate he used as a bedside table.

'It looks like you've got a message.'

To her relief, Sean pulled away. As he read it, his face darkened.

'What the fuck . . .'

'What is it?' Bea scrabbled to the side of the bed, ready to take flight.

'It's an *Echo* update. But, but . . . it can't be right.' He frowned.

'What is it?' Bea was practically shouting now and her heart juddered against her ribs in fear.

'An old lady was done over this morning and the police are calling it attempted murder,' said Sean. His breaths were coming fast and Bea could see he was sweating.

'I don't get why you're upset. It wasn't us.'

'Because, you fucking idiot, the police think it was.' He thrust the phone at her and Bea read, open-mouthed, that the police were indeed investigating the strong possibility it was another attack by the 'Con Couple', who they were seeking in connection with other distraction burglaries.

'But we've been here all day,' she cried.

'No shit. Someone's copied us and now everyone thinks it's us. If the old lady dies, we're fucked.'

Terrified, Bea burst into tears. 'I want to go home,' she sobbed, sounding like the child she was.

'Shut the fuck up and let me think,' said Sean. He rubbed his chin as he paced the room. Dark stains spread across the armpits of his red T-shirt; Bea had never seen him so worked up. 'We need to get rid of the clothes first. I'll chuck them away or something. Then we need to stop seeing each other for a bit. Put some distance between us. I'll get my old man to say I was here all day, but you need to find your own alibi. Say you were in town shopping or something.'

Bea's heart suddenly soared. For weeks she had wanted nothing more than to never see Sean again. Now, at last, she had a reason not to.

8

Maggie's frustration boiled over as the door to the relatives' room clicked shut behind Della. She was convinced Della had lied about being unable to describe the missing photograph from memory. But why?

The most obvious reason was that Della had taken the frame herself because she knew its exact value. She wouldn't be the first person to exploit a burglary by hiding valuable items so a false claim could be made against a home insurance policy. From there it was a leap to wondering whether Della could even have attacked her grandmother herself. She was, after all, Sadie's sole heir. But as the house was only rented and would revert back to the housing association for someone else to occupy if she died, what else would Della stand to inherit? Maggie also doubted Della had the physical strength to hit Sadie with the bottle. That was some whack to the back of the head.

With a sigh, Maggie pulled her notebook from her bag and recorded as much of her conversation with Della as she could remember verbatim – her notes would need to stand up in court under the scrutiny of a defence barrister. Her lips pursed as she wrote down Della's comments about

Sadie's wedding and engagement rings. If Della had taken them, their sentimental value must be worthless in her eyes.

She was writing down their final exchange about the photograph when the door to the relatives' room opened again and the male nurse who'd let her into HDU appeared.

'Oh good, you're still here,' he said. 'There's a message for you. They said they couldn't reach you on your mobile.'

He handed Maggie a scrap of paper with 'Call DI Gant URGENT' scrawled across it in black biro.

'I put it on silent,' said Maggie, retrieving her phone from the pocket of her overcoat. The display showed five missed calls, one from DS Renshaw, the others from the Family Liaison coordinator for their force, DI Gant.

She immediately suspected the calls were connected. DI Gant only ever rang when he was assigning her to a new case; assuming he'd already cleared it with her DCI at Mansell CID, as protocol dictated, she guessed Renshaw was calling because she wasn't happy to lose Maggie from the robberies investigation and wanted to vent. Maggie knew which of them she'd call back first.

'He rang through to the nurses' station but didn't give his number, said you already had it.'

'I do, thank you.'

'You'll have to go outside to ring him back,' the nurse said snippily. 'Mobile use is restricted here.'

'I know – that's why mine was on silent.'

'Well, good,' he huffed as Maggie followed him out of the room. 'The door code to get back in is 3749.'

Maggie didn't think she'd need it. If DI Gant needed her deployed elsewhere, this would be her last involvement with the case for now and she'd have to hand her hunch about

Della lying over to Renshaw. She said thank you to the nurse and made her way back to the lifts. As she stepped inside the first to arrive, her phone lit up to signal Renshaw was calling again. She let it ring.

Outside the hospital entrance Maggie squinted as her eyes adjusted to the sunlight. The sky was bright blue and virtually cloudless but the temperature was at least ten degrees below agreeable, typical for November. The cold stung her face and she wished she'd remembered her gloves as she clutched her phone against her ear with numbed fingers to call DI Gant back.

The second he picked up she knew something was wrong. He sounded harassed, which wasn't like him.

'About bloody time, Neville,' he snapped. 'Don't you ever answer your phone?'

'I was in HDU, sir. I had it on silent.'

'Fine. Don't move from that spot.'

'Sorry?'

'Have you heard about the attempted murder-suicide in Trenton?' He didn't wait for her to answer. 'The female victim is on her way to Mansell General. Her injuries are serious but not life-threatening and the SIO has asked if you're available to be her FLO. I've checked with your DCI and you are.'

Maggie's mouth went dry and her pulse quickened.

'Who's the SIO?'

'For now it's DCI Umpire. His new Homicide and Major Enquiry Team are working with Trenton CID on this one.'

Umpire had asked for her. A tremor shot through her and she gripped her phone tighter. She couldn't decide whether she was excited or nervous but at least she'd get to talk to him face to face. He hadn't returned any of the messages she'd left him last night or that morning.

They'd both been at the Old Bailey in London yesterday for the sentencing hearing in the Rosie Kinnock case. As the senior of the two FLOs assigned to Rosie's parents, Mack and Lesley, Maggie had been asked to read out a victim impact statement on their behalf before the judge considered appropriate jail terms for the accused, who had pleaded guilty at an earlier hearing. What Maggie read to the court was a harrowing and heartbreaking account of a family devastated by a nefarious act of greed; it would take the Kinnocks a very long time to come to terms with what had happened to their child and the entire court was bowed by emotion by the time Maggie finished.

As she and the rest of the investigating team had hoped, the judge used the maximum sentencing powers gifted to him and afterwards they celebrated at the Viaduct Tavern pub across the road from the court. The crowd included Maggie, Umpire, Renshaw and DC Belmar Small, the other FLO on the case. Conspicuous by his absence was DC Steve Berry, who'd recently quit the police and now worked for a private security firm as head of its CCTV division.

By her third glass of wine Maggie was drunk. So drunk, in fact, that when Umpire mentioned he wasn't catching the last train back to Buckinghamshire with the rest of them but instead planned to hail a black cab to his estranged wife's house in Finchley so he could have breakfast with his kids the next morning, Maggie reacted with unguarded jealousy. Out of earshot of the others she forcibly told him she wasn't interested in being messed around and he should go back to his wife. That morning, after waking with a clanging hangover, she rang to apologize but her call went through to voicemail and subsequent messages went unreturned. She could've kicked herself for the emotional outburst, but the fact Umpire had asked for her now hopefully meant he was no longer as angry as he'd been when he stormed out of the pub to flag down a taxi.

Ignoring her churning insides, Maggie tried to sound businesslike as she answered DI Gant.

'What do we know about the victim, sir?'

'Hold your horses. Your DCI has cleared you to be the FLO on this but on the understanding you continue with some of your current caseload. I've had DS Renshaw on the phone too saying she can't spare you from the distraction burglaries investigation, so we've agreed you'll do both cases in tandem.'

'Both?'

'Yes, it looks like we'll have to share you. I did offer some-one else from the roster to DCI Umpire as I'm only allowed to deploy one FLO to this case, but he wanted you.'

'But I thought there always had to be two of us?'

'That's what the guidelines say, but budget cutbacks mean I can't sanction the use of anyone else right now. Look, I don't know how long the stabbing victim will be in hospital but you won't need to be with her all the time and when you're not with her you'll carry on with the other case.'

Gant made it sound easy but Maggie didn't share his optimism. Could she realistically juggle the two? It wouldn't be the same as having a few CID cases on the go, with the same senior officer to report to and working out of the same office. She didn't relish the idea of being split between

Umpire and Renshaw, but when she tried to say that, Gant cut her short.

'Don't be difficult, Maggie. We've been shaved to the bone by cutbacks, as you well know. Policing levels are nearly the lowest they've been for decades and now there aren't enough officers to go round. I've pretty much lost half my roster because I'm being told my FLOs can't be taken away from their day jobs.'

Maggie could hear the frustration in his voice and felt sorry for him. Gant had worked tirelessly in the years she'd known him to reverse the opinion of more cynical colleagues who saw Family Liaison as bringing little more to investigations than tea and sympathy. Policy changes to improve both perception and training were brought about after the murder of London teenager Stephen Lawrence in 1993, when the subsequent Macpherson Report into the Met Police's handling of the case criticized the Family Liaison allocated to his parents as inadequate. Since then FLOs had been acknowledged as a vital function of policing and at one point Gant's roster of officers had swelled to more than a hundred. But she knew he wasn't exaggerating about being hit hard by budget cuts.

'I did read something in the *Police Oracle* a while back about FLOs on other forces working two or even three cases at a time,' said Maggie. 'I didn't realize it was happening within ours as well.'

'So you know what I'm talking about. Of course it's better if you're in pairs so you can prop each other up when it all gets too much, but working alone is something you might have to get used to,' said Gant glumly. 'I don't like it, it's not how I want to run things, but there's little I can do.'

'Sir, it's fine, I can manage both,' she placated him. 'I do have a question though: why is HMET involved if it's only attempted murder?'

HMET was the force's new flagship unit set up to tackle gangland-related crimes and terrorist attacks on UK soil. It had been established under the auspices of Assistant Chief Constable Marcus Bailey and he'd appointed Umpire to head it up. Maggie had been thrilled when Umpire told her: the next time they met for dinner they'd ordered the most expensive bottle of champagne on the menu to toast his promotion.

'ACC Bailey thought it would be a good one for HMET to begin with. The husband's name is Simon Bramwell and he runs a recruitment agency that sends specialist engineers to work with oil companies in the Middle East. Until we know for sure what went on in that house, ACC Bailey reckons Bramwell's business connections mean nothing can be ruled out. At the moment he's under police guard at the Princess Alexandra hospital in Trenton, still unconscious,' Gant said. 'So, can you stay put at Mansell hospital until the wife arrives?'

'Of course. What's her name?'

'Eleanor Bramwell.'

'Can you give me any more details about her?'

'Don't have any,' said Gant. 'You'll be briefed by DCI Umpire or whoever else comes down from Trenton with her.'

'It might not be him?' said Maggie, trying not to sound too disappointed.

'I imagine he'll want to stay at the scene. It might be

someone from Trenton CID or even your old partner, DC Small.'

'Belmar?' exclaimed Maggie. 'I thought you said I was the only FLO on the case?'

'You are. DC Small is off my roster, as of two weeks ago.'

'What?'

'Didn't you know? He's joined HMET.'

Maggie's jaw dropped. Her and Belmar's partnering on the Rosie Kinnock case had blossomed into a firm friendship and she now regularly socialized with him and his wife, Allie. He hadn't breathed a word about quitting when she'd seen him at the Old Bailey yesterday, nor afterwards in the pub.

'He's no longer a FLO?'

'No, he's not. Another good officer I can no longer use. At this rate I'll have to assign myself to cases.'

Gant chuckled but Maggie didn't mirror his amusement. Her mind was too busy trying to work out the reason why Belmar hadn't told her. If anything, Allie not saying anything made Maggie feel worse. She had confided in Belmar's wife about her conflicted feelings for Umpire and Allie would've known what Maggie's reaction would be to Belmar joining his new unit.

Whatever Belmar's reason was for keeping quiet, it had better be good.

9

Lou Neville hated doing the afternoon school run. Her fourteen-month-old daughter Mae had recently dropped her morning nap and as a consequence her post-lunch sleep was now longer. Every afternoon Lou was faced with either waking Mae up and carting her to Scotty's school screaming her head off, or being late for the 3.30 p.m. pick-up and receiving a lecture from his teacher about the importance of timekeeping. Today they were on time but Mae was making her displeasure known by wailing loudly from the confines of her buggy. Ignoring the looks from other parents, Lou plugged a dummy in her daughter's mouth and prayed she wouldn't spit it out.

What irked Lou most was the fact she wouldn't have to do the school run at all if the head let Scotty walk home on his own like she'd requested. They only lived a few streets away and Scotty was nine now, old enough in Lou's mind to make the short walk unaccompanied or at least with the other kids who lived on the same road. But the head kept citing safety issues and parental responsibility and eventually Lou gave up asking.

At least she didn't have to worry about her eldest child,

Jude. Now eleven and in his first year at secondary school, he got himself home every day with no questions asked. Lou had pondered getting him to collect Scotty on his way but their schools were too far apart for him to make it there in good time and three out of five days he was at after-school football practice, which he loved. It seemed unfair to make him give that up just so she had an easier life.

A gust of wind whipped across the playground and Lou shivered as it hit her full in the face. She re-angled Mae's buggy so the toddler was shielded from the icy blast then stuffed her own hands deep into her coat pockets. There was a parents' room in the main school building where they could've waited in the warm, but she preferred to stand outside on her own these days. Waiting in the cold was preferable to the faux sympathy and concern she'd receive from the other mums inside.

None of them really wanted to know how she was doing – it was just an excuse to find out any additional juicy bits from the Rosie Kinnock trial that hadn't already been published and picked over in newspapers and on the Internet. Lou had told them enough times that she never went to court herself and that it was her ex-husband, Rob, who'd given evidence, not her, but still they asked. As her sister, Maggie, was also involved in the case they assumed Lou must know everything.

They also assumed – because one of the mouthier mums had said it outright to her – that Lou must've known what Rob was up to before it was laid bare in court. Surely she could've guessed from his size that he was taking illegal steroids, even if she didn't know he was dealing them? Lou had lost her temper then, screaming that of course she had no idea, until a teacher intervened and asked her to calm down or she'd have to leave the school grounds.

The Rosie Kinnock trial had taught Lou one thing though: however devastated she'd been that Rob had left her for another woman, she should count herself lucky he was someone else's problem now. It was therefore with relief, not regret, that she'd signed their divorce papers two months ago and reverted from his surname, Green, to her maiden name. She wasn't completely shot of him because he still had access to Mae but yesterday she'd discovered some news about him and Lisa, the woman he'd left her for, that suggested the situation might soon change. At the same time she'd found out that Maggie already knew but hadn't told her. Furious at her sister, Lou was biding her time until she confronted her about it.

The bell went to signal the end of the school day and the first class was released like a pack of wild dogs into the play-ground. Parents surged forward to collect their offspring, taking hold of book bags and water bottles and garish paint-ings that would probably go straight into the recycling bin when they got home. One of the dads reminded Lou a little bit of her new boyfriend, Arturs, and a shiver of excitement ran through her. Tonight he was taking her out for a drink and – shit, she'd forgotten to check Maggie could still babysit. Scrabbling for her phone, Lou kept an eye on the double doors into the main building in case Scotty's class was out next.

'Hey, sis, can you talk?'

'What's up?' said Maggie.

'Can you still babysit tonight? Remember I asked you last week? I'm off out with Jeannie, one of the school mums.'

Lou wasn't stupid. If she was going to lie to Maggie about who she was going out with, it was better to use the name of someone her sister didn't know. At some point she would tell her about Arturs, but it was still early days and she wanted to enjoy the romance for a bit longer before she held it up to her sister's scrutiny. Maggie might be the younger sister, by three years, but she acted as though she was the gatekeeper of Lou's life, vetting anyone who came into it. She'd never liked Rob and had been openly hostile to him at times, so quite how she'd react to Arturs, a Latvian-born builder who'd been in the country for less than a year, Lou could only guess. Maggie certainly wouldn't be happy that, at twenty-two, he was ten years younger than Lou and she'd also be concerned about the boys being introduced to a new boyfriend when they were still raw from the departure of their stepdad, Rob, who they both adored. Concerns that, if Lou was being honest, she also shared.

'Oh God, I'd forgotten all about it. I'm so sorry, Lou, but I don't think I can. I've got two big cases on the go, and I'm at the hospital right now waiting to interview a relative on one case and a victim on another. I could be hours.' Maggie spoke in a rush, the way she always did when she was coming up with an excuse.

'Oh for fuck's sake,' said Lou, not caring who overheard her. 'I asked you last week.'

'I'm really sorry, sis. I forgot.'

'What am I meant to do? I don't want to cancel.'

'Maybe your friend could come round to yours instead? Get a bottle of wine and a takeaway?'

'But I want to go *out*. I never get the chance any more,' said Lou.

She wasn't exaggerating. She had been twenty when she'd had Jude, his birth coming only five months after his dad, Jerome, her then fiancé, was killed in a road traffic accident. She was still a single mum when Scotty was born just over two years later: his dad, Carl, had been one of Jerome's old school friends and he'd done a runner the day after she'd peed on the stick and the two lines came up. She hadn't heard from him since.

Rob had been her salvation, coming into her life when she was twenty-seven. He'd been happy to take on the role of doting dad to the two boys and Mae's arrival had completed their happy family – until Lisa came along. Now Lou was on her own again and sometimes it was simply too much to cope with. She was only thirty-two and she wanted to have some fun. She deserved it after everything she'd been through.

'I know you don't,' said Maggie, 'but there's really nothing I can do tonight. Maybe your friend could rearrange for another evening and I'll make sure I'm definitely free?'

Lou swore again and hung up. She was about to ring Arturs to break the bad news when Scotty's class spilled out into the playground. Stepping forward to greet her middle child, a thought popped into her head. There *was* someone else she could ask to babysit. Someone she'd never considered before, but who she trusted just as much as Maggie. Someone who wouldn't let her down. As Scotty tossed her his book bag and started rifling in the basket beneath Mae's buggy looking for snacks, Lou broke into a smile.

10

Caroline Dennison was in the kitchen preparing the vegetables for the family's evening meal when Bea arrived home. She smiled as Bea entered the room but her face fell when she caught sight of her daughter's expression.

'What's the matter, darling?' she said, letting go of the courgette she was slicing and dropping the knife onto the wooden board with a clatter. She quickly wiped her hands on a tea towel. 'You look terrible.'

'Don't feel well,' mumbled Bea.

She had walked all the way from Sean's flat instead of getting the bus, hoping the journey on foot would clear her head. Every step was an effort though, like she could barely lift her feet, and her excitement at not having to see Sean any more had given way to an awareness that she was in more trouble than she could imagine. She felt utterly alone.

Bea slumped into one of the chairs spaced around the scrubbed wooden table that was covered in old newspapers, school textbooks, discarded receipts, hairbands, cap-less Biros and other bits of paraphernalia that proclaimed family life. The kitchen was the hub of their house, the room where Bea, her parents and her younger sister, Esme, migrated to at the end of every day. The rest of the house wasn't as lived in, more pristine than messy, and didn't exude the same warmth. Yet sitting at the table, her head in her hands, Bea found no comfort in its sunshine yellow walls and white, wood-panelled units. Not even the family cat, Smudge, could rouse her spirits as he rubbed against her legs, purring loudly.

Caroline came over and asked Bea to sit up. She laid her palm on Bea's forehead.

'You feel very hot, darling. Did you start to feel ill at Clara's?'

Clara was the friend whose house Bea had lied about going to after school. Although Clara was willing to cover for her as payback for Bea keeping the secrets she'd shared herself, she didn't like Sean and the girls weren't as close these days. The mention of her friend's name made Bea perk up – now she didn't have to give all her time to Sean, maybe they could hang out again. The same went for all the other friends who had drifted away. Feeling slightly more optimistic, she gave her mum the most convincing smile she could muster.

'I'm fine. I just haven't eaten much today.'

Caroline clicked her tongue and frowned.

'Oh, Bea, you must eat. We don't want you wasting away again. There's nothing of you as it is. Look at your arms, they're like twigs.'

Bea knew her mum was speaking out of concern but she didn't imagine Dr Reynolds would approve of how she was saying it. What was the advice he'd tried to drum into her parents? 'If you want to help Beatrice to get better, don't blame or judge her, and don't comment on her appearance.'

Naughty Mummy.

'I'm hungry now,' Bea lied. The thought of eating made her shake, even though her stomach growled appreciatively at the prospect.

'Make some toast while I finish dinner,' said Caroline, returning to the chopping board. 'I've got some of that nice farmhouse bread you like. Oh, and Dad's working late tonight, so I thought after dinner you, me and Esme could have a *Friends* marathon. I've bought some of your favourite Ben & Jerry's too.'

Tears streamed down Bea's face so suddenly that they surprised her as much as Caroline, who stood frozen in shock, courgette in hand, as her daughter sobbed her heart out.

'Bea, what on earth is going on?'

'Don't be nice to me,' Bea howled, her thin little body wracked with grief as the torrent of emotion poured out of her. 'I don't deserve it!'

She repeated the words over and over until her mum pulled her into an embrace. Bea melted into Caroline's arms with relief, breathing in the sweet, almost chocolatey smell of the cocoa butter her mum rubbed into her skin every day after her morning shower. In her mum's arms she felt safe again.

'You're scaring me, sweetheart,' said Caroline, kissing the top of Bea's head. 'Whatever is the matter? What is it you think you don't deserve?'

Swaddled in her mum's arms, Bea began to relax. But with calmness came the realization she mustn't tell Caroline the truth. If she did, her mum would call the police, because she was the kind of person who would do that, who always did the right thing. And if the police came, they'd lock Bea up and she wouldn't see her any more. She squeezed her eyes shut as her mum stroked her hair and made the same soothing noises she used to when Bea was little and upset. The soft, rhythmic stroking planted the germ of an idea in Bea's mind.

'It's my hair. I hate it,' she said. Her voice was muffled where her face was pressed against Caroline's chest.

'What?'

'My hair,' said Bea, reluctantly disentangling herself. 'I don't like it any more.'

Caroline looked like she didn't know whether to laugh or be angry.

'That's why you're so upset, because of your *hair*?'

'It's awful. I hate the colour. I wish I'd never dyed it,' said Bea.

Another lie. She actually liked the blue-black shade because it made her look older than fourteen and more sophisticated. Someone in her class said she reminded them of Kendall Jenner, which was just about the best compliment ever. But if she wanted to not get caught, she needed to get rid of it. Four victims had seen her with this hair.

'Can I dye it back, Mum, please?'

Caroline looked doubtful as she picked up a strand and rubbed it between her fingers.

'I don't know, darling. It's so dark now it'll cost a fortune to strip out the colour, if it can be done at all. You'll probably have to lose some of the length too, because the ends are so split now.'

Bea knew the cost wouldn't be an issue, whatever her mum protested. Her dad was CEO of a global design and marketing agency in London, commuting there every day from Mansell. His six-figure salary was why Caroline was able to quit her own job in marketing to be a stay-at-home mum. Her dad hated Bea's dyed hair too, so she knew he would happily cover the cost.

'Please, Mum. I can't stand it.'

'Okay, I'll ring my hairdresser and book you an appointment. But I can't take you until Saturday. I expect the process will take a few hours and there won't be time to do it after school.'

'Thanks, Mum,' said Bea. She threw her arms round Caroline and squeezed with all her might. Her mum laughed.

'I'm pleased you want to get rid of it. I'll be glad to get my little girl back.'

Bea smiled too but inside she was gripped by fear. Yes, but for how long?

11

The ambulance swept into the bay outside A&E with its blue lights flashing and police outriders bringing up the front and rear.

'Bit much, isn't it?' said the porter loitering next to Maggie. He sucked noisily on his cigarette. 'I heard her old man was in a coma. Does she really need a police escort if he's out of it?'

Maggie ignored the porter as he exhaled a plume of smoke in her direction and instead kept her focus on the ambulance, impatient for the rear doors to open and reveal which officer had accompanied Eleanor Bramwell on her journey to Mansell. As they swung open, her breath caught as a familiar figure stepped down onto the tarmac.

Belmar.

Pushing her disappointment aside that it wasn't Umpire, she smiled at her friend, who looked nervous as he approached, pulling at the collar of his navy wool overcoat, which he wore over a charcoal grey three-piece suit. Maggie always marvelled at how meticulous Belmar was in appearance, especially as she looked so ramshackle by contrast. He looked like a menswear model; her clothes were usually retrieved from her bedroom floor rather than her wardrobe and it was a good day if she remembered to brush her shoulder-length dark blonde hair before she left the house.

'Hey, Maggie,' he said. 'Bit of a surprise, I bet.'

'I'll say. How come you didn't tell me you were joining HMET? Last night, when we were talking about work, you didn't say a word. Did you think I wouldn't be pleased for you? Because I am: it's a bloody fantastic move.'

Belmar grinned. 'Thanks. I did want to tell you, trust me. I nearly blurted it out in the pub but I was told I couldn't say anything until after I'd started. It's actually my first day today so I thought we'd catch up at the weekend. I didn't know we'd end up working together on day one.'

Maggie frowned. 'You couldn't tell anyone or just me?'

There was that sheepish look again.

'Well?' she pressed.

'You. Ballboy didn't want me to tell you.'

Ballboy was the nickname bestowed upon Umpire by the ranks as a pun on his surname's tennis connection. Maggie never used it.

'Why not?' she said hotly.

'Haven't a clue. He said I shouldn't broadcast it to you until I'd started, so I didn't.'

Why the hell didn't Umpire want her to know? But although she was reeling at the revelation, Maggie was careful to shrug it off in front of Belmar, sensing a fissure in the trust they'd built up. She didn't want him running back to tell Umpire she was upset. What if they had laughed at her behind her back as Belmar agreed to keep their secret?

'Fair enough,' she replied as nonchalantly as she could.

'He probably thought I'd try to talk you out of giving up Family Liaison. You've only been doing it for a year.'

'You'd have been wasting your time. No way was I going to turn HMET down.'

Over his shoulder Maggie could see the paramedics unloading Eleanor Bramwell from the ambulance. Even in her unconscious state she was still an arresting sight, with bright blonde hair, smooth, unblemished skin and pronounced cheekbones. Did Simon Bramwell have good looks to match, Maggie wondered?

'How's she doing?' she asked Belmar.

'She's sedated but the doctors think she'll be fine. The knife was still embedded in her right shoulder when she was found and she needed multiple stitches under general, but the other wounds were superficial by comparison.'

Around the side of the ambulance came an older woman with blonde hair. She said something to one of the paramedics then looked over at Maggie.

'Who's that?' Maggie murmured.

'Trenton CID.'

'You must be DC Neville,' said the woman, smiling as she approached. 'I'm DI Deborah Green, Trenton CID.' They shook hands. 'Someone was meant to warn you that we're doing this in tandem with HMET.'

Green's accent was rich, Northern – Maggie guessed at Yorkshire – and she was almost disconcertingly cheerful.

'Yes, DI Gant told me,' said Maggie.

'Good.'

The paramedics pushed Eleanor into the hospital as Belmar, Green and Maggie fell into step behind them.

'How's the husband doing?'

'He's had his stomach pumped but it's touch and go,' said Green. 'Docs are worried he might succumb to organ failure. They don't know how many pills he ingested but it looks like a lot and he swallowed them down with neat vodka.'

'You think a third party might be involved because of his line of work?' Maggie directed this at Belmar. 'DI Gant said that's why HMET got the shout.'

'That's our brief, but there haven't been any threats reported against him and so far no hint of shady dealings that could've incited retribution. We're still looking though. The next-door neighbours heard the Bramwells rowing late last night and again in the early hours of this morning and didn't hear any voices other than theirs. But that's not to say someone else wasn't there.'

'Who found them?' asked Maggie.

'A bloke who lives across the street was backing his car out of his drive to go to work around eight this morning when he looks in his rear-view mirror and sees Eleanor Bramwell staggering out of her front door with the knife still stuck in her shoulder,' said Green. 'She told him she'd passed out in the bathroom but wasn't sure for how long and when she came to she found her husband sparked out on their bed. Then she collapsed again and has been sedated ever since.'

'Any kids?' asked Maggie, thinking what a horrible scene for a child to bear witness to.

Green shook her head. 'They've been trying for a baby and are having IVF. Their third round just failed and Mrs Bramwell wants to try another but her husband thinks it won't work again and costs too much. The neighbour who heard them rowing last night said they'd openly discussed it at another neighbour's barbecue in the summer.'

'He thinks they can't afford it? I thought he ran a business that was doing well?'

'Maybe it's not,' said Belmar. 'And IVF isn't cheap you know.'

There was something in the brittleness of his reply that stopped Maggie short. His wife, Allie, had confided in her a couple of months ago that she was keen to start trying for a baby and said Belmar was eager too. Had they hit a stumbling block already?

Belmar fiddled with the knot of his tie as he looked away. Maggie let it slide.

'How old are they both?' she asked.

'He's forty and she's thirty-eight,' said Green. 'Been married nine years.'

The hospital's chief administrator was waiting in A&E with a consultant. After a brief discussion it was decided Eleanor would be taken up to a side room in HDU and a uniform officer posted outside her door.

'Her going to HDU makes my job easier,' Maggie remarked to Belmar in a low aside.

He frowned. 'Meaning?'

'The victim of a case I'm working is already up there. I've got to interview her next of kin again, so waiting for Mrs Bramwell to come round gives me an excuse to hang around the ward until they're ready to talk.' Maggie glanced at her watch, a chunky silver men's Seiko that was a present from her parents one Christmas. There was a scratch on the glass and the strap was too loose round her wrist. 'Shit, it's already gone three.'

DS Renshaw was holding a briefing on the distraction burglaries in a few hours and she was expecting Maggie to have re-interviewed Della in time to report back. Renshaw had already made it clear during a tense phone call shortly after Maggie had spoken to DI Gant that she was not going to cut her any slack as she juggled the two cases. She'd even implied that by being the FLO on the Bramwell case Maggie was singularly letting down the elderly victims, conveniently overlooking the fact she did not volunteer to join the investigation.

'What am I meant to tell Sadie Cardle when she comes round?' Renshaw had sniped. '*If* she comes round, that is. "Sorry, we're one man down now but we'll do our best"?'

'But you're not an officer down,' Maggie had shot back, not bothering to hide her irritation. 'I'm still on the case; I'm just doing the other one in tandem. I'm struggling to see what the problem is. It's me who'll be stretched, not you.'

'But what happens when Ballboy monopolizes your time? I can hardly tell him to take a run and jump, can I?'

Maggie wished she could tell Renshaw to do exactly that herself, but she'd never get away with it now there was a rank separating them.

'It's up to me to manage my time and I'll make sure neither case is neglected.'

After that Renshaw had grudgingly dammed her tirade long enough to allow Maggie to repeat what Della had said when she questioned her.

'Why would anyone lie about a photo?' Renshaw had mused out loud when Maggie finished.

'My thoughts exactly.'

'Okay, let's get Della to give us her movements for this

morning and also for last night. Even though forensics believe the break-in happened this morning, I want to check her alibi for the entire time, in case she was at the house before she said she was. Then push her again on the photograph. Don't say outright we think she's lying, but imply that we do. Can you do that, DC Neville?'

Biting back a sarcastic retort, Maggie had said, yes, she could.

'In the meantime, I'll go back to Audrey Allen to get her opinion on the relationship between the grandmother and the granddaughter – there may be some issues between them that she knows about. I'd bet good money on this being the Con Couple again but we need to cover all bases. I want you to speak to Della then report back to the station at six thirty for the briefing.'

Maggie had hesitated. 'I've been told to wait for Eleanor Bramwell to arrive from Trenton. I don't know when that will be.'

There had been a loaded pause before Renshaw spoke again.

'As you said yourself, Neville, it's up to you to make this work. See you at six thirty.'

12

The consultant entrusted with treating Eleanor Bramwell in HDU was perturbed to see the three officers waiting to speak to her.

'I don't know if it's a good idea to present her with a crowd when she wakes up,' he remarked.

'Call it a welcoming committee,' Green shot back, slipping off her overcoat to reveal a deep burgundy trouser suit worn over a cream silky camisole-style top. 'No need to put out bunting though.'

Maggie was rapidly warming to Green. She guessed the DI's age to be somewhere in the late forties: faint vertical lines marked her décolletage and crow's feet puckered around her eyes. She was about five foot four and all soft edges, from her round face and top-heavy build to the bobbed blonde hair that curled flatteringly round her face and into the nape of her neck. Maggie decided it would be a welcome change to work with a senior female officer who didn't take herself as seriously as Renshaw did.

'You might have a long wait,' said the consultant exasperatedly.

'Don't you worry about us, we'll be fine,' said Green.

As the consultant stalked off, Maggie suggested she would use the wait to speak to Della Cardle again and check on her grandmother.

'Makes sense,' said Green, as Belmar nodded. 'We'll call you if we need you.'

Sadie was in a room with three other patients. The curtains had been pulled round her bed for privacy and Maggie spoke softly through the folds.

'Are you there, Della? It's DC Neville.'

She heard movement on the other side of the curtains then a small hand appeared through a gap to pull them aside. Della greeted Maggie with a forlorn look, her bloodshot eyes revealing she'd been crying again. Behind her on the bed, Sadie's chest rose with every whoosh of the ventilator.

'I need to ask you a few more questions,' said Maggie. 'I thought we could do it over a cup of tea.'

Della had removed her coat; the black roll-neck jumper she wore with dark blue skinny jeans accentuated her frailty. As she shook her head, her whole body trembled.

'I don't want to leave her,' she said.

'It won't take long, I promise.'

Della looked torn. Then she turned and kissed Sadie on her bandaged forehead. 'I'm just going outside, Nan. I'll be right back,' she whispered.

'Bring your coat with you,' said Maggie. 'There's a garden on the ground floor. I don't know about you but I could do with some fresh air.'

Ten minutes later they were sitting side by side on a

bench by a small patch of grass and some empty flower beds, cradling steaming hot cups of tea.

'What did you want to ask me?' said Della. 'If it's about the photograph, I still can't remember.'

Her eagerness to convince Maggie her memory had failed her made it seem even more like a lie. Maggie decided to build up to it.

'Let's talk about what you can remember then. What time did you say you found your nan?'

Not being quizzed about the photograph again seemed to make Della relax. She settled back on the bench and took a sip of tea. Maggie set hers down on the floor by her feet and flipped open her notebook.

'It was about ten past one. My lunch break starts at one and it doesn't take that long to drive there,' Della answered.

'What do you do for a living?'

'I'm an administrator at the Langston Hotel.'

'The one at the top of Bishop's Hill?'

'Yes. I work full-time, Monday to Friday.'

'When did you last see your nan before this morning?'

'Sunday. I went round to cook lunch for her. I did a roast.'

'So you didn't see her at all yesterday, not even in the evening?'

'No, but I never do on Mondays. Nan always goes to bingo on Monday nights with her neighbour Audrey, from about seven thirty to nearly ten.'

Maggie jotted down Della's comment but added a question mark. What was to say she didn't deviate from their normal routine yesterday? She could've gone round after Sadie had returned home from bingo. They'd have to check whether Audrey remembered seeing Della later on.

'I know you've already told this to the officers who arrived at your nan's house first, but I'd like you to go through what happened again when you found her,' said Maggie.

Della nodded. 'I parked outside the house like I usually do. I have my own key so I let myself in.'

'Front or back door?'

'Front. I do have a key for the back, but I never use it.'

'Then what?'

'Usually I shout out that it's me when I come in and Nan shouts hello back. When she didn't say anything I went straight to the sitting room and that's when I found her. At first I thought she'd had a heart attack like Granddad, but when I got closer I saw the blood by her head.'

Della huddled over her cup of tea, face etched with grief. Something deep inside, a gut feeling, told Maggie she wasn't responsible for the assault on Sadie.

'Did you touch her?'

'What?' Della looked alarmed.

'Did you touch her hand or face? Was her skin warm?'

'Oh, I see. Yes, she was. The room was really hot too, like the heating had been left on all night. Nan sometimes did that when it was very cold.'

Was it cold enough last night to warrant that? Maggie didn't think so and made a note of it.

'What time does she normally get up?'

'Usually it's just before seven. She's always been an early riser.'

That gave them roughly a five-hour time frame during which Sadie was attacked, as she was already up and dressed when it happened.

'So what did you do next?'

'I called 999 then sat with her until the ambulance came. I knew I shouldn't move her in case I made the injury worse.'

'Did you notice if anything else was missing? I know her rings were gone, but was there anything else that springs to mind?'

Della shook her head forlornly.

'I wasn't paying attention. All I could think about was making sure Nan was okay. I'd have to check again to see what's gone. I mean, I don't remember seeing if her purse was still there.'

'It was. One of our officers found it in her handbag. Her money and cards weren't touched.'

'So they only took her rings?'

'We won't know for sure until you've checked the contents of the house again, but right now it looks that way.' Maggie paused. 'Well, her rings and possibly the framed photograph from the hall.'

Della flinched and her face paled.

'Are you going to tell me the truth now?' said Maggie gently.

'I don't know what you mean,' Della stuttered.

'Okay, let me put it another way. I think you're lying about not remembering the photograph.'

Della slopped tea over the edge of the polystyrene cup onto her hand but didn't seem to notice. Maggie took the cup from her.

'Tell me about the photograph,' she said.

Della buried her face in her hands and began to sob.

'I'm serious, Della. The more you lie, the guiltier you make yourself look. And I don't think you're guilty. So put me out of my misery so I can concentrate on finding out who is.'

Della raised her head. Her cheeks were blotchy and streaked with tears.

'The photograph is of my mum and me,' she breathed, 'taken on the day I was born.'

Maggie had been expecting something far more dramatic; Della's distress seemed disproportionate when presented with the explanation.

'Do you have any idea why someone might want to take it?'

'It's in a big silver frame. An expensive one.'

Maggie paused to give Della time to wipe her eyes. 'Then I imagine that's why it was taken. Why didn't you want to tell me about it?'

'I . . . I . . . it's just that I don't like talking about Helen – that's her name. She walked out on me when I was three. I haven't seen her since and I don't know where she is and it hurts to talk about it.'

'What about your dad?'

'He doesn't know I exist. He was visiting town and he and my mum had a one-night stand. All I know is his name is Andy. I'm sorry, I know I should've told you sooner about the photograph but I'm pleased it's gone because I hate it. All it does is remind me that she didn't want me.'

'I still need a description of the frame to circulate but I'm glad we've cleared that up.'

As Maggie leafed through her notebook to start a new page, she was struck by a thought.

'Can I ask you something about your mum?'

Della nodded warily.

'Okay, this might be a silly question, but is there any chance she took the picture herself?'

'None whatsoever,' said Della bitterly. 'My granddad told me Helen threatened to leave and not come back and she's stuck to her promise for seventeen years so far.'

'Was her departure acrimonious?'

Della nodded. 'I was only little when she went, but I vaguely remember a lot of shouting and screaming indoors, like really big rows.'

'You really have no idea where she is?' said Maggie. She felt desperately sorry for Della that Helen could just walk out like that. She didn't see much of her own mum, Jeanette, since she and her dad, Graeme, had moved to the south coast, but she still couldn't imagine life without her.

'Nan and Granddad reported her missing but nothing came of it. She was twenty-two years old, she could do what she wanted.'

'It must've been tough for them too.'

Della nodded. 'My memories of her are so patchy that I suppose it's easier for me to put her out of my mind. But I know not a single day goes past without Nan wondering where Helen is or what she's doing.'

Maggie's phone beeped in her pocket. It was a text from Belmar.

She's awake.

'I'm needed in HDU. Don't worry,' she added hastily as panic crossed Della's face, 'it's for another case I'm working on.'

Relieved the message wasn't about Sadie, Della said she wanted to stay outside for a bit longer. Maggie left her on the bench, lost in thought.

Back in HDU, Maggie heard raised voices as she approached Eleanor's room and recognized one of them as Belmar's. The uniformed officer keeping guard outside made a face as she knocked on the door and let herself in.

'I am NOT talking to you.'

Eleanor Bramwell was indeed awake – and she was beside herself with anger.

'Mrs Bramwell, we do need a statement from you about what exactly happened,' Belmar said, who was standing at the foot of the bed with DI Green next to him.

'What else is there to say? That bastard husband of mine tried to kill me!'

Belmar looked relieved as Maggie stepped into the fray. Green smiled grimly.

'Best introduce yourself,' she said.

'Mrs Bramwell, I'm DC Maggie Neville and I've been assigned as your Family Liaison Officer. I'm here to help you.'

Eleanor eyed Maggie suspiciously.

'Help me with what? I don't need your help.'

'I want to assure you that you're safe here,' she said. 'Your husband is in hospital in Trenton and is under police guard.'

Eleanor's eyebrows knitted in confusion.

'What do you mean, he's in hospital? But he's dead, isn't he? I saw him. He was dead.'

Maggie flashed a look of surprise at her colleagues.

'I was about to tell her,' said Belmar tightly.

'Tell me WHAT?' Eleanor shrieked. She tried to sit up but the tube attached to the cannula in the back of her hand impeded her movement.

'Your husband is in a critical condition but he's still alive,' Belmar explained.

Stricken, Eleanor slumped back against her pillow. 'Oh God, oh God, no, no.'

'It's okay,' Green reassured her. 'He's a long way from here.'

'We do need to know what happened,' Belmar tried again. 'You're definitely sure it was your husband who attacked you and not someone else?'

'Are you stupid? Who else could have done it? There was no one else there but us.'

That ruled out any third-party involvement. Belmar looked disappointed.

'I'm sorry, I had to ask,' he said.

Eleanor ignored him and addressed Maggie.

'You said you're here to help me?'

Maggie assumed the question was Eleanor's acceptance of her position. Now she would give her the spiel she always gave at the start of an investigation, when she outlined what relatives could expect from her as their FLO. She'd begin by telling Eleanor she would keep her up to date on the progress of the investigation and that she'd be recording their conversations in her logbook so they could go over any points that were raised along the way, but she'd omit to mention it also gave her and the team the means to check any discrepancies in her account. She'd then tell Eleanor she might not be able to share certain information if it could jeopardize an arrest or subsequent conviction and, finally, she'd mention that the rules laid down for FLOs dictated she couldn't offer counselling herself, but she could put Eleanor in touch with Victim Support, who had trained specialists available to talk through how she was feeling. The no-counselling rule, designed to protect FLOs from becoming emotionally overburdened, was the one aspect of Family Liaison Maggie disliked. When she was with relatives round the clock, it was hard to bite her tongue when they wanted to vent or unburden themselves: in her mind it put up a wall that was unnecessary and unhelpful.

'Yes, I'm here to help—' Maggie began.

Eleanor cut her off.

'If you want to help, make them leave,' she said, firing a dirty look at Belmar and Green. 'And when you've done that, you can bloody well piss off too.'

13

'We can't force her to talk if she's not ready,' said Maggie, as an agitated Belmar paced up and down outside Eleanor's room. They had conceded to her demand that they leave her alone but it was with much reluctance on his part.

'The gaffer won't be happy,' he fretted.

'We'll try again later,' said Green.

'I know but—'

'This isn't about you, DC Small. I know you want to make a good impression in your new job,' Green continued, 'but she's just woken up in a strange place and she's trauma-tized because her husband tried to kill her a few hours ago. It's not like you've got to rush through her statement to secure an arrest either. Simon Bramwell's not going any-where.'

Belmar stopped pacing.

'You're right. Let's leave it for now and I'll let my DCI know what's going on. I'm not sure how involved HMET will be now we know it's a domestic and nothing to do with the husband's business.'

'My DCI' rang in Maggie's ears and her mind was sud-denly swamped with questions she wanted to ask Belmar about Umpire. *Did he say he was mad at me after last night? Is he coming to Mansell today?*

She shook her head as if that would dissolve them. She needed to get a grip.

'I have to go back to my station for a briefing on my other case,' she said. 'As soon as I'm done I'll come straight back here. Maybe Mrs Bramwell will have calmed down by then.'

Green nodded. 'Okay.'

Maggie was almost at the exit from HDU when Belmar caught up with her.

'I am sorry I didn't tell you about the new job. You should've heard it from me.'

'It's okay, I understand.'

'I think you're right – Ballboy probably didn't want me to say anything in case you talked me out of it.' He gave her a grin then strolled back to where DI Green was making herself comfortable on a plastic chair outside Eleanor's room.

Maybe that *was* the reason for the secrecy. Umpire knew how passionate Maggie was about Family Liaison yet had tried more than once to persuade her to give it up and train in a new specialism that made it easier for her to go up a rank. Very few detective sergeants were FLOs because their caseloads wouldn't allow it. Maybe he didn't want Belmar to be held back either.

She dug her phone out of her bag to check if he'd messaged her but there were no new texts or voicemails waiting. Realistically she knew he'd be busy now the investigation was under way but the radio silence still unnerved her. This was the longest they'd gone without contact in months.

Before she could dissuade herself, she sent Umpire another text. They were meant to be going out for dinner the following evening – surely a sufficient enough reason to message him again.

Hey, are we still on for tmw night?

To her surprise, a text pinged back from him almost immediately. Her hands shook as she read it.

No.

14

Shortly before 9 p.m. a nurse appeared at Sadie's bedside and announced to Della that visiting hours were about to end for the day.

'But I want to stay with her,' said Della, who had expected to continue her vigil throughout the night. 'What if she needs me?'

'We'll call you if there's any change.'

The nurse was a new arrival for the night-time shift and not one of the staff who had spent all day checking on Sadie and administering her pain relief. Della decided she couldn't possibly know enough about her nan's condition to justify sending her away and for once tried to stand her ground.

'Can I please speak to the doctor? He might be fine with me staying,' she said.

There was more than a hint of impatience in the nurse's voice as she intoned that the consultant wouldn't be available until the morning and Della really would have to leave. Realizing she was beaten, Della pulled on her coat. If she'd known she couldn't stay she'd have asked Alex to hang on and give her a lift home. He'd turned up at the hospital just after 8 p.m., apologizing for not arriving sooner because he'd been held up at work. When he asked one of the nurses about Sadie's prognosis and relayed to Della that she was 'stable but critical', Della didn't have the heart to say she already knew that and it had been unchanged all day. She could see how exhausted he was, and when he started yawning less than twenty minutes later, Della told him to go home and get some sleep.

'I am knackered,' he'd said as he gave her a grateful peck on the lips. 'It's been a rough day at work.' Then he'd caught himself. 'Oh God, I'm sorry. That was really insensitive of me. It's hardly been a good day for you either.'

'It's all right, Alex, I know what you meant.'

Assuming, like her, she'd be there all night, he promised to call her in the morning, told her he loved her then left.

As Della kissed Sadie goodbye and walked quietly out of the room, her mind churned over the events of the day. The same pair who'd targeted the other elderly women in Mansell were surely the people who'd attacked Sadie, but Della couldn't stop thinking about another possibility. It was that female detective, Maggie, who'd set her mind on to it, after their conversation in the hospital garden.

What if Helen *was* behind it?

The idea wasn't as implausible as Della had led Maggie to believe – there was, in fact, a good reason why Helen might have suddenly returned to Mansell after all these years.

Della's birthday was four weeks away, on 11 December. She was turning twenty-one and would mark the occasion by inheriting £3,000 from her grandfather's savings that was placed in a trust fund for her when he died. As far as Della was aware, only she and Sadie knew of the fund's existence, but what if Helen also did? Her grandparents could've discussed setting it up for Della long before they actually got round to it. What if Helen had returned to claim what was rightfully hers as Sadie and Eric's heir?

Della nervously wound a strand of hair round her finger as she walked down the corridor and out of HDU, a habit begun in childhood that she'd never been able to break. Should she mention to the police about her birthday and the money, in case it was relevant? She wished she could ask Sadie if there was a possibility Helen knew about it.

Too tired to think straight, Della trudged to the bus station to catch the 141 home. Halfway through her journey a sudden realization pierced through her jumbled thoughts. If Helen had come back to get her hands on the pay-out she would need all the paperwork relating to it – and the uniformed officers who arrived first at the house that morning had told Della that Sadie's personal documents, kept locked in a bureau in the dining room, were not disturbed during the break-in.

She slumped back in her seat and stared dejectedly out of the window as the bus continued to wind through the streets of Mansell, past rows of parked cars and houses with Christmas decorations hung prematurely in their windows.

It was silly of her to think Helen had returned after all this time – yet it surprised her how much she wished it was true.

15

Maggie watched Della leave HDU from her vantage point outside Eleanor Bramwell's room, but did not call out to her. The young woman looked exhausted and troubled and as Maggie had no other questions for her at that time, it seemed kinder to leave her to go home and get some rest.

'It's gone nine,' Maggie said to Belmar, who was fidgeting on the hard plastic seat next to her. 'How much longer do we give it? Eleanor has made it clear she's not going to talk to us this evening.'

Three times they'd gone in to ask if she was ready to make a statement; three times Eleanor had screamed at them to get out. After the third time, DI Green ruefully said that she was going to head back to Trenton. 'I can make myself more useful up there than I can sitting here.'

Belmar got to his feet and stretched.

'I'll call Ballboy to see what he says but I think we should call it a night,' he said. 'As long as uniform stay here on the door, I don't see why we need to as well.'

Maggie nodded. It felt strange to be taking direction from Belmar when it had been the other way round on the Rosie Kinnock case, with her the more experienced FLO in their partnership. Belmar's position as one of the investigating officers with HMET meant he could call the shots over her now, even though they shared the same detective rank.

'I'll go outside,' he added. 'I don't want a nurse telling me off for using my phone in a restricted area.'

Maggie had no desire to check her own phone for messages, not after that last text from Umpire. Who knew one tiny word could cause so much hurt? It was worse than if he'd fired off a huge, expletive-filled rant. Now, she wasn't expecting to hear from him again unless it was work related.

Keen to distract herself from how upset he'd made her, Maggie mulled over the subject of whether Lou had forgiven her yet for forgetting to babysit. How long would her sister sulk for this time? The record was three weeks, back in their early twenties when Maggie had had to duck out of a week's holiday with Lou and the boys at a caravan park in Great Yarmouth because of work. The silence had dragged on far too long for Maggie's liking and only ended when she booked and paid for another trip to make up for the one she'd missed.

Maggie's friends often remarked that she was too deferential towards Lou and that it was wrong she always apologized for the slightest upset, especially when an apology wasn't warranted. Only Maggie knew that her saying sorry had less to do with her actions in the present and more to do with the past – specifically the death of Lou's fiancé, Jerome.

Maggie had had a secret affair with Jerome when she was eighteen, and she blamed herself for his death. Walking home from an afternoon's drinking in a pub while her pregnant sister was at work, Maggie had tried to kiss Jerome but he'd ducked out of her grasp, fearful someone might see them and tell Lou. He'd run backwards onto a zebra crossing without checking the oncoming traffic first and died almost instantly after being struck by a car.

More than once Maggie had come close to blurting out the truth to Lou, worn down by the guilt that festered inside her like a rotten appendix. If she hadn't tried to grab Jerome, if he hadn't run out, if he'd seen the car approaching, if she'd turned down his advances in the first place . . . So many 'what ifs', and she was haunted by them all. But she always stopped short of confessing because Lou didn't deserve her heart to be broken any more than it already had been: discovering the man she'd planned to marry had been having sex with her little sister would devastate her as much as his death had. So Maggie had learned to live with her secret and tried to make amends by devoting as much time and as many resources to Lou as she could spare, including paying a generous stipend into her bank account every month to help cover her bills.

Belmar returned smiling. 'Umpire says we can call it a night. He wants you back here first thing to try again with Mrs Bramwell.'

'What time? Shall I meet you in reception before heading up?' Maggie got to her feet and pulled her coat on.

'It won't be me coming, it'll be Ballboy. He said be here at eight.'

Maggie managed to keep a straight face as her insides somersaulted.

'He's coming himself? Why's that, if there's nothing to suggest a link to Bramwell's firm?'

'He didn't say. Fancy a drink before we head home?'

'Not tonight. I've got to pop round to Lou's. Tell you what, we'll go out and celebrate your new job properly when this case is done.'

'Allie will be pleased. She said it felt like we were lying to you when we saw you the other week and didn't say anything.'

Keeping the truth from someone was not the same as lying – as Maggie well knew. 'Tell her it's fine.'

'Good, I will.' He reached for his own overcoat, which was draped neatly on the back of his chair. 'We could both do with a night out to let off some steam.'

Maggie shot him a look. 'Is everything okay with you two?'

'Yeah, we've just got a lot going on at the moment.'

Maggie decided not to push him again – if he wanted to confide in her, he'd do it in his own time.

Downstairs in the hospital's main reception, she was relieved to see the newsagent's concession was still open.

'I need to pick up something for Lou,' she told Belmar. 'I'll speak to you in the morning. Tell Allie I said hi.'

He gave her a quick hug and left.

There were slim pickings inside the shop as most of the shelves needed replenishing after a busy day. Maggie grabbed a carton of Roses chocolates and a copy of *Heat* magazine with Taylor Swift on the cover. As a peace offering it would have to do.

16

The drive from the hospital to the street where Lou lived took less than five minutes. It was close to the railway line that carved through Mansell and a train heading in the direction of London thundered past as Maggie got out of her car. With a start it reminded her again of Umpire and the time they hopped aboard a train to dine out in Soho, their excitement building as the rolling Chiltern fields that encircled Mansell gave way to the densely packed streets of west London as they drew closer to Marylebone, their final stop. Smarting with regret, she watched the train disappear from view down the tracks.

Lou's house was in the middle of the terrace and Maggie was surprised to see that the upstairs lights were still on as she approached. Reaching the front door, she could hear children's voices shrieking inside and was even more taken aback. Lou never let the boys stay up so late on a school night.

She rapped on the front door with the knocker but the noise inside was too loud for it to be heard. So she thumped on the door with her fist and suddenly everything went quiet. As the seconds ticked by, she thumped again and called out, 'Hey, Lou, it's me!'

She could hear scuffling inside until at last the door opened and Maggie found herself staring down at her eldest nephew, Jude.

'What are you doing still up?' she asked with a bemused smile.

'Nothing,' he said sheepishly.

Maggie frowned. He was a terrible liar.

'Jude, what's going on?

'Nothing.'

'Where's your mum?'

Jude wouldn't meet her gaze. Maggie pushed past him into the house, stepping straight from the front doorstep into the lounge, where she found Scotty bouncing on the sofa as a *Ben 10* cartoon blared out from the TV in the corner. Like Jude, he was in his pyjamas. On the coffee table there was an empty family-sized packet of cheese-flavoured Doritos, a discarded chocolate bar wrapper and two Robinson Fruit Shoots. No wonder Scotty was so hyper. Maggie marched over and turned the TV off, ignoring the howls of protest from him.

'Lou?' she called out. 'Are you upstairs?'

'She's not here,' giggled Scotty as he resumed his bouncing.

Maggie was horrified. 'She's gone out and left you on your own?'

'No, I'm babysitting,' said Jude defiantly and for a second Maggie was reminded of his dad. Jude took after Lou in appearance, with the same hazel eyes, aquiline nose and open features, but the older he got the more his temperament mirrored Jerome's. The easy-going little boy Maggie adored was becoming cocky and strong-willed as he hurtled towards adolescence.

'You're only eleven, Jude. You're far too young to babysit Scotty, let alone Mae.'

'That's not what Mum said,' he huffed.

'Is Mae with her?'

'No, she's upstairs asleep in her cot.'

Maggie was overcome by anger. What the hell was Lou thinking, leaving the children alone? What if one of them had hurt themselves? Didn't she realize she could be accused of abandonment or even neglect? Lou had pulled some stunts in her time but this one went beyond the pale.

'Right, you two, upstairs to bed,' she ordered. 'I'll wait down here until your mum gets home.'

She must've looked angry because neither boy argued as she ushered them upstairs. To her relief Mae was sleeping soundly in her cot in Lou's bedroom. Maggie tiptoed out and went into the room the boys shared.

'Has Mae been okay?' she asked Jude as he slid beneath his duvet on the top bunk bed. Despite his junk food excesses, Scotty was already drifting off in the bunk below.

'Yes,' he said sullenly, clearly unhappy that Maggie had taken charge. 'Mum left a bottle of milk in the fridge for me to heat up if she woke up. I know what I'm doing.'

'I know you do, Jude, you're terrific at helping with Mae. But that doesn't alter the fact you are way too young to be looking after her and Scotty on your own. Do you know where your mum's gone tonight?'

'She didn't say. She just said to call her if there was a problem.'

Maggie thought for a moment. Given her current mood, Lou would probably ignore her if she rang.

'Where's your phone, Jude?'

'There,' he said, pointing to the desk in the corner of the room. Lou had picked the desk up second-hand in a junk shop but it was Maggie who'd spent a weekend sanding it down and repainting it bright blue, the boys' favourite colour.

'I need to borrow it. I'll take it downstairs so I don't wake Mae. Go to sleep, sweetheart.'

Back in the lounge Maggie flicked through the contacts on Jude's phone to find Lou's number. She was gratified when her sister picked up after only two rings.

'Jude, what is it?' There was music playing loudly wherever Lou was and she had to shout to make herself heard. A man was laughing raucously very close by.

'It's not Jude, it's me.'

'Maggie? Why have you got Jude's phone?' Lou demanded to know, her panic evident. 'Has something happened?'

'No, thank God. But I came round to see you and found the kids on their own. I can't believe you went out and left them.'

'I'm only up the road at the Hand & Racquet,' Lou protested. 'I left Jude to babysit.'

'He's eleven,' Maggie hurled back. 'How could you be so irresponsible? You do know you could be done for leaving the kids at home alone?'

'Get off your high horse,' Lou snapped. 'If you hadn't let me down, I wouldn't have had to leave them.'

'I should've known you'd blame me. But you know what, Lou – for once I am not going to let you. Get back here *now*.'

'Oh, but I'm having such a good time,' her sister whined. 'I'm really sorry I left them and I promise never to do it again, but please, Maggie, can't you stay with them now you're there?'

Against her better judgement, Maggie could feel herself wavering.

'Please, Maggie,' Lou implored. 'I just want a night out. You know how hard it is for me.'

Maggie bit her lip.

'Come on, sis,' Lou tried again, her voice hardening. 'You owe me. Don't pretend you don't. I know what you've been keeping from me.'

Maggie went very still. 'What?'

There was a long pause that was filled by Liam Gallagher wailing the words to 'Wonderwall' in the background.

'It doesn't matter,' said Lou eventually. 'Will you stay or not?'

'I'll stay,' said Maggie quickly.

Lou hung up and Maggie slumped back on the sofa. For a horrible moment she'd thought her sister was going to say she knew about her and Jerome. But there was no way Lou wouldn't have come out with it straight away if she had found out. She'd go ballistic and would make sure everyone else knew about Maggie's betrayal too. And how would she ever find out anyway? The only other person who knew about the affair was Jerome and he was dead. He'd taken their sordid, shameful secret to the grave and it would remain there with him, buried forever.

17

Bea poked the porridge in front of her with her spoon. She wasn't hungry and had only managed a mouthful so far. Esme, who was sitting next to her at the table, had already finished hers and was now jabbering on about what she wanted for Christmas.

Bea's phone lay silent on the table beside her bowl. It felt odd not to have received any texts from Sean since leaving his flat yesterday. Normally there would be a steady stream of messages from him throughout the evening, which Bea would explain away to her parents as being a friend from school texting her. She'd saved his number under 'Nicole', just in case.

'Eat up, Bea,' her mum chided from across the kitchen, where she was unloading the dishwasher. 'You can't go to school on an empty stomach.'

Bea tried another mouthful and almost gagged. The porridge was cold now and it cemented to the roof of her mouth.

Her dad bundled into the kitchen in a rush, his overcoat half on as he fastened his watch.

'Anyone seen my keys?'

'Hanging up,' Bea, her mum and Esme all intoned simultaneously, before the latter two dissolved into giggles. Every day it was the same skit: Dad would rush in pretending he couldn't find his keys but they were where they always were, hanging on a hook in the hallway. It was a family in-joke but today Bea couldn't see the humour in it.

She caught her dad staring at her with concern and quickly ate another spoonful of porridge as he came over and stroked the back of her head.

'You okay, sweetheart?' he asked.

She nodded and pointed at her full mouth to show she couldn't answer him.

'Mum told me you want to go back to your natural hair colour. I can't say I'm not pleased,' he said with a smile.

'Oh, thank God for that,' squeaked Esme. 'That colour is so rank.'

'Enough, Esme,' said her mum sharply. 'Leave your sister alone.'

Esme rolled her eyes and returned to writing her Christmas wish list, top of which was an iPhone 6, followed by getting her ears pierced and a trip to London to see *Wicked*. Bea felt a pang of guilt – Esme was always being told to stop bothering her, like she was a porcelain ornament that mustn't be handled in case she shattered.

'She's right though,' said Bea. 'It is rank.'

She pulled a funny face at Esme, who grinned back. Their dad smiled at them both.

'Will you be back late again tonight?' Caroline asked him.

'I hope not. It depends if my meeting at four overruns. What have you got planned today?'

'I've been asked if I can go into the shop.'

Bea began to tune out of the conversation. The charity

shop in town where her mum volunteered and was in charge of marketing their fundraising events held little interest for her.

'You don't normally do Wednesdays.'

'No, but Sheila isn't coming in today and they need someone to fill in.'

'What's her excuse this time?'

'Actually, I don't think she's pulling a fast one for once. Her sister, Audrey, lives next door to a woman who was robbed in her home yesterday, Sadie something.'

Bea suddenly sat up, all ears.

'It sounds nasty – the woman was beaten and now she's in a critical condition at Mansell General. Sheila's sister is very upset, so Sheila wants to stay at home with her today.'

'Hmm,' said Chris distractedly.

Bea fumbled her spoon and it clattered onto the table. Her parents didn't notice.

'It's awful that these elderly women are being attacked in their own homes,' said Caroline. 'Did you see what they wrote in the *Echo*?'

Her husband didn't answer as he leaned across Bea to grab a banana from the fruit bowl on the table and put it in the brown leather Mulberry messenger bag he used for work.

'I can't blame Sheila for wanting to be with her sister,' her mum went on. 'It must've come as a terrible shock, happening right next door.'

Bea found her voice again but it shook as she spoke.

'Won't the old lady get better?' she asked.

Caroline came over and kissed the top of her head.

'I don't know, honey. Right, you two, it's nearly time to leave for school. Have you got your bags ready?'

Esme nodded, but Bea stayed still, her mind in a whirl. All she could think about was the old lady lying in hospital and, even though she knew she and Sean weren't responsible, it still felt like it was their fault. She couldn't go to school until she knew the woman was going to be okay.

'I don't feel well, Mum. I – I made myself sick last night.'

She felt Caroline tense up behind her and Bea hated that she was lying about something that had caused her parents so much anxiety over the past couple of years. But she needed an excuse to stay at home and she knew it would do the trick.

'After dinner?' said her mum hoarsely.

'Yes. I'm sorry, Mum.'

Looking round, she saw her parents exchange worried glances.

'You can stay at home today, Bea,' said Chris, as Caroline nodded. 'But we'll have to make an appointment to see Dr Reynolds again.'

'I'll call the shop and tell them I won't come in,' said Caroline.

'No! Don't do that. I'll be fine on my own. I don't want you to worry.' Bea groped around for a better explanation. 'I did tell you about being sick and I didn't have to. That's good, isn't it? I'm not keeping it a secret like last time.'

Her parents exchanged another look.

'Well, yes, it is,' said Chris eventually. 'Are you sure you'll be all right on your own?'

Bea nodded. She wouldn't be staying indoors though. As soon as her mum left to go into town, she would slip out and catch the bus to the hospital. She didn't know if they'd let her see the old lady, but she had to try. She had to say sorry.

18

Lost in thought as she hurried into Mansell General's ground-floor reception, Maggie didn't notice Umpire until he darted in front of her and waved his hand in her face.

'Didn't you hear me calling you?'

'Oh! You made me jump. I was miles away.'

She'd been thinking about Lou. They still hadn't discussed what had happened last night – Lou was weaving drunk when she got home at midnight so Maggie had put her straight to bed, then slept on the sofa in case Mae needed feeding or changing in the night. When she left an hour ago to nip home to shower and change before going to the hospital, her sister had been awake but monosyllabic. Maggie didn't want to start a row in front of the children so she left with a promise to go round later. They needed to discuss Lou's behaviour and whatever it was Lou felt she had over Maggie would have to wait until they were able to have a face-to-face conversation.

Umpire's interruption dragged her into the present. 'Coffee?' he asked. 'Need you up to speed.'

The brevity of his speech did not strike her as unusual: Will Umpire was not the kind of man to use many words when a few would do. What she minded was the fact he seemed reluctant to look in her direction, as if making eye contact with her was the last thing he wanted to do. Nor had he called her by her first name, as he had done every time they'd spoken for the past six months. Maggie was crushed but tried not to show it.

The Costa Coffee concession was already busy for 8 a.m., with hospital staff queuing up alongside members of the public. She stood beside him in the queue and kept quiet as he busied himself plucking pound coins from the stash of change in his pocket.

'Latte, isn't it?' he asked her when it was their turn to be served.

As she nodded, Maggie was overcome by the urge to break the impasse between them. Being in such close proximity made her realize how desperate she was to make amends for Monday evening. She wanted them to go back to how they were.

'Will—' she began tentatively.

He cut her off abruptly. 'DC Small filled me in on what happened with Mrs Bramwell when you tried to question her. When we get up there I want you to go in on your own first, see if she feels less threatened by just you. I'm happy for you to take her initial statement informally if that makes her more comfortable but if she doesn't cooperate at all I'll have to take over, DC Neville.'

Maggie felt winded, like he'd just delivered a well-aimed punch to her stomach. She had expected him to be a bit brusque with her, but he was acting as though they barely knew each other and she hated that it upset her so much.

'If that's what you think, *sir*,' she said evenly. 'Will DI Green be joining us?'

'No.'

A barista called out their order and Umpire grabbed both cups of coffee. Maggie trailed him to a table near the entrance to the concession. He was six foot three and lean in frame and struggled to fold his long legs under the table. Maggie could tell he hadn't shaved that morning and his chin bristled with more grey than his natural strawberry blond. It suited him.

'Is the husband still unconscious?' she said briskly, placing her notebook on the table in front of her. If he could be detached, so could she.

'Yes. The doctors are saying it's too early to tell whether any of his organs are damaged, because they still don't know exactly how much diazepam he took.' He sipped his coffee. 'I need Mrs Bramwell's testimony before the CPS will consider charges. His prints were found on the knife used to stab his wife but the defence could argue that's because he regularly used it in the kitchen.'

'But it still looks like he attacked her?'

'Yes.'

'Belmar – I mean DC Small,' she said hastily, 'seems to think HMET won't continue with the case now there's no link to Mr Bramwell's line of work.'

'I think DC Small is getting ahead of himself. Nothing can be ruled out until Mrs Bramwell tells us what happened. That's why I've come down myself, to make sure it gets done.'

Maggie wrestled with what to say next. She had so many questions for him: why did he send such a sharp text in reply to her checking about dinner? Did that mean they weren't even friends any more? Why did he order Belmar not to say anything to her about joining HMET? But now wasn't the time. He couldn't have made it clearer that personal talk was not welcome.

'Is there anything else in particular you want me to raise?' she said, pen poised again.

'It would help to know how much diazepam was left in the prescription packet her husband emptied, as it's her name on the label. Find why she takes it too,' he said. 'I also want to know what room she was in when the attack began – from the blood we've found it looks like she moved between a few of them. Even if Bramwell doesn't recover and we can't charge him, we still need a full account before we can close the case. I'll wait outside while you talk to his wife, if she deigns to be interviewed this time.'

Maggie frowned. It wasn't like him to speak disparagingly about a victim.

'She was very distressed when she came round yesterday. I imagine that's why she didn't want to talk straight away,' she made a point of saying.

Umpire said nothing as he swirled his cup and drained the dregs of his coffee.

'Right, let's go.' He pulled a face as his phone rang. 'Fucking solicitors,' he muttered under his breath as he killed the call.

'CPS causing problems?' she asked, presuming the call was connected to either this case or another.

'No. My soon-to-be-ex-wife being difficult about when I have the children.'

Maggie was stunned. From the conversations they'd had

over the summer, she believed Umpire's estranged wife was happy to split custody of their two children, Flora and Jack, once their divorce was finalized. What had happened to change that? Her eyes raked over his face, searching for any clue, but his expression remained stony. By confiding what the call was about, was he expecting her to ask? Her answer came a second later as he rose from his seat and headed out of the seating area towards the lift.

'Come on, Neville,' he snapped.

Deeply unsettled, Maggie trailed behind him. Even if they did manage to resolve their row and get back to how they had been, would it always be like this, with him dictating how it was between them because she had no choice but to defer to him while they were at work? Was it even possible for them to have a personal relationship on an equal footing when at work it was the opposite? As Umpire continued to avoid eye contact with her as they queued for the lift, she began to seriously doubt that they could.

19

A night's rest had done nothing to improve Eleanor Bramwell's mood. She ordered Maggie to leave as soon as she saw it was her who'd knocked on her door and not a nurse or doctor.

But Maggie stayed where she was at the foot of the bed, acutely aware that Umpire was right outside expecting answers.

'You do need to talk to us at some point, Mrs Bramwell. Isn't it better to get it out of the way now, so we can leave you in peace?'

Eleanor's face creased into a scowl, but she didn't tell her to leave again, which Maggie took as a hopeful sign.

'Why don't we talk for five minutes then have a break? Five minutes, that's all.'

A while back Maggie had read a newspaper article on the subject of procrastination, in which a clinical psychologist was quoted as saying that people with a tendency to stall should set themselves a five-minute time limit when they began a task to make it seem less insurmountable. Once the five minutes was up they could stop, but more often than not they'd find they were happy to continue and would complete the task in full. Maggie found that applying the rule when interviewing trickier witnesses often had the same effect.

'Okay,' said Eleanor warily.

'Can I sit down?'

She nodded and Maggie settled herself in the hard plastic chair by her bed, stealing a glance as she pulled her notebook from her bag. Eleanor's complexion was wan and her long blonde hair tangled and in need of a brush, but on the whole she didn't look too bad for someone who'd been through such an ordeal.

As if she was aware of what Maggie was thinking, Eleanor looked her squarely in the eye.

'Go on then, what do you want to ask me?'

'It would be helpful if we could establish a timeline of what happened. Can we do that?'

Eleanor's eyelids squeezed shut for a moment and Maggie thought she was going to ask her to leave again. Then she realized she was trying to stop herself from crying.

'It's okay, Mrs Bramwell. You're safe now.'

Eleanor nodded frantically as tears began to seep down her face. Her right arm was in a sling so she could only use her left hand to wipe them away.

'I know. It's just—' she fought back a sob and squeezed her eyes tighter, but continued to talk. 'Simon slept on the sofa because we'd had a row the night before. I went to bed around one a.m. and fell asleep. The next thing I know he's crashing into the bedroom screaming his head off. Before I could say anything, he . . . he stabbed me in the leg. At first I didn't realize what he'd done. Our duvet is very thick so the knife only nicked me through it. But then he did it again and again. I screamed at him to leave me alone and then I got out of bed.'

Eyes still closed, Eleanor shuddered.

'What happened next?' Maggie gently asked.

Eleanor's eyes flew open and she stared at her coldly.

'You do understand how hard this is for me?'

'I appreciate how difficult it must be to relive what's happened, but it's important we establish the facts, and the more you tell me now, the less likely it is I'll have to keep coming back with more questions. I don't want to prolong this experience for you any more than I have to.'

'Is my husband dead yet?'

Maggie was taken aback by the bluntness of her question. 'No. He's still critical.'

'But he's going to die, isn't he? I mean, given the amount of pills he took. And all the vodka.'

Maggie jumped on the comment.

'Actually, we can't be sure how many tablets he ingested. I understand the diazepam was prescribed to you?'

'Yes.'

'When did you receive the prescription?'

'A fortnight ago. There are twenty-eight pills in a packet, but I don't take one every day, just when I need to. There must've been at least twenty-three tablets left.'

Maggie jotted down the number then Eleanor asked if she could help her get more comfortable. As Maggie helped her sit up straighter and settled her against the pillows, she noticed Eleanor was still wearing a hospital-issue gown.

'Would you like me to arrange to have some of your things brought in from home?'

For that she received her first smile.

'God, yes please. This thing is so itchy,' said Eleanor, tugging at the gown's neckline. 'I don't think the hospital understands the concept of fabric conditioner.'

'You can give me a list of what you'd like at the end,' said Maggie. She quickly glanced at her watch and noted five minutes had passed. She didn't say anything and resumed her questioning.

'Where do you normally keep the diazepam?'

'In the bathroom cabinet.'

'Can I ask why you take it?'

'No, you can't,' said Eleanor bluntly. She appeared more in control of herself: her eyes were dry again. 'It's not relevant.'

Maggie shrugged off the rebuke. They could come back to it.

'How did you get away from your husband in the bedroom?'

'I managed to push him over and ran to the bathroom, but he came after me and stabbed me in the shoulder as I was closing the door. The pain was horrendous and I passed out on the bathmat.'

'Do you remember what time you first entered the bathroom?'

'It must've been about three minutes past five.'

'That's quite specific. What makes you so certain it was then?' said Maggie carefully.

'When Simon came into the bedroom I turned the bedside light on and I saw on my alarm clock that it was five a.m. on the dot. After he started stabbing me it could only have been a matter of minutes before I got into the bathroom.' Eleanor shuddered. 'He was so drunk it wasn't that hard to get away from him.'

'Do you have any idea what time it was when you came round?'

'No, but it was still dark outside.'

Maggie thought for a moment.

'Okay, so with the clocks going back, it's not light until about seven twenty most mornings. Was it dark for quite a while?'

'No. If I had to guess I'd say about half an hour, then it started getting light.'

'Based on those timings you were unconscious for well over an hour.'

'If you say so.'

'No, Mrs Bramwell, *you* say so – according to the times you've given me. I need you to be clear on this,' said Maggie. 'Are you sure it was five-oh-three that you went into the bathroom?'

'I am,' Eleanor snapped back.

'What did you do between regaining consciousness and going outside?'

Eleanor chewed her bottom lip as high spots of red formed on her cheeks. Suddenly she seemed less sure of herself.

'I freaked out because I had a knife sticking out between my shoulder and my collarbone. I thought about pulling it out but it was agony so I pressed a towel around it. And then I waited.'

'For what?'

'To see if I could hear Simon. I didn't want to leave the

bathroom in case he attacked me again. I waited until I thought it was safe.'

'When you couldn't hear anything?'

'Yes. Once I thought it was safe I came out and went to the top of the stairs with the intention of going straight down, but then I saw Simon through the doorway to our bedroom.'

'Where was he?' said Maggie, even though she already knew the answer from the briefing Belmar and DI Green had given her yesterday.

'Laid out on our bed. At first I thought he was passed out – he'd drunk a lot of red wine and vodka even before we rowed – but I could see his lips and fingertips had this odd bluish tint. I went into the bedroom and I thought he was dead, so that's when I ran downstairs and went outside for help and my neighbour found me.' Eleanor slowly exhaled as she reached the end of her account.

'Thank you, Mrs Bramwell, that's very helpful. Now I'd like, if you don't mind, to go back a bit further, to the actual row itself and what started it.'

Eleanor began to protest but Maggie raised a hand to placate her.

'Let me explain why we need to know what triggered it. Should your husband regain consciousness, he'll almost certainly be facing criminal proceedings based on what you've told us so far and the forensic evidence we've gathered. His defence lawyer may present a different version of events though, or try to argue mitigating circumstances, so we need to know what caused the row to make sure your husband can't try to claim that he acted in self-defence and armed himself with the knife because he felt threatened by you.'

Eleanor paled. 'Are you serious?'

'Yes. It's what defence lawyers do – they try to present the best case to get their clients acquitted. My job is make sure we have all the facts to disprove it.'

'There is no way he could say it was self-defence, no way at all,' said Eleanor, shaking her head angrily.

'Why's that?'

'He attacked me after accusing me of having an affair. He came at me when I was lying in bed, not the other way round. He stabbed me clean through the duvet; it was all torn up,' said Eleanor bleakly. 'And I'm not seeing anyone else, before you ask. Simon's just paranoid about other men and always has been, ever since we got together.'

'Did he say who he thought you're having an affair with?'

'No, that's the craziest thing about it. He said I must be, because I've been going to the gym a lot and that I must be doing it for another man. But the reason I'm trying to stay fit is to improve our chances of having a baby.'

Eleanor's gaze wandered to a spot on the wall above Maggie's head and her fingers plucked nervously at the blanket covering her.

'I have what doctors call unexplained infertility – apparently there's no medical reason why I shouldn't be able to conceive naturally. We've already had three rounds of IVF that haven't worked; my useless body won't allow an egg to implant, and the doctors can't tell why.'

It struck Maggie as an odd way for Eleanor to describe herself, like her body was a third party separate to the rest of her. Or maybe detaching herself from the process was the easiest way to deal with it failing.

'Simon thinks we should wait a bit before trying again

because it's so expensive. I thought going to the gym might improve my chances of getting pregnant naturally while we save up for our next cycle. He didn't believe me when I said that's why I was going out and the row started when I got back late from a class last night.'

Maggie made a note to suggest to Umpire that they confirm Eleanor was at the gym when she said she was. There was no reason to disbelieve her – it was simply a case of being thorough.

'Is that it?' said Eleanor. 'I'm tired now.'

Maggie had enough information to go on for the time being, but a final question niggled away at her.

'Yes, we can wrap it up for now,' she said. 'But before we do, I was wondering if your husband made any attempt to break down the door to the bathroom once you were locked inside?'

Eleanor's expression hardened. 'What?'

'Well, it sounds like he was in an agitated state when the attack commenced and I'm wondering if he made any attempt to get at you in the bathroom.'

'He banged and kicked on the door after I locked it and I thought he was going to knock it off its hinges so I screamed at him to leave me alone. After that it went quiet and then, as I've already told you, I passed out from the pain,' said Eleanor with more than a trace of annoyance. 'Please, I'm very tired now. Can we stop?'

'Yes, of course,' said Maggie. 'Do you want to tell me what items you'd like brought in from home? I'll arrange to have them picked up.'

After writing down the list of things, Maggie gathered up

her coat and bag and said goodbye to Eleanor, who was far warmer saying farewell than she had been with her greeting.

As Maggie closed the door behind her, another question popped into her mind and when Umpire rose to his feet in readiness for an update, she fired it at him.

'Sir, when Simon Bramwell was found on the bed, was the empty packet of diazepam with him?'

Umpire's forehead creased into deep lines as he stared at her.

'No, he crushed up the pills in the kitchen. The empty packet was on the side along with the vodka bottle. Why do you ask?'

'I'm wondering how he got hold of them when Mrs Bramwell had locked herself in the bathroom. That's where she said she kept them.'

'He must've taken them downstairs before the row started, which . . .' His eyes locked on Maggie's and she knew what was coming next.

'. . . suggests this was premeditated and that Simon Bram well had every intention of killing his wife last night and committing suicide afterwards. It wasn't heat of the moment,' Umpire concluded.

But something still wasn't adding up for Maggie and she shook her head to convey her doubt.

'If he really did plan to kill her all along, why stop halfway through? Okay, he was drunk, but why not make sure the job was finished? Mrs Bramwell said he almost took the bathroom door off its hinges to get to her then changed his mind. Why?'

'Perhaps he decided he couldn't go through with it but felt guilty for what he'd done so he tried to top himself anyway.' Umpire gave her a searching look. 'You're not buying it though, are you?'

'No, I'm not. She's being so spiky towards us when we're trying to help her that it makes me think she's not being entirely truthful.'

'Well, you're in the best position to find out if she isn't. Keep questioning her account, but do it subtly.'

'I know what to do, sir,' Maggie said, more abruptly than she intended.

The grin Umpire flashed her was so unexpected that it almost wrong-footed her. Then it disappeared just as quickly, the impenetrable mask slipping firmly back into place.

'I know you do,' he said coolly, 'which is why I asked for you to be assigned her FLO in the first place. So far the circumstantial and forensic evidence backs her story, but if you think Eleanor Bramwell is lying, find out why.'

20

Lou was dozing in bed when a sudden burst of light forced her eyes open. Raising her head off the pillow, she blearily made out Jude's silhouette in the doorway of her bedroom, the light streaming in behind him rendering his face almost pitch-black and featureless.

'I've made you some tea downstairs, Mum. It's time to get up. We've got to get to school.'

He went across the room and pulled open the curtains. Lou groaned and covered her eyes with her hands.

'It's too bright,' she said, pulling the duvet over her face.

Her head throbbed and her mouth was parched. How much had she had to drink in the end? The evening had started with them ordering beer, that much she did remember. When her second pint started to sour her taste buds, she switched to bottles of cider and then she had a vague recollection of Arturs ordering some tequila shots, of which she downed at least one. She groaned again. How could she be so stupid to drink so much on a Tuesday night?

'Is Auntie Maggie still here?' she asked in a muffled voice from beneath the cover.

Her sister had stuck her head round the door first thing

to wake her up but Lou had been in no mood to listen to a lecture about being irresponsible and had ignored her until she took the hint and went back downstairs.

'No. She had to go to work,' said Jude. 'I made Scotty get dressed and gave him his breakfast and I gave Mae her milk and I changed her nappy.'

She could hear the pride in his voice and for a moment felt vindicated. Jude was a responsible kid – why couldn't he babysit his brother and sister? But Maggie's angry words still rang in her ears and deep down she knew her sister was right. She should never have left him to look after Scotty and Mae while she went to the pub.

Lou lowered the duvet and turned onto her side so she was facing away from the window. As she moved, her back gave a sharp twinge and she realized her buttocks also felt sore. Through the fog of her hangover she remembered how Arturs had cajoled her into the back of his work van in the pub car park after she told him that he couldn't come home with her because of Maggie and the children. The recollection made her giggle – it had been years since she'd had such frantic, urgent sex.

'What is it?' asked Jude, looking concerned.

'Nothing, sweetheart,' she said quickly. 'Thanks for sorting breakfast. I'll get up now.' She tried not to wince as she pulled back the covers and eased her aching body out of bed. 'Did you say Scotty's dressed for school?'

'Yep. Our bags are ready too.'

She flashed him a grateful smile. 'Thanks, hon. I'll get dressed and be right down.'

There was a three-quarter-length mirror on the front of the wardrobe door. When Jude had gone, Lou stripped off the old T-shirt she wore as a nightgown and stood with her back to it, twisting her head over her shoulder to see if there were bruises on her back and bum from contact with the van's metal floor. From what she could see, there were none. She turned straight ahead again and appraised her body in the mirror. The toll of carrying three babies could be seen in her flattened breasts and the way the skin across her stomach dimpled, though she'd lost weight in the past six months and her thighs and bum were trim again. But it was in her face that she saw the greatest transformation. Despite her thumping headache and greasy hair, her eyes shone and her cheeks were flushed with an excitement she hadn't felt for a long time. Arturs made her feel sexy and wanted again.

As she quickly dragged on her underwear and a pair of jeans and a jumper, Lou told herself she'd have to smooth things over with Maggie about leaving the kids. She couldn't afford a falling-out with her sister: aside from the fact she relied on her for emotional support, she also couldn't manage without the money Maggie gave her every month.

She knew she took advantage of her sister's kind nature but she couldn't help it. Her life was such a struggle and Maggie was always there for her, willing to help out. She had been since Jerome's accident. Lou knew it was because her sister was chewed up with guilt that she wasn't able to stop Jerome being hit by that car, but it wasn't Maggie's fault – she just happened to have been there. The only person Lou blamed was Jerome, for drinking so much that he couldn't see straight as he crossed the road.

Pottering downstairs, a sudden flash of memory came to her. There *was* something Maggie needed to apologize to her for, the thing Lou had alluded to on the phone last night.

She'd found out on Monday from a mutual friend that her ex-husband, Rob, was planning to move to Majorca with his fiancée, Lisa, now the Rosie Kinnock trial was behind them. The friend, who trained at the same gym as Rob in the centre of town, said Lisa's parents owned an apartment in Palma and the two of them were planning to pick up some bar work on the Spanish island before they got married over there in April.

The ramifications of Rob leaving the UK were huge. Not only would Mae hardly ever see her dad if he moved abroad, but it would also be much harder for Lou to chase him when he was slack with his maintenance payments, which he often was. And if Rob and Lisa started a family of their own, she feared Mae would become even more of an afterthought.

Shocked by the news, Lou had texted her mum, Jeanette, to tell her, and it turned out she already knew – because Maggie had known about it for weeks from the witness liaison officer who had been dealing with Lisa ahead of her giving evidence at the trial. Lou couldn't fathom why Maggie hadn't told her something so important the second she heard about it and was determined to have it out with her.

Keeping a secret like that just wasn't what sisters did.

21

Alex wiped an arc through the mist on the inside of the windscreen with his gloved hand and peered up at Sadie's house. A strip of blue and white police tape hung loosely from the front gate.

'Are you sure we're even allowed in?' he asked Della. 'Isn't it still a crime scene?'

'I don't know. I rang the police before we left but there was no answer on the number I was given,' she fretted. 'I thought I should check on the house before I went to the hospital though, because I don't know if the police locked up properly. I don't want anyone else getting in.'

'I can't imagine anyone would attempt another break-in after yesterday.'

His hot breath made the windscreen steam up again. It felt even colder today than it had been yesterday and even though she was bundled up in her thick coat Della still felt chilled to the bone. She was exhausted too, having lain awake all night, petrified the hospital was going to call at some point to say Sadie had died.

'You think we shouldn't go in?' she said.

'I think it'll be okay. If the police didn't want anyone here they'd put someone outside to keep guard. You need to get inside so you can get the ball rolling on the insurance claim.'

Della flinched. It felt wrong to be discussing money while her nan was in hospital, like they were being grubby and underhand. Alex had first brought up the subject when he'd turned up at her flat last night, saying it would give her something else to focus on, but she didn't share his conviction.

She'd been surprised to see him on her doorstep, given how shattered he had been when he'd left the hospital a couple of hours earlier, but he said he felt bad about her being on her own and she'd fallen gratefully into his arms. When Alex was with her she felt more able to cope.

She watched as he leaned forward to wipe the windscreen again. He was good looking, with a body kept fit by thrice-weekly runs and thick brown hair he spent half an hour every morning coaxing into a quiff. He resembled nothing of her previous two boyfriends, who were both blond and, like her, on the skinny side, and while she believed it was a bit shallow to think so, she liked being seen out with Alex. He made her look good.

'Have you phoned the insurance company yet?' he asked, wiping the windscreen for a third time as it misted back over.

'No, not yet.'

'You need to be quick about these things.'

'I thought I should see what's actually missing first. I haven't given a complete list to the police yet.'

'Oh. Well, yeah, I suppose you should do that first. I wonder if your nan had valuables stashed away you didn't even know about?' he mused.

'I doubt it. We had a big tidy up when I moved out last year and I didn't come across anything then that I didn't know about already.'

Alex gave a sly grin. 'Maybe you missed them. It's always worth putting down for a few extra things when you stick in the claim, like bits of jewellery or maybe a camera.'

'You mean lie?' said Della, shocked.

'Come on, those insurance companies make a fortune on premiums. What's the price of another necklace to them?'

'No, I can't do that. It's wrong.'

Alex held up his hands. The black wool glove he'd used to wipe the windscreen appeared soaked through.

'You're right, forget I mentioned it. Shall we go in? I haven't got long before I need to get to work.'

'Are you sure you can't take the day off?'

His expression clouded. 'I really can't, Del. I do want to see your nan but it's so manic at work right now and you know what Geoff is like. I'll try to pop up to the hospital in my lunch break.'

She knew he would try. Alex got on well with Sadie and he understood and respected the importance of Della's relationship with her. But, still, she was disappointed and ducked her face behind the upright collar of her coat to hide it.

The entire hallway was covered in a filmy black dust – the banister leading upstairs, the doors and door frames between the hall and the living room and kitchen, the picture frames and ornaments on the walls. Immediately Della's eyes fell upon the gap left by the missing photograph. She noticed there was a partial handprint in the dust next to it.

Alex bundled into the hallway behind her.

'So if your nan doesn't pull through, you'll get the house?' he asked.

'No, it reverts back to Quadrant Homes,' said Della as she peered through the doorway into the sitting room. She hastily backtracked when she saw the dark stain on the carpet by the sofa.

'Who?'

'The housing association. But can we not talk about that, please? I want Nan to be okay.'

'You what?'

The sharpness of Alex's voice made her swivel round. He frowned at her.

'What did you say?'

'I said I want Nan to be okay.'

'No, before that.'

Exhaustion was making it hard for her to think straight. 'Before? You asked me about the house.'

'You mentioned something called Quadrant.'

'Oh, right, yes. That's the housing association which manages this place.'

'I thought your nan owned this house.'

Della shrugged off her coat and hung it on the bottom of the banister. The heating must have come on with the timer as the house was stifling. Sadie always liked it to be tropically warm.

'No. She and my granddad always rented.'

She caught the surprised look on Alex's face and grew defensive. 'My granddad wasn't well paid and Nan gave up work so she could look after me and they could never scrape together enough to buy their own home. Some families can't. There's no shame in it,' she added hotly.

'I'm not saying there is. I just assumed this would be all yours one day.'

'No, it won't.' Suddenly she was overcome and began to cry.

'Hey, come here.' Alex wrapped his arms round her. 'I didn't mean to upset you.'

'I can't bear the idea of someone else moving in. If Nan dies, they'll want the house back straight away.'

'They can't do that—' Alex pulled away as his phone pinged in his pocket. 'Shit, it's Geoff asking when I'm coming in. Sorry, I have to go.' He kissed her hard on the lips. 'Call me if you need me.' Then, after a pause, he cupped Della's face in his hands and stared directly into her eyes. 'You know I love you, right?'

She nodded. 'I love you too.'

'Good. Right, I'll see you later. Oh, and have a think about what I said about the insurance claim. If we got a bit of extra cash we could go on holiday when all this is over, somewhere nice and hot.'

22

The automatic doors slid seamlessly open but Bea couldn't bring herself to step through them. Ahead of her was a mass of people and the noise and bustle was too daunting. She took a step backwards and the doors slid shut, cutting her off from the clamour.

'Hey, stop mucking about with those doors.'

Bea looked round to see a man in a fluorescent yellow jacket bearing down on her, his face twisted in a snarl. Terrified, she shot forward again. As the doors slid open and the milling crowd swallowed her up, she turned to see the word 'Security' emblazoned on the breast of the man's jacket and she felt a stab of relief. He wasn't the police.

Bea picked her way round the edge of the reception area as she debated how best to find out where the old woman was being treated when all she had to go on was her first name. Eventually a desk marked 'Information' loomed into view on her right, staffed by a man and a woman. Bea sped over to it and settled herself in the woman's queue.

'Yes?' said the woman when it was Bea's turn. She didn't bother to look up from her computer.

'I'm . . . I'm . . .' Bea looked helplessly around for inspiration. She couldn't just ask to see the old woman when she wasn't a relative: hospitals had strict rules about that, which she remembered from the time her dad had an operation on his knee. Then her gaze fell upon the posters on the wall behind the receptionist's head and one in particular, adorned with the words, 'CAN YOU HELP?'

'Volunteering,' said Bea excitedly. 'I want to know about becoming a volunteer.'

The woman, who was older than Bea's mum, raised her head to look at her, then swivelled her chair round on its casters to see what she was pointing at. When she wheeled round again her expression was curiously triumphant.

'You can't do that. You're too young,' she said.

'Is there an age limit?'

'Yep. Seventeen. Can't have anyone younger. Rules and regulations.' The woman's eyes narrowed. 'Why aren't you at school?'

To Bea's relief, the middle-aged man also behind the desk butted in. He gave Bea a little wink and a smile, the latter of which she returned.

'Come on, Pamela, let's not put her off from helping out. It's not often we get young ones coming forward. Yes, there is an age limit,' he said to Bea, 'but if you're sixteen you can get your parents to give written permission for you to volunteer.'

'You'll still need ID though,' his colleague chipped in.

'Pamela, why don't you see to this gentleman,' said the man. His voice was calm but it did nothing to pacify Pamela, who tut-tutted as she snapped her attention to the person in the queue behind Bea.

'The volunteer scheme is run by a service called PALS.

Their office is on the second floor,' the man told Bea. 'I can give you directions, if you're sure you want to sign up?'

He gave Bea such an intense stare that she almost took a step back. Why would he doubt her?

'I am sure,' she said, nodding.

'Well, good for you. If only more young people were as community-minded,' he said, smiling. 'Here, this is the way.'

Using a bit of space on a leaflet offering advice on depression, he drew Bea a rough map.

'Thank you,' said Bea, taking it from him.

'I hope we see you here again,' he said with a smile.

Pamela looked less convinced.

The woman manning the PALS office was as nice as the man on the information desk and apologized to Bea when she said they couldn't lower the age limit under any circumstances.

'If you were sixteen your parents could vouch for you,' she explained, 'but I'm guessing you're a bit younger than that?'

For a moment Bea considered lying. She did have some fake ID that one of Sean's mates had procured for her so she could go to the pub with them. But using it might be more trouble than it was worth. What if she got found out and it led the authorities back to Sean?

'I'm fourteen,' she admitted.

The lady gave her a sympathetic look. 'I'm sorry, I'm afraid you'll have to come back in a couple of years if you want to volunteer. But you could help us through fundraising until then.'

Bea brightened. 'Would that get me onto the wards?'

'Oh no,' said the woman with a laugh. 'I meant by doing a sponsored silence or a cake sale.'

Dejected, Bea thanked the woman for her help then left the office and meandered her way back down the long corridors towards the lifts. She was almost there when a man in an orderly's uniform stopped her and asked if she was lost. He was quite elderly and his eyes appeared unfocused. Bea wasn't sure if he was even looking at her.

'I can help you if you want,' said the man. He spoke slowly and over-enunciated his words.

'That's kind of you, but I'm okay,' she said.

'Visiting someone, are you?'

Bea was suddenly inspired.

'Actually, I am a bit lost. I'm looking for my, um, nan's friend. She came to hospital yesterday and her name is Sadie. My nan is called, um . . .' she groped for the name her mum had mentioned over breakfast. 'Sheila, that's my nan's name. Her sister, Audrey, lives next door to Sadie . . .'

'So Audrey's your great-aunt?'

Bea paused for a moment. The man wasn't as slow as he appeared.

'Yes, that's right. My great-aunt's neighbour is a woman called Sadie and she got burgled and was badly hurt. She came in yesterday and I thought I'd pop in to see her but I'm not sure where she is.'

'If it's serious, she'll be round the corner, in the High Dependency Unit.'

'I think that's where she'll be,' said Bea, feeling wretched. The *Echo* report had made it sound like Sadie was in a very serious condition.

'Right. Follow me, young lady.'

Bea followed the man until they reached a set of double doors. He keyed a code into the panel on the wall and the doors scraped against the linoleum floor as they opened.

'Through here,' he said.

The orderly marched Bea up the corridor to a desk behind which sat two nurses. Both smiled as they approached.

'Hello, Trevor,' said one of them.

'This young lady wants to visit someone.'

The nurse who'd said hello glanced at the clock on the wall. 'There's still five minutes until morning visiting begins. Who are you here to see?'

Bea's throat constricted and she couldn't speak.

'The woman brought in after the burglary yesterday, Sadie,' Trevor said for her.

'You'll need to sign in,' said the nurse, pushing a visitors' book across the top of the desk towards Bea. 'Are you a relative?'

'She knows her very well. Her nan Sheila is best friends with the patient.'

Bea couldn't bring herself to correct Trevor's inaccuracy. She was in far too deep to start telling the truth now.

'She's still unconscious,' said the nurse. 'But she's doing better. She's in the fourth room down on the left.'

Bea nodded as she signed the visitors' book, deliberately scrawling her name so it was virtually indecipherable.

'Mrs Cardle's granddaughter should be here soon as well.'

Bea was seized by panic. It hadn't occurred to her that the woman might have other visitors, ones who would undoubtedly ask questions about why she was there.

'I won't stay long,' she mumbled. 'Got to get to school.'

Trevor gave a little bow. 'If that's all, I best be getting on.'

'Thank you,' said Bea. She tried to smile but her fear made it appear more like a grimace.

'If you come back for elevenses, Trevor, we'll let you have the first Hobnob,' said the nurse.

He beamed, did another little bow, then left.

'So it's fourth room down?' Bea confirmed.

'Yes, on the left. Come and see us if you need anything.'

Bea's legs turned to jelly as she made her way down the corridor. There was a voice in her head screaming at her to turn round and run as fast as she could out of the hospital but she kept going, mindful that the nurses at the desk might be watching her and wondering why she didn't get a move on.

At the entrance to Sadie's room she faltered. What would Sean say if he could see her now, see what she was about to do? She was about to risk them being caught and all because she felt the need to say sorry to a woman she didn't even know. But it was a need she couldn't ignore. It was their fault that poor woman was lying there because someone had copied them.

She inched slowly into the room, terrified of what state she might find Sadie in. But to her relief there were no injuries to the woman's face and if it hadn't been for the bandage round her head, Bea would've assumed she was simply asleep.

She forced herself to move closer to the bed. She had to be quick.

'Hello. I'm . . . well, it doesn't really matter what my name is. You don't know me. We've never met until now.'

Bea stopped for a second. In the deathly quiet room, her

voice sounded alien to her, as though someone else was speaking. She swallowed hard.

'I wanted to say I'm sorry you're in here. I didn't mean for any of this to happen and, well, I hope you get better soon.'

A tear slid down her cheek. What a lame apology, she scolded herself. As if that could make up for what had happened.

'I wish I could find out who did this to you,' she said mournfully. 'Then you'd know it wasn't us—'

'Oh my God,' said a voice behind her. 'It's you.'

23

Closing the front door behind Alex, Della made a mental note to ask the police how long she had to leave it before she could clean the house. The officer in charge of the case, DS Renshaw, hadn't answered her call that morning but she was hoping she might see her at the hospital when she visited Sadie and could ask her then. Morning visiting hours started at ten so Della placed a call to a local cab firm to collect her at 9.40 a.m to take her there.

She went into the small dining room, which could only be accessed through the kitchen. Here, the evidence of the police investigation was less pronounced: nothing had been disturbed during the break-in and it looked as though the intruders hadn't ventured into the room at all, so the finger-print powder residue was minimal.

The bureau where Sadie kept her personal papers was still locked and Della was cross with herself for entertaining the thought that Helen might've come back for its contents. In the cold light of day she knew her mother turning up was the last thing she needed when she already had so much to deal with; she'd managed this long without Helen and had no use for her now.

She was about to shut the dining-room door when a piece of paper sticking out from beneath the bureau caught her eye. She stooped down to pick it up and was surprised to see it was an old Kodak photograph she'd seen many times before, of Sadie and Eric on their honeymoon in Jersey. The last time she'd seen the picture was when she'd been flicking through one of Sadie's photo albums; the white cardboard triangles that had anchored it to the page still covered the corners now, like they'd been ripped off when it was removed.

Della went to leave the photo on the table to put away later when she remembered she needed to find a photograph of Sadie wearing her wedding and engagement rings to give to Maggie for the purposes of identification. The honeymoon picture wouldn't do: Sadie's hands were hidden from view in it.

Sadie kept her photo albums – six altogether – on a shelf within the tall Ercol cabinet set against the far wall of the dining room. The albums were kept in date order but as Della reached for the one the honeymoon picture was usually kept in, she saw they were muddled up. She pulled out the first album in the row then gave a start as dozens of loose photographs fluttered from between its pages to the floor – some with the triangle corners intact, some without. She flipped through the album to discover every picture had been pulled out of position. It was the same for the next album, and the next.

As she reached the last one and slowly opened the pages expecting more loose pictures to tumble out, her puzzlement turned to shock. There were no photos inside at all, not even unsecured ones. She leafed through the stiff cardboard pages from beginning to end and back again but there wasn't a single image trapped within them.

She checked the inside flap and saw Sadie's handwriting: 'Della, b. December 11, 1995'. She gasped. This was *her* album, the one in which her grandmother had captured her every milestone from babyhood to teens.

Every picture was missing.

24

'What now, sir?' asked Maggie. They were back on the ground floor, Umpire nursing a second cup of coffee. Sitting side by side on plastic chairs screwed into the concrete floor in the quietest part of the reception area, she'd spent the last ten minutes repeating Eleanor's statement in full.

Her question went unanswered as Umpire stared at her intently. Yet she knew he wasn't looking *at* her: it was what he did when he was thinking. Once, over dinner, she'd teased him that when he went into staring mode it was like he was a cyborg in a *Terminator* film with a computer screen on the inside of his eyeballs to call up data, and he'd laughed and said he would love someone to invent contact lenses that could do that, because it would make his job easier. They'd then spent the rest of the evening coming up with madcap inventions that could help policing, each one sillier than the last.

The memory of that night stung now. They'd dined at Durazzo, an Italian restaurant in Mansell that served calzone the size of pillows and the best tiramisu Maggie had ever tasted. It was where they had been due to eat at again that evening.

Umpire suddenly snapped to attention.

'You need to write the statement up. If the husband regains consciousness, he'll be looking at an attempted murder charge. If he doesn't survive, the investigation closes but there will be an inquest into his death, so you won't be excused as Mrs Bramwell's FLO until after then.' He took a final swig of coffee. 'Right, I'm off.' He got to his feet and started looking around for a bin in which to deposit his empty take-out cup.

The abruptness of his farewell floored her. Was that it? She almost grabbed his arm to stop him but instead spoke forcefully.

'We still have things to discuss . . . sir.'

He appraised her coolly.

'Such as?'

She almost said *us*, but common sense and self-preservation prevailed.

'Mrs Bramwell wants some of her own things from her house. Who do I speak to about getting them sent down? Unless . . .' she hesitated, 'you want me to get them personally?'

'You don't need to travel up to Trenton.'

There was a firmness to his voice that indicated his decree was non-negotiable and made Maggie flinch. He was right, of course: at this stage, with Eleanor in hospital, there was no need for Maggie to attend the crime scene. But surely he must be aware that she could take his comment another way – that there was no need for her to go to Trenton because it was where he lived and whatever it was that existed between them no longer did? Had her drunken rant in the pub really been that bad?

'Send the list to Trenton CID to sort out,' he added. 'I want Mrs Bramwell's statement to me by mid-afternoon.'

Maggie swallowed her dismay and got to her feet. Although above average height at five feet eight, she still felt dwarfed by Umpire, who was seven inches taller. Standing close to him made her uncomfortable and she took a step back.

He turned as if to go, but something drew him back and he rubbed his chin roughly, something else he did when he was ruminating. Maggie hated that she knew his habits and tics so well now.

'Look, the point you raised about him suddenly stopping when he was breaking down the bathroom door is a good one and I think you're right to have doubts about Eleanor's account,' he said, his voice softer than it had been at any point during their conversations that morning. 'While you were interviewing her, I had a chat with her consultant and he remarked how lucky she was that her wounds are relatively shallow. A couple of them barely punctured her skin. But if her husband attacked her as frenziedly as she says he did, why aren't they much deeper?'

'She said he stabbed her through their duvet when the attack started and apparently it's very thick. Maybe that's why.'

'Perhaps. The knife that went into her shoulder was up to the hilt, but then again the blade was only four centimetres long. Must be the smallest type of paring knife you can buy for a kitchen. Why not use a carving knife for maximum injury?'

'Who knows? Maybe because he could hide it better?'

'But he burst into the bedroom. There was no ambush that would have required him to conceal it.'

'I'll bring it up with Mrs Bramwell again and let you know what she says.'

'Fine.'

They stood facing each other for a moment and Maggie was heartened to see he appeared as hesitant to leave as she did. He made a show of checking his watch then muttered something about having to get back, but didn't shift from the spot.

'I'm really sorry for what I said on Monday night Will,' she said quietly.

He stared at her for a moment then shook his head. His voice became brittle again.

'Someone will be in touch with any updates, DC Neville.'

It wasn't the worse brush-off Maggie had ever experienced but it was up there on the scale of most painful. If she couldn't say what was really on her mind, she could at least have the last unspoken word.

With a curt nod, she walked away first.

25

The voice made Bea jump. She spun round to see a woman in a hospital gown standing in the doorway, her hand clutching a stand from which hung a plastic bag half filled with clear liquid. The patient's skin was pale, her hair limp around her face. She stared at Bea for a second then smiled.

'Silly me, I thought you were her granddaughter.' The woman's eyes flickered towards Sadie on the bed. 'Della was here all day yesterday, didn't leave her bedside.' She turned back to Bea. 'It's uncanny how alike you are. You could be sisters.'

Bea was unsettled by the way the woman peered at her and her heart pounded with fear.

'Do you know the family?' asked the woman, moving slowly into the ward. Her knuckles were white where she grasped the stand, her only means of support. A tube twisted and looped from the bag into the crook of her elbow.

Bea panicked. She had to get out of there, fast. How long would it be before Sadie's granddaughter turned up and started asking questions too?

She leapt from her chair and shoved past the woman, who yelped in protest, and scurried to the exit. As she flew past the nurses' station, one of them yelled after her, 'Hey, you're supposed to sign out!'

Trembling from head to foot, Bea prayed the lift would hurry up and arrive. She kept shooting glances at the doors into HDU, fearful a nurse was going to suddenly appear and drag her back inside to explain herself. When the lift arrived she shot inside before the doors had fully opened and squeezed into the far corner, her back against the wall. An elderly couple shuffled in after her but Bea kept her head down, unable to bring herself to look at them.

It was warm inside the lift and Bea clawed at the scarf round her neck, the sensation that it was choking her growing by the second. By the time she reached the ground floor, she was gasping for air and half ran, half staggered to the main door, ignoring the quizzical stares of people watching her leave.

Only when she was outside, gulping in mouthfuls of fresh air, did she begin to relax and her limbs lost the quivery sensation that follows a burst of adrenaline. As her breathing steadied, she began to berate herself for leaving so hastily. She'd made a spectacle of herself, which might prompt unwelcome questions when she returned.

Pulling her coat tighter around herself as she walked away from the hospital, she knew there was no question of her not going back. Seeing Sadie lying there all bandaged up had strengthened her resolve, not weakened it. She would go back every day until Sadie woke up so she could say sorry in person and explain it wasn't her and Sean who'd attacked her. But for now she'd go home and keep up the pretence of being ill again.

As Bea waited to cross the approach road to the hospital

to head back into town, she heard someone shout a familiar name.

'Della?'

Her head whipped round as she frantically looked for anyone who might resemble Sadie's granddaughter in the vicinity. Then she realized the woman in the trouser suit who'd called out Della's name was walking towards her. She was some distance away still and her eyes were squinting against the sun, but she was definitely looking at Bea.

'Della?'

Alarmed, Bea shook her head and turned on her heel, darting across the road between two cars that had pulled to a halt. She didn't dare look over her shoulder to see if the woman was following her and instead kept running until she reached the familiar imposing outline of the shopping centre and darted inside.

Scurrying past shops and coffee bars on the cut-through to the bus station, Bea considered how bizarre it was that she'd now been mistaken twice for Della. Were they really that similar? It was probably her dyed hair, she decided – everyone said that being brunette made her look older.

The bus she needed to catch was about to leave, its engine ticking over impatiently as the driver waited for the last few stragglers to board. Tagging on to the back of the queue, it occurred to Bea that her resemblance to Della might work in her favour when Sadie did wake up – if Bea reminded her enough of her granddaughter, Sadie might be quicker to accept she had nothing to do with her being attacked.

Bea twirled a strand of her hair round her finger and held it up to examine it. She didn't know if her mum had booked an appointment with the hairdresser on Saturday to strip the dye out, but if she had Bea would find a way to cancel it. Her hair needed to stay exactly as it was.

It might just be her saving grace.

26

Maggie's stomach was in knots as she left the hospital. Umpire had every right to be annoyed with her for barracking him in the pub about going back to his wife, but she never imagined for a moment it would end their friendship as well as kill the chance of anything else developing. Walking slowly towards the car park up the paved slope running along the side of the hospital she hoped he'd come after her. Halfway up, unable to stop herself, she turned round to check, but the only person on the path behind her was Della Cardle.

Except it wasn't Della. After calling her name and walking towards her, Maggie realized it was Della's double – a teenage girl with the same shade of hair and similarly waifish build. Startled to see Maggie approaching her, the girl turned on her heel and ran across the road. Maggie let her go.

In the car park her frostbitten Toyota had to be coaxed to life with a few pumps on the accelerator pedal but five minutes and a complicated configuration of mini roundabouts later Maggie pulled into the rear of Mansell police station. Immediately she felt calmer. This was her domain, the place where she felt most at home. Even her own flat, where she'd lived for more than three years, didn't give her the same sense of reassurance as the police station that had been her place of work for the past eight. As she relaxed, she told herself there was no point obsessing about the situation with Umpire when she had no control over it right now. At some point, God knows when, she would try again to raise the subject of *them*, but until that moment presented itself she would bury her feelings as effectively as he'd seemed to.

The front of the police station, overlooking the main thoroughfare leading to Mansell High Street, was an old but beautifully maintained red-brick facade with wood-frame sash windows. Behind it, though, the bit the public never saw unless they were handcuffed and being brought into the custody suite to be booked in, was a concrete box of smoked glass windows and steel doors. The station's two faces. Maggie liked the contradiction.

CID was up on the third floor. The department was open plan and envied by the uniformed officers and civilian personnel shuttered in the rabbit warren of corridors and rooms on the lower floors.

Maggie had just stepped out of the lift when DS Renshaw bore down on her.

'Ah, good, you're here. I need you to do me a favour,' she said.

The politeness of Renshaw's approach and the smile that accompanied it caused Maggie's hackles to rise, primed for the attack she was sure would follow.

'Can you go round to see Della Cardle? I've just spoken to her and she's in a right state about some more missing pictures. I couldn't really get much sense out of her. I'd go myself but Nathan and I are meant to be seeing the first two victims this morning, as I want to go over the discrepancies in their descriptions of the Con Couple. That okay?'

Maggie was lost for words. She'd never known Renshaw to be so polite.

'I know you've got a lot on with the attempted murder-suicide,' Renshaw added, 'but Della's rung me five times. We should check she's okay.'

Were they giving out frontal lobotomies in the canteen as a side order to sausage and chips? Maggie marvelled inwardly. It was surely the only possible explanation for Renshaw's sudden niceness.

'I can go round now,' she replied, unable to hide her bemusement.

'Thanks, I appreciate it.'

Maggie gaped at the unprecedented expression of gratitude but Renshaw didn't notice because at the same time she was yelling across the room to tell Nathan to get a move on. The young DC sprang from his chair, grabbed his coat from the back of it and hurried across to them, unbothered by the loud summons. He and Renshaw got on well and their easy rapport reminded Maggie of how it used to be between her and Steve Berry when he was still in CID. Like Renshaw and Nathan, she and Steve had shared the same way of thinking and the same approach to policing, but an error of judgement caused Steve to slip up on the Rosie Kinnock case and he quit the force before he could be disciplined. Maggie had tried to talk him out of resigning but he was resolute: his wife, Isla, had just had a baby and his new job for a private security firm meant family-friendlier hours. Watching Renshaw give Nathan a rundown of the descriptions the two witnesses had previously given as he pulled his coat on made

Maggie wistful for Steve. She hadn't gelled with anyone else in CID in quite the same way since his departure.

Noticing Maggie was still rooted to the spot, Renshaw broke off.

'I haven't got anything else to brief you on at the moment,' she said. 'That may change after we speak to these victims again, but you can get going if you want.'

Again Maggie waited for a rebuke to be tagged on to the end of the sentence but none came. She scanned Renshaw's face for signs of insincerity – a sly jerk of an eyebrow, a subtle twist of the mouth, narrowed eyes – but there was nothing. Disconcerted, she said that when she got back from seeing Della, she had to write up a witness statement for Umpire, who wanted it by the afternoon.

Renshaw nodded her consent.

'I'll make sure you're left alone to do it. Right, come on Nath, we need to get going.'

Renshaw strode off towards the exit. Maggie grabbed Nathan's arm before he could follow.

'What's up with her?' she hissed in an undertone. 'Why is she being so nice?'

'She's always all right to me,' he said. 'Maybe if you stopped being so snarky to her, she wouldn't be like it back.'

Jolted, Maggie dropped her hand from his arm. Was Nathan right? Was her reciprocal attitude not the defensive response she thought it was but actually the fuel igniting the flame? No, a voice cautioned firmly inside her head. Renshaw had been a bitch to her since day one. If she was being pleasant all of a sudden, there was a reason for it.

Maggie had a feeling she wasn't going to enjoy finding out what it was.

27

By the time Della had finished, the dining room looked as though it had been ransacked. She'd upended every book, ornament, envelope, document and stray piece of paper but couldn't find any of the missing photographs from the album. She flew upstairs to Sadie's room and went through every drawer in there but the result was the same. Nothing. She was about to start on the living room when the doorbell rang.

'Oh, thank God,' she cried when she saw Maggie on the doorstep. 'You have to see this. Look, in here.'

Della shot down the hallway with Maggie trailing in her wake.

'Wait—' the officer called after her.

Della stopped abruptly in the doorway to the dining room, causing Maggie to stagger into her.

'I can't find them. I've looked everywhere,' said Della, whipping round.

'Can't find what?'

'The photographs of me. Every single picture of me growing up. They've been taken. I think you were right. It's *her*. It has to be.'

She fired the words at Maggie so quickly that the officer held her hands up as if to deflect them.

'You need to slow down, Della. Do you mean the missing pictures you spoke to DS Renshaw about earlier?'

Della ignored her again and dashed across to the cabinet, where she'd left the empty album. She shook with excitement.

'Look, they've all gone. Every single one!'

She opened the album and shoved the empty pages at Maggie, who pulled back in surprise.

'You were right,' Della went on. 'She was here, in the house. I can't believe it. Nan won't believe it either.'

Maggie took a step back and folded her arms across her chest.

'Della, calm down.'

The firmness of her voice stopped Della in her tracks but she couldn't stop herself smiling.

Helen had been *here*.

She had come back.

'Now, do you want to start at the beginning?' said Maggie. 'And take it slowly this time . . .'

Della gulped down a huge intake of breath before she spoke again.

'I was checking through my nan's belongings like you said to, in case I'd missed anything, and I found a photograph on the floor, over there.' She pointed to beneath the bureau, now an empty wooden shell with its contents scattered far and wide across the dining-room floor. 'I didn't know how it got there as it's from one of Nan's albums. When I went to put it back, I realized that all the photographs had come loose. Not just in that album but four of the others too. Look.'

Maggie followed her over to the tall cabinet. Saying nothing, she watched intently, arms still folded, as Della leafed through the albums to show her the photos and where the white cardboard corners holding them down had been ripped out.

'Then I opened the last one,' said Della breathlessly. 'The photographs aren't just missing from the pages, they're missing completely.'

She handed the album to Maggie, who with the very edges of her fingertips slowly turned every page. Then she went back to the beginning and read the inscription. Her lack of urgency sent Della spinning again.

'See, you were right when you said my mum could've been here. I think she's the one who took them!'

'Hang on, that's not what I said, Della. I asked you if it was possible your mum had returned but you were adamant she hadn't.' Maggie handed the album back. 'Isn't it more likely your nan removed them and hasn't mentioned it?'

'Why would she throw away every picture of me?' Della demanded. 'That makes no sense.'

'But why would someone else want to take all your photographs?'

'It must be Helen,' Della parried. 'What if she came back? What if,' she went on, her voice rising an octave, 'she came back for me and my nan didn't like it and they argued and Nan fell and that's how she got hurt and now Helen won't come forward because she's worried she'll get into trouble when it was an accident?'

Maggie took her time before answering. When she did, her tone was gentle.

'We believe a glass bottle was used as a weapon to hit your nan and it doesn't appear to have been accidental. The back door showed signs of forced entry, and her rings being stolen from her person also indicate this was a robbery.' Della opened her mouth to protest but Maggie raised a hand to stop her. 'I do think the theft of the photograph in the hallway is significant, in that it was taken because the frame was worth something. But I'm not sure we can say the same about these pictures.'

Della groped for something she could say that might convince Maggie otherwise.

'Don't you have a duty to investigate all possibilities?' she pleaded. 'Isn't that what you said to me when you asked if any of Nan's friends were capable of hurting her, that you had to check every line of inquiry?'

'Every credible line of inquiry. I'm sorry, Della, I know you're going through a very stressful time right now, but we don't have the resources to investigate an empty photo album. Forensics checked this room and they were satisfied the intruders hadn't entered it—'

There was a loud banging on the front door. Feeling too overwrought to deal with whoever was making the noise, Della let Maggie answer it. She made out a man's voice she didn't recognize then heard Maggie say something in response. She shut the dining-room door to block them both out. Then she slumped to the floor cradling the empty album of lost memories and began to cry.

28

The minicab driver on the doorstep didn't care who paid the fare, as long as someone did. 'I've been out here with the meter running. She told me to wait.'

'How much is it?' said Maggie.

'Twenty-two quid.'

'Really? That seems a lot.'

'I've been out here half a bleedin' hour,' said the driver, who didn't sound local. 'I'm freezin' me knackers off.'

'Hang on, I'll see if she's got any cash.'

'Don't she want taking to the hospital now?' said the driver irritably. 'Have I been wasting my time?'

'Not if you're getting paid. Just wait a minute.'

Maggie ducked inside. She found Della cross-legged on the floor of the dining room, hugging the album to her chest like a teddy bear. It took a few attempts, but she managed to elicit a response and Della got the money from her purse.

'I'll drive you to the hospital myself when you're ready,' Maggie told her.

The driver had returned to his minicab, engine running and the heating cranked up. The radio was also at full whack, a commentator on 5 Live giving a rundown of the previous night's football results. Maggie rapped on the window to get the driver's attention, which made him jump. The window slid open.

'Here you go,' said Maggie, bending down to hand over £25. She didn't ask for change and nor did the driver offer any.

'Cheers. 'Ere, is that the house where that old lady got clobbered?'

Maggie straightened up. 'You can go now.'

'Ah, you're a copper. I should've guessed. I can tell by the way you walk.'

Maggie rolled her eyes and the driver gave a friendly blast of his horn as he drove off. The noise must have disturbed Sadie's next-door neighbour, because Maggie noticed movement behind the net curtain in the downstairs window and a moment later Audrey Allen threw open her front door and beckoned her up the path.

'I do hope you don't mind me disturbing you, officer, but I was wondering if there was any news on Sadie. I haven't wanted to go round and ask Della because she looks so upset,' said Mrs Allen, who looked equally stricken as she wrung her hands.

'I'm about to take Della to the hospital so we'll know more then, but the last I heard Mrs Cardle was in a critical but stable condition.'

'She's stable? Oh, that's good to hear.'

'I'll ask Della if you can visit, if you want?'

Audrey Allen brightened at the suggestion.

'Oh, that would be lovely. I've been ever so worried. I hadn't seen Sadie for days before all this happened.'

Maggie frowned as she remembered what Della had said

about the two women usually going out on Monday evenings.

'You didn't go to bingo with her?'

'I went, but Sadie cried off this week. She said she was expecting someone.'

That was news to Maggie. There had been no mention of Sadie having a visitor in any of Renshaw's briefings.

'Did she say who?'

'She didn't give much away, but she said someone was coming to talk to her about her father. He had a bit of a claim to fame, you see. After the war he was a cabinetmaker at Perry's – you know, the furniture factory that used to be on Chapel Lane until it shut down. Well, one day, just like that, he was handpicked to make a writing desk for Winston Churchill to use at Chequers.'

Maggie was impressed. Almost twenty miles north of Mansell, Chequers had for a century been the country residence of prime ministers and was one of the nation's most famous houses. Being commissioned to make the desk for Churchill would've been a huge honour for Sadie's father.

'So she was being interviewed about that?'

'I think so. That's what it sounded like. She was very excited.'

It dawned on Maggie that the interview might explain why the photo albums were in disarray: Sadie could have been looking through them for images of her father to accompany the story.

'Did she say who the interview was for?'

'I presume the *Echo*, but I can't be sure. She was being very cloak and dagger about it.'

'Did you mention this to DS Renshaw yesterday?'

Audrey looked concerned. 'I'm sorry, I didn't. The lady only wanted to know if I'd heard anything in the morning, like glass breaking. We didn't talk about the day before.'

'It's okay. We'll ask Della if she knows anything about it,' said Maggie, experiencing a frisson of excitement. Discovering Sadie hadn't been alone the evening before she was attacked put a new slant on the investigation and tracking down the reporter would now be a priority for the team.

'I must say, it was a bit of a shock when I saw the reporter leave,' Audrey said.

'You saw them?'

'Oh yes, it was a young woman. I watched her coming out of the house as I arrived home after bingo. It was about ten p.m. and my friend had dropped me off over there,' Audrey pointed across the road, to a parking space on the opposite side. 'We were saying goodbye when the girl came out of Sadie's. She gave me the fright of my life!'

'How come?'

'You know Sadie has a daughter? Silly me, of course you do – she's Della's mum. Well, I've lived here as long as the Cardles have and this girl was exactly how I remember Helen before she went. Long dark hair, slim like Della is. Uncanny, it was.'

'But it can't have been Helen,' said Maggie with a frown. 'I mean, she would be much older now. You said it was a girl?'

'When you get to my age everyone seems like a girl,' Audrey laughed. 'She was perhaps in her thirties. But I didn't say it *was* Helen – only that it looked like her. Whoever the reporter was, she looked exactly as I imagine Helen would now.'

157

29

Maggie drove Della to the hospital in silence. She wasn't about to share Audrey Allen's sighting with her, not until it had been thoroughly checked out. She doubted Della would react rationally to the news that someone who resembled her long-lost mum had been seen visiting Sadie the night before the attack.

And what if it actually *was* Helen? Maggie's mind raced as she mapped out the investigation in her head. Starting points would be checking with the DVLA to see if Helen held a driver's licence and tracing her address through her National Insurance number – if she had one. She may also have changed her name through marriage or by deed poll, which would take longer to look into. There were many avenues the police had to explore before Della was informed.

A quick sidelong glance as they drove along the approach road to Mansell General also reiterated to Maggie that it would be cruel to mention the sighting to Della until they were absolutely sure of the woman's identity. Della appeared diminished in the passenger seat next to her, her face pinched with worry and exhaustion. It wouldn't be fair or responsible to heap more stress on her right now.

After dropping Della off outside the hospital reception, Maggie drove back to the station. The open-plan office was fairly empty when she returned – no sign of either Renshaw or Nathan – so she settled down at her desk to write up Eleanor Bramwell's statement, her priority with Umpire's afternoon deadline looming. Yet as she tried to concentrate, pecking away at the keys of her computer, the image of Della slumped down in the passenger seat tugged at her mind. She needed to call the *Echo* to confirm whether it was one of their female reporters who had visited Sadie on Monday evening – and happened to coincidentally look like Helen – but it would have to wait until she had finished the statement. The only *Echo* hack she knew by sight was Jennifer Jones, the chief reporter, and it couldn't have been her because she had light brown, curly hair and was more curvy than slight.

The words on her computer screen swam in front of her eyes as she continued to type. Cursing under her breath, Maggie pushed her chair back roughly from her desk and stood up. She knew it wasn't the question of the reporter's identity that was bothering her – it was the question of what really happened to Helen after she went missing all those years ago. Della's distress had hit a nerve – now Maggie couldn't rest until she found out too.

She strode across the office to a bank of six desks where the CID admin support assistants sat. The most senior of them, Pearl, was busy inputting a document, her chunky fingers flying unchecked across the keyboard as she chatted to the colleague next to her.

'Hey, Pearl, have you got a minute?'

Pearl was overweight to the point of morbidly obese and

her eyes almost disappeared beneath her enormous cheeks as her face lifted in a smile. Her mouth was thickly coated in her signature bright red lipstick.

'Always for you, Maggie,' she said, her fingers still moving rapidly back and forth across the keys.

'I need to dig out a case file for a miss per. It's from quite a while back – August 1999. Any chance you could help me?'

Pearl stopped typing and picked up a pen.

'What's the name?'

'Helen Cardle.'

Pearl's eyes narrowed. 'Is she to do with the robberies case? Isn't the most recent victim a Cardle?'

'It's the victim's daughter. She went missing from Mansell in August 1999. There's no connection to the case, I just want to read the file.'

Pearl gave Maggie a wry smile. 'If it's reading you're after, I've got the latest Cathy Kelly novel in my bag.'

'Okay, you've got me,' said Maggie, grinning back. 'I want the file because I'm curious. There are a couple of things about the break-in that are sort of linked to the daughter but she hasn't been home for seventeen years. I'm hoping the file might shed some light on them.'

'Don't let DS Renshaw hear you say that,' the assistant sitting next to Pearl said with a giggle. A pretty Asian school leaver called Omana who was the youngest in the department by about twenty years, she had a reputation for speaking her mind. Maggie liked her a lot. 'She's looking to tie this one up by catching the Con Couple and earning herself a pat on the back.'

Pearl dug a fleshy elbow into Omana's side.

'Now, now. Let's be nice about our new detective sergeant.'

Maggie grinned. It was nice to know her dislike of Renshaw was shared.

'Oh, come on, she's so full of herself. Did you hear her going on about what happened at that federation do, to raise money for that PC who died? You know, the one in the accident?'

Omana was referring to a traffic officer from Trenton killed two months earlier when his patrol car crashed while in pursuit of a stolen vehicle. Umpire had attended the benevolence fundraiser for the officer's family and Maggie wondered what connection there had been between the dead officer and Renshaw that she was also invited.

'All she's done since is bang on about that bloke she hooked up with there. Reckons he's some big hotshot in the force but she won't tell us his name. "It's complicated",' said Omana, mimicking Renshaw's voice and making speech marks in the air with her fingers. 'Apparently he's taking her out somewhere posh tonight.'

That would explain Renshaw's chipper mood today, thought Maggie. The poor bloke had no idea what he was letting himself in for, whoever he was.

'Do you think it will take long for you to track down the file?' Maggie asked Pearl.

'I doubt it, but if I come up against a brick wall I'll let you know. You know what the bureaucracy in this place can be like.'

'You could always get Renshaw to pull some strings with her hotshot,' Omana chipped in.

'And end up owing her a favour?' retorted Pearl. 'No thank you.'

'Hey, she's not that bad,' Maggie suddenly felt obliged to say. The admins' desks might be tucked away in the corner but the open-plan layout of the office still meant their conversation could be overheard and slagging off a senior officer could get them all into trouble.

Pearl raised an eyebrow.

'You of all people are defending her? The way she talks to you?'

'She's being nice at the moment.'

'Hmm. If she's being nice it's because she's after something or she knows something you don't. She's like a slow loris, that one.'

'A what?' said Omana.

'A slow loris. It's one of the cutest mammals that exists, all big brown eyes and fluffy fur like a cuddly toy, but it's one of the most poisonous too. When it feels threatened it shoots a toxin out of its elbows that can cause a fatal anaphylactic shock. My Jamie did a project on dangerous animals at school,' Pearl explained to Maggie in an aside.

'So it's not Renshaw's sharp elbows I should be worried about but her poison-spitting ones?' said Maggie, amused.

'Exactly.'

30

The boys had only been home from school for half an hour but were already driving Lou to distraction as they bickered over what television programme to watch before they did their homework. Scotty wanted *Scooby Doo* but Jude, with all the smug maturity of a big brother on the cusp of teenagehood, denounced it as a show for babies and flicked on a repeat of *Ice Road Truckers*, causing a major tantrum to erupt from the other end of the sofa. Then Mae joined in with Scotty's wailing and the combined noise made Lou's still-throbbing head feel like it was about to explode.

It was a long time since she'd experienced such a brutal hangover. Her temples felt like they were being squeezed in a vice and the Nurofen washed down with Pepsi Max that she'd taken earlier – her usual fail-safe hangover cure – had done nothing to alleviate the pain. It hadn't been so bad when the boys were at school as she'd managed a brief doze while Mae napped. But now her headache had returned with a vengeance and the only thing she knew would help was the bottle of Pinot Grigio chilling in the fridge. Hair of the dog, her second fail-safe cure for a hangover.

She never drank before the kids were in bed as a rule, but

with Jude wanting to stay up later the older he got she was becoming more inclined to bend it. A swift mouthful of wine as she cooked dinner did no harm, even sometimes straight from the bottle. Lou's mouth watered at the thought of the wine in the fridge and she stole into the kitchen, leaving the boys to argue it out. She'd just opened the fridge door when her phone rang and she jumped guiltily, as if the person at the other end could see she was about to have a sly swig.

It was Arturs, wanting to know if she could go out again that evening.

'I really can't. I can't leave the kids again.'

'Oh, come on, Lou,' he cajoled. 'They were fine, weren't they? Just a couple of hours.'

She liked the way her name rolled off his foreign tongue. The way he said it made it sound exotic. It made *her* sound exotic.

'I'm sorry, but I can't risk getting into trouble.'

'Because of what your sister said? So ask her to babysit. Problem solved.'

He made it sound so simple but Lou knew that phoning Maggie to ask for her help meant having to listen to a lecture about her behaviour last night and about shirking her responsibilities. She didn't want to hear it, not today. She was sick of everyone judging her. It was all anyone had done for the last six months since her idiot ex-husband got himself caught up in the Rosie Kinnock abduction, like it was somehow her fault.

'I want to see you,' Arturs breathed huskily down the line. 'My work no good today when all I think about is you in my van.'

A smile spread across Lou's face. The sex really had been amazing.

Keeping her phone tucked between her ear and her shoulder, she yanked open the fridge door, took out the bottle of wine, unscrewed the cap and swallowed a mouthful. Fuck it. If she wanted to see Arturs tonight she would. Jude could babysit again. He was doing fine before Maggie arrived.

'Are you still there?' asked Arturs.

'Yes I am. So . . . where shall we meet?'

31

The *Mansell Echo* operated out of a shop unit on the side of town deserted by most retailers in favour of the new shopping centre. It was sandwiched between a T-shirt printing business on one side and a takeaway chicken outlet on the other. Hardly Fleet Street but Maggie knew the road well, because the dental surgery she'd gone to as a child was opposite the *Echo*, above an estate agent. The dentist, a lovely man called Mr Cope who had long since retired, had once appeared on *Blue Peter* and became something of a celebrity as a result. It didn't take much to make it big in Mansell.

The paper's receptionist sat behind a polished wooden counter. She reacted coolly to Maggie's request to see the editor, assessing her warrant card with something approaching disdain.

'The editor's not available.'

'Can you get hold of him? I need to speak to him urgently.'

'He's not free right now.'

'Any idea when he might be?'

'No.'

Maggie usually had patience in spades but after the morning she'd had, compounded by the stress of her row with Umpire, and from dealing with Lou and the children last night, her reserves were depleted.

'Could you try to get hold of him?' she snapped.

The receptionist, who was matronly both in appearance and dress, gave a shrug. 'Not right now, sorry.'

Her name badge said she was called Joyce.

'You don't sound sorry, Joyce. Do you know what happens to people when they obstruct a police investigation?' Maggie didn't like resorting to threats but she was in no mood to be mucked around by someone clearly on a power trip.

The threat worked.

'He's meeting with the advertising director,' said Joyce huffily.

'Interrupt him then.'

'They're not on site. The meeting is at our head office in Reading.'

'Who's his second-in-command?'

'He doesn't have a deputy editor.'

It was like getting blood from a stone.

'Do you think you could try to be a bit more helpful?' said Maggie angrily. 'Why don't you just tell me who is available who can help?'

The woman's face mottled. She wasn't happy being barked at. Maggie thought she was quite possibly the least suited person to be the welcoming face of a company that she'd ever come across.

'We only have a small reporting team based here now. The production of the newspaper is done in Reading. I suppose I could see if our chief reporter is free.'

'Jennifer Jones?'

'Yes. She's probably busy but she's in the office at the moment.'

Maggie had had a few run-ins with Jennifer during the past couple of years that she'd worked on the *Echo* and found her to be annoyingly persistent and inquisitive. Great qualities for a reporter, granted, but Maggie didn't want to be badgered into giving too much away about the visitor to Sadie's house on Monday evening if the person turned out to have nothing to do with the *Echo*. She'd have to be careful what she said.

'Sure, I can speak to Jennifer.'

'Take a seat,' said Joyce sourly.

Maggie remained standing and smiled wryly as Joyce put on a warm, friendly voice as she patched herself through to Jennifer and told her someone in reception wanted to see her.

'It's a police officer,' said Joyce. 'A woman detective.'

The door separating the reception area from the rest of the building flew open less than ten seconds later. Jennifer Jones bolted through the open doorway with a grin on her face.

'DC Neville, what a surprise! Have you got a story for me?'

Immediately Maggie's guard went up. Her mistrust of journalists, particularly *Echo* reporters, stemmed back to the inquest into Jerome's death. The reporting of the hearing had been sensationalist, with the paper headlining their story 'Boozed-up dad-to-be drank six pints before road death', with no regard for how Lou and his parents would feel seeing it in print. The story itself wasn't much better, painting Jerome as an unemployed waster who regularly indulged in daytime drinking and implying he was only marrying Lou because he'd got her pregnant.

'I don't, no. The conversation we're about to have is strictly off the record.'

Jennifer's eyes lit up. 'Ooh, that sounds interesting. Follow me, we can use the editor's office as he's not here.'

Maggie trailed Jennifer down a short corridor lined with blown-up images of *Echo* front pages, from its very first, published back in 1897, to a more recent one featuring TV personality and author David Walliams landing in a school playground in a helicopter for World Book Day. As they walked, Jennifer launched into a chatty monologue about why it was great when they could talk face to face with the police like this, as the reporting system for the force had changed and the *Echo* no longer had its morning briefing at Mansell police station but instead had to follow an online wire of news digests written by the press team at force HQ and of course that was fine but there really was nothing like talking in person, especially when you wanted to build contacts. She only ran out of steam when they reached a small office packed with desks and people who looked up with mild curiosity as they entered.

'This is the newsroom but we also share it with the advertising and sales teams,' explained Jennifer. 'We don't need as much space now the subbing and designers have been hubbed in Reading.'

Maggie had no idea what that meant but didn't ask her to explain. She wanted to be in and out as quickly as she could. She followed Jennifer into a small side room with floor-to-ceiling glass walls that gave an overview of the office.

'We call this the Goldfish Bowl. Take a seat,' said Jennifer, positioning herself in the editor's chair behind his desk. She was tiny in stature, barely scraping five feet, and her boots only just reached the ground. There was something likeable about her – she had wild, Titian brown curls, a freckled face and wide smile – but Maggie didn't trust her. Mindful of staying on her guard, she explained that she needed to check if any of the *Echo* reporters had been working on Monday evening.

Jennifer's eyes narrowed slightly and Maggie could see she desperately wanted to ask why the police wanted to know that, but instead sensibly provided an answer to the question. She must've sensed the reaction she'd get if she tried to interrogate Maggie now.

'I was at a district council meeting until eleven but I don't recall there being anything else in the diary to attend,' said Jennifer. 'As chief reporter it's my job to make sure any big evening events or council meetings are covered by either myself or the other reporters.'

'Who's responsible for the nostalgia pages in the paper?'

Maggie had familiarized herself with the *Echo*'s content ahead of coming to the office and decided that if Sadie was being interviewed about her father receiving a commission from Winston Churchill, the feature would most likely be published in the section devoted to stories about Mansell and its residents from bygone eras.

Jennifer's eyes narrowed further. It must be killing her not to know why I'm asking, Maggie thought. She suppressed a smile.

'One of our junior reporters, David Mendick.'

Maggie's hopes were dashed. They were looking for a female interviewer, not a male.

'There's no one else who does that old stuff? No female writers?'

Jennifer pushed a loose curl out of her eyes. 'Why don't you just tell me what you need to know, DC Neville? It'll be much quicker than batting back and forth like this. We'll be here for hours at this rate and I've got some copy to file to the subs by noon.'

Usually Maggie liked it when people were direct with her but her reluctance to reveal the truth made Jennifer's approach more irritating than helpful. With a sigh, the reporter laid her hands on the desk in front of her. They were almost childlike in size, the nails bitten down to the quick.

'Look, we've already established this chat is off the record. I'm not going to print a word of it. I'm not writing anything down or recording it.'

Maggie had no reason to believe Jennifer would stick to her promise – but equally no reason not to. What she did know for sure was that they needed to find out who was at Sadie's house on Monday evening as a matter of priority. Jennifer was right when she said it would save them both time if she just came out with it.

'Okay, but please understand that if you print a single word from this conversation, I'll come after you for contempt.'

'I can only commit contempt if I jeopardize criminal proceedings that are active,' said Jennifer snippily.

Maggie raised her eyebrows to show she wasn't impressed

by Jennifer's legal knowledge, even if it was technically correct.

'Fine,' said the reporter. 'I understand.'

'The reason I'm asking you is we believe the elderly woman found injured in her home on Tuesday after being attacked was visited by a female reporter on Monday evening who was apparently interviewing her for a nostalgia piece. We need to trace who the reporter was.'

'The latest robbery victim? Bloody hell,' Jennifer breathed. 'I wasn't expecting that. Well, it definitely wasn't someone from here. You sure it was a woman?'

'Yes, with long dark hair. Does David ever outsource his work to freelancers?'

'No, there's no budget to do that.'

Maggie pondered Jennifer's comments for a moment. If the interviewer wasn't from the *Echo*, who sent her?

'Do you know what the victim was being interviewed about?' asked Jennifer.

'It was to do with a member of her family, but as we're not confirming her identity yet that's all I can tell you.'

Jennifer didn't bother to hide her disappointment. 'It's not like we'd hound them if we knew.'

'Still not telling you.' Maggie got up to leave.

'If she was being interviewed for a nostalgia piece, the reporter could've been from a special interest magazine, like a history title. There are tons published now. Go into WH Smith's and you'll see rows of them.'

Maggie suppressed a groan. By casting the net of possibilities wider Jennifer had just made her job much harder.

'Well, thanks for your help anyway.' She was reaching for the door handle to let herself out when a thought struck her.

'Do you have every issue of the paper archived here? Would you have copies going back, say, seventeen years?' She was wondering if the *Echo* might've covered Helen's missing person's case.

'Yes, but the system is pretty archaic. The most recent copies are saved in an online library, but if you want to go back that far, you'd have to use the microfiche.'

'Have you got a machine here?' asked Maggie.

'Yes, upstairs. It's a bit knackered and we never use it, but it still works. There are literally hundreds of boxes of film. Unless you can narrow down the date of the issue you need, you'll be there for days.'

32

The invitation to meet for a drink came in a phone call as Maggie arrived home just before seven. She was more than happy to turn round and go straight back out but when she arrived at the Cross Keys, one of the few town centre pubs not sequestered by students from the local college and that still served wine in bottles and not on draught, her nerves kicked in and she fumbled her step as she walked inside to the bar. The person waiting for her laughed as they watched her totter forward.

'Have you been drinking already?'

Maggie blushed as she took off her coat, sweating already. The bar was stiflingly warm compared to how bitterly cold it was outside and before coming out she'd changed into a pair of skinny blue jeans and a slouchy green jumper that went halfway down her thighs.

'No, but I'll have a glass of Sauvignon Blanc, seeing as you're asking.'

Allie Fontaine repeated Maggie's order to the barman then added a request for a red wine for herself. 'Make them both large,' she said.

Maggie was pleased Belmar's wife had called asking to

meet for a chat but now, face to face, she found herself at a loss for what to say, the awkward topic of Belmar's new job hovering over them like a rain cloud. Luckily Allie had no qualms about bringing it up and dived straight in with an apology.

'I'm so sorry we couldn't say anything. I didn't want to keep it from you, believe me, but Bel was under orders. God knows why,' said Allie, handing the barman a £20 note in exchange for their drinks. 'Shall we sit over there?' she said a moment later as she slipped her change into her purse.

Maggie led the way to a table in the corner that was flanked by two low stools. The pub wasn't busy for a mid-week evening and the music piping through the room was thankfully not loud enough to drown out conversation. Allie set the drinks down on the table then slipped off her coat. She was still wearing her work attire of a fitted dove grey skirt suit but had updated her make-up for the evening with slicks of emerald green eye shadow and a deep burgundy lipstick that were vivid against her black skin. Like her husband, Allie was fastidious about her appearance. Their flat in Trenton was like a show home.

'Belmar told me it was Will who asked him to keep quiet,' said Maggie, using Umpire's first name as she always did with Allie.

'Well, have you asked him why he didn't want you to know? Being a typical bloke, Bel never bothered to question it.'

'When did he apply for the job?' said Maggie, deflecting Allie's question. She took a sip of her wine and the inside of her mouth tingled as the ice-cold liquid washed through it.

'He didn't as such. Will asked Bel to put himself forward for it. The process must've started about two months ago.'

'Two months?' said Maggie, agog. 'What, in September? Why didn't he say anything? Why didn't he . . .' She trailed off, reluctant to finish the sentence.

Why didn't Umpire trust her enough to tell her?

'Has something happened with you two?' said Allie perceptively.

Maggie delayed her response by drinking more wine. Although she'd previously told Allie how she felt about Umpire, she was reluctant to say anything now in case she relayed it to Belmar. It was too close for comfort.

Allie set her glass down.

'If you're worried about me saying something to Bel, don't be. I haven't said a word about what you've told me. I'm not one of those wives who subscribes to the theory you should tell your other half everything.'

Maggie grinned. She should've known better than to think Allie would go running to Belmar with her secrets. From refusing to take his surname to bucking the trend amongst black women to relax their hair by keeping hers in its natural Afro state, Allie danced to no one's tune but her own. Deep down, Maggie wished she could be more like her.

'So come on, what's the latest with you two?'

By the time Maggie finished, Allie had drained her glass.

'You shouldn't have kicked off at him for staying over at his ex-wife's to see his kids,' Allie wagged a manicured finger at Maggie, who cringed, 'but Will's being a first-class prick by blanking you now. He owes you an explanation as to why he won't return your calls or talk to you, if nothing else.'

'I don't think that will happen,' said Maggie with a sigh.

'Honestly, you should've seen how he was this morning. It was like we didn't know each other.'

'But, Maggie, do you actually *want* anything to happen? I'd say the fact that you've not taken it any further already is a pretty big sign, wouldn't you? Maybe he got fed up waiting. I've seen how the two of you are together and it isn't him who is playing hard to get.'

About a month ago, before the Rosie Kinnock trial was due to start, the investigating team had met for a post-work drink and Allie had tagged along with Belmar. It was after that evening Maggie had confided in her about her con-flicted feelings for Umpire.

'It's not me holding off, it's him,' Maggie protested. 'He's the one going through the divorce.'

'He's also the one asking you out for dinner,' said Allie gently. 'Do you see what I'm getting at?'

Maggie did see – and it confused the hell out of her. Was it really her who'd stopped them progressing beyond friend-ship? Had Umpire got fed up with her stalling? But surely her reaction to him staying at his ex's showed she *did* care? With a sigh, she drained her wine.

'I feel like I'm going round in circles thinking about it. Same again?'

Allie hesitated. 'I probably shouldn't.'

'Why? You're not driving, are you?'

Allie had a new job working in HR for a law firm in London and commuted there from Trenton. Her parents lived in Mansell, however, so sometimes she stopped off on her way home to see them before catching a later train to continue her journey.

'I did. I'm just not meant to be drinking much at the moment.'

'Are you on a health kick?'

'Not exactly.' Allie's eyes glistened as she looked at Maggie across the table. 'You know how I said we wanted to try for a baby? Well, we actually started five months ago but nothing happened and I had this feeling something wasn't right. I mean, we were at it constantly and I'd even been using one of those ovulation kits to work out when I was most fertile. So I went to see our GP and she said we had to keep going for a year before we'd be referred for tests, but I didn't want to wait that long so we went private. The tèsts showed Bel's sperm are the biological equivalent of couch potatoes. The lazy little shits won't move from their comfy spot, so it's impossible for us to get pregnant naturally.'

Maggie could see Allie was trying to make light of it but her pained expression gave away how agonized she was. Maggie reached over and squeezed her hand.

'I'm so sorry to hear that,' she said, thinking back to how prickly Belmar had been when the subject of the Bramwells having IVF was raised. 'What are your options?'

'We're going to start IVF in January. I'm injecting myself every day with these drugs to boost my egg production, which is a bitch because my eggs were fine in the first place and these fertility drugs do your head in. You ask Bel – I'm like a walking time bomb. Say the wrong thing and I'll rip your head off.'

Maggie's mind flashed up an image of Eleanor Bramwell screaming at them to leave her alone.

'Is that a common side effect?'

'Apparently. Imagine the worst kind of PMT and multiply

it by a million. That's how bad you feel. One minute I'm as happy as Larry, the next I could kill someone. Poor Bel is too scared to open his mouth because he never knows how I'm going to react.'

'Hopefully it'll be worth it in the end though.'

'I hope so too,' said Allie morosely. 'I've always assumed Bel and me were rock solid but doing IVF really tests your relationship. We've had more rows in the past two months since I started taking the drugs than we've had in the entire ten years we've been together. If you were on shaky ground to begin with, I don't fancy your chances of still being together at the end of it.' Allie thrust her empty glass at Maggie. 'Sod it – I will have another. If I go back drunk, Bel will be relieved. Better I pass out than we have another row.'

Waiting at the bar to be served, Maggie's thoughts returned to Eleanor Bramwell. Had IVF pushed her and her husband Simon to the brink too? Their neighbour said they'd talked about the treatment being a financial drain: had it depleted them emotionally as well, and was that why Simon Bramwell snapped? Maggie glanced over at Allie, who was staring absent-mindedly into space. It was hard to imagine Belmar's easy-going wife ever losing her temper as explosively as she'd just described.

But would Eleanor Bramwell's friends say the same of her?

33

The next day was Thursday and Bea managed to persuade her mum and dad not to send her to school again. There was a caveat to their agreeing though: she was booked in to see Dr Reynolds on Monday, no argument. Bea knew the paediatric dietician wouldn't find anything amiss physically – her weight had remained steady for the past year and despite what she'd told her parents yesterday, she hadn't made herself sick for many months – but she'd go along with the request if it meant she had the morning free to visit Sadie again.

She set off early, like the day before, as soon as her mum had left to go to the charity shop. Caroline was working another extra shift because her colleague Sheila was still comforting her sister, Audrey. The ripple effect caused by the attack on Sadie spread far.

There was no hesitation from Bea today as she walked through the sliding doors into the hospital reception area. She bypassed the information desk and the lines of plastic chairs filled with waiting outpatients and headed straight for the lifts to take her up to HDU. It was two minutes to ten and she hoped that by arriving just as the morning visiting session began she would avoid bumping into anyone from Sadie's family. But if she did, she would simply stick to the lie that she was Sheila's granddaughter and had met Sadie when she visited her great-aunt Audrey's house. Who would bother to check something like that?

Besides, it was a risk worth taking because she had to see if Sadie had regained consciousness yet. After another sleepless night she was desperate for Sadie to tell the police that whoever attacked her wasn't the same couple who'd burgled the other victims. Bea couldn't undo what she and Sean had done to those poor women, but was it fair they should be blamed for something they had no hand in? In her mind there was a big difference between stealing someone's purse and caving their head in.

In her backpack was her school copy of *To Kill a Mockingbird*, which she was studying in English. She'd done some research on the Internet last night and discovered that it sometimes helped to read to people who were unconscious and she thought Sadie might like the story. Reading aloud to her might even trigger her to wake up, if she hadn't already.

Bea dutifully signed in at the nurses' station, taking care again to disguise her writing. The nurse behind the desk watched her carefully.

'Weren't you here yesterday morning?'

Bea nodded.

'I couldn't stay long. I only had one free study period at school.'

The lie slipped out effortlessly. She was getting good at telling them.

'Right. Well, make sure you sign out this time. We need to keep track of when visitors leave.'

'Of course,' said Bea, setting the pen down on top of the visitors' book. 'Is there anyone else here?'

'No, you're the first.'

Her confidence rising, Bea made her way to the side ward where Sadie's bed was. Walking along the corridor, she glanced through a doorway and saw the woman who'd mistaken her for Della yesterday sitting up in a bed. She gave Bea a sharp look as she passed.

There was no change in Sadie's physical appearance but her surroundings were homelier than they had been yesterday, with a 'get well soon' card propped up on her bedside table, a pale lilac dressing gown draped across the foot of her bed and a pair of fluffy cream slippers embroidered with pink flowers on the floor beneath it. Bea drew up a chair.

'Hello, Mrs Cardle, it's me again,' she said in a low voice. 'I came yesterday morning.' She chewed the inside of her cheek, unsure how to proceed. If there was a chance Sadie could hear her, she had to be careful. She mustn't say anything too incriminating.

'I'm sorry you've been hurt, I really am,' she said. 'I know it wasn't the Con Couple this time. Did you see who it was? If you tell the police they'll be able to catch them.'

Sadie didn't so much as twitch in response and Bea started to feel a little foolish. She reached into her backpack and pulled out the novel, turning to the start of chapter one. Her voice faltered as she began to read but soon she found a rhythm and quickly became absorbed in the story. She had no idea how long she'd been reading when she heard a voice behind her.

'I, um, hello . . . who are you?'

The book clattered to the floor as Bea shot out of her chair. Standing behind her was a woman with long dark hair wearing a Puffa jacket with an enormous collar. She looked confused.

'I'm a friend,' said Bea, trying to keep her composure, even though her heart was slamming against her ribs in panic.

'Whose friend?'

'Your nan's,' said Bea, guessing the woman must be Sadie's granddaughter because there was a clear resemblance to herself. The woman was skinny like her and her hair exactly the same colour, although the woman's looked way more natural. 'Well, kind of. My nan's sister lives next door. That's how I know her.'

There was a long pause as the woman stared at Bea, who tried to keep her gaze level like she had nothing to hide.

'You're related to Audrey?'

'Yes.'

'Why are you here so early?'

A simple question, but one that still made Bea falter.

'Well . . . I . . . my nan is very upset and I said I'd come and see how your nan was, so I could tell her. I'm going round hers now.' Bea grabbed her backpack from the floor. 'I'll go now. I didn't mean to get in the way.'

Suddenly the woman's face softened and she fluttered her hands in front of her as though she was nervous.

'I'm sorry, I didn't mean to be so rude. It's lovely you came to visit. My name is Della.' Her eyes locked on Sadie and immediately they filled with tears. 'I thought she'd be awake by now.'

As Della wept for her grandmother, Bea was filled with self-loathing. It didn't matter that she and Sean weren't the ones who'd put Sadie in hospital: they were still responsible because someone had copied what they'd done to the other victims. Then, in a flash, it came to her – the solution to sorting out this horrible mess. There was, she realized, another way that the police could find out who hurt Sadie without her waking up to tell them.

'I should go,' she said, choking on her words as the enormity of what she was about to do hit home.

'Thanks for coming. It was really nice of you.'

Bea shot out of the ward. By the time she reached the exit on the ground floor she was shaking with fear, knowing that going through with her plan meant having to live with the consequences however bad they might be. Yet she knew it was the right thing to do, what her parents would want her to do.

With a heavy heart but a determined pace, Bea set off in the direction of the police station.

34

A few minutes passed before Della noticed the girl had left behind her copy of *To Kill a Mockingbird*. She retrieved it from the floor and as she leafed through the pages she was seized by nostalgia. It was a book she remembered studying at school and had adored for the character of Scout, the fearless little girl she wished she could've been more like as a child. Scout had lost her mother too, but she hadn't let it define her like Della had.

There was a stamp on the inside cover: *Property of Mansell High School for Girls*. For a brief moment she wondered whether she should return it, then put it on the bedside table next to the card she'd written to Sadie yesterday. If the girl didn't visit again she could give it to Audrey to pass on to her.

Della heard voices at the door and turned to see the consultant entering the ward with a young man and woman in tow. The consultant looked just as dishevelled today as he had done when Della met him in the relatives' room two days ago, his hair seemingly not brushed since.

'Ah, hello there, Miss Cardle,' he said. 'Do you mind if these two tag along? They're my students.'

She said it was fine, then sat quietly as he gently lifted

Sadie's eyelids and shone a small light at her pupils before checking her pulse. Then he pulled out the chart at the end of the bed and spoke in an undertone to the students, who listened intently. Then he came over to Della's side of the bed.

'Your nan's making good progress I'm pleased to say. The CT scan we ran yesterday showed the swelling on her brain is reducing and her vital signs are strong. I'd like to keep her sedated for another twenty-four hours or even a little longer to give the brain a bit more time to recover but if she continues on this trajectory I'd say the prognosis is good.'

'So she's not going to wake up yet?'

'Not yet, but only because we don't want her to, not because she can't,' said the consultant, giving Della a reassuring smile that was mirrored by his two students. 'If I were you, I'd go back home and get some rest while you can.'

'I will, thank you.'

As the trio trooped out of the room, Della felt her mood lift for the first time since finding Sadie on Tuesday morning. It was a welcome change to how awful she'd felt yesterday, a day that had ended as it had begun with her sitting on her nan's dining-room floor, crying over the empty photo album. She'd gone back to the house alone after spending the day at Sadie's bedside because Alex had had to work late. It was gone midnight before she'd dragged herself upstairs to fall asleep on the single bed in her old bedroom.

When she woke that morning she'd been feeling more pragmatic – Maggie was right, of course, when she said the police couldn't investigate the missing photographs and it was silly of her to have suggested it. There was bound to be a perfectly good explanation for why the pictures had disappeared, that Sadie would tell her when she woke. As for what she'd said about Helen coming back, well, that was her emotions getting the better of her. The stark reality made much more sense: Helen had missed so many milestones in Della's life that she was hardly going to come back to Mansell after a seventeen-year absence for the sake of a few snapshots.

Della decided to take the consultant's advice. She would go back to Sadie's house to tidy up the dining room. Visiting hours resumed in the afternoon and she would come back then.

Hundreds of loose photographs were still scattered across the carpet along with reams of documents and old newspapers that Della had pulled from the bureau when she was searching for the missing pictures. With a heavy sigh she slipped off her coat, hung it on the doorknob, then dropped to her knees and began scooping the photographs into neat piles. It was going to take her hours to put them all back in their rightful places.

Once she'd piled the photographs together, she reached for the newspapers, most of which were old and yellowed. Della wondered why Sadie had hung on to them. The first one she picked up was a copy of the *Daily Express*, a newspaper she'd never known either of her grandparents to read. The story on the cover was about the official French report into the death of Diana, the Princess of Wales: Della checked the date and was shocked to see it was Saturday 4 September 1999 – exactly two weeks after Helen left

Mansell. The actual date of her mum's departure – Saturday 21 August 1999 – was as unforgettable to Della as her own birthday.

She reached forward for the next paper, another *Daily Express*. That one was from 30 August 1999. The next one, the *Mirror*, was from 2 September 1999. The penultimate paper in the pile, a copy of the *Sun*, was dated the 29th of that month. Della flicked through them but nothing jumped out as a reason for why Sadie had kept hold of them.

At the bottom of the pile was a copy of the *Mansell Echo* from 27 August 1999 – the Friday after Helen went. Della found the answer to why Sadie had kept that particular issue on page five. The entire page, bar an advert for a cleaning firm in the bottom right-hand corner, was devoted to coverage of the Mansell Show, a glorified fete that used to be staged every year in the town's main park until attendance tailed off and its organizers stopped bothering.

In the centre of the page was a photograph of Helen sitting on the grass with a group of people who looked to be the same age as her. Just behind them families milled about food stalls and a games stand where goldfish were being handed out as prizes. Behind those was a stage with a banner running above it, flapping in a breeze that had been frozen in time. The banner was too far away to make out what was printed on it.

Della's throat tightened as she stared at the photo. She didn't recognize the others posing with her mother, who was wearing a knee-length black dress with spaghetti-thin straps, covered in daisy motifs. Squatting next to Helen, an arm wrapped round her shoulder, was a redhead dressed in a low-cut black vest top, cut-off denim shorts and purple platform sandals. Both women were smiling widely and Helen wore a garland of real daisies in her hair like a crown.

Three men flanked them. The tallest was heavy-set and had a Panama hat perched on his head at a stupid angle; the fair-haired man standing next to him was trying to tip it off. The only one of the group not smiling was the dark-haired man in jeans and a white T-shirt crouched down next to Helen. The cigarette hanging from his lips made him look even more sullen and his hand was clamped on Helen's thigh.

Della lifted the newspaper up so she could read the small caption beneath the photograph.

The gang's all here: (from left) Niall Hargreaves, 24, Helen Cardle, 22, Fleur Tatton, 21, Ross Keeble, 24, and Kelvin Cruickshank, 23.

Were these her mum's friends? Were they the ones Helen had preferred to go out with rather than stay at home and look after her? Della's skin felt hot and prickly as she studied their faces. She was certain she'd never heard any of their names mentioned by her grandparents. Helen's best friend back then had been a girl called Gillian Smith, who lived a couple of streets away and had gone to the same school – and Gillian wasn't in the photo.

As Della pored over the image, the enormity of what she was looking at hit her. She sat back on her haunches and covered her mouth with her hand to stifle her mounting shock.

For as long as it ran, the Mansell Show had always been staged on a Saturday afternoon, every year without fail. The

Mansell Echo, meanwhile, went on sale every Friday morning. The newspaper Della was looking at was datelined Friday August 27 1999, which meant – if the *Echo* had published its coverage of that year's fair in its next available edition, which she assumed it would have – the Mansell Show that year must've been held on Saturday 21 August.

In other words, the exact same day Helen left Mansell for good.

The pages of the newspaper crumpled as Della gripped them tighter. This photograph was most likely the last one taken of Helen in Mansell . . . and the four other people in the frame quite possibly the last to see her.

35

It was only supposed to be a flying visit to the hospital so Maggie could check that the belongings Eleanor Bramwell had requested had arrived from Trenton. There had been no follow-up questions after she sent Eleanor's statement to Umpire yesterday afternoon and with Simon Bramwell still unconscious there was nothing to update Eleanor with from the police's point of view either. But when Maggie arrived to sign in at HDU, the ward clerk delivered some surprising news that instantly ruled out her speedy return to the station.

'The consultant wants to discharge Mrs Bramwell today,' the ward clerk told Maggie.

'Already? Is that wise?'

'It was him who said it, not me.'

'Sorry, I didn't mean to snap. Can I speak to him?'

'He's not on the ward right now but I can page him if you want?'

'Yes please.'

It felt far too soon for Eleanor to be released. Even if her knife wounds were healing well, the trauma of her experience surely warranted a longer stay. If they needed to free up her bed, why not move her to a general ward?

The issue, it quickly became apparent, wouldn't be getting the consultant to change his mind but persuading Eleanor to stay put. She was already dressed, ready for the off, when Maggie found her in her room. Wearing grey jeans that looked new and an off-white wool sweater – her belongings had arrived then – she was perched on the edge of the bed trying to comb her hair. She was having difficulty lifting her right arm and as the comb snagged in her hair, she swore.

'Here, let me help,' said Maggie.

As she untangled the comb, Maggie took in the full face of make-up Eleanor had managed to apply. Clearly she was determined to leave.

'Are you sure you're ready to be discharged? It looks like you're still in pain,' she said, releasing the comb and handing it back.

'It's not up to you,' Eleanor retorted. 'I want to get out of here and the doctor says I can go.'

'Okay, but I'll have to check with DCI Umpire that you can return home. It might be better for you to stay with family or friends for the time being.'

'Absolutely not,' said Eleanor.

Maggie had found it strange that Eleanor's family hadn't visited after the attack but she had insisted they be kept away, saying her parents were elderly and she didn't want them any more upset than they already were. She'd also refused to allow any friends to visit either because they were mostly people Simon knew from before they married and she feared their loyalty would be to him.

'I don't want to go back to Trenton anyway. I want to stay here until all this is over.'

Maggie imagined that by 'over' Eleanor meant when her husband was either dead or had been formally arrested.

'I suppose I could ask if one of our safe houses is available,' she said. 'We have a few properties across the county that we use to house victims and witnesses in cases where their safety has been compromised. I can't say for sure that you meet the criteria as your husband is unconscious and under police guard, so not posing a threat right now, but I could ask.'

'No, I want to stay in a hotel.'

Maggie frowned. There was no way the force would fund that.

'I don't think a hotel stay is something we could cover if that's your preference,' she said carefully, 'and it could end up being expensive for you. Let me find out about a safe house.'

'No, I want to stay in a hotel and I don't expect the police to pay for it. I have some money put aside that I can use.' She paused. 'It's what I call my running-away fund.'

Maggie knew what a running-away fund was, but was perplexed by the unexpected admission that Eleanor had one. It was essentially money that women in abusive relationships were advised to set aside for an emergency departure, but why was Eleanor secretly making provision to leave her husband at the same time she was undergoing IVF to have a baby with him?

'How long have you been saving up?' she asked.

Eleanor wouldn't meet her eye.

'A while . . . two years.'

'Do you mind if I ask what prompted you to start?'

'Well, my marriage . . . things haven't been good for a while. Not good at all. I feared the day would come when I needed to leave and I wanted to make sure I had enough money to do it.'

If there was a history of abuse, Eleanor needed to give them chapter and verse. It would strengthen their case should Simon regain consciousness.

'I take it your husband has no idea you've been setting money aside?' said Maggie gently.

'No. I didn't put it in a bank account in case I was sent letters and he saw them. I've been hiding sums of cash.'

'Where?'

Eleanor brushed off the question.

'One of the nurses told me about a hotel called the Langston. I'd like to stay there please.'

It was the second time in two days the Langston had been mentioned to Maggie: it was also the hotel where Della Cardle worked. It had a three-star rating and wasn't the best establishment Mansell had to offer, as Maggie pointed out.

'I don't care,' said Eleanor stubbornly. 'That's where I want to go. The nurse said it's tucked away on a hillside a distance from the town centre and it should be nice and quiet. It sounds perfect.'

'Sure, if that's what you want.'

As she watched Eleanor stand up to pack away the last of her things, Maggie chewed over her query about the Bramwells trying for a baby, wondering the best way to frame it. Of a highly personal nature, she could guess what Eleanor's reaction would be but she felt it was a wrath worth provoking. The reservations she had about Eleanor's account of her husband stabbing her were playing on her mind – namely, if he burst into the bedroom and began stabbing her immediately, how come she found time to switch on her bedside lamp and check the time to the minute? And why did he give up trying to get into the bathroom if he was that determined to kill her?

'Mrs Bramwell—' she began.

'Call me Eleanor, please.'

'Okay, Eleanor, can I ask you something about your IVF treatment?'

The woman eyed her warily. 'Go on.'

'I'm wondering why you were putting yourself through all that to have a baby, if at the same time you were saving up to leave your husband?'

Eleanor inhaled sharply, her shock evident. Maggie readied herself for the rebuke but instead Eleanor sank back down onto the bed.

'I want a baby so badly and I thought that if I got pregnant, Simon would change.' She choked on her words. 'I thought he wouldn't hurt me again if I had his child.'

'Is Simon violent towards you?'

Eleanor couldn't answer and buried her face in her hands. Maggie sat down next to her.

'I'm sorry to have to ask, but the more we know about the true state of your marriage, the easier it will be for us to build a case against your husband if he survives.'

Eleanor's head snapped up and her eyes bored into Maggie's. 'You think he's going to live?'

'To be honest, I have no idea.'

'But your colleagues, the ones with him in Trenton, they must have said something.'

'I spoke to them this morning and there's been no change in his condition. But even if he does recover he won't be allowed anywhere near you.'

'It's not that. I know Simon and I know that if he does wake up he'll try to put the blame on me. That's what he does. He tells people I'm clumsy and that's why I walked into the door or fell down and broke my arm.'

'He broke your arm?'

'He slammed the car door on it and fractured my forearm. He said I'd tripped over and people believed him. Everyone believes Simon,' said Eleanor as tears began to roll down her cheeks, taking her newly applied mascara with them. 'Our friends, people at work, even my parents. He's so charming and such a good liar. I bet you'll end up believing him too.'

'People will believe you this time. I mean, how is he going to explain away your wounds?'

'He'll make it sound convincing,' said Eleanor. 'Is it bad that I want him to die?' she whispered.

Maggie thought very carefully before she answered, mindful that she wasn't allowed to counsel Eleanor.

'I think you've been through a terrible ordeal and how you're feeling is probably normal in the circumstances,' she said. 'Look, I should probably ring DCI Umpire and let him know you're being discharged . . .'

As if on cue, the consultant arrived. He seemed as taken aback as Maggie had been to see Eleanor already dressed and packed.

'Ah, I see you're ready. Well, I'm afraid you have to stay just a bit longer as we need to get your discharge drawn up.

But it shouldn't take too long,' he said distractedly as he checked his pager.

'Mind if I have a word?' said Maggie.

'By all means.'

'In private?'

'Oh. Okay. Do excuse us, Mrs Bramwell.'

When the door was firmly shut between them and Eleanor, Maggie asked why he hadn't thought to inform the police before telling her she could go.

'I don't have to explain my medical decisions to you. I wouldn't ask you to explain yourself to me,' he blustered.

'No, but it's been less than thirty-six hours since she was admitted and she's a vulnerable patient.'

The consultant shook his head. 'My remit is to assess her medical condition, not her psychological state. Her wounds are healing well. She has no other medical concerns that she should be detained for.'

'Really? She's just been attacked by her husband and left for dead. Fine if you can't keep her up here in HDU, but at least get her on a general ward for another twenty-four hours.'

'I can't justify taking up another bed when there's no clinical reason for her to stay.'

Maggie bristled with frustration but she knew it wasn't his fault.

'Fine, discharge her if you have to, but you still should've warned us. There are protocols we need to follow in a case like this, like making sure she's got somewhere suitable to stay first. She doesn't want to go home, understandably.'

The doctor's shoulders sagged.

'I'm sorry, you're right. We should've let you know. I did

mean to, but the nature of the department, it never slows down enough for me to get everything done.'

Maggie felt sorry for him. The poor man looked dead on his feet.

'Can you at least keep her here until this afternoon? Give us some time to make arrangements?'

'Yes, I can do that.'

With that agreed, Maggie headed outside to call Umpire. Butterflies took off in her stomach as she dialled his number but their flight was cut short when he didn't pick up. Frustrated, she left a message asking him to call back, but when her phone rang less than a minute later it wasn't his name that flashed up but Belmar's.

'Hey, we got your message. What's this about Eleanor Bramwell being discharged?'

Umpire had listened to her message but refused to call back himself? Disgruntled, she gave Belmar a rundown of the morning's events so far.

'Well, if that's what the consultant thinks,' said Belmar. 'It's not our call anyway.'

'Sorry?'

'Trenton CID are running the show on their own now.'

'Since when?'

'About an hour ago. ACC Bailey said that now we know it's definitely got nothing to do with Bramwell's business connections it's no longer HMET's concern.'

'If I hadn't called, was anyone going to bother to let me know?' said Maggie hotly.

By anyone, she meant Umpire.

'Of course. Ballboy's just finished briefing the new SIO.'

'Who might that be?' She knew she must've sounded petulant but didn't care.

'It's DI Green. Either she or someone else from CID will give you a call.'

It wasn't often Maggie was made to feel as though her position as FLO was so far down the pecking order it didn't count, but this was fast turning into one of those occasions. It was bad enough Umpire wouldn't talk to her, but was she now meant to wait on tenterhooks until DI Green deigned to contact her too?

'What am I meant to do in the meantime with Eleanor Bramwell?'

'Do as she's asked. Take her to the hotel. She's paying, so it's not like you need to clear it. Look, I need to go,' said Belmar. 'Call Trenton if you need anything. Oh, and one more thing – thanks for sending my wife home drunk last night.'

Despite her sour mood, Maggie couldn't help but smile. 'Sorry, we got a bit carried away.'

'I'll say,' he laughed. 'She threw up when she got in and was still feeling sick when she went to work this morning.' His voice suddenly dropped to a whisper. 'Allie said she told you about us doing IVF.'

'Um, yeah, she did.'

'You won't say anything to anyone, will you? It's just that, well . . . it's my fault and it's embarrassing.'

'Belmar, you know I wouldn't. But you shouldn't feel embarrassed. It's not like you have any control over it.'

'That's easy for you to say,' he said abruptly. 'Look, I just want it to stay between us, okay?'

'Of course, I promise. Look, I'd better go too. Good luck with whatever case you're on next. Drink soon?'

'Yes, let's get a date organized. Wait, hang on a sec.'

Maggie heard muffled voices, as if Belmar had put his hand over the receiver. Then he was back.

'DCI Umpire says thanks.'

'For what?'

'Doing a good job, of course.'

'That's it?'

Belmar laughed. 'What else were you expecting?'

Maggie could think of a dozen things, but what was the point.

'Nothing,' she said. 'Nothing at all.'

36

Bea took two wrong turns on her way to the police station. This side of town was alien to her, far away as it was from the invisible boundary surrounding the shopping centre and six-screen cinema that she and her friends never strayed beyond.

The first time she went up a cul-de-sac into a dead end she simply doubled back on herself, but on the second occasion she'd been paying far less attention, absorbed in her phone and a WhatsApp chat going on between a couple of her friends that she'd been included in. When she finally looked up, she had no idea where she was. She went to open Google maps to check her location but her phone battery chose that moment to die on her.

Bea chewed nervously on her thumbnail. She was in a residential street lined with trees and parked cars. It wasn't like the road where she lived, where all the houses had driveways – here the properties were knotted together in one long line, and you had to look hard to see where one ended and the next began. The exteriors revealed signs of neglect from their occupants – paint flaking off window frames, dirty net curtains suckered against smeared glass – and the pocket front gardens were either overgrown or cultivating piles of rubbish. This must be one of those streets her mum referred to as a no-go area.

Bea walked back to the end of the terrace to check the street sign but was still none the wiser when she saw it: Clarendon Road. For a second she wavered. Why didn't she just go home? She could ask someone for directions to the bus station and jump on the 365. Life would be so much easier if she didn't tell the police.

An elderly man with a shock of white hair was walking towards her with his dog straining at its leash. Displaying a confidence she didn't feel inside, Bea stopped him.

'Can you help me please? I'm lost,' she said.

He smiled. 'Where are you trying to get to?'

Looking into his kind, weathered face, Bea had a sudden flashback to the last break-in she and Sean had committed. She remembered the victim's expression as she cowered in her hallway and begged Sean not to hurt her; Bea had tried to reassure the woman it would be okay but Sean had shouted at them both to shut up and then he hit the woman hard across the face. Flooded with shame, Bea knew what she had to do.

'The police station,' she said firmly.

'Are you all right?' asked the man with a trace of concern.

'I will be, yes.'

He gave her directions to get back to the main road.

'It should be signposted from there,' he finished.

'Thank you,' said Bea, and she bent down to pat his dog, a glossy-coated Golden Retriever. The dog butted his head up to meet her hand.

'He likes you,' said the man. 'Take care now.'

Bea bade them both farewell and continued in the direction the man had outlined. There would be no going home, not today. She had to tell the truth. Maybe, a little voice inside her head reassured her, the punishment wouldn't be so bad because she was handing herself in and this would be the first and only time she'd ever been in trouble.

Maybe.

But as the police station loomed into view, Bea's legs buckled beneath her and she began to shake. Twice she tried to step off the pavement to cross the road to get to it and twice she had to pull back as she thought her legs might give out. She was about to attempt it a third time when a hand suddenly encircled her upper arm and gripped it tightly, causing her to yelp.

'What the fuck do you think you're doing?' Sean whispered in her ear.

Keeping hold of Bea's arm, he yanked her back from the kerb. A woman bustling past with shopping bags shot them a look.

'I'm not doing anything!' Bea protested. 'I'm – I'm on my way home. I had an appointment.'

Sean squeezed her arm even tighter and she began to cry.

'Don't lie to me. I heard you ask that old bloke for the way to the police station.'

Bea struggled to make sense of what Sean was saying. How did he know about the man with the dog? Then it dawned on her.

'Have you been following me?' she squeaked.

'Too right I have. First you go to the hospital two days on the trot, now you're heading to the police station. Are you out of your mind? What are you playing at?'

He reeled her round to face him, so they were almost nose-to-nose. Sean's face was twisted in a snarl and Bea recoiled from the fury that burned off him like heat.

'Well?'

She was too terrified to answer.

'Take another step towards that nick and I'll push you under a fucking car.'

Crying harder, Bea tried to pull away but Sean grabbed her other arm and yanked her towards him. He wrapped his arms round her body; anyone walking by would think they were hugging. Only close up would they see the terror stamped on her face.

'I am not going to prison because some silly little kid can't keep her mouth shut, do you hear me?' he hissed in her ear.

Bea nodded frantically.

'I've warned you what will happen, haven't I? Social services will be round to your house quicker than you can say boo hoo. And it won't be just you they take away – it'll be that sister of yours too.'

She didn't doubt he knew what he was talking about. Sean had told her, with some pride, that he'd been dabbling in petty crime since junior school and a previous arrest for stealing a car had earned him a community service order and his own social services case file.

He pushed her back a fraction so she could see his sneering face. 'She's a looker, your sister. Maybe I should get to know her as well.'

'She's only twelve,' said Bea hoarsely.

'So?'

Fear ripped through her at the thought of what he might do to Esme given half a chance.

'I won't say anything, I promise,' she said. 'I'll go home now and I won't go back to the hospital.'

'Too right you won't. What the hell were you doing going to see that woman? Do you want people to think it was us who did her over?'

'I know it's stupid but I wanted to say sorry that someone had copied us.'

Sean rolled his eyes. 'You are such a fucking sap.'

'She didn't hear me though, she's unconscious.'

'Just as well. Now, you're going to go straight home like a good little girl and forget all about hospitals and police stations, aren't you?'

'Yes,' she stammered.

He released her arm and stepped backwards, smiling as though nothing was amiss and he hadn't threatened her life.

Bea hesitated for a second then slowly began to walk away, fearful he might grab her again at any moment. She hadn't gone more than ten paces when he called her name and jogged after her.

'In case it hasn't sunk in yet, I'll be keeping a close eye on you, Bea. Anywhere you go, anything you do, I'll know about it.'

37

Leaving Eleanor to cool her heels until her discharge, Maggie headed back to the station. There was a growing tightness in her chest, a reminder she was juggling two cases requiring her full and absolute attention. For the next couple of hours at least, it was Della's turn.

When she arrived back in CID, Pearl was waiting for her.

'Don't say I never give you anything,' she said, thrusting a file at Maggie.

'Is this . . . ?'

'Yep. Everything we've got on Helen Cardle.'

The file felt flimsy and light in Maggie's hand.

'Not a lot by the looks of things,' she said, disappointed.

'Nope. It's pretty clear from the witness statements that she'd been talking about leaving for a while. My take on it, for what it's worth, is that she didn't want to be found.'

Helen wouldn't be the first missing person to fall into that category. Of the 200,000 or so people reported missing in the UK every year, at least two thousand went untraced.

'I ran the usual background checks too, but nothing came up,' Pearl added. 'She's covered her tracks well.'

'Or she could be dead for all we know.'

'I did look for a death certificate under the name of Helen Cardle but there was no match.'

'Thanks for trying,' said Maggie.

Pearl's enormous shoulders lifted in a shrug. 'I'm not sure it's going to be of much help.'

Maggie dropped into her chair and opened the file on her desk. Across the office, she could see Renshaw was on the phone, talking animatedly. She looked up and caught Maggie's eye and smiled. Maggie overcame her shock quickly enough to fire a bemused smile back. Then she turned her attention to the file.

The preliminary police report revealed Helen Cardle was reported missing a month after her last sighting in Mansell on Saturday 21 August. Her father, Eric Cardle, had become concerned they'd had no contact with her whatsoever in that time. Maggie flicked through the papers to find the statement Sadie had given to officers once the investigation began. It didn't make particularly comfortable reading: she'd effectively washed her hands of her 'errant' daughter, saying she had threatened to walk out so many times she assumed she'd made good on her threat. 'Attention-seeking' was how she'd labelled it.

Helen wants everyone to make a fuss of her and beg her to come home but I've had enough. We've done it too many times already and our poor darling granddaughter doesn't know whether she's coming or going as far as her mum is concerned. Right now I don't care if Helen never comes back.

Maggie wondered what Della would make of that last sentence in Sadie's statement. At least Eric was more forgiving:

Our daughter will always have a home with us if she wants it.

The file also included a witness statement from one of Helen's friends, Gillian Smith. The two of them had gone shopping in Mansell town centre on the morning of Saturday 21 August and had stopped for a burger in McDonald's for lunch. Afterwards Helen said she wanted to look in on the Mansell Show on their way home and Gillian was surprised – the show was something mostly old people and families went to. She suspected there might have been a man involved, although as far as she was aware Helen hadn't arranged to meet anyone and when they got there they'd wandered around aimlessly for a bit.

The statement then revealed Helen had provoked a row by bringing up an ex-boyfriend of Gillian's who'd mistreated her. According to Gillian, Helen knew it was a touchy subject for her and in hindsight she thought Helen had mentioned it so she would get angry and leave, which is exactly what happened. Gillian had stormed off, unaware it was the last time she would ever see her friend.

The officer who conducted the interview had pushed Gillian on why she should be so sure Helen had deliberately engineered the row.

I think she set the whole thing up so she could leave that day. Helen has been very unhappy lately. She doesn't enjoy being a mum, although I think she does love Della. Why is she unhappy? Well, she's always talking about the places she wants to travel to and how having a baby ruined her chance of going. Did her parents tell you that last summer she took off for three weeks without telling anyone? When she came back she refused to say where she'd been but I think it must've been somewhere in this country as her dad said she didn't take her passport. Actually, my money's on the Isle of Wight, because a few weeks earlier a funfair had come to Mansell and Helen slept with this bloke who ran one of the rides. We'd been talking to him for a bit before they went off together and he said the fair was off to the south coast and then to the Isle of Wight and the dates tallied. I can't remember his name though and to be honest she didn't mention him after that night. He was young, about our age.

Maggie flicked through the file but could find no mention of whether the funfair was followed up as a line of inquiry. She wasn't wholly surprised it hadn't been: as Pearl said, everything stacked up to suggest Helen had left of her own accord. Also, unbeknown to her parents, she'd withdrawn her savings a week earlier and while shopping with Gillian on the morning of 21 August had purchased new underwear and several changes of clothes. Her passport was also missing. With no sense of criminality playing a part in Helen's leaving, Maggie could see why the case was quickly closed.

'What's that you're reading?'

She hadn't noticed Renshaw come up behind her. The DS eyed the file suspiciously. In the interests of prolonging their new harmonious relationship, Maggie decided to be honest.

'Actually it's the miss per file for Sadie Cardle's daughter.'

'Why are you looking at that?'

'Della has this crazy theory her mum might somehow be involved in the break-in, so I wanted to read up on her. Also, Audrey Allen thought she saw someone who looked a lot like Helen leaving Sadie's house on Monday evening. Audrey forgot to mention when you questioned her that Sadie didn't go to bingo as normal because she was due a visitor.'

Renshaw's reaction was surprising. Far from being annoyed, her usual default setting when Maggie took the initiative, she was excited.

'Actually, I'm all for crazy theories today. I just had a call from Imaging. They've been going over the crime scene photos from Sadie Cardle's kitchen and noticed something we didn't pick up – and by "we", I mean forensics too. You know how there was glass on the floor where the window-pane in the door was smashed?'

Maggie nodded.

'Everyone assumed the glass was punched in from the outside so they could get to the lock, because that's what it looked like at the scene. But Imaging now reckons it might've been staged to look like that. They think it was the other way round and the glass was scooped up from outside and spread over the floor,' said Renshaw as she made sweeping gestures with her hands. 'Apparently the pattern of broken glass doesn't quite fit with what it should be had the window been smashed inwards. I've put a rocket up Paul to get a shift on with his forensic report, especially regarding fingerprints on the back-door key. If we only find Sadie's or Della's prints on it, that means the key wasn't turned in the lock by someone trying to get in from outside . . .'

'. . . Because Sadie had already let them in the front and they broke the glass to make it look otherwise.'

'Exactly!' said Renshaw triumphantly. 'It's not the Con Couple's usual MO for them to both come in the front and the gin bottle being used as a weapon doesn't fit with them either. If we are looking at other suspects, maybe there is something in Della's theory about her mum. Do you have any more info on this lookalike who went round there on Monday night?'

Maggie filled her in on Sadie being interviewed about her furniture-making father and revealed that she'd spoken to Jennifer Jones at the *Echo* and had ruled out the reporter being anyone else from the paper.

'Audrey said the resemblance to Helen was uncanny, but I don't know how reliable her memory is. She hasn't clapped eyes on Helen for seventeen years.'

'If it was Helen, why pretend to be a reporter?' Renshaw mused. 'Why not return home as the prodigal daughter?'

'Della's due to inherit some money next month when she turns twenty-one. Not a substantial amount but if Helen wanted to get her hands on it, she probably wouldn't want Della to find out and stop her. She could've rung first and pretended to be a reporter to set up a time to go round – it's feasible Sadie wouldn't have recognized her voice after all this time and she'd have been none the wiser until Helen turned up on the doorstep, by which time it would've been too late to let Della know. Helen would also have known about the Churchill desk to use it as an opening. But what makes me doubt that the reporter was Helen is the very fact she *hasn't* surfaced anywhere in the past seventeen years.'

Pearl ran a check through the usual channels and she found no trace of her,' Maggie explained.

'People can live off-radar though. There are websites now dedicated to showing you how. Clearly they don't get the irony.'

'Okay, but what about the fact Audrey said she watched the reporter leave around ten p.m.? I thought we were putting the time of Sadie's attack as the following morning, based on how long the paramedics thought she'd been lying there.'

'We can go over all the timings again to see if there is a chance Sadie could've been there all night before Della found her. If she did, that puts the so-called reporter on our list of suspects alongside the Con Couple.' Renshaw screwed her face up as she thought for a moment. 'Do you honestly think there's something in this Helen-coming-back theory?'

'I don't know, but it's worth checking out,' said Maggie.

'I'll get some of the others to do some digging on her, see if we can find anything Pearl might've missed. Is there anything else?'

'Don't you want to wait for the briefing at ten?'

Renshaw did a funny little side-to-side shake of her head.

'No, let's get on with it. It's better if we share info as we go along.'

Maggie couldn't help herself.

'Okay, now I'm worried. What the hell have you done with the real Anna Renshaw?'

Renshaw grinned and held up her hands.

'It's a fair cop. Someone recently gave me some good advice about trying a different approach, that's all. Be less uptight, that kind of thing.'

'Who?'

Renshaw looked startled and reddened.

'Why do you need to know that?'

'Because I think we should organize a whip-round to say thanks.'

Renshaw laughed and it was only then that Maggie noticed her hair was loose on her shoulders and she was wearing one of the tight pencil skirts she used to shimmy around in before her promotion. She was also wearing make-up again. Maggie was intrigued by the switchback in appearance but managed to bite her tongue before a sarky comment tripped off it. If she was honest, she was enjoying the friendliness too much to want to ruin it.

'Once I've finished reading this I was going to head back to the hospital if that's okay. Eleanor Bramwell is being discharged,' she said.

'Oh. How's that going?'

'It's a waiting game to be honest.'

Renshaw gave her a quizzical look.

'To see if the husband lives or dies,' said Maggie.

'I hear HMET are off the case.'

Maggie was impressed by Renshaw's insider knowledge. Belmar had made it sound as though the decision to relinquish the case to Trenton CID had only just been made.

'Yep. Do you know DI Deborah Green at Trenton? She's taking over as SIO.'

'Don't know her but if she gives you any aggro, let me know. So far you've managed both cases really well and I don't want that to change.'

Maggie pretended to faint. 'Did I hear you pay me a compliment? Bloody hell, I'm starting that whip-round now . . .'

Nathan walking up to Maggie's desk cut short their laughter. She took one look at his face and knew it wasn't good news.

'Has there been another robbery?' she asked.

'No, it's worse than that,' he said. 'The hospital rang. Sadie Cardle died twenty minutes ago.'

'Shit,' said Maggie, envisaging Della's reaction. 'I thought her condition was improving.'

'So did the doctors,' said Nathan. 'The hospital is launching an investigation. They suspect she might've been given an incorrect dosage of pain medication by mistake. The doctor who prescribed the drug and the nurse who administered it have both been suspended.'

Maggie and Renshaw were stunned.

'You're telling us the attack didn't kill her but someone's cock-up might have?' said Renshaw. 'How the hell are we going to explain that to her granddaughter?'

'She already knows. They called her first.'

38

Della had no recollection of phoning Alex but she must've done because suddenly he was there, taking her in his arms and telling her how sorry he was and how she would get through it and that he would help in any way he could. Yet his embrace was of no comfort to her. Instead it made her feel claustrophobic and inexplicably angry and she wanted to scream at him to leave her alone. How could she even begin to get through it, whatever *it* was?

The hospital administrator who had delivered the news by telephone was sorry too. Three times she had to repeat what had happened because Della was too shocked to take it in.

'There will be an inquiry into what happened . . .'

Inquiry into what, exactly, she'd asked. Someone had hurt Sadie and now she was dead and she'd never see her again and she was all on her own. What else was there to say? She'd ended the call without a goodbye.

As another wave of grief slammed into her, Della made a noise that was somewhere between a wail and a sob. Alex patted her on the back and said 'there, there' like she was a baby being winded and it annoyed her with such intensity that she shoved him away from her, the violence of her action surprising them both.

'Hey, there's no need for that,' he admonished as he made a show of rubbing his chest.

Her own chest heaved as she struggled to catch her breath.

'Then stop treating me like a child.'

He looked hurt. 'I know you're only being like this because you're upset.'

She didn't know whether to laugh or scream at him. He didn't get it.

'If you want to make yourself useful, take me to the hospital,' she said.

'Are you sure? I mean, is there much point now?'

Della stared at him, incredulous.

'What I meant,' he said, stumbling over his words, his expression suggesting he wished he could take back what he'd said, 'is that it's not like she's there any more. I'm sorry.'

'I know she won't be there,' Della spat, 'but I'm still going to say goodbye.'

'Of course, if that's what you want,' Alex replied hastily.

Della was in the hallway pulling on her coat when the doorbell rang. She wasn't surprised to find Maggie outside: the hospital administrator who'd rung had said the police were being informed too.

She jumped in first. She didn't want to hear the message of condolence she could tell Maggie was on the verge of delivering.

'I'm going to the hospital,' she said.

'I can take you,' Maggie offered. 'Unless . . .'

She looked past Della's shoulder to where Alex had appeared. He extended a handshake.

'I'm Alex Morgan, Della's boyfriend. I'm going to take her, thanks all the same.'

Maggie shook his hand but kept her gaze trained on Della.

'We do need to talk about what happens next . . .'

This time the grief hit Della like a physical blow, knocking the wind right out of her. She pitched forward as if she was fainting but Maggie was there to catch her.

'Let's sit you down inside.'

'No, no, I want to go to the hospital.' The words clawed at her throat. 'I need to say goodbye.'

Maggie took charge. 'I'll drive you both in my car. Come on.'

Alex tried to get in the front passenger seat but Maggie demoted him to the back, saying she wanted to talk to Della as she drove. He huffed loudly as he got in.

'Did the hospital explain what the inquiry would involve?' Maggie asked Della as she turned out of Frobisher Road. 'It won't change our investigation but it may complicate things a bit.'

'I was too upset to take in what they were saying.'

Maggie indicated left and pulled into a parking space at the side of the road. She shut off the engine and turned to face her.

'The hospital believe your grandmother may have been given an incorrect dosage of pain relief that was fatal. A nurse and a doctor have been suspended pending the investigation.'

Della gasped and Alex swore in the back seat.

'They killed her?' he said. 'Oh my God.'

'The inquiry will establish exactly what happened. In the meantime, our police investigation into who attacked her will continue. Nothing has changed on that score.'

Della felt weak and dizzy, as though the blood was draining from her body.

'I can't believe it. She was getting better and they gave her the wrong amount of medicine? Who makes a mistake like that?' she said, choking back tears.

'I'm afraid there will have to be a post-mortem to establish exactly what happened,' said Maggie. 'It will take place later today.'

'She's going to be cut up?' Della cried, her mind suddenly filled with an image of her nan's body flayed open. She'd watched enough police dramas on TV to know exactly what a post-mortem looked like. Bile rose in her throat.

'This is insane. How could they have let this happen?' said Alex from the back seat. He sounded as upset as Della.

'I can't speak for the hospital and it's probably not healthy for either of you to speculate until you know the outcome of the inquiry. In the light of your nan's death it's been decided by my senior officers that I will be your Family Liaison Officer going forward,' Maggie added. 'Any questions you have, just ask me. We are still determined to find out who attacked her.'

At first Maggie's words didn't register. But as Della repeated them in her mind as the car pulled away from the kerb and rejoined the flow of traffic, the significance of what Maggie had said hit home.

'You don't think it was the same ones who attacked the

other old people.' She posed it not as a question but as a statement.

They pulled up at a red traffic signal and Maggie cast her a sideways glance.

'They're still our main suspects but we do have a couple of other leads we're looking into.'

Alex unbuckled his seat belt and leaned forward so his face loomed between the front seats.

'Such as?' he said.

'I can't tell you at this stage I'm afraid. I know that's frustrating to hear, but as soon as I have any concrete information to pass on I will.'

The traffic lights changed and Maggie eased the car forward. She kept her eyes on the road.

'So we just have to wait?' Alex demanded.

'Mr Morgan, please can you sit back in your seat and buckle up? I can't be distracted while I'm driving,' said Maggie.

Alex did as he was told. Della watched him in the sideview mirror and saw he wasn't happy at being told what to do.

'To answer your question, Mr Morgan,' said Maggie, after waiting until he had put his seat belt on, 'yes, I'm afraid so. We need to make sure we investigate as thoroughly as possible. We don't want to arrest the wrong person, do we?'

Della kept her eyes on the side mirror. Leaning back in his seat, Alex looked pensive.

'I'd like to come round later, once you're back from the hospital, and go through a couple of things,' said Maggie to Della.

'Like what?'

'Just some paperwork.'

'What paperwork exactly?' Alex chimed in.

'We can talk about it later.'

Della turned her head to look directly at Maggie. Why was she being so vague? Then she noticed Maggie's gaze flit between the road and the rear-view mirror far more than was necessary.

She was watching Alex too.

Della's pulse quickened. Surely the police didn't suspect him? She tried to think of reasons why they might believe Alex was involved and immediately she recalled his reaction to finding out she wouldn't inherit the house if her nan died . . . What if he hadn't been at work when he said he was? But Della couldn't bring herself to imagine Alex hurting Sadie. Her mind simply wouldn't entertain it. This was Alex she was talking about, Alex who loved her and who got on well with her nan. No, it was someone else. It had to be.

As Della floundered for any kind of explanation that made sense, Maggie suddenly mentioned the name Gillian Smith.

'Do you remember her at all?'

Oh God, please don't bring up Helen now, thought Della, not with Alex in the car. He thought her mother was dead because that's what she'd told him. He wouldn't react well to finding out that she was lying all this time.

'She and your mum were best friends apparently. Does her name ring a bell?'

'Kind of,' Della stammered. 'I don't remember her at all, though Nan sometimes talked about her. But why are you – I mean, what has she got . . .' She tailed off, wanting the conversation to stop.

'I read the missing person's file for your mum. I was wondering if Gillian was still in Mansell.'

Della shuddered as Alex piped up.

'Missing person?' he exclaimed. 'I thought your mum was dead.'

Maggie glanced at Della, clearly surprised. Della prayed the pleading look she flashed her back adequately conveyed her message: please don't tell him.

'She's dead now, like I told you,' Della said to Alex. 'She went missing first. The police knew.'

Maggie kept her eyes firmly on the road and Della was grateful she did not contradict her. Later, when they were alone, she would explain to Maggie why she hadn't told her boyfriend, why it was no one's business but hers.

Reassured that Maggie wouldn't counter her, Della mentioned she'd found a new picture of Helen. 'It's from the day she went missing.'

'How do you know it was from that day?'

'It was in a newspaper.'

Della felt the car swerve a fraction as Maggie expressed surprise. Fighting a tide of emotions, she explained how she'd stumbled across the photo in the copy of the *Echo* that Sadie had stashed away.

'I don't know who the others are in the photo, but they were with her in the afternoon before she left. I want to find out where they are now.'

Alex spoke up from the back seat. 'Why do you need to find them if you already know what happened to your mum?'

His tone was curious and Della clammed up, fearful she'd roused his suspicion.

'The only friend who was interviewed at the time of Helen's disappearance was Gillian,' said Maggie in an aside. 'Do you have any idea if she still lives around here?'

'I don't think she does. Nan would've known for sure, but I can't ask her, can I, because she's dead.' Della's voice rose as her emotions got the better of her. 'She's left me on my own.'

'You're not on your own,' said Alex, reaching over and squeezing her shoulder. 'I'm here.'

Della shut down again. A few moments later the car turned a corner and the hospital loomed into view. Nan's last resting place – an ugly, five-storey mass of grey concrete and metal.

'It shouldn't be too hard to find Gillian,' said Maggie casually. 'Tie up some loose ends.'

Della caught the look Maggie gave her and her mind began to whirl. Was she suggesting Gillian might know something about the people in the photo? Then it hit her. What if Gillian knew where Helen was now? What if Helen had got in touch with her and they were friends again after all these years?

'The advancement in technology has made it easier to track people down. It's much harder to disappear without leaving a trail now,' said Maggie. 'Same goes for committing a crime.'

Her eyes drawn to the side mirror, Della watched as Alex shifted awkwardly in his seat.

39

The headache that had plagued Lou from the moment she woke up was getting worse under the supermarket's strip lighting. Wincing from the pain caused by last night's excesses, she pushed the wire trolley up the dairy aisle towards the shelves heaving with plastic containers of milk.

Mae flailed angrily on the green plastic seat at the front of the trolley – now her little legs were getting used to walking she hated being forced to stay seated and she was noisily voicing her anger. Lou ignored her and the stares of other shoppers as she chucked two four-pint cartons of whole milk into the trolley. Her eyes were then drawn to the ready-made milkshake on the shelf above that she sometimes bought the boys for a treat. A rough calculation in her head told her she couldn't afford it this week. Not with money even tighter than usual.

Years of coping as a single mum had taught her to budget well. For a short time when Jude was a baby she'd returned to work part-time as an admin assistant at the skip hire firm she'd joined straight from school, leaving Maggie or her mum to mind him. But once Maggie began her police training and her parents moved to the south coast, Lou couldn't afford proper childcare so she stopped work altogether to be supported by the state. It wasn't how she wanted to live and she prided herself on accepting the bare minimum in government handouts, getting by on the money she received each month from Maggie and also from Jerome's parents. After his death they had also gifted her the deposit to buy the house where she and the children now lived.

Her own parents, Jeanette and Graeme, gave her little. While they would never dream of voicing it, Lou could tell they were uncomfortable with Jude and Scotty being mixed race and her dad had made every excuse not to hold the boys after they were born. His immediate acceptance of Mae, white-skinned and born within wedlock, upset Lou deeply and it was out of fury and protective pride for her sons that she'd rejected her dad's offer to loan her some money 'for Mae's sake' now she and Rob were divorced. Besides, even if she did take the loan she had no way of paying it back. Every penny she received was accounted for – or had been until she started seeing Arturs.

Their nights out were burning through her cash at an alarming rate. Halfway through November and she barely had enough money to see her through to the weekend, let alone to the end of the month. The only saving grace was that she received her child benefit payments weekly, so the next two instalments would tide her over. But there was nothing spare for emergencies.

Her guilt grew as she swung the trolley into the next aisle. She knew it was irresponsible to be using money meant for the children and for bills on enjoying herself and she had tried to tell Arturs last night in the pub that she couldn't go out as much. She'd risked enough leaving Jude in charge again, but to her relief the evening had passed without incident and when she got home, earlier and marginally less inebriated than she had been the night before, all three children were fast asleep in their beds.

Arturs hadn't been impressed when Lou said she'd have to scale back their nights out though, and made his irritation known by doing the one thing he knew would hurt her – chatting up another woman. He'd waited until Lou had gone to the toilet before scooting over to the next table to talk to a girl barely in her twenties. He'd even eyeballed Lou directly as he nuzzled the girl's neck while leaning in to whisper something. His message to Lou was crystal clear: you're easily replaceable.

Lou's eyes pricked with tears as she reached for the cheapest baked beans on the shelf. Once was a time when she'd never let any man treat her with such casual disdain but it was like she'd forgotten how to stand up for herself. Rob leaving her for Lisa had crushed her confidence to the extent that instead of doing what she should've done, which was to walk out and leave Arturs to it, she'd ended up apologizing for upsetting him. The upshot was they were going out tonight for the third evening running while Jude babysat again. She had briefly toyed with asking Maggie to watch the kids but realized she couldn't risk Jude or Scotty letting slip she'd left them and Mae alone the night before as well. It was two days since she'd spoken to her sister and she missed her.

'Mama,' said Mae suddenly, reaching for Lou with her chubby fingers. Her little face was curdled with worry.

Lou quickly wiped her eyes and forced a smile.

'Hey, Mummy's fine,' she said.

She bent down to kiss her but Mae clung on to the front of her coat.

'Mama!' she wailed.

Lou scooped her out of the trolley and hugged her tight. She hated the kids seeing her upset. Even when Rob walked out she wouldn't cry in front of them. The only person she ever allowed to see her at her lowest was Maggie.

Mae screamed and bucked wildly when Lou tried to get her back into the trolley so she hitched her onto her hip and pushed it with one hand. The next aisle was crisps and nuts and Lou was about to swerve to avoid it when her guilt got the better of her.

'Why don't we get your brothers a snack for after school? How about some crisps or popcorn?' She couldn't afford either but if she was going to spend money on going out again, the boys deserved a treat too. As she browsed the aisle, Mae excitedly clapped her chubby hands together and Lou smiled.

As long as the kids were okay, she'd manage.

40

Thirteen point five togs of duvet and a blanket covered her fully clothed body but still Bea shivered as though she was freezing cold. She burrowed further down the mattress until only the top of her head was visible on the pillow. If anyone came into her bedroom they might have to look twice to notice her lying there.

She'd gone straight to bed as soon as she'd arrived home. She wanted to hide away and shut out all the bad things that were happening. For the first time in a long time her phone was switched off and still at the bottom of her bag.

The curtains in her bedroom were lined with blackout material and since pulling them shut she'd lost all track of time. At some point, after dozing off, she became aware of noises downstairs. Either her mum was back from the charity shop or school had finished and Esme was home. Bea shuffled further down the bed and stuck her fingers in her ears to shut out the muffled sounds of family life being played out below.

She didn't hear the knocking on her door at first. Eventually the raps grew louder and more insistent, rousing her from the depths of her bed.

'Yes?'

'Can I come in?' said Esme.

'No.'

'Please, Bea. I've got something for you.'

'I don't want it.'

Her sister evidently wasn't prepared to take no for an answer and flung the door open.

'Why is it so dark in here?'

Without asking if Bea minded, Esme switched on the overhead light and plonked herself down next to her on the bed. Her right hand was behind her back and she was holding something in it.

'Have you been in bed all day?' said Esme with a smile.

Bea replied with a scowl. They got on okay as a rule but her sister's unrelenting cheeriness wound her up at times. Esme viewed the world through a prism of optimism, never crying and rarely getting upset. Even as a baby she'd hardly ever grizzled. She had the same blondish-brown hair and big brown eyes as Bea, but unlike her Esme wore a permanent smile. People who met them guessed immediately they were sisters but Bea's slighter, shorter frame meant they usually assumed Esme was the eldest.

In some ways Esme *was* the more mature sister – certainly she was in temperament. When Bea's bulimia was diagnosed and their parents became frantic with worry, Esme had been exposed to conversations a child of ten would not normally be privy to and had been forced to grow up quickly as a consequence.

'I'm not in the mood for a telling-off,' Bea said.

'Don't be nasty, I've bought you a present.'

Emse's hand came out from behind her back holding a Kinder egg.

Bea couldn't stop the smile spreading across her face. 'Oh wow, I haven't had one of those in years!'

'I hoped you might like it,' said Esme, looking pleased. 'I thought it was something you could manage to eat. I heard Mum say you're seeing Dr Reynolds again on Monday.'

Bea was touched. Esme tried so hard to understand her complicated issues with eating and she loved her for it. She took the Kinder egg from her, unwrapped it and broke off a piece of the two-tone chocolate. It melted against her tongue.

'Want some?'

'No, it's all yours. Hey, something funny happened on my way home from school. This boy stopped me and said I had nice hair. Can you believe it!' said Esme, giggling.

'That's only because you've brushed it for a change,' Bea teased as she wolfed down the rest of the chocolate. She set the plastic egg on her bedside table, feeling too old for the toy it concealed.

'He was really hot.'

'From the boys' school?'

'No. That's why it was so brilliant, cos he was old. Not old old, but grown up, like twenty or something. Amelia was so jel.'

Bea tensed. 'What did he look like?'

She listened with growing horror as her little sister described Sean right down to the silver ring he wore on the middle finger of his right hand.

'Do you know what he said then?' Esme squealed, her cheeks reddening. '"Hope I see you around." Me! *He* hopes to see *me!*'

Bea feigned a giggle but inside she wanted to scream. Sean was never going to leave her alone and now he was going after Esme too. She couldn't bear to think what he might do to her dear, sweet, smiley sister if he got his hands on her.

'He sounds way too old,' she said, pulling the duvet back up to her chin so Esme couldn't see she was shaking.

'I'm nearly thirteen! He was only paying me a compliment.'

'Stopping a schoolgirl in the street like that is creepy. Mum and Dad would go nuts if they knew.'

Esme instantly looked worried. She usually did as she was told and didn't like getting into trouble – Bea suspected she tried so hard not to be a nuisance to their parents because they'd had so much on their plate for the past couple of years with her illness.

'Please don't tell them. I didn't really talk back to him. All I did was smile.'

'All right, I won't say anything. But if he ever stops you again, you must tell me, okay?'

Esme nodded but concern lingered on her face.

'I will, I promise. Can I get in with you?' She kicked off her school shoes. 'Can we watch *Friends* for a bit? There's bound to be one on.'

'Sure.' Bea shuffled across to make room. A small, flat-screen TV was attached to the wall at the end of her bed and she flicked it on using the remote. The room filled with the sound of American accents and studio laughter, and Bea hooked her arm round her sister's shoulders, pulling her close. As Esme snuggled against her and laughed at the TV, Bea began to relax.

Here they were safe.

41

The mood in HDU was even more sombre than usual. The ward clerk was the same one who'd been on duty that morning and she tensed as Maggie approached her desk, her eyes red and tumid.

'Can I help you, officer?'

'I'm here to collect Mrs Bramwell.'

The woman's shoulders dropped a fraction and the rigidity eased from her expression. She must've thought Maggie was there because of the inquiry into Sadie's death, yet it wouldn't be a police matter unless it was discovered the incorrect dosage had been administered deliberately. From the details that had been passed to Nathan earlier by the hospital administration it was being treated as human error.

'I don't think her discharge has been signed off. Her consultant . . .' The clerk's voice grew tight again, as though it was an effort for her to talk. 'He's not here right now.'

So the consultant treating Eleanor was the same one suspended over Sadie's death. Maggie recalled their last conversation, how exhausted and overworked he'd seemed, and she felt a pang of sympathy. The poor man's entire career could be in jeopardy because the demands of his job had made him too tired to think straight. As a police officer she understood how easy it was to reach that point, but then she wasn't dealing with matters of life or death. If the consultant had caused Sadie's death, unwittingly or not, he couldn't go unpunished.

'Is there anyone else who can do it?'

'Let me find out for you.'

'Thanks. We need to get it done now.'

'Why don't you wait with Mrs Bramwell and I'll find someone straight away,' said the clerk. 'It shouldn't take long.'

Maggie felt contrite for putting pressure on HDU staff when the department was in a state of turmoil but now she was FLO to both Eleanor and Della she had to manage her time carefully between them. Taking Eleanor to the hotel while Della was viewing Sadie's body seemed like a sensible use of it. Alex had said he would arrange for them to get a taxi home when Della was ready, then Maggie would go round later to check on her. Hopefully by then Eleanor would be settled at her new digs.

As she watched the ward clerk reach for the phone to page another doctor, Maggie knew at some point she'd need to sit down and fill in her log for both cases. Every FLO was required to fill out a daily log detailing conversations they'd had with relatives and anyone else they came into contact with who was relevant to the investigation. In the case of Sadie Cardle that meant Della and her questionable boyfriend. Maggie tried to avoid making snap judgements about people as a rule – her detective brain automatically fished around before she formed a deciding opinion – but there was something about Alex that made it hard for her to warm to him. He was almost too good to be true: attentive, caring, accessible – yet experience and training had taught her it was those relatives a FLO should be most wary of, as eagerness to help could often be a mask for guilt. So, after dropping the pair of them off at the morgue, she'd called Renshaw to suggest they look into his alibi for Monday evening and Tuesday morning, just in case.

Twenty minutes later Maggie carried Eleanor's overnight bag as they walked towards the car park. Eleanor's right arm was in a sling to support her injured shoulder and she'd been given an outpatients appointment for Monday to have her dressings changed. With no friends or relatives to help, the task of getting her to the appointment would probably fall to Maggie. She had to hope there was no cause for Della to need her at that time too.

'I'm concerned about leaving you alone at the hotel,' said Maggie. 'What if you start to feel worse?'

'Then I'll call reception for help. Please, I want to get out of here. I hate being surrounded by so much illness and death,' said Eleanor with a shudder. 'Just this morning a lady died in the room along from mine. She was old, but still.'

Maggie guessed she was talking about Sadie but made no acknowledgement of the fact.

'She was alone too when it happened. It made me think of Simon. In spite of everything, I hope he's not on his own. His parents are both dead but he has a lot of friends. Do you know if anyone is with him?'

'He's under police guard so I don't imagine visitors are permitted,' said Maggie. 'I can ask when I speak to DI

Green, who you met on Tuesday. She's now in charge of the case.'

They eventually reached Maggie's Toyota. After helping Eleanor into the passenger seat and putting her small suitcase of belongings in the boot, Maggie opened the rear door behind the driver's seat to toss in her own bag but she threw it too hard and the contents spilled out. Pages from Helen Cardle's missing person's file, which she'd been planning to take home that evening to study further, scattered across the back seat. She gathered them up as Eleanor peered over her shoulder.

'Is that another case?' she asked as Maggie slid a headshot of Helen back into the file.

'Not exactly.'

'Who's the woman?'

'A missing person,' said Maggie reluctantly, uncomfortable discussing another case with Eleanor.

'Is she to do with the woman who died this morning? They have the same surname, don't they?' Eleanor shrugged. 'I heard the nurses talking about her after she died and they said her name. It's the same one on the front of the file.'

'I can't discuss it I'm afraid,' said Maggie, tucking the file under her handbag and shutting the rear door. She climbed into the driver's seat as Eleanor remarked: 'Your job must be fascinating.'

Maggie was stumped for a response. It wasn't often a victim expressed a keen interest in what she did for a living, much less one of a very recent and very violent crime. Their concern was usually limited to the investigation relating to themselves and she could only conclude that Eleanor's questions were a way of deflecting any conversation about her own situation.

Mansell was spread across the floor of a basin in a part of Buckinghamshire known as the Chiltern Hills. A chalk escarpment more than forty miles long, stretching through Buckinghamshire into the neighbouring counties of Oxfordshire and Bedfordshire, the area was characterized by steep hills soaring over deep vales.

The Langston Hotel was built on the brow of the steepest bluff overlooking the town. The hotel had undergone a refit since Maggie last had occasion to visit, for a friend's thirtieth birthday party two years ago. A waist-high glass wall now flanked the walkway from the car park to the front door, up a set of steps into which small, round spotlights had been set at regular intervals. Maggie carried Eleanor's suitcase and offered her other arm for support, but Eleanor gingerly pulled herself up the steps holding on to the top of the glass wall, which was freezing cold to the touch. Her face was pinched with pain and again Maggie worried how she'd manage in the hotel on her own.

When they reached the door, Eleanor stopped.

'I don't want anyone here knowing who I am,' she said firmly. 'You mustn't tell them.'

Maggie hesitated. 'But what if you need someone to help you, if your shoulder starts playing up?'

'Then I'll ask for help. But there's no reason for anyone to know how I got injured. Okay?'

'I can't guarantee the press won't track you down to here,' Maggie cautioned. 'Your name is already circulating.'

'I'll worry about that if and when it happens. But I mean it: I don't want anyone at the hotel to know why I'm here.'

Maggie wasn't happy about it, but she nodded. She appreciated Eleanor's desire for privacy but it made her job harder if there wasn't anyone else looking out for her when she couldn't be there.

She kept quiet as Eleanor checked in. The Langston was a fairly big hotel and there were a number of rooms available, including a studio-style double room that came with a small kitchenette. It was the priciest of those on offer, but Eleanor liked the idea of catering for herself whenever the mood took her.

'I just want to shut myself away,' she told Maggie, which sparked an inquisitive look from the receptionist. 'In fact,' she went on, pulling Maggie aside so the receptionist couldn't hear them, 'I don't want you checking up on me while I'm here. I don't need babysitting.'

Maggie wasn't easily deterred.

'I'm afraid it's not that simple,' she said pragmatically. 'My job as your FLO is to maintain regular contact and keep an eye on you. I also thought you'd like me to take you for your outpatients appointment.'

'I'll get a taxi.'

'Really? Because I can pick you up.'

'No, I'll go alone,' said Eleanor. 'Please, I don't want any fuss.'

'Fine,' Maggie sighed. 'Look, I get that you don't want me popping in constantly, but is it okay that I stay in touch with you by phone?'

'Do I get a say in it?'

'Not while the investigation is ongoing.'

From the corner of her eye she could see the receptionist watching them. Eleanor noticed too, and lowered her voice.

'After what I told you about my marriage, I thought you'd understand. I want peace and quiet. No more shouting. No more threats. No more fearing for my safety.'

Years of apparent pent-up grief cast a shadow across Eleanor's face. Maggie knew she should back off.

'I do understand and I promise I'll only call you if there's important information to pass on, or when we need to check something with you.'

Eleanor's eyes suddenly filled with tears.

'All I want to hear from you is that my husband is dead and can never hurt me again. I want this to be over.'

42

Maggie settled Eleanor at the hotel and was driving back to the centre of town when her phone rang. It was Alex Morgan and he sounded upset.

'It wasn't at all what I expected. I've never seen a dead body before and I thought she'd just look like she was asleep. But she didn't. She looked dead. It was horrible,' he said, his voice cracking. 'Della's in pieces now.'

'I'm so sorry. I should've come with you.'

'I don't think you being there would've made any odds to the experience. It was . . .' He tailed off.

'Why don't I come round now and see you both?'

'I don't think Della's in a fit state to talk to anyone. That's why I'm ringing. Can we please leave it until tomorrow? With everything that's happened, and now this hospital inquiry, Della needs some time to herself.'

'Are you sure?'

'I am. It's getting late in the day now anyway.'

Maggie glanced at her watch. It was already five o'clock and dusk was creeping its way across an already moody sky.

'If Della does need someone to talk to, I can arrange for Victim Support to come round. Their counsellors are fantastic and talking about it might help her begin to process what's happened.'

'Maybe tomorrow.'

'Why don't I call you in the morning to let you know what time I'll be round? I do have more questions to go through with Della. In the meantime, if there's anything you need, don't hesitate to call. I'll keep my phone on all night.'

'Fine. I'll let her know.' Alex paused for a second. 'What questions?'

'I need to check some details about her grandmother's movements on the day prior to her being attacked,' Maggie fudged, deciding Alex didn't need to be privy to the mysterious reporter coming round on Monday evening.

She could almost hear him frowning down the phone. 'I'll have to make sure I'm here when you ask them. I don't want Della upset again.'

'Nor do I,' said Maggie.

To her surprise he hung up without another word.

When she reached the CID office she went to find Renshaw to ask if Alex's alibi had been checked yet, but the DS was nowhere to be seen. She made a beeline for Nathan's desk instead.

'Is Anna around?'

He glanced up briefly. 'No, she's got something on. She had to leave.'

'To do with the burglaries?'

'No, hot date.'

'Lucky her.'

'What's up?' asked Nathan. 'Anything I can help with?'

'Do you know if Alex Morgan's alibi for Monday night and Tuesday morning has been established yet?'

'Sorry, I don't. She must've asked someone else to do it.'

Maggie decided to check her computer to see whether the information had been uploaded onto the system yet. Returning to her desk she saw someone had left a Post-it note stuck to her computer screen asking her to call DI Green. There was a mobile number to go with it. Maggie used the landline phone on her desk to call it back and Green answered on the first ring.

'Ah, about time we had another chinwag, DC Neville,' she said. 'How's it going with our victim? Is Mrs Bramwell still being a madam at helping us with our inquiries?'

'She's not the easiest of witnesses, no. But I think anyone in her position would be on edge, ma'am.'

'Point taken. Now stop with that ma'am nonsense, it makes me sound bloody ancient. Guv will do fine,' said Green with a throaty chuckle. 'Right, I read the statement you took from her yesterday and it's a bit Swiss cheese in places.'

Maggie was unnerved. Was the DI implying she'd missed something?

'Don't hit the panic button,' said Green sagely, as though she could hear Maggie's mind galloping. 'You asked the right questions – it's her answers I'm not happy with, especially the bit about him stopping halfway through breaking down the bathroom door. Do you think she's telling the truth about what happened?'

'I don't think she's being entirely honest, no. She has kept information back, including the fact that her husband abused her.'

'How bad?'

'Broken limbs bad.'

'Hmm. I shall be interested to see what Mr Bramwell says about that.'

'That's my point. If she wants us to believe that he tried to kill her, why not tell us immediately about the history of violence? Why withhold it?'

'Fear? Shame? There are plenty of reasons why wives don't speak out against their abusive spouses. What we need now is his side of the story, which I'm hopeful we can get in the next couple of days. He's been kept under because the docs were worried the overdose might've damaged his brain, but his vital signs have improved and they're going to try to bring him round tomorrow morning.'

Eleanor's last words to Maggie rang in her ears: *All I want to hear from you is that my husband is dead and can never hurt me again.* She didn't relish the next conversation they'd have if he regained consciousness.

'I think I need another face-to-face with Mrs Bramwell before I question him,' Green mused. 'I can get to Mansell by nine a.m. tomorrow. I'd like you to meet me at the hospital.'

'Actually, Mrs Bramwell was discharged today. She's now staying at a hotel in the town. She didn't want to go back to Trenton.'

'Discharged? Why didn't I know that?' A discernible flintiness sharpened Green's voice.

'I was told to wait for your call,' said Maggie, careful not to sound defensive. 'I did ask if she could be moved to a general ward but there was no clinical reason for her to stay in hospital.'

'Her wounds are not that bad then?'

'Not enough to keep her in hospital, no, but she's still in

a lot of discomfort. She's said she doesn't want me checking up on her constantly though.'

'Tough,' said Green. 'Simon Bramwell seemed intent on killing himself with all those pills but he didn't do such a good job on his wife, did he? I want to get to the bottom of why.'

'He might not have intended for either of them to die. Maybe the row spiralled and he attacked his wife without thinking of the consequences.'

'Nice theory, DC Neville, but I'm not using that one to build our case against him,' said Green. 'If I'm going to charge him with attempted murder, I need premeditation and previous broken limbs gives me that. We need to know what he's done to her over the years, so let's meet with Mrs Bramwell in the morning, get this one wrapped up. Where is she staying?'

Maggie gave her the Langston's address.

'Let her know we're coming, will you?' Green added. 'There's no point in spooking her even more by turning up unannounced. Right, I'm calling it a day here and I suggest you do the same, unless your other case needs you? I had a call from DI Gant earlier and he's let me know the score on you doubling up as FLO with this case and the robbery victim's granddaughter. If you start feeling overworked, let me know. I did Family Liaison on a couple of cases way back when I was a DC. Didn't suit me – I couldn't cope with all the grief. Drains you.'

'It can do, but only if you let it.'

'That's where I went wrong. Just let me know if the two cases do get too much, DC Neville. I need you on top of things and I don't want anything or anyone slipping through the net.'

43

Maggie stayed in the office to answer a few urgent emails and to fire off some of her own. Afterwards she did a PNC trawl to double-check there wasn't anything else on Helen Cardle aside from what was included in the file Pearl had dug out for her. It didn't matter that Renshaw had tasked someone else on the team to do exactly the same: Maggie's curiosity drove her to seek the answers herself.

Where had Helen been for almost two decades? Why did her parents stop looking for her? Had something or someone stopped her coming back? Yet nothing came up on the PNC and Maggie's extensive Google search for any related news items and any social media mentions was equally unrewarding.

It was gone nine when she finally got home. Her flat occupied the top floor of a converted Victorian townhouse on a street a few minutes' drive from the town centre. It was the first and only property she'd viewed when house-hunting, but it wasn't just its location, high ceilings, sash windows and two bedrooms that had convinced Maggie it was the perfect home. Thanks to its close proximity to the railway line that shuttled passengers and freight between

London and the Midlands it was also the most affordable, with an asking price far less than that of identical properties in quieter locations. Almost every visitor to the flat remarked on the noise, wondering how she could stand it, but Maggie found the deep rumble of trains passing beneath her windows oddly comforting.

She'd previously rented out the spare bedroom to bring in some extra cash to help cover Lou's bills as well as her own, but it had recently dawned on her she could just about manage on her salary alone and she'd decided she would rather live by herself than go through the rigmarole of finding a new lodger. The last one, a veterinary assistant called Susan, had been disappointingly antisocial, shutting herself away in her room any time Maggie was also home.

She changed out of her work clothes into thin grey cotton trousers designed for yoga but which she'd never used for their intended purpose, a cable-knit sweater she'd nicked off her dad the last time she'd visited her parents near Portsmouth and the thickest socks she possessed to keep out the evening chill. Then, after summoning the energy to cook herself a vegetable stir-fry with noodles and chicken, she cranked the heating up to high and slumped down on the sofa to flick through the channels, eventually settling on a repeat of *Game of Thrones*.

She must've dozed off because she was woken at 11.15 p.m. by the sound of the doorbell buzzing through the intercom. Still half asleep, she stumbled into the hallway, presuming it was another late-night pizza delivery for the couple who lived on the ground floor. Callers always got their doorbells mixed up and Maggie made a mental note to put a sign up spelling it out.

She held down the talk button on the intercom.

'Yes?'

'It's me.'

Suddenly she was wide awake.

'Will?'

'Can I come up? We need to talk.'

Umpire's sentence slurred to a finish and she hesitated. If he'd been drinking, any attempt at a meaningful conversation would probably end in even more misunderstanding. But her keenness to see him shoved the misgiving aside.

'It's open,' she said, pressing down firmly on the button with a key symbol on it to unlock the main front door downstairs.

Maggie yanked open the door to her flat and listened as Umpire plodded up the three flights of stairs. At one point she heard him stumble and swear as he collided with either the wall on one side or the metal-railed banister on the other.

When he reached the tiny landing outside her flat, she realized he was the most drunk she'd ever seen him. His eyes slipped in and out of focus as he stared at her, their whites shot through with red, and the smell of alcohol clung to him like fog.

'Maggie.'

He said her name with such foreboding that in an instant she forgot that he was drunk, forgot that she was embarrassed for him to see her in such slovenly clothes, forgot that she was annoyed with him for telling Belmar to lie to her and for the way he'd dismissed her at the hospital.

'What's wrong?' she rasped.

His answer was to stagger forward, cup his hands round

her face and plant his lips firmly on hers. Her mind screamed *what the hell?* but her mouth quickly succumbed, not caring that his lips and tongue tasted of stale whisky and cigarettes. The feelings she'd held back for months erupted inside her and she kissed him back as ferociously as he kissed her.

Later, she wouldn't remember which of them pulled away first, but she would always remember it was him who said, 'This is wrong.'

'*What?*'

'I'm sorry. I have to go.'

He backed away from her on the landing, his hand feeling behind him to make contact with the banister.

'Will, wait. You can't just turn up and then . . . then leave. What's going on?'

'I'm sorry, Maggie. I can't do this to you.'

'What does that mean?'

'I can't do this to you. You're amazing. The most amazing woman I've ever met.' He groaned and clasped his hand to his forehead. 'I'm . . . I'm a shit. A total shit. You deserve better.'

'Why don't you let me decide what I deserve?' said Maggie in frustration. The imprint of the kiss thrummed through her. She didn't want him to leave: she wanted him to stay the night. She wanted him to stay every night.

'I did something,' he said.

'Did what?'

'Something I can't undo. Something you'll hate me for.'

'To do with us?'

'Yes, but . . .' He floundered. 'No, it's to do with me. My life.'

His eyes met hers and there was something so wretched

about the way he looked at her. Her mind raced through every possible explanation until, finally, she landed on it.

There was someone else . . . that's why he'd been holding back all those months . . . she wasn't the only one.

Instantly her stomach gave way, like someone had ripped it out and thrown it at her feet.

'I think you should go,' she said quietly, trying not to cry.

Somewhere over her shoulder, inside the flat, her phone was ringing. Or was it? Was she imagining she could hear it, wanting some other noise in her head to drown out this agonizing silence? But Umpire had heard it too.

'You should get that,' he said. 'It might be important.'

She nodded, not trusting herself to speak, and went to close the door, but he moved forward again and took her hand.

'Maggie . . .'

'Don't,' she said, but she didn't pull away.

'How I felt about you was real,' he slurred. 'Really fucking real. You need to know that.'

How I felt.

Past tense.

Maggie yanked her hand from his, stepped inside her flat and shut the door. She waited for a moment, her forehead pressed against the cool wood surface, listening to him retreat down the steps and hoping he'd change his mind and come back. He didn't.

Her phone was still ringing as she moved away from the door. She stumbled through the flat in search of the noise and found her mobile on the floor by the sofa. Caller ID said it was Lou and Maggie choked up at the sight of her sister's name and picture flashing up in front of her.

'Oh, sis, your timing is perfect . . .'

A loud wail from Lou cut her off.

'Maggie, you've got to come! My babies!'

There was so much background noise that Maggie could hardly hear her.

'You need to speak up. What's going on?'

'The house . . . it's, oh God!'

There was a loud bang and the sound of glass shattering. Maggie's knees buckled.

'The house,' Lou sobbed. 'It's on fire.'

44

Maggie fought her way through the crowd of rubberneck-ers, screaming 'Police!' and shoving her badge into the face of anyone who objected to being elbowed out of the way.

Two fire engines and an ambulance were blocking the street outside Lou's house and the acrid stench of smoke filled her lungs long before Maggie reached them. She staggered to a halt outside number seventeen. No flames were visible but the white facade of Lou's house was black-ened with soot and the windows on the ground floor smashed. Water pooled around the open front door where two hosepipes snaked inside.

Maggie's heart caught in her throat and she looked around frantically until her gaze landed on the ambulance parked a little way down the street. Two children were huddled together on the steps.

'Jude?'

Her nephew looked up, his shell-shocked face streaked with tears. Slumped against his side was Scotty, his small, filthy hand clinging to the blanket that covered them both. Maggie ran over and flung her arms round them, letting out a sob of gratitude that they were both safe. It was a few moments before she could bring herself to let go.

'Where's Mae?' Her voice wobbled as she tucked the blanket firmly round them.

'In here,' said Lou's voice from inside the ambulance. Maggie craned round the door to see her sister sitting on a bench attached to the ambulance wall with Mae, an oxygen mask covering her tiny face, lying across her lap. Maggie's eyes filled with tears as Lou began to cry.

'I'm so sorry, I'm so sorry,' she said.

'It's okay, you're safe and the children are safe,' Maggie reassured her.

'You can come inside,' said the paramedic watching over her sister and niece. Maggie realized she knew him.

'Roy, isn't it? I'm DC Neville, with Mansell CID. We've met before.'

'Oh yeah. I thought you looked familiar.'

'This is my sister. Can you give me a minute with her? Keep an eye on the boys out here for me?'

'Sure.'

She stood aside to let him down the steps and watched as he crouched down next to Jude and Scotty and asked if they wanted some more water to drink, to which they both nodded. Maggie climbed into the narrow space he'd vacated.

'What happened?' she asked Lou.

Her sister closed her eyes and nuzzled her lips against Mae's forehead. Aside from the mask, the sleeping toddler appeared remarkably unscathed.

'Lou?'

'It was some cauliflower cheese, in the microwave.' Tears dripped from Lou's chin, wetting Mae's fine blonde hair. 'I forgot you can't microwave foil containers and it caught fire. I . . . I tried to get it out with a tea towel, but that caught fire and . . .' She exhaled with a shudder. 'It all happened so quickly.'

'But you're all okay?'

Lou nodded. 'Jude got Scotty and Mae out before it got too bad. Oh, Maggie. The house. The kitchen's gutted and the smoke's got everywhere.'

'Houses can be fixed, lives can't. Be thankful you and the kids are okay.'

'But where are we going to stay?'

'With me,' said Maggie firmly. She'd already decided on the drive over that she'd take her sister and the kids in until the house was habitable again. 'You and Mae can have my bedroom and the boys can sleep in the spare room. I'll use the sofa.' When Lou began to protest, Maggie cut her dead. 'We'll manage. I've called Mum and Dad too. They're on their way.'

Lou was horrified. 'Why did you do that?'

'Because they want to help.'

Maggie wasn't surprised by her sister's reaction: Lou had an uneasy alliance with their parents and rarely asked them to lend a hand. Yet Jeanette and Graeme Neville's immediate response to Maggie's call was to get straight in their car to make the journey from the outskirts of Portsmouth to Mansell. If the roads were as clear as they should be at that time of night, they'd be there in a couple of hours.

Maggie called outside to Roy.

'Are you going to take them to A&E to get them checked out?'

'Well, we can, but your sister isn't keen on them being

admitted. None of them are suffering from smoke inhalation – we're only giving the baby oxygen as a precaution. They got out well before the fire took hold.'

Maggie swung back to face her sister.

'I think you should all go to hospital, just to be on the safe side.'

Lou shook her head violently. Mae woke up and tried to pull the oxygen mask off her face. As she grew distressed, Maggie went to her aid.

'Let's take this off for a sec, sweetheart,' she said, removing the mask. Mae gazed up at her aunt, her eyes like huge orbs. Maggie gently stroked her cheek with the tip of her index finger until Mae's eyelids drooped again and she settled back into sleep. Then she replaced the mask.

'I really think you should have a doctor look them over,' she said to Lou in a low voice. 'The boys are clearly in shock.'

Her sister's face drained of colour.

'We can't go,' she whispered.

Maggie grew exasperated. 'Why ever not?'

'Because the doctors might ask questions and I can't risk it.' Lou grabbed Maggie's hand. 'Can't you tell them we're fine and that we just want to go back to yours?'

Maggie knew her sister as well as she knew herself. She could tell in a heartbeat whether Lou was troubled, sad, pissed off or – as she was right now – hiding something.

'Not until you tell me the truth. What aren't you saying?'

'I can't tell you here.'

Maggie glanced outside. Roy was sitting with his back to them on the step alongside Jude and Scotty, showing them a piece of ambulance equipment that looked a bit like a water pistol. Both boys were enthralled, their ordeal forgotten for a moment. The ambulance's other paramedic, a short, stout woman with cropped dark hair, was a short distance away, chatting to one of the firefighters.

'No one's listening now,' Maggie hissed to her sister.

There was a long pause before Lou spoke. Her voice was soft and low.

'I wasn't at home when the fire started.'

Maggie's jaw dropped. 'Tell me you're joking.'

Fresh tears streaked Lou's face.

'I'd gone out and left Jude to babysit. I thought they'd be okay. I was only down the road at the Crown,' she said, referring to the pub at the bottom of her street, a horrible dive frequented by surly locals who threw dirty looks at any outsider who dared to venture inside. Maggie hated it.

'Scotty didn't know that foil containers can't go in the microwave, so when he tried to heat up the cauliflower cheese it caught fire. Jude tried to put it out but couldn't. So he got Scotty and Mae out of the house and called me. I was back in less than a minute,' said Lou desperately as Maggie shook her head in disbelief. 'None of the neighbours saw me. They only came out of their houses once the fire engines turned up. Everyone thinks I was here when the fire started.'

Maggie was so angry she had to clench her fists to stop herself raising her voice.

'How could you be so irresponsible?' she whispered angrily. 'What did I say about leaving Jude in charge of Scotty and especially Mae? She's only fourteen months old for God's sake.'

'I know, I just . . .' Lou trailed off, aware that no excuse in the world would cut it. 'Please don't say anything.'

'We have to.'

Lou flared up at her sister. 'So it's okay for you to keep it a secret that Rob's moving to Spain and marrying that cow, but when I need you to keep quiet for me, you won't?'

'Is that what you meant on the phone the other night? For crying out loud, Lou, it's not the same.'

'It is,' said Lou stubbornly.

Maggie tried to think logically. As furious as she was with Lou, her instinct was still to protect her and the kids. Her sister wasn't a bad mum but social services might not see it that way if they found out where she'd been that evening and what she'd done. It would mean putting herself on the line, but in that moment she couldn't see any other alternative. Shielding her family was her only consideration.

'Roy?' she called out. The paramedic swivelled round, as did Scotty and Jude. 'Is there any chance you could ask one of the neighbours to make my sister a cup of sweet tea? I know it's not your job, but she doesn't want me to leave her.'

Luckily for Maggie, Roy was the amenable sort.

'Yep, I can do that. Won't be a tick.'

As he went off, Maggie called the boys inside the ambulance. 'Come and sit here,' she said, gesturing to the bench next to their mum. 'I want to talk to you about this evening.' She waited until they were settled, then crouched down in front of them. 'It's really important neither of you tells anyone that Mummy wasn't at home this evening. Do you understand? The fire was an accident but Mummy shouldn't have left you on your own and she might get into trouble if anyone finds out. So it's our secret, okay?'

Maggie's insides churned as she spoke. She hated having to get the boys to lie when she'd always encouraged them to be honest. It was also a secret that could potentially mar her career.

Both boys nodded. She turned to Lou.

'How many people were in the pub tonight?'

'Why does that matter?'

'Were you *seen* by many people?'

'No, no, I don't think so. We sat outside under one of the heaters. I only went to the bar once, right when we got there. The place was virtually empty then.'

'We?'

Lou flicked her head towards the boys. 'Please, not now.'

A man. Someone Lou hadn't told her about. She'd find out why later.

'Aside from whoever you were with,' said Maggie, rolling her eyes, 'are you sure no one else saw you?'

'Pretty sure.'

'That's not good enough, Lou,' Maggie snapped again.

'Stop it, Auntie Maggie, you're upsetting her.'

Jude, always the defender. He glared at Maggie.

'I'm not trying to upset her, buddy. I'm trying to make sure she doesn't get into trouble.'

'I know, but don't tell her off when she's already crying.' Brow furrowed in anger, Jude put his arm round his mum while Scotty got up and moved to Lou's other side so he could do the same. The sight of them protecting her sister, little jaws jutting out defiantly, made Maggie want to cry too.

Instead, she tried to keep calm. One of them had to think and act straight.

'Right, I'm going to talk to the fire crew, see what they're saying. Stay here, all of you,' she ordered. 'I won't be long.'

Jude squeezed his mum tighter.

45

It didn't take Maggie long to find the sub-officer in charge
of the two crews, identifiable by the two black stripes on his
yellow helmet and the matching silver bands on the collar
of his tunic. He was intrigued by Maggie's presence – she
introduced herself by showing him her warrant card – until
she explained her relationship to Lou.

'Your sister's bloody lucky,' he said. 'Because they all got
out quickly and called us, the damage is a lot less than it
could've been, not to mention no lives were lost. The kitchen's scorched, but the rest is mostly smoke damage.'

Maggie looked up at the small terraced house and had to
swallow hard to stop herself from welling up. She couldn't
bear to think what the outcome might've been had Jude not
reacted so quickly.

'My sister said the fire was caused by a foil container
being put in the microwave by accident.'

'Yep, that's what it looks like. The seat of the fire is in the
corner, on one of the worktops.'

'Maggie?'

She turned at the sound of her name and was stunned to
see Craig, a firefighter she'd dated briefly the previous year,

256

coming towards her. In all the drama it hadn't occurred to her that he might be among the crews answering the shout.

'You two know each other?' asked the sub-officer.

'Yeah, sort of,' said Craig, smiling. He removed his helmet and his short dark hair was slick with sweat. 'You all right?' he directed at Maggie.

She nodded, embarrassed. Their romance had been short-lived because her heart hadn't been in it. It wasn't that she didn't like Craig – he was lovely and kind and he made her laugh – but after a few weeks she'd been forced to admit to herself that she simply wasn't sexually attracted to him. Lou had howled with laughter when she'd told her. 'He's a six-foot-tall firefighter with a six-pack and his own hose,' her sister had giggled, 'how can you not fancy him?' But when they kissed there was no spark, at least not for Maggie. Craig had been gracious when she broke it off, although she'd stopped short of telling him the truth. The line she'd spun him was that work was too busy for her to fit in a relationship as well. Bad timing, and all that.

'It's your sister's house, isn't it?' said Craig.

'Yes, it is.'

'I thought I'd recognized it, and her.'

Maggie remembered he and Lou had met once, when she'd brought him round for Sunday lunch.

'I want to take my sister and the kids home,' she said to the sub-officer. 'They seem fine but they're exhausted. They need sleep.'

The sub-officer nodded. 'We're pretty much done here too. Does your sister own the property?'

'Yes, it's hers.'

'Well, the house is structurally safe so we don't need to

let the council building control know, but your sister will need to call a glazier out to secure the windows, then call the utility suppliers to make sure everything stays switched off for now. Don't turn anything on until they've come and done a proper assessment, understand?'

'I do. Thank you.'

'Not a problem,' he said, shaking her hand. He marched off, leaving her, Craig and an awkward silence in his wake.

'I should get back to my sister,' said Maggie after a few moments.

'Aren't you even going to ask me how I am?' he grinned.

Although it hardly felt like the time for a catch-up, Maggie didn't want to appear impolite.

'Yes, of course. How are things?'

'Great. Really great,' he said. 'I'm engaged. Set the date for next May.'

Maggie was pleased for him; he was a nice guy and deserved to be happy.

'That's good news, congratulations.' She allowed a few more seconds to lapse before saying, 'Right, I really do need to get them home.'

'Right.'

'Well, bye then.'

Craig titled his head to one side.

'I don't suppose you fancy a drink sometime?'

She stopped. 'A drink?'

'Yeah, a catch-up for old time's sake.'

He made it sound like they were exes of a few years and not just a few weeks.

'Now's not the time, Craig. My sister . . .'

'No, you're right, it isn't. You've got my number though, give me a call.'

She gave him a bemused smile. 'What about your fiancée? Won't she mind?'

'It's just a drink, Maggie,' he said mockingly. 'Just two friends having a drink.'

Flustered and embarrassed, Maggie told him that's what she thought he'd meant. 'A drink would be nice. I'll give you a call.'

Craig smirked as she walked away.

Back inside the ambulance Scotty had fallen asleep with his face pressed against Lou's side while Jude was also close to losing his battle to stay awake, his head jerking as his chin drooped towards his chest. Roy, the paramedic, nodded his consent when Maggie said she was going to take them home.

'Just be mindful that they might suffer from delayed shock. If they do, either take them to their GP or call 111 for advice,' he said.

'I will, thank you.'

A couple of neighbours came forward to help Maggie get Lou and the children out of the ambulance. One, a genial Irishman in his sixties named Frank who lived three doors down from Lou, lifted sleeping Scotty and carried him to Maggie's car parked down the street. Maggie put her arm round Jude and led him in the same direction, while Lou followed with Mae.

'Shit, I haven't got their seats,' said Maggie as she unlocked the vehicle. The baby seat for Mae and the booster for Scotty were in the charred wreck of their house.

'I don't think you need to be worrying about that,' said

Frank, laying Scotty down on the back seat. He ushered Jude in after him and shut the door as softly as he could. 'You get these babbies home as quick as you can. They're flah'ed out. Their mum too,' he added, nodding to Lou, who had climbed in the front passenger seat with Mae in her arms. 'I knows a fella who does windows. I'll call him now and get him round to fix some boards up. We'll keep an eye on the place until the morning.'

The tears Maggie had fought so hard not to shed for the past hour suddenly sprang from her eyes. She laid her hand on his arm.

'Thank you, Frank,' she said, overcome. 'That's really kind of you.'

'It's the least we can do, lassie,' he said gruffly as he patted her hand. 'That's some lucky scrape they've bin through tonight. It's a miracle they're here at all.'

46

Bea never walked to school with Esme if she could help it. It wasn't cool to be seen hanging out with a younger sister, even if the journey took less than ten minutes from their house. Usually she ditched Esme at the end of their drive to walk with her friends, or if she was alone she'd make her sister walk on the other side of the road from her. Trying to persuade Bea to let Esme accompany her was a battle their mum had long given up trying to wage, so her shock was evident when, as casually as she could manage, Bea announced over breakfast on Friday morning that she'd walk Esme to and from school that day.

'Really?' said Caroline, astonished.

Bea shrugged. 'I don't mind just this once.'

Except it wouldn't be a one-off. She planned to walk with Esme every day now she knew Sean had her little sister in his sights. The thought of him touching Esme the way he had her made her heartbeat accelerate in terror.

'Are you sure you feel well enough to go today?' said Caroline.

Bea proffered the slice of granary toast she'd slathered in butter and Marmite. 'Yes. Look, I am eating.'

'We're still seeing Dr Reynolds on Monday though. I've made the appointment for right after school. I'll pick you up and Esme can make her own way home.'

'No! Can't she come with us?'

Across the table, her sister pulled a face.

'That's not fair, I don't want to,' said Esme.

'She's right, it wouldn't be fair,' said Caroline, earning herself a beaming smile from her youngest daughter and a scowl from her eldest. 'She'll get bored sitting in the waiting room all that time.'

Bea tried to pretend she wasn't bothered but inside she was frantic with worry. If she couldn't be there to walk Esme home, who'd protect her if Sean followed through on his threat to go after her?

'Right, you girls need to get going. It's nearly twenty-five to nine.'

After watching them wriggle into their winter coats and pull on gloves and scarves, Caroline kissed both of her daughters on the cheek, shoved their bags into their hands and ushered them out of the front door. The cold blast of air that shot into the house made her shiver violently.

'Quick, before you let all the heat out.' She'd shut the door before they reached the end of the drive.

Esme broke into a skip as they reached the pavement.

'Don't do that,' said Bea. Her voice was muffled from where she'd buried her chin and mouth in the depths of her scarf.

'What is wrong with you? You're being a right moody so-and-so.'

But Bea wasn't listening. Her eyes darted back and forth across the street, searching for any sign of Sean. When they reached the main road she relaxed a little, the increase in pedestrians and the vehicles flowing past making her feel more secure. Still, she wasn't taking any chances, and in the pocket of her coat her gloved hand tightly clutched her phone, just in case.

They were barely twenty yards from the school gate when Esme let out a squeak of excitement.

'Oh my God, it's *him*,' she said, her words coming out in a high-pitched rush.

Bea didn't need to look to know the 'him' her sister was talking about, but she did anyway. Sean was sitting on the brick wall outside the caretaker's house, the final property between the rest of the street and the school perimeter. His long legs were stretched out in front of him, crossed at the ankles, and to her horror she realized he was wearing the same black Primark jeans he'd worn during each of the burglaries. She would bet anything the matching black T-shirt was under his bomber jacket. He had a beanie hat pulled down low over his head and Bea was taken aback to see a tuft of bright blond hair escaping the rim. Had he dyed his hair?

Sean wasn't looking at her though. He was staring at Esme, who quivered with excitement beside Bea, her face scarlet. 'Oh my God,' she said over and over under her breath.

'Is that the guy you were talking about, the one who said about your hair?' Bea asked her, even though she already knew the answer.

'Yes, that's him,' her sister giggled. 'OMG, he's so fit.'

Bea couldn't lie and pretend Sean wasn't attractive because he was. Judging by the looks being thrown his way by other girls streaming through the school gates ahead of them, she and Esme weren't alone in thinking it either. But where she once saw beauty she now saw only danger. She grabbed at the sleeve of Esme's coat and tugged.

'Come on, we'll be late.'

'But he might want to talk to me again,' Esme protested, pulling away from her.

'Look at him,' said Bea furiously. 'He's, like, so old. He shouldn't be hanging around talking to girls your age. It's messed up. I'll tell your teacher.'

Esme was still of an age where the authority of teachers actually counted for something and Bea knew the thought of getting in trouble would fill her with dread. Immediately she stopped the tug-of-war with her sleeve and started moving, albeit slowly, towards the school gate, shooting looks over her shoulder at Sean as she went. Bea fought the urge to look back herself but couldn't resist one final glance as she stepped into the safe haven of the playground.

As she did, Sean pointed to his eyes with two fingers then pointed them directly at her.

I'm watching you.

47

Maggie stirred another sugar into her mug of tea. Normally she didn't sweeten her drinks but this morning she needed every stimulant she could get, so shattered was she after being up until the early hours consoling Lou. Her eyeballs itched with tiredness and even though she'd showered before coming to work she was convinced the smell of smoke still lingered in her hair.

Across the table from her sat DI Green with a copy of Eleanor Bramwell's statement laid out next to the cup of tea and bacon sandwich she'd ordered from the canteen servery. Green had texted Maggie just before eight saying she wanted a chat before they went to see Eleanor and could they meet at Mansell police station instead of at the hotel. The diversion made no odds to Maggie: she was too exhausted from dealing with the previous evening's events to mind. With the fire at Lou's house dominating her thoughts, she hadn't even begun to process Umpire's surprise visit to her flat, although she did keep checking her phone in the vain hope he might contact her. Every time she saw there was no message she felt even more deflated.

'You don't share DC Small's opinion of Mrs Bramwell, do you?' said Green. 'He thinks she's aggressive and a bit shifty.'

'When he met her she'd just regained consciousness. You saw what she was like – distressed, confused and in unfamiliar surroundings. I'd have probably shouted at us too, if I were her.'

'Fair dos. Maybe he needs to work on his bedside manner,' said Green sardonically, taking a sip of tea. 'Now, I'm going to lead the questions, but feel free to hop in if anything occurs. I prefer my interviews to be more like a chat than an inquisition. Am I right in thinking Mrs Bramwell still hasn't got anyone with her, no friends or relatives?'

'That's right. She's adamant she wants to be left alone. Her friends are mostly people her husband knew before they married, so she doesn't want them around her.'

'There's always one in a relationship who brings more to the party. I couldn't stand my husband's friends when I first met him and got rid of them sharpish. He didn't mind,' said Green, catching the look on Maggie's face. 'He couldn't stand them either.'

Maggie grinned. Green's company was fast becoming the balm she needed after only two hours' sleep. The DI carried herself in a way that commanded respect, but her humorous asides made Maggie think she'd be great fun on a night out.

Maggie didn't plan to tell her about the fire though, finding it preferable to switch off and concentrate on work. Her parents, who'd arrived in Mansell at 3 a.m. after numerous toilet stops slowed their journey, had taken over the task of keeping an eye on Lou and the children, and when Maggie left for the station they were all crammed into the living room of her flat, deciding the day's plan of action. Top of the to-do list was arranging for the utilities to be turned off and contacting the firm with which Lou held her buildings and home insurance. After that they would go back to the house and see what they could salvage from the ground floor.

DI Green drove them to the Langston Hotel, with Maggie giving directions.

'I'd forgotten how bloody hilly Mansell is. Gonna bugger my clutch going up this,' said Green as she crunched into second gear halfway up Bishop's Hill. With some effort on the part of her ageing Audi, seconds later they swung into the forecourt of the hotel. Green parked efficiently in front of the glass-walled walkway and peered out of the windscreen.

'Not a fancy place, then.'

'It's not the best hotel in Mansell, no. But one of the nurses recommended it and Eleanor insisted this was where she wanted to stay. I guess it suits her being a cheaper option – it'll make her running-away fund stretch further.'

'Her what?'

'It's what she calls the money she salted away to escape her marriage.'

Green let out a low whistle. 'That bad, eh?'

'So she says.'

The two of them got out of the car. It was half past nine and Eleanor was expecting them – Maggie had called ahead to let her know DI Green wanted to question her. Eleanor wasn't happy but Maggie had made it clear it wasn't optional.

They found her hovering nervously in the small and

perfunctory reception area. Eleanor didn't give DI Green the opportunity to re-introduce herself before she leapt in.

'Is there any news on my husband?'

'Actually, there is,' said DI Green. 'Shall we go somewhere private to talk?'

'No, tell me now.'

Green stood firm. 'I really think we should find a nice, quiet corner.'

Eleanor looked to Maggie for reassurance.

'DI Green is right. Can we go to your room to talk?'

'No, you can't. Let's go in here.'

As Green and Maggie raised eyebrows at each other behind her back, Eleanor led them into a room filled with bright orange easy chairs and low tables. There was a small bar in one corner, its beer pumps and bottles of liquor and wine locked out of temptation's way behind a metal grille.

'The receptionist said we could use this while the other guests have breakfast in the dining room,' said Eleanor. She grew agitated as Green took a seat and motioned for her and Maggie to do the same.

'Please, tell me what's going on.'

'The doctors treating your husband are hoping to bring him out of his coma this morning. There may be some lasting damage to his kidneys that will require further treatment but the signs are that he's going to recover,' said Green.

'NO!'

Eleanor jumped out of her seat and screamed so loudly that both officers jolted in surprise. The scream continued until Green leapt up and forcibly grabbed Eleanor by her upper arms to hold her still.

'You need to calm down, Mrs Bramwell,' she said in a

loud, firm voice, as a man in shirtsleeves and tie bolted into the room.

'Is everything okay? I'm the manager . . .'

Green addressed him with the same forcefulness. 'We're fine. Mrs Bramwell's just received some bad news. We'll take care of her.'

Bewildered, the manager's eyes darted from Maggie to Green to Eleanor.

'You can go now,' Green ordered.

'I don't think I should,' he blustered.

'DC Neville, can you speak to the gentleman outside?'

Maggie shot out of her seat and ushered the manager out of the bar.

'Can we talk in your office?'

He took Maggie to a small room behind the reception area filled with three cluttered desks – all presently unoccupied – and shut the door behind them so the receptionist couldn't overhear their conversation.

'We can talk freely in here,' he said.

When Maggie explained that she and Green were police officers and were there to interview Eleanor he was aghast.

'Your receptionist should've informed you we were here,' she added.

'Why are you here to see my guest?'

'She's a witness to a crime. I'm afraid that's all I can tell you for now.'

His eyes widened. 'Is she in danger? Should she be staying here? Because I have a responsibility to all my guests, not just her.'

'I give you my word she's not at risk and nor is anyone else. Here, this is my card. If you have any concerns during her stay, give me a call. But there's really nothing to worry about.'

The manager seemed not in the least bit mollified by her reassurance. His long, slim fingers grasped the card by one of its corners, as though the rest of it was contaminated. He peered at it through the narrow, rectangular lenses of the glasses perched on the end of his beaky nose. Everything about him was long and thin, including the strands of hair he'd combed over his head to disguise his baldness.

'One whiff of trouble and I shall make a formal complaint,' he warned.

As Maggie fought the urge to say something equally snippy in response, it suddenly dawned on her that the backroom office was where Della Cardle worked and that this man must be her boss.

'I'm working on another case at the moment involving one of your employees,' she said.

He seemed taken aback.

'Oh, you mean Della? Such an awful business with her grandmother.' There was a fraction of a pause. 'I was hoping Della might be back to work today. I spoke to her yesterday and she said her grandmother was doing well. We're rather short staffed without her, as you can see.'

He didn't know Sadie had died.

'I'm very sorry, Mr . . . ?' Maggie looked for a name badge but there wasn't one attached to his shirt.

'Kendrick. Tim Kendrick. Sorry for what?'

'I'm afraid Della's grandmother died yesterday.'

Mr Kendrick gasped and raised a hand to his mouth. It was a few moments before he could speak.

'Oh, oh, that's awful. Poor Della. I had no idea. Who would do such a thing?'

Maggie let the comment hang; it wasn't her place to mention the hospital investigation. Mr Kendrick sank into one of the empty chairs and stared into space as he processed the news. Eventually he looked up, his face marked with sadness. 'Is there anything I can do to help?'

'You could start by giving Della as much time off as she needs. Her grandmother was her only family, so she's got a lot to deal with on her own.'

'Of course, yes, absolutely,' he said, visibly choked. 'Anything she wants. Maybe we could help her with the funeral. Have the wake here.' He shook his head. 'What terrible, terrible news. I knew it was a nasty attack but, well . . . I thought she'd get better. Poor Della.'

He clearly cared. Maggie was touched.

'I'm sure Della will appreciate whatever support you can give her.'

Blinking back tears, Mr Kendrick gathered himself together.

'I'll let you get on, detective. Would you like me to bring you some teas and coffees?'

'That would be terrific, thank you.'

Thinking that Della was lucky to have a considerate employer, Maggie re-entered the bar. Then, as her eyes focused on the scene in front of her, she stopped in her tracks.

DI Green was on the floor, out cold, her head resting at an awkward angle.

Eleanor Bramwell was nowhere to be seen.

48

Maggie darted across the bar and pressed her fingers against the side of Green's throat in search of a pulse. To her relief she found one instantly, strong and regular. There was no obvious sign of injuries but a red mark was forming on the DI's cheek. Maggie called control on her radio to request an ambulance and to summon back-up to the hotel.

'Can someone help me in here?' she hollered as she clipped the radio back onto her belt.

A few seconds later Mr Kendrick dashed into the room. The manager went ashen when he saw DI Green on the floor. 'What happened?'

'Did you see Mrs Bramwell leave?' Maggie barked at him.

'No, I was in the back office still.'

'I need to find her,' said Maggie. 'What room is she in?'

'317, third floor.'

'Stay here with DI Green, but don't move her. She might be injured internally and moving her could make it worse.'

He nodded.

The digital display above the hotel's only lift said it was on the third floor already. Too impatient to wait for it to descend, Maggie raced up the stairs, her lungs burning by the time she reached the top.

The third-floor corridor was empty except for a tray bearing used crockery, a scrunched-up napkin and a half-eaten croissant on the carpet outside one of the rooms. Maggie checked the first door she came across: Room 300. She was at the wrong end.

She took off in the opposite direction, her footsteps muffled by the navy patterned carpet. She wasn't entirely sure what she was looking for – was it Eleanor who'd attacked DI Green or a different assailant altogether? And if it was Eleanor, why on earth had she done it? Maggie got the answer to her first question a moment later when, as she rounded the corner at the end of the corridor, she was smacked full in the face by a small suitcase. As she fell back against the wall with a groan, blood pouring from her nose, Maggie caught a glimpse of long blonde hair flying past her.

Eleanor.

She staggered forward onto her hands and knees as the blood from her nose flowed onto the carpet like water from a tap. Then, with some effort, she forced herself to her feet. Woozily she began to run, her hand slapping along the wall for support. Reaching the corner she saw there was no sign of Eleanor near the lift or the door to the stairs so she aimed for the former. Her legs felt too shaky to negotiate three flights of steps.

The lift seemed to take ages to reach the ground floor and Maggie cursed its slowness. She'd managed to stem the bleeding from her nose by removing her coat and using the suit jacket she wore underneath as a hanky-cum-bandage. Her nose and cheeks throbbed painfully but her pride was battered more. She'd been too trusting with Eleanor Bramwell.

The receptionist shrieked as Maggie stumbled out of the lift covered in blood.

'I'm okay, it's just my nose,' she reassured her. Her voice was thick though, like she was bunged up with a cold. 'One of your guests, Mrs Bramwell, did she come through this way?'

'She just left.' With a shaky hand the receptionist pointed towards the exit.

Maggie raced outside in time to see DI Green's Audi screech out of the car park.

Swearing under her breath, she returned to the hotel and made her way back to the bar. Green had come round and was sitting in one of the orange easy chairs clutching an ice pack against the side of her head. She smiled ruefully when she saw Maggie.

'Got you too, did she?'

'With a suitcase.'

'Ouch. I should count myself lucky she only punched me. This,' said Green, pointing to the mark on her cheek, 'I got hitting the table on my way down.'

'What's your car reg?' Maggie asked.

'ML59 0GR. Why?'

Maggie made a face as she pulled her radio off her belt and called control to put out an ANPR alert so that traffic cameras in the area would automatically pick up DI Green's car registration. Eleanor hopefully wouldn't get far.

'She nicked my keys while I was unconscious?' said Green angrily. 'Oh, wait until I get hold of her.'

'What happened before she hit you?'

'You saw the state she was in when I told her about her husband – after you stepped out, she started begging me to let him die. Told me to tell the doctors not to bring him round. When I said I couldn't do that, she socked me. Next thing I know, Mr Kendrick's fanning me with a bar menu to wake me up.'

Green grinned and so did Maggie.

'I don't know how you can find this funny,' said the manager in a tight voice.

'Gallows humour,' said Green. 'It's the only thing that keeps us sane. Right. We need to get into Mrs Bramwell's room. You got a master key?'

Mr Kendrick nodded obligingly. 'I'll go and fetch it.'

When he was gone, Green gingerly got to her feet.

'So, DC Neville, do you think Mrs Bramwell flipped out because she's scared her husband will come after her once he's conscious?'

'If he has been abusing her then, yeah, she's probably terrified.'

Green pulled a face that suggested she didn't agree.

'Why, do you think there's more to it?' asked Maggie.

'She didn't seem scared when I told her we couldn't let him die. In fact, she was spitting mad. She went into a total rage. So the question I'm asking myself now is whether she's really scared of him – or is she frightened *we'll* come after her once her husband's conscious and tells us he didn't swallow those pills willingly?'

49

Lou woke with a start. The curtains were drawn and the room near pitch-black and for a second she wondered where she was, until it all came rushing back: the fire; Jude calling her; running up the road; Maggie taking them home. Her skin was clammy as she rolled over in her sister's double bed but her heart soared to see Mae fast asleep next to her, her pudgy little arms splayed out. Lou gently stroked her daughter's forehead, smoothing back a feather-light lock of blonde hair flopping across it. Mae stirred but didn't wake.

Lou rolled onto her back and stared at the ceiling. She couldn't believe how stupid she'd been to risk her children's safety like that. She didn't blame Arturs for putting pressure on her to go out and leave them at home alone – it was her fault for not refusing and for putting her own needs above theirs. He had tried to help when Jude called to say he couldn't put the blaze out: he'd run up the road with her to the house and it was him who called the fire service. But then he'd panicked at the sight of the children and the smoke billowing out of the open front door and had legged it, saying he didn't want any trouble. She wouldn't be seeing him again.

She eased out of bed, taking care not to wake Mae. The poor mite needed her sleep as it had taken them ages to settle her in Maggie's bed when they'd finally got back. She was missing Snuggle, the floppy bunny she'd slept with since birth, and she hadn't taken kindly to being given warm milk in a mug rather than a bottle either. Lou hadn't thought to salvage anything from the house before they left and the T-shirt that Mae currently wore as a nightgown was one of her aunt's, the sleeves rolled up and the bottom hacked off with scissors to shorten it. Luckily Maggie did have a few nappies at her flat left over from when Mae had stayed before, but Lou would need to buy everything else from scratch.

Lou heard giggling as she approached the lounge, then Scotty yelped excitedly: 'Granddad, you're meant to shoot it, not drop it!'

She stopped, surprised. Her dad was playing with the boys? Normally Graeme Neville would decline to join in their games, no matter how much they begged him. He wasn't rude to their faces, just distant. Yet when he and their mum Jeanette had finally arrived, he'd gone straight to Maggie's spare room to check on Jude and Scotty as they slept.

'I just want to see for myself that they're okay,' he'd said gruffly, standing over their slumbering forms. 'You've all been very lucky.'

Lou was gladdened by the shift in his attitude and as the giggles grew louder as she entered the lounge, she prayed it would continue.

'Mum! You're awake!'

Jude and Scotty raced over and threw their arms round

her. Her dad was a bizarre sight, kneeling on the floor holding a Nerf gun. He flashed her a concerned look.

'How are you feeling?'

'I'm fine. I hope these two haven't been running you ragged.'

'Not at all,' he said with a wry smile. He used the arm of the sofa for support as he got to his feet and handed the toy to Jude, who immediately took aim at Scotty, who dived under the sofa cushions with a squeal. Neither of them seemed too affected by what had happened – they were thrilled to be kept off school more than anything else – but Lou knew appearances could be deceptive and Jude in particular was good at masking his feelings.

'Where's Maggie?' she asked.

'She's at work. You know how it is for her.'

'Never off-duty,' said Lou, but she wasn't annoyed. All she felt towards her sister right now was an immense sense of gratitude for covering up for her.

'Cup of tea, love?' said her dad.

'Yes please. Where did the Nerf gun come from?' she asked as she followed him into Maggie's small kitchen. Her mum said hello as she busied around the stove. Lou wasn't wearing her watch and guessed it must be nearly lunchtime as she watched Jeanette decant a tin of baked beans into a saucepan.

'I nipped out this morning to pick up some things and they had them in the Tesco superstore.'

'Thanks, Dad, that was lovely of you.'

'Well, they're good kids.'

It was the nicest – perhaps only – compliment she could ever recall him paying her sons. Her tears fell fast.

'Oh darling, don't cry,' said her mum, giving her a hug. 'It's going to be okay.'

'I know, but I keep thinking about what could've happened . . .'

She let her mum hold her for a moment, then pulled away and wiped her eyes with the backs of her hands. 'I'll be fine. It's just the shock.'

'You'd better tell her,' said her mum sombrely.

'Tell me what?'

She could see her dad wavering. Jeanette prodded him in the side.

'Go on, love.'

'The insurance company rang back while you were asleep. They're saying there's a problem with one of your policies. Your buildings insurance is fine, but they haven't received the last two payments for your contents and they're saying it means you're not covered for the fire damage. I told them it's bound to be a mistake, but you need to call them back pronto.'

Lou's cheeks burned with shame. There was no mistake to rectify. She paid her buildings insurance in a lump sum once a year, which was why it was up to date, but there hadn't been enough money in her account to cover the last two Direct Debits for the contents. If her policy was invalidated it meant anything damaged inside the house she would have to replace herself. The cost could run to thousands.

'I'll call them and sort it out,' she assured her dad.

She wasn't ready to tell him the truth, in no mood for a fatherly lecture about her finances. Instead she'd talk to Maggie when she was back from work. Her sister would know what to do and she'd be fine about her and the children staying until Lou sorted out the mess that was her life now. Whatever else happened today, tomorrow or in the coming weeks, she knew she could rely on her sister. Men like Arturs might disappoint her but Maggie never did.

50

Della's hand shook as she dialled the number written down in the battered, leather-bound address book balanced open on her lap. It was Sadie's address book and the sight of her nan's handwriting made her throat seize with grief. While the line connected and somewhere in the UK a mobile phone began to ring, with a fingertip she gently traced the digits and names on the page, recorded in old-fashioned fountain pen ink.

As she waited for the call to be answered, Della heard a noise from the other side of the bathroom door and froze. Was that Alex coming into the room? Her ears strained for a follow-up but there was none: it must've been him moving around the kitchen instead.

The tiny dimensions of her studio flat meant that if she opened the bathroom door and stretched her arm out, she'd almost be able to touch her sofa, which folded down every night to a bed. The living space was separated from the kitchen by a glass-bricked wall and Alex was in there now, washing up their breakfast cups and plates. He'd asked for the day off because he was worried about her and for once his boss had looked kindly on his request.

Her plan had been to go outside so Alex couldn't over-hear the phone call but a sudden downpour forced her into the bathroom instead, where she was now perched on the closed toilet seat. The room was freezing cold – it was so small there was no room for a radiator, only a toilet, a sink you could barely fit two hands in at the same time and a cramped shower cubicle – but the call couldn't wait. Or rather, she couldn't wait. As a voice came onto the line, she reached over and turned on the shower so Alex wouldn't hear her over the torrent of running water.

'Hello?'

Della took a deep breath.

'Is this Gillian Smith?'

There was a long pause. The background din suggested the person was outside, near a road.

'Yes, this is she.'

'I . . . I don't know if you remember me, but my name is Della Cardle. I'm Helen Cardle's daughter. I found your number in my nan's address book.'

Gillian gave a little cry.

'Della? Oh my word, this is a turn-up!'

Her reaction made Della tremble with relief. It was during the early hours, unable to sleep, that she had decided to call Helen's best friend and tell her about Sadie dying in the hope she could ask her some questions about her mum. She had no inkling of the response she'd receive or if Gillian still had the same mobile number Sadie had jotted down in her address book. If it hadn't worked she was going to follow Maggie's suggestion and try to track her down online. Whatever it took. All she knew was that she needed urgent answers and Gillian might be the person who had them.

'I guess it must be a bit of a shock,' said Della, stumbling over her words. Lying in bed, she had gone over and over what she planned to say to Gillian once she'd got her on the phone but now she was stumped. It didn't help that she had to keep her voice low because of Alex. Last night he'd questioned her about the conversation regarding Helen in Maggie's car, about why the newspaper clipping had made her so agitated. She'd managed to explain it away – 'I'm grieving for Nan. Everything is upsetting me right now' – and he let it drop, but she had a feeling it wasn't the last conversation they'd have about it. If he knew she was talking to Helen's friend, it might make him even more suspicious.

'It really is a surprise – you were a little girl the last time I saw you. You must be well into your teens now.'

'I'm about to turn twenty-one.'

Gillian laughed. 'Really? That makes me feel very old. So to what do I owe the pleasure?'

'Um, I have some bad news, actually. I thought you'd want to know.'

There was a sharp intake of breath down the other end of the line. When Gillian spoke again, her voice was strained.

'They haven't found her after all this time have they?'

It took Della a few seconds to fathom what she meant.

'You mean my mum? No, she's not the reason I'm phoning. We still have no idea where she went.'

'Oh. I just thought . . . well, I thought you were ringing to say there was finally some news. So if it's not about Helen, why are you calling?'

'Nan died yesterday. I'm letting people know.'

That wasn't strictly true. The only person who had been informed so far was Sadie's neighbour Audrey and that was more through chance than planning. Audrey had been coming out of her house to go shopping when Della and Alex arrived back after viewing Sadie's body. Poor Audrey collapsed in tears upon hearing the news and had to be helped back indoors by her sister.

'I'm so sorry to hear that,' said Gillian. 'Sadie was such a lovely woman. She was always so nice to me and never minded that I was round at hers every day. In fact, she was like a second mum to me growing up.'

Della's eyes filled with tears. She knew exactly what Gillian meant.

'When is the funeral? I'd like to come.'

'I don't know yet.'

'Have you got someone to help you get things organized? I'm happy to do whatever I can from here.'

Della stalled. 'It's not that . . .'

'What is it?' said Gillian, sounding concerned.

'There was a break-in and Nan was attacked. I can't organize the funeral until the police tell me it's okay to do so.'

Gillian gasped. 'Oh God, that's awful. Poor Sadie. And poor you, you must be devastated.'

Della had no comeback to that.

'Please, if there's anything I can do to help, you must let me know,' Gillian added.

'Actually, there is. You can tell me about Helen leaving. I want to know everything that happened before she went. I know you were with her that day.'

The line went quiet for a moment.

'Della, are you sure this is the time for that? I mean, I'm happy to talk to you, but now?'

'I think there's a connection.'

'What do you mean?

Della explained to Gillian about the picture taken from Sadie's hallway, the photographs ripped from their albums and the disappearance of all the pictures of herself.

'You think your mum might be involved? What do the police say?'

'Will you help me or not?' said Della, dodging the question.

'Well, yes, of course.'

'I'd like to talk to you in person. I could come to your house.'

Gillian didn't sound too happy with that suggestion. 'I don't think so. I'm not local.'

'I could get the train. Where do you live?'

'No, it's too far. I don't want you coming all the way here.' The line crackled and for a horrible moment Della thought she'd lost the connection. Then Gillian spoke again, her voice warmer this time.

'Look, I suppose we could meet in London. My work sometimes brings me there. I could maybe combine a trip in a couple of weeks.'

Della couldn't wait that long and said so.

'Could you come tomorrow?'

'Tomorrow? I don't think –'

'Please. I'll pay for your travel and for a hotel if you want. I have to talk to you as soon as possible. If Helen has anything to do with Nan being attacked, I need to know.'

'Shouldn't the police be the ones finding out?'

'Please.'

Gillian finally relented. 'Okay, I'll come down tomorrow. The train from where I live goes into Liverpool Street. Can we meet there?'

'Yes, that would be great. Thank you,' said Della with a rush of gratitude.

They arranged to meet at 2 p.m., to give themselves both time to get there.

Della was elated when she hung up, her grief bypassed for a moment. Speaking to Gillian might help her make sense of—

The door to the bathroom flew open with no warning. Alex stood in the doorway. He looked cross.

'What the hell is going on, Della?'

51

Maggie refused further medical treatment, as did DI Green.

'It probably looks worse than it is,' Maggie remarked after the attending paramedic was sent on his way. Her nose didn't feel broken and now that the bleeding had stopped it was more sore than painful. Eleanor hadn't hit her as hard as she'd initially feared.

'You're going to cop for two nice shiners though,' said Green. 'Skin's already going purple.'

'How's your head?'

'Tough as titanium.'

They were in room 317, surveying the few belongings Eleanor had left behind in her haste to leave: a Max Factor mascara, a pair of socks and her toothbrush. Slim pickings.

'Do you think she planned to run or hadn't got round to unpacking yet? After walloping me she must've come straight up here to get her case,' Green said to Maggie as they checked through the drawers and cupboards in the tiny kitchenette area, both wearing protective gloves. Downstairs, uniform were taking statements from the hotel staff, including Mr Kendrick the manager, about their dealings with Eleanor in the hope it might shed some light on where she was headed.

'I don't know,' said Maggie. 'What if she did just panic about her husband waking up and coming after her? She knows she'll have to face him if we pursue charges against him and the case goes to court. Maybe it's too much of a leap to assume her running away is a show of guilt?'

Green banged a drawer shut with her hip.

'You could be right,' she conceded, 'although that doesn't excuse her clobbering us both. I've made a request for her medical records so we know exactly what he did to her. Hang on, let me get this.' Green stripped off her right glove to answer her phone. 'He has? Terrific. I'll head back now, although I'm gonna have to borrow a car. What? Nah, mine's gone. It all went tits up down here . . . I'll explain when I see you.' She paused. 'Can you get someone round to the Bramwells' house in case the wife turns up? Yes, *that* wife.' She rolled her eyes at Maggie and mouthed the word 'idiot'. 'And get everyone together for a briefing in two hours. I'll talk to him at the hospital first then head back to the station, do the briefing.'

Maggie had already guessed the latest development but Green spelled it out anyway.

'Simon Bramwell's awake. Groggy, but he's able to talk. Docs have said I can have ten minutes with him. Trust me when I say it'll end up being longer. Right, where can I get a bloody car from?'

'If we get uniform to take us back to the station, I'm sure you could use one of the pool ones. What do you want me to do in the meantime?'

'Well, seeing as you're currently Family Liaison to a

person who's gone AWOL, not much. But when we do catch up with Mrs Bramwell, I'll want you to sit in on the interview, that's for certain. You're the only person she's talked to so far. Let's keep in touch for the time being and you can get on with your other case.'

Maggie scanned the room one last time. She noticed there was a battered paperback on the bedside table, *The Lemon Grove*. She picked it up and flicked through the pages. Tucked in the middle was another key card. Without a word, she went outside, shut the door then tried to open it again by putting the card in the slot. The light below the slot stayed red. She knocked on the door and Green opened it with a quizzical look on her face.

'This isn't a key for this room,' said Maggie.

'Come on.'

They went down to reception to find Mr Kendrick.

'Can you tell us if this key is one of yours?' DI Green asked him.

'Of course,' he said with a nod. He went behind the reception desk and checked the card.

'It is, for room 202.'

Maggie and DI Green exchanged glances.

'Whose room is that?' asked Maggie.

The receptionist scooted out of the way so the manager could use her computer.

'The room was paid for in cash,' he announced. 'It was booked out over a week ago and the guest paid in advance for a fortnight's stay.'

The receptionist piped up. 'It was Mrs Bramwell who booked it. I did think it was strange she asked for a second room when you came in yesterday but what with you being the police, I didn't like to mention it.'

Mr Kendrick pursed his lips so tightly the flesh of them went white. 'You should've told me, Josie.'

'You always say we have to respect our guests' privacy,' said Josie defiantly. 'Besides, she didn't use the same name, so I got confused.'

'She what?' Maggie exclaimed.

'Josie's right,' said Mr Kendrick, frowning as he checked the screen again. 'Our records show room 202 was booked under another name – Helen Cardle.'

52

Maggie reeled back in surprise. 'You're kidding me. Are you sure that's the name Eleanor Bramwell used for the first room?'

Josie nodded. 'Yes, Helen Cardle.'

'Who's Helen Cardle?' asked Green.

'Those distraction burglaries we're investigating? Helen Cardle is the daughter of the most recent victim. The thing is, she did a runner from Mansell seventeen years ago and hasn't been back since.'

'That's bloody weird. Could it be a coincidence that Eleanor's used the same name?'

'I'd be surprised. It's quite an unusual name.'

'Only one way to find out.'

On their way up to the second floor Green called for a forensic investigation team to be dispatched to the hotel while Maggie had a similarly hurried conversation with Renshaw to let her know what was going on. She and Nathan were now on their way to the hotel to join the search.

Maggie and Green came to a halt outside room 202. A 'Do Not Disturb' sign hung from the handle.

'You ready?' asked the DI.

Maggie nodded as adrenaline pumped through her. Green opened the door and flung it wide open.

Room 202 was shrouded in darkness, the curtains pulled closed. Wearing latex gloves again, Green switched on the overhead light and Maggie's gaze immediately fell upon the bed. Strewn across the queen-size mattress were dozens of photographs of the same girl. Moving closer, she recognized her immediately.

'This girl is Helen Cardle's daughter, Della,' she said, her own gloved hand reaching for a photograph of Della, aged about six, riding a bright pink bike. 'These pictures were nicked from a photo album belonging to her nan; Della was raised by her grandparents after Helen's vanishing act.'

Green looked shocked. 'So our Bramwell case is connected to your burglaries?'

Maggie looked around the room. On the desk opposite the end of the bed, next to the TV and a tray holding a small white plastic kettle, sachets of instant coffee and tiny plastic cartons of milk, was a large silver-framed photograph of a young woman cradling a newborn baby. Maggie went over for a closer look. Lying next to the frame was a plain gold wedding band and a diamond and sapphire engagement ring.

'All of this stuff was reported missing by Della,' said Maggie.

Green shook her head in wonderment. 'What, you think Eleanor broke in and attacked the old woman and stole it all? But why?'

Maggie was equally baffled and said so.

'We found a partial handprint where that frame was removed from the wall,' she added. 'We can cross-match it against Eleanor's prints taken from her house in Trenton. Then we'll know whether it was her or not.'

'Well, we can definitely rule out Eleanor being the long-lost Helen,' said Green, staring down at the picture of Della and her mother. 'They look nothing alike. But what could possibly be her motive for going after this family?'

Green began to slowly move around the room, checking drawers and opening the wardrobe. It quickly became obvious there was nothing else in the room other than the photographs and the rings.

'Did Eleanor know you were working on the Cardle case?'

'Initially she had no idea – I was assigned as her FLO by DCI Umpire and DI Gant while she was unconscious and being brought down to Mansell General. But she has found out since, as I had the missing person's file for Helen Cardle in my car yesterday and she saw it.'

'We need to work out the connection between Eleanor and Helen. When did you say the grandmother was attacked?'

'Sometime between Monday night and Tuesday lunchtime, when Della found her.'

'If it was Eleanor, it must've been before five a.m. on Tuesday, as that's the time she said Simon Bramwell attacked her. Maybe he's at the heart of it all,' Green mused. 'I need to get back to Trenton to talk to him, see if he can shed some light on all this.'

'Della said she never knew her dad, as he and Helen only had a one-night stand. What if Simon is actually him, and Eleanor found out? Maybe he wanted a relationship with his daughter after all these years and she objected? We know they're struggling to have a family of their own.'

'Simon Bramwell could be Della's dad?' said Green, bemused. 'Bloody hell.'

'Della thinks her dad's name was Andy, but Simon Bramwell could've given Helen a fake name, if it was a one-night thing and he didn't want her tracking him down afterwards. One step up from giving someone the wrong phone number.'

'A DNA test would certainly prove it, but before we go down the Jeremy Kyle route let's see what he says when we interview him. In the meantime, ask Della if she knows or has heard of Eleanor.'

'I'll go round now and talk to her in person, but I'll need to check something out on my way.'

'What's that?'

'I've got this hunch and, if I'm right, it might establish a link between Helen and Eleanor.'

Green regarded her for a moment and Maggie thought she was going to demand a fuller explanation. Maggie wouldn't blame her if she did – Green didn't know her, so why should she trust her judgement without questioning it? But Green simply nodded.

'Best get on with it then.'

53

The row had petered out but the atmosphere in Della's tiny studio flat was thick with tension still. Alex was deeply affronted she hadn't told him the truth about Helen's disappearance and equally upset she'd arranged to meet Gillian without discussing it with him first. Round and round they had gone, him shouting that it made a mockery of the trust between them, her trying to explain that she was too ashamed her mum had abandoned her as a child to tell him the truth. A stalemate was only reached when Della finally yelled at him. 'This is not about you! Why does everything have to be about you?'

Now he was sulking, banging plates on the small kitchen unit as he made them a sandwich for lunch. She wasn't hungry and nor did he ask her what filling she wanted, but she feared he'd start shouting again if she said anything. Better to force down whatever he dished up and keep quiet.

She was sitting on the folded-away sofa bed making a list of everything she needed to organize in the coming days. Top of the list, written with some reluctance, was 'House'. She wanted to delay telling the housing association for as long as possible that Sadie was dead, because it would set in motion the process for clearing the house out to make it habitable for another family. The thought of emptying the home she'd grown up in devastated her; all those memories swept away with a flick of a duster. She had no idea how long they'd give her to clear out but Alex seemed to think it was a week. Her only hope was the police might insist the property be left alone as a crime scene until after the investigation was completed, buying her more time. She wrote down 'Ask Maggie' on the same line as a reminder to raise the subject when she came round.

Alex came into the room with a cheese sandwich for her, which he handed her unsmilingly on a plate.

'I don't think you should go to London tomorrow to meet that woman.'

Della took her time answering. One wrong word would be all it took to start the row again.

'I've said I'd go. I can't back out now.'

Alex sank down onto the sofa beside her. He didn't look angry, she was relieved to see. In fact, he looked concerned.

'Is it a good idea though? Raking up all this stuff when your nan's just died? I'm worried you're fixating on your mum because you don't want to deal with what's going on.'

His perceptiveness surprised her. She hadn't banked on him being so attuned to what was now her preoccupying thought.

'Maybe I am a bit, but I also think it's somehow tied together. I know it sounds crazy,' she said hastily, seeing his expression cloud, 'but doesn't it strike you as odd that the intruder took the photo of me and Helen from the wall as well as all the pictures of me from the album?'

'I thought the police didn't think the album had anything to do with the break-in.'

'Well I do. It's too much of a coincidence for it not to be.'

Alex gently took her hand.

'What do you think this Gillian person is actually going to know? You said yourself that she hasn't seen your mum since the day she left seventeen years ago. What's she going to know about the photos?'

'I'm not expecting her to know anything about them, Alex, I just want to talk to her. I know this is difficult for you to understand but I need to do this. There's this big part of me that feels incomplete and has done since I was a little girl. I wish I could pretend that it doesn't matter that Helen didn't want me, but it does. It really does. And now that Nan's gone, it feels even more important. Even if Gillian tells me one thing, like Helen's favourite subject at school, or her favourite TV programme, I'll have filled in that gap a tiny bit. It's awful that I hardly know anything about her. I want to know.'

She exhaled deeply. It felt good to finally admit to him how she felt.

'I'm worried about you,' he said.

As Della looked deep into her boyfriend's eyes, her mind flickered back to ten months earlier, when she and a friend were having a drink in a pub near her flat. A surprise interruption: Alex, all smiles and charm, his beautiful brown eyes fixed on Della for the entire conversation. Her heart thundering in her chest when it dawned on her he was flirting with her. He had chosen *her*.

'It's so sweet you're concerned about me, but I'll be fine.'

'But you don't know this Gillian at all.'

'If you're that worried, come with me.'

'I wish I could but I can't. I'll have to go in tomorrow to make up for not working today.'

'But it's Saturday.'

'I know, but I'll get behind if I don't.'

Della sighed and turned her attention back to the notepad. 'I need to ask Maggie about the house. Quadrant Homes will have to be informed about Nan, but I'm hoping the police might want us to hold off.'

'Your nan's death is on the Internet already, because of the hospital inquiry.'

Della blinked at him, surprised. 'Is it?'

'Yeah. The *Echo* has done a piece on its website.'

'I don't want journalists coming round asking questions about Nan,' said Della, horrified.

'Don't worry, the hospital told the *Echo* her identity won't be released on the grounds of medical privacy. Do you want to see what they've written?'

She shuddered. 'No I don't. How long do you think the inquiry will take? Will we have to wait until it's over to have the funeral? I was hoping that now they've done the post-mortem,' she bit down hard on the word, 'they wouldn't need to hang on to Nan. I want to lay her to rest.' She wrote 'funeral?' next to Maggie's name. 'Did Maggie say what time she'd be here?'

'She said this morning, but it's almost one now. She should've called to say she'd be late,' Alex sniped. 'You know, I'm not sure about her. I don't think she's up to the job.'

'I like her. The other policewoman was a bit frosty. I'd rather deal with Maggie than her.'

Alex pulled a face and pointed to the plate he'd given her.

'Aren't you going to eat that? I hope you're not going to let it go to waste.'

Della gave him what she hoped was a convincing smile. Then she took a bite and forced it down.

54

It took Maggie a good few minutes to convince Jennifer Jones to leave the room so she could go through the *Echo*'s microfiche files alone.

'Don't you want me to show you how it works?' Jennifer asked.

'I'm pretty smart; I'll figure it out. Just show me where the on-off switch is.'

'The boxes of film are all stored in these filing cabinets. They should be in order.'

Maggie walked over to the nearest. Judging by the pencil-thick layer of dust coating the top of it, the filing cabinet hadn't been touched in years.

'You don't use these ever?'

'Nah, there's no point. Most of what background information we need we can find online these days. This room,' said Jennifer, sweeping an arm in front of her, 'is pretty much a dumping ground.'

She wasn't wrong: it was a health and safety inspector's nightmare. Old desks were stacked haphazardly on top of each other, with a few chairs thrown on the pile for good measure, while the other side of the room was crammed with bulging filing cabinets that looked like they'd topple over the moment you pulled out a drawer.

'What are these?' asked Maggie, running a hand over an enormous fabric-bound folder that had been left on the floor.

'Those are old copies of the *Echo* going back to the last century. No one ever looks at those.'

All that history, discarded on the floor like used chewing gum.

'That's a shame,' said Maggie. 'I bet you could learn a lot about the town by going through these.'

'Be my guest. Personally I can't think of anything more boring.'

'You're not from Mansell, are you?'

'No, I'm from Manchester. I only ended up here because the *Echo*'s got a good track record for its reporters ending up on nationals.'

'Any joy with that?'

Jennifer's face clouded. 'Not yet.'

'Right, I should get on. Thanks for letting me do this,' said Maggie, hoping Jennifer would take that as her cue to leave.

'I think I'll stay and watch.'

The reporter's eyes flickered over Maggie's face, which was slightly more presentable since she'd washed the blood off and reapplied her make-up, using extra concealer to hide the emerging bruises. She'd also changed her suit jacket and shirt, putting on the emergency outfit she kept in a battered leather holdall in the boot of her car specifically for Family Liaison duty. It wasn't unusual for Maggie to stay overnight with relatives during an investigation if they requested it, as she had done with Rosie Kinnock's parents when the teenager was initially reported missing, and she liked to be prepared.

'I don't think so. This is a police inquiry and journalists aren't invited.'

'These are our files.'

'I could get a warrant to confiscate the lot. Up to you.'

Jennifer pulled a face as she relented.

'How about I leave you alone and you give me the exclusive on whatever it is you're looking for and how it relates to whatever case you're working on, when it's okay to do so. We could do a story on how the *Echo* archives have helped solve a modern-day crime. Deal?'

'Sure, I can do that,' Maggie bluffed, knowing there was no way she would be divulging anything.

'Great. See you in a bit.'

As Jennifer closed the door behind her, Maggie found the filing cabinet with the microfiche versions of the *Echo* dated August and September 1999. The machine was fiddlier than she thought it would be and it took her a few moments to work out how to spool the film onto it. There were four issues saved on each reel, so she had to wind through all of August to reach the final issue with the coverage of the Mansell Show. She went straight to the group shot of Helen and her friends that Della had told her about and noted down their names. Then she scanned the rest of the page, leaning so close to the screen that her nose was practically touching it.

It took a while but finally Maggie spotted the face she'd hoped to find, in the background of a photograph of some children throwing balls at a coconut shy.

Although the image was indistinct, it was clear that Eleanor Bramwell was much less groomed back then in her twenties. Her hair, a much darker blonde than it was now, was centre parted, falling lankly around her face, and she was wearing a shapeless navy maxi dress and flip-flops.

The caption at the foot of the photograph only listed the names of the children in the foreground. Disappointment rose inside her. All it proved was that Eleanor was in Mansell on the same day Helen went missing – there was nothing to show they knew each other and it certainly didn't explain why Eleanor appeared to be targeting the Cardle family now. In her notebook Maggie jotted down a few theoretical questions to follow up with DI Green:

Did they go to the same school – bullying? Helen bully, Eleanor victim?

Family friends – parental feud?

Potential boyfriend issue – did they share same ex?

Did Eleanor also know Niall/Fleur/Ross/Kelvin from the other photo?

As she rested her pen on her notebook, rereading the questions she'd written down, Maggie had another thought, one almost too horrifying to contemplate. She scrabbled for her phone to call DS Renshaw.

'Hey, what's up?' Renshaw answered. 'I'm at the Langston now.'

'I think we should check the hospital CCTV for the hours before Sadie Cardle was given that incorrect dose to see if Eleanor Bramwell went anywhere near her.'

Renshaw swore loudly. 'Seriously?'

'Yes. I think because of the photographs we found in room 202 we can assume Eleanor was behind the break-in at Sadie's house and not the Con Couple. And if she attacked Sadie at her home and left her for dead, it's not unfeasible to think that she might've decided to finish her off when she saw her at the hospital.'

'Do you think Eleanor asked to be transferred to Mansell General for that reason?'

'I don't think she could've – she was unconscious when the decision was made and she wouldn't have known Sadie had survived at that point. Also, think about it – would you ask to come back to Mansell if you'd just committed a crime here? My guess is it was most likely a toss-up between bringing her here or taking her to John Radcliffe in Oxford and she just got unlucky.'

'Or lucky, if she did manage to kill Sadie after all. We'll check the CCTV and I'll also get a picture of her to show Audrey Allen, to see if she IDs her as the reporter who was at Sadie's house on Monday evening,' said Renshaw.

'Audrey said the woman had long dark hair,' Maggie pointed out. 'Eleanor's a blonde.'

'She could've disguised herself with a wig to avoid detection. The girl in the Con Couple is a brunette – maybe she deliberately made herself look like her so we'd blame them for another break-in. The sodding *Echo* has printed so many details about the first burglaries that it wouldn't be a stretch for anyone to copy them. Incidentally, the medical examiner has confirmed Sadie could've lain there all night, which means Eleanor could've attacked her before Audrey saw her leave around ten p.m. If the heating was on all night it would've prevented Sadie developing hypothermia and may well be why she didn't die at the scene. I've already instructed the team to start liaising with DI Green's lot at

Trenton to establish the connection between Eleanor and the Cardle family. At the moment we've got nothing concrete.'

'I might have something. I'm at the *Echo* at the moment, going through their archives.' Maggie quickly explained that Della had found an old copy of the *Echo* at Sadie's house featuring Helen at the Mansell Show, taken on the day she left town.

'I've found a picture of Eleanor at the same show.'

'In the same photograph?'

'No, that's the problem. She's in the background of another one.'

'It just proves they were at the same event, nothing else. Do we know that Eleanor's originally from Mansell?'

'I haven't thought to ask her but she hasn't mentioned it being her hometown.'

'We'll keep digging. I'm going to stay here at the hotel for a bit, then head back to the station. Are you going to see Della?'

'I am, after I've finished here.'

'Ask her if she knows Eleanor but don't tell her why you're asking.'

'Okay. Look, this is awkward, but who do I report to now, you or DI Green? If the cases overlap, I mean?'

'Both of us for the time being, until someone higher up the greasy pole decides otherwise.'

After ringing off, Maggie unspooled the film from the microfiche then replaced it with the one for September 1999.

What she hoped to find was a news report about Helen's missing person's case. If the police at the time had followed protocol, there should've been a public appeal for information. But all thoughts of it were forgotten when she called up the front page of the first issue for that month. Next to a headshot of Fleur Tatton, the woman pictured next to Helen at the Mansell Show, was the headline: THREE DEAD IN WOODLAND CRASH.

With a sharp intake of breath, Maggie read the text beneath it.

Three young friends died in a car accident at the notorious 'Death Corner' black spot in Barnes Woods in the early hours of Sunday 22 August.

Fleur Tatton, 21, Ross Keeble, 24, and Kelvin Cruickshank, 23, all from Mansell, were travelling in a Ford Transit minivan when they were in a head-on collision with a Rover SD1 driven by Malcolm McMinn, 62, from Henley, Oxfordshire.

Miss Tatton, of Raleigh Road, and Mr Cruickshank, of Frogmore Close, both died at the scene. Mr Keeble, also of Frogmore Close, passed away in hospital two days later from his injuries. The driver of the minivan, Niall Hargreaves, 23, of Layton Road, is in a critical but stable condition, while Mr McMinn suffered a broken leg and concussion.

Police have confirmed the minivan veered off the road and rolled down a steep embankment . . .

Maggie sat back, stunned. The accident had occurred only hours after they were at the Mansell Show with Helen; if she'd stayed with her friends and been in the car too, Sadie and Eric would've been informed. Had her decision to leave Mansell that day actually saved her life?

Maggie snapped an image of the front page on her phone and made a note of the issue date. She rewound the film and carefully removed it from the machine. There was no point sitting there for hours looking for more mentions of the crash: any further information she needed she could probably find in their own records.

Jennifer reappeared as she was shutting the machine off. 'You done?'

'Yep, found what I needed, thanks.'

'I've just seen one of your old colleagues on Sky News.'

'Oh, who?'

'DCI Umpire, the one in charge of the Rosie Kinnock investigation.'

Maggie hastily turned away to pick up her handbag from the floor so Jennifer couldn't see her face. Just hearing his name made her feel wretched.

'Don't you want to know why?'

'Something to do with his new unit?'

'Actually, it was about an attempted murder-suicide in Trenton. Apparently some husband tried to kill his wife and now she's gone AWOL in Mansell. Umpire was appealing for her to come forward. Know anything about it?'

Maggie frowned. 'Are you sure DCI Umpire was talking about that case?'

'Yes. Kay Burley said he's the officer in charge. My editor wants me covering the story now there's a Mansell connection. Got any leads?'

Maggie's mind was too full of questions to pay attention to Jennifer. Why were Umpire and HMET back on the Bramwell case? What the hell had happened to DI Green? Did that mean she'd have to report to HMET again? In a heartbeat she knew she couldn't. She'd have to quit the case. She couldn't continue if it meant having to deal with Umpire.

'Do you know anything about why Eleanor Bramwell was in Mansell?' Jennifer pressed.

'No, why would I?'

'Wouldn't it be a matter of courtesy to tell the local police if the victim of a major crime was being hidden on their patch?'

'Hidden? That's a bit dramatic.'

'Well, wouldn't they have told your lot?'

'Probably, but I haven't been privy to any conversations.' Maggie hated lying, especially to a journalist, but she wanted to get out of the room. Her nostrils felt like they were clogged up with dust and she couldn't breathe.

'I've got to go.' She shoved the boxes of microfiche film back into the filing cabinet drawer and slammed it shut. The cabinet wobbled precariously but stayed upright as the noise reverberated around the small space.

'If you hear anything will you let me know?' said Jennifer. She pressed a business card into a reluctant Maggie's hand. 'Here's my mobile number. It would be great if you could return the favour for me letting you in here.'

'Sure. I'll call you.'

On her way back to her car Maggie passed a raised, bricked flower bed containing a few perennial plants that were just about weathering the autumn wind. She took Jennifer's business card and shoved it between them.

55

Safely ensconced in her car, Maggie called Green.

'Why is DCI Umpire giving interviews to Sky News and not you?'

'Ah, I wondered when you might ring,' said Green with a throaty chuckle. 'Not just Sky News – I think the boys from the Beeb were there too.'

'So HMET are running the Bramwell case again?'

'No, I'm still SIO and my team are still investigating. ACC Bailey apparently thought it would look better if the DCI did the call-out for Mrs Bramwell as HMET were first on the case and he's the force's rising star after Rosie Kinnock.'

'But that's not fair. You're in charge; you should've done it.'

'Umpire's got a better face for TV than I have. Not worth losing sleep over.'

Maggie bristled at the inference that DI Green couldn't cut it in front of the media like Umpire. Was it a gender thing or an age thing? Whatever the reason, it annoyed her intensely and she was surprised Green wasn't more pissed off about it. Or maybe she was used to being passed over in favour of her male colleagues.

'Well, I'm pleased you're still SIO.'

'Not a fan of the DCI, are we?'

'You have no idea,' said Maggie, managing a weak smile.

'I won't ask why. Right, the bad news is there have been no sightings of Eleanor Bramwell yet, but the good news is my car's been found.'

'Where?'

'Mansell train station, which means she could've hopped on a train to London or to Trenton and beyond. We're checking the CCTV now and that should hopefully point us in the right direction.'

'Have you spoken to her husband yet?'

'Just about to: I'm outside the Princess Alexandra now. He was napping when we got here and the docs wouldn't let us wake him.'

'I can't wait to hear what he says. I wonder if he is Della's father? It's the only motive for Eleanor's behaviour I can think of.'

'I'll call you afterwards with an update. And thanks for what you said: it's nice to know at least one person is happy with me at the helm.'

Della was pleased to see Maggie when she at last made it to her flat. She'd gone to Sadie's house first, thinking Della might be there, but a quick phone call revealed her whereabouts. Alex, on the other hand, was less than welcoming.

'What time do you call this? You said you'd be here this

morning and it's two o'clock. Della's got dozens of questions for you and she's been waiting anxiously to ask them.'

'I'm sorry I've kept you waiting. There was nothing I could do to get away sooner.'

Della appeared at the door beside him.

'It's okay, Alex; she's here now. What happened to your face?' she asked Maggie.

'I lost an argument with a suitcase. It's a long story. Shall we sit down?'

The sofa creaked in protest as Maggie lowered herself onto it. It was more comfortable than it looked, however, and it took all of her restraint not to flop backwards: she was reaching the stage where she was so tired she was unable to think straight. At some point she needed to take a break and get something to eat, but after she'd finished with Della her plan was to pop home to check up on Lou and the kids. She felt bad she hadn't checked in with them all day.

'How are you?' she asked Della.

'I'm okay. I'm glad yesterday is over.'

Alex made a noise that could've been a snort or him clearing his throat; either way, it was clear she couldn't have a conversation with Della with him in the room.

'Alex, could you please give me a few minutes to talk to Della alone?'

He reacted with surprise but quickly recovered.

'Anything you have to say to her I want to hear.'

'That's not how police investigations work, I'm afraid. Sometimes we have to talk privately to family members.'

'I'm her boyfriend. That practically makes me family. You talk to her, you talk to me.'

What an odious prick, thought Maggie. She stood up.

'Fine, if you won't do as I ask I'll have to take Della down to the station with me.'

'Are you arresting me?' Della yelped, horrified.

'No. I just need to talk to you privately and it doesn't seem like we can do that here.'

'Alex, please,' Della implored her boyfriend, who had turned puce. 'Let's not have another row.'

Maggie clocked the look that passed between them and wondered what else they'd been rowing about. Maybe she'd find out once she got Della on her own but Alex didn't look like he was going to back down. Time to intervene.

'Right, let's get going, Della. I haven't got time to argue about this.'

'Fine, have it your way. I'll go and get some more milk.' Alex stropped out of the room and a few seconds later they heard a door slam. Della flinched.

'Sorry, but I really do need to speak to you on your own, without interruption.'

'You think Alex has something to do with it, don't you? I saw you watching him in the car, and now you don't want him to listen to us talking. But I know he didn't hurt Nan or have anything to do with it, he couldn't have done!'

'No, Alex isn't a suspect right now. We've checked his alibi for Monday evening and Tuesday morning and he was at his office.'

'Why would you need to know where he was on Monday evening?' said Della with a frown. 'I thought whoever it was broke into Nan's on Tuesday morning.'

'That's what we need to discuss now,' said Maggie, sinking further into the sofa with another creak. 'Did you know your nan didn't go to bingo with Audrey on Monday evening as usual?'

'No, I didn't know that.'

'Audrey told us your grandmother cancelled going because someone was coming to interview her about the desk your great-grandfather made for Winston Churchill. I take it from your expression that she hadn't told you?'

'No, she didn't mention it,' said Della, shocked. 'Interviewed by who?'

'We don't know. We've ruled out the *Echo*, but it could've been for another newspaper or some kind of special interest magazine. I would've thought she'd have shared the news.'

'I don't understand why she didn't. It's not like her to keep something like that to herself. She would've been excited – she was very proud of her dad's connection to Churchill. He actually met him, when he delivered the desk to Chequers.'

'All I can think is that whoever it was asked her not to say anything. Does the name Eleanor Bramwell mean anything to you?'

Maggie watched Della intently for any sign of recognition but she seemed bewildered.

'I've never heard of her. Is she the reporter?'

'We don't know,' said Maggie, 'the name's just cropped up.'

'You said the reporter might have asked Nan to keep the interview quiet – why would they do that?'

'Sometimes journalists want to protect their stories – maybe that's why. I wonder, did Sadie write down her appointments in a diary at all?'

'No, she has a calendar on the back of the kitchen door. She writes . . .' a flicker of pain crossed Della's face. 'I mean, she wrote – stuff down on that. If she made a note of it any-where, it'll be on that.'

'Are you fine for me to go to the house and check?'

Della nodded. 'I wanted to ask you about the house actu-ally. I need to let Quadrant know about Nan, but the minute I do they'll say I've got to clear it out for the next tenant to move in.' Her eyes filled with tears. 'I'm not ready to do that.'

'You know what, we probably need the house left as it is for now. I'll talk to them for you.'

'Oh, thank you. I want to hang on to it for as long as I can. It's going to take me a while to sort through Nan's belongings.'

'Have you removed anything from the house so far?'

'No, not yet.'

'If the house is unoccupied, it's probably wise to remove all the valuables and also any important paperwork. Talking of which, did you find the documents relating to the money your granddad left you?'

'Yes. They were locked away in the bureau.'

'Right.'

Della looked at her quizzically. 'You almost look dis-appointed.'

Maggie fished for her next sentence, knowing she mustn't give too much away at this stage.

'New information has come to light that suggests it wasn't the same couple who attacked the other pensioners.'

'What information?'

'I'm afraid I can't tell you at the moment. Our priority is finding out who else might have had reason to target your nan.'

'I've been thinking about that too, and I keep coming back to Helen. She's the only person I can think of who might have had a grudge against Nan, because of what happened before I was born.'

Falteringly, Della told Maggie how her mother hadn't wanted to continue with her pregnancy but Sadie had pressured her.

'You think Helen might've resented your nan all this time?'

'Perhaps. Maybe. I mean, Helen's life would've turned out differently if I hadn't come along, wouldn't it? She might blame Nan even after all this time. There must be some way of finding out where she is. Bank records or something.'

'We've tried the usual channels but nothing has come up.'

'She could've changed her name.'

'If she did, she hasn't done it officially. There is no record of a Helen Cardle changing her name either by marriage or through the deed poll registry.'

'But she must've been in touch with someone after she went,' said Della with evident frustration. 'She can't have just vanished.'

'Some people don't want to be found,' said Maggie as gently as possible.

'Well, I'm seeing Gillian Smith tomorrow. Maybe she knows more than she let on back then.'

'You tracked her down?'

'Yes, Nan had her number in an old address book. I'm going to show Gillian that photograph from the *Echo* to see if she knows the people who were with Helen on the day she went.'

Maggie felt uneasy. Della was becoming obsessed with finding her mother and confirming she was behind the assault on Sadie.

'Gillian's statement to the police said she had no idea who Helen might've met at the Mansell Show that day,' she pointed out.

'That doesn't mean she wouldn't recognize them still if they were locals.'

'I guess that makes sense.'

'Can you come with me to meet her?'

Maggie faltered. 'If I can make time, I'll try. But with the investigation ongoing . . .'

'It's okay, I understand. But if the others turn out to still be living locally, you could talk to them, couldn't you?'

Maggie knew she had to proceed carefully. While telling Della about the accident wouldn't impede the investigation, it might make her even more distressed than she already was and her job was to help Della, not make her feel worse.

'I'm afraid that's not going to be possible. They were all from Mansell but the evening after the show, the group was involved in a road traffic accident. I'm sorry to have to tell you that some of them suffered fatal injuries in the crash. One did survive, but I haven't tracked him down yet.'

Della's face drained of colour. 'They're dead?'

'All apart from one of the men, Niall Hargreaves.'

'But Helen wasn't with them?'

'No. The newspaper report I found only mentioned four of them being in the vehicle. I'm sorry. I can imagine how upsetting it must be to hear this.'

Della looked devastated.

'I can't believe they were in an accident the exact same

day. I really thought that if I could find them and speak to them I'd find out where Helen went. For years I haven't cared but now, with Nan, it feels really important that I find her.'

Maggie faltered. 'I can see that, Della, but please understand we only have so many resources available to us.'

'You think finding her is a waste of time,' said Della, her face hardening.

'I never said that. I just don't want you to be disappointed if the search comes to nothing.'

'It won't. We'll find her.' Della looked embarrassed for a moment. 'I know this is going to sound crazy, but the more I think about her, the more I feel like she's here, in Mansell.'

To Maggie's immense relief, Alex chose that moment to return, laden with shopping bags that he plonked down noisily onto the kitchen counter.

'Everything all right here?'

Maggie glanced across at Della, who was hugging her arms to her scrawny frame. Her eyes were glazed over, like she was in a trance.

No, everything was definitely not all right.

56

The end of the school day followed the same pattern it always did: hundreds of pupils streaming through the gates with their heads bent low as they frantically checked the phones they hadn't had access to all day. The head teacher at Bea's school had issued a decree a couple of terms earlier that all phones must be turned off and shut away in lockers during the day; the constant interruption they'd caused in the classroom had driven her and other teachers to distraction.

Bea was one of only a few girls looking up and ahead as the throng surged forward. She stood on tiptoe to scan the sea of blonde, red, brunette and black hair as she looked for Esme. They'd arranged to meet just inside the school gate but Bea was terrified her sister might have forgotten, this new routine of walking to and from school together not one she was used to yet. Or, worse still, she might have decided she would rather journey home alone. The thought of Esme bumping into Sean without her being there to protect her turned Bea's insides to liquid.

Then Bea saw her, standing to the right of the gate, looking up hopefully at the girls who passed her, and when she clapped eyes on her sister, Esme beamed. Bea was bowled over with affection for her little sister and barrelled through the crowd to reach her, hugging her fiercely.

'Ow, you're squeezing too tight!'

'Sorry,' said Bea, letting her go with a grin. 'What'd you get up to today?'

'Not much. Stacie Clarkson got sent to the head again for swearing at Miss Berwick. She used the c-word,' said Esme with a giggle.

'Hmm,' said Bea, only half listening as she steered her sister out of the gate. Her heart pounded as she looked back and forth across the road for a sighting of Sean but mercifully he wasn't anywhere to be seen. She caught Esme also scanning the street and for a fleeting moment her sister looked disappointed.

'Expecting someone?' said Bea, unable to help herself. Esme went bright red.

'No,' she squeaked. 'I was only looking.'

Bea hooked an arm round her shoulders. 'Come on, let's go. Mum should be back early today.'

'Hang on, my phone's buzzing.'

Bea waited patiently while Esme burrowed in her backpack for her mobile. She giggled as she read the message she'd been sent.

'Who's it from?' said Bea sharply. She didn't doubt that Sean or any of his shady mates would know of a way to get hold of Esme's number.

'Amelia. She's wondering where I am.'

'Didn't you tell her you were walking home with me?'

'Well, yeah, but she said you'd probably change your

mind. She was all, like, who wants to walk home with their kid sister? But I'm glad you were waiting.'

Bea smiled. 'Me too.'

'Oh, Mum's texted as well.' Esme frowned as she read the next message. 'She's going to be late home because she's going to see Sheila from the shop. That old lady Sheila knows died yesterday. Aww, that's sad.'

Bea let out a low moan as everything in the street began to spin. The pavement, lampposts, houses, the cars jostling for space outside them, even Esme. Bea tried to clutch on to something to steady herself but her hands just grasped at air.

'Hey, are you okay?' said Esme.

'No, no, no,' Bea moaned. 'Make it stop.' She put her hands over her face but the spinning became faster and she couldn't breathe.

Poor Sadie was dead.

Dead.

Dead.

DEAD.

Bea screamed and collapsed to the floor.

57

Easing her Toyota into the station car park, Maggie was overcome by tiredness. Turning off the engine, she rested her head against the steering wheel for a moment and closed her eyes. The last time she remembered feeling this exhausted was the night Jude had been born, when she'd paced the corridor outside the birthing suite at Mansell General while Lou screamed the place down, their mum, Jeanette, at her side alternately urging her to push and breathe. Every time Lou had called out for Jerome, cursing him for dying and leaving her to give birth to their child alone, Maggie's heart had broken a little bit more.

A sharp rap on the window made her sit up.

'You okay?' said Renshaw, after Maggie had lowered it.

'Yeah, I'm a bit tired.'

'I'm not surprised. Why didn't you tell us about the fire at your sister's last night?'

Maggie was taken aback. 'How do you know about that?'

'The fire service passed it on to us this morning. Down-stairs are dealing,' said Renshaw, referring to their uniform division, 'but they let the boss know because of you and he told me just now.'

'Why are we involved?' said Maggie, trying to stay calm as she got out of her car and locked it. 'It was an accident caused by something catching fire in the microwave. The sub-officer at the scene confirmed it.'

'Apparently there's been a tip-off that the circumstances of it starting might be suspicious. You know how it is – some busybody rings in and we have to look into it. I'm sure it'll come to nothing.'

'Suspicious? In what way?'

'I don't know the details and I think it's best you don't either. Stay out of it.'

'I can't. This is my family you're talking about.'

'I mean it,' said Renshaw sternly. 'You can't get involved. Don't make it any worse.'

Maggie slumped against her car as she fought back tears, hating herself for it. She didn't want Renshaw to see her upset. What would happen to the children if the investigation revealed Lou had left them at home alone when the fire started?

'Hey, it's okay,' said Renshaw, patting her awkwardly on the arm. 'It'll blow over.'

'I don't understand why someone would want to stir up trouble,' said Maggie. She rubbed her eyes. 'I'm not upset. I'm just really tired because I was up all night.'

'That's why you should've told me this morning. We could've shared your caseload out and I could've gone to see Della earlier.'

'I didn't want to let anyone down. DI Green was waiting for me to speak to Eleanor Bramwell and I'm Della's FLO too.'

'Well, I'm sending you home now. Get a good night's

sleep tonight, then you can hit the ground running tomor-row.'

'No, I can't. I've got to make some calls on the Cardle case.'

'What calls? Can't Nathan or I do that? Look, let's grab a coffee and you can fill me in and then you can go home.'

'Why are you being so nice to me?' Maggie blurted out more forcibly than she intended to.

Renshaw shot her a look. 'If you don't want me to, we can go back to biting each other's heads off.'

'But why the sudden change?'

'I told you,' said Renshaw, blushing to her roots, 'I was given some good career advice from someone and it included not wasting energy on petty office politics.' She laughed. 'They told me this saying: "A wise man gets more use from his enemies than a fool from his friends." Turns out they were right.'

Maggie froze. She was familiar with the saying herself, and had heard it more than once. The first time, ironically, to illustrate to her that it wasn't worth getting caught up in arguments with Renshaw.

'Who told you that?' she croaked.

'Just someone I'm seeing,' Renshaw replied airily.

As Maggie stared at her colleague with mounting horror, Renshaw's eyes widened and she swiftly averted her gaze, as if she knew she'd said something she shouldn't.

Maggie clutched the roof of her car for support. There was only one person she'd ever heard use that saying. But it couldn't be . . .

'Who is he, Anna?' she said, almost choking on the sentence.

Renshaw's cheeks burned even darker. 'I don't talk about my private life at work,' she replied brusquely. 'Come on, let's go in. We've a lot to get through.'

Maggie took her response as all the confirmation she needed.

It was Umpire who'd told Maggie the saying.

He was Renshaw's 'hotshot'.

58

The noise filtering down the stairwell as Maggie climbed the three flights to her flat half an hour later made her want to turn back. She could hear the boys laughing – high-pitched and unselfconscious shrieks of unadulterated joy that only children make – but she wasn't sure she could cope being around them.

It had taken every ounce of professionalism she possessed to sit down with Renshaw in the face of what she'd just learned about her and Umpire and brief her on Della's response to Sadie not going to bingo on Monday evening. Ordeal over, now she just wanted to curl up and cry. But first she had to break the bad news to Lou about the police looking into the fire.

Mae squealed with delight and toddled down the hallway to greet her as she let herself into the flat. Maggie scooped her niece up and squeezed her tightly, making the little girl giggle even more. That lasted a couple of seconds until Mae demanded to be put down, but Maggie couldn't let her go. She wanted to hang on to her for as long as she could.

'What's wrong?'

Lou had appeared in front of them. From the frown on

her face, she'd guessed something was amiss; Maggie's own expression must've betrayed her. She put Mae down and watched as her niece gambolled back down the hallway towards the voices of her two brothers, who were laughing again. Maggie could hear the TV was on.

'Sis, what's happened?' asked Lou worriedly.

'The fire investigators were at your house this morning. It was meant to be routine, them just checking that the fire had started in the microwave like you said. But someone tipped them off that there might be more to it than they've been told. I don't know exactly what's been said but the fire is being treated as suspicious and the police have been informed. All I can think is that someone found out you weren't there when it started.'

Lou clamped her hand over her mouth as tears sprang to her eyes.

'The police will want to talk to you,' Maggie went on, fighting back tears of her own, 'but you stick to your story and we'll get the boys to stick to theirs and hopefully it'll be okay.'

Her sister's shoulders shook as her tears turned to sobs. Maggie stepped forward and embraced her.

'It's going to be okay,' she said, feeling far less positive than she sounded.

'I've been such a fucking idiot,' Lou cried. 'I should never have left them to go out drinking.'

Maggie didn't contradict her, but she wasn't about to pile on more guilt either.

'Look, it's done now. What's important is that you're all okay. We'll sort this out, get the house fixed and get back to normal.'

'The insurance won't pay out,' said Lou, pulling away from her.

'Because of the police being involved? I told you, we'll get that sorted.'

'No, it's not that. I haven't been able to afford the monthly premiums for my contents insurance. I let the payments lapse so I'm not covered.'

The last vestige of Maggie's energy drained away.

'Oh, Lou.'

'I know. I should've said something rather than stop paying. Don't hate me.'

'Hate you? That's a crazy thing to say.' Maggie mentally scrolled through her finances. 'I have some money in an ISA I can take out. I can pay for whatever needs to be replaced.'

Lou shook her head vehemently. 'No way, you already do too much for me. I'll ask Mum and Dad.'

'We can all help.'

'But what about the tip-off? What if the police find out I wasn't there?'

'Keep your voice down,' Maggie cautioned. 'You don't want the boys to hear what's going on. I said we'll deal with it.'

'How? Can you speak to whichever of your lot is dealing with it?'

'I can't get involved to that extent; it wouldn't look good if I interfered. But I can speak to someone I know at the fire service and find out from them what's been said.'

'You mean Craig? I thought I saw him there last night.'

'Yes, I mean Craig. I'll ask him to do some digging for me.'

'Really? Do you think he'll help?'

Maggie had a feeling from the way he'd asked her out

for a drink that he would be receptive. 'I think so. I'll call him this evening.'

'You are amazing. I don't know what I'd do without you.'

Maggie managed a half-smile as she eased off her coat and hung it on the rack of pegs near the front door. 'Is there anything to eat? I'm starving.'

'Dad went grocery shopping and Mum's made a lasagne that could feed fifty.'

'How's Dad getting on with the boys?' Maggie asked, aware of Graeme's strained relationship with her nephews.

'Actually,' said Lou, brightening, 'he's been great with them. He's been playing with them and even did some spellings with Scotty. Proof that miracles do happen.'

'I'm glad he's making an effort,' said Maggie as she trailed her sister along the short hallway into the living room. 'Did Dad get any wine with the shopping?'

'Did I get any what?' asked Graeme Neville, who was on the sofa watching *The Incredibles* with Scotty glued to his left side and Jude to his right. The sight of them cuddled together made Maggie's heart lift then plummet. If her colleagues did discover Lou had left the kids alone when the fire started, she could be prosecuted and social services would get involved, a scenario too awful to contemplate.

'Wine. I need wine. Lots of it,' she said, leaning over the back of the sofa and kissing her dad and the boys on the tops of their heads.

'Bad day, love?'

'You could say that.'

Her mum bustled into the front room from the kitchen. 'Oh, Maggie, look at the state of your nose. How did that happen?'

Lou peered at her. 'I didn't even notice. Sorry.'

'What, you think I always look like this?' said Maggie as everyone else laughed. The sound wrapped itself around her like a hug and she began to relax.

'Will that chap of yours join us for dinner?' asked Jeanette. 'There's plenty of food to go round.'

'What chap?' said Maggie, aghast.

'Sorry, blame me. I told her about you going out for dinner with Umpire,' Lou confessed in an aside. 'I did say you were more friends than anything else.'

Maggie cringed as her mum waited for her to answer, eyebrows raised expectantly.

'No, he won't be. In fact . . . he's seeing someone,' said Maggie as nonchalantly as she could manage.

'You're fucking kidding me!'

'Louisa, you shouldn't swear like that in front of the boys,' her mum admonished.

Lou ignored her, but did take Maggie by the elbow and steer her into the kitchen, away from little ears.

'Who's he seeing?'

'Anna Renshaw.'

Maggie was mollified that Lou looked as stunned as she had felt in the car park earlier.

'I don't believe it,' said Lou, huffing out a breath. 'He's going out with that bitch? When the hell did that happen?'

'Please, can we talk about something else?' said Maggie. She yanked open the fridge door and reached for the bottle of white wine chilling in the side rack. 'Want one?' she asked, moving across to the cupboard where she kept her wine glasses.

'No, I'm not drinking any more.'

'You don't need to quit completely.'

'I do. I need to make better decisions and drinking stops me doing that. Now stop changing the subject. How did you find out Umpire's seeing Renshaw?'

'I said I don't want to talk about it,' Maggie snapped. Just then their mum poked her head round the door.

'Sorry to interrupt but I can hear your phone ringing in the hallway, love.'

'Saved by the bell,' Lou remarked drily.

Maggie dashed into the hallway but her phone had stopped ringing by the time she wrestled it out of her coat pocket. The missed call was from DI Green.

Maggie rang her straight back.

'You got a tank full of petrol?' was Green's opening gambit seconds later.

'Pardon?'

'I need you up here in Trenton.'

Maggie's heart sank. All she wanted was to fill her stomach with food and curl up with a glass of wine in front of a film.

'You want me to drive up now?'

'Unless you've got a helicopter that'll get you here quicker, then yes, get in your car and get a move on. I've just this minute finished talking to our man Simon Bramwell.'

'Oh, what did he say?'

'It's quite some story he's told,' said Green sombrely. 'Look, I know it's Friday evening but I'll be briefing the team in an hour and I want you there. You really need to hear this in person.'

59

Della had spent the rest of the afternoon at Frobisher Road sorting through her grandmother's belongings. She had been more relieved than upset when Alex ducked out of going with her, his excuse being that he needed to tidy his own flat. She knew it was a lie – he had a cleaner who came every Thursday and the place was always still spotless a day later – but she didn't mind. After the stress of the past seventy-two hours she craved some time to herself to reflect and also to plan.

Even if Maggie did manage to stall Quadrant Homes from taking possession of the house it wouldn't be indefin-itely. Fifty years of living needed to be carefully sorted through and stripped away and with no other family to bequeath Sadie's belongings to, the arduous task of deciding what to keep and what to bin was down to her alone.

At least she had a weekend's grace. Maggie's parting shot had been that she should leave the downstairs rooms as they were in case forensics needed to return but if she wanted to begin clearing out upstairs, she could go ahead. Della began in the smallest room, which had been hers as a young child. The décor had not been altered since – flimsy pink curtains decorated with images of Polly Pocket and her friends still hung at the window. When Della was nine, after her grand-dad had told her the truth about Helen, she had moved into the second biggest bedroom, which had been left, shrine-like, while her mother was supposedly recovering from her illness.

It didn't take Della long to clear the first room, as it was fairly empty to begin with. There were a few old outfits of Eric's in the wardrobe, a pile of jigsaw puzzles Sadie hadn't got round to taking to the charity shop and some old Mills & Boon novels stacked on top of the bedside cabinet. Della decided to donate the lot, so she shoved the items into black bin bags and left them on the bed. Working quickly, without thinking, made it easier to keep a lid on her feelings. If she stopped to pick over each item she feared she'd start crying and never stop.

She used the same approach in hers and Helen's old room, which again was fairly clear. All that remained were some books, CDs and a few childhood keepsakes Della hadn't been able to shoehorn into her studio flat. She hadn't missed them in the year since she'd moved out so they were earmarked for donation too.

After that she tackled the bathroom, spending an hour scrubbing it clean. It wasn't dirty to begin with but Della thought her grandmother would appreciate her making the effort, even if the housing association didn't. It was almost 6 p.m. by the time she peeled off the Marigolds protecting her hands. As she left the gloves hanging over the edge of the bath and wearily got to her feet, she heard a knock on the front door, tentative at first then becoming more insist-ent as she descended the stairs.

'Hang on, I'm coming,' she called out.

Her unexpected visitor was Audrey Allen, Sadie's neighbour.

'I wondered if it was you. I heard water running out of the drain at the back.'

'I was cleaning the bathroom,' said Della.

'Really? Well, I suppose it's good to stay busy at a time like this.'

Della peered over Audrey's shoulder. When she'd arrived at Frobisher Road mid-afternoon the sun had been making a valiant effort to poke through the broken cloud cover, but now dusk had fallen the sky was obscured by a thick, dark, low-hanging mass.

'It looks like the heavens are about to open. Do you want to come in?'

'Oh, I don't want to disturb you. I just wanted to check it was you here and not someone from the association. I know what that lot's like. My sister knew someone who lived in Burleigh Road and when he died they didn't even wait until he was in the ground before taking the house back,' said Audrey with a disapproving sniff.

'The police have said they can't have the house yet so don't worry. If you hear anyone moving around, it will only be me or my boyfriend, Alex.'

Audrey promptly burst into tears.

'It's so dreadful. I still can't believe she's gone. Why would anyone want to harm dear Sadie?'

'Please don't cry,' said Della, reaching forward to take Audrey's arm. 'Come on, come inside and I'll make us some tea.'

'I should be comforting you, not the other way round,' Audrey lamented as she trailed Della into the small kitchen.

'I'm okay. Well, I'm not, obviously, but you know what I mean. Tea?'

'Yes please.'

'Let me get you a seat.' Della went into the dining room and retrieved two chairs. She carried them into the kitchen and shut the door behind her. 'We can't go in there at the moment, or in the front room, so we'll have to sit in here.'

'Why's that?'

'The police might need to come back and have another look around.'

Audrey's eyes brimmed with fresh tears.

'I keep thinking I should've done something to stop it. Me and your nan, we were always in and out of each other's houses. I should've known something was wrong.'

'I doubt there was anything you could've done,' said Della kindly.

'The attack must've been sudden or she would've screamed and I would've heard it. You know how paper-thin these walls are. I used to hear your granddad snoring at night and your nan used to say the same of my Malcolm.'

Della smiled as Audrey's remark triggered a memory of herself as a little girl being kept awake by both men making a racket through the walls. When Audrey's husband Malcolm had died a few years after Eric she couldn't sleep for weeks because it was so eerily quiet.

'Why didn't she call for help?' said Audrey despairingly. 'I could've done something.'

Della pondered the comment as she plopped three tea-bags into a teapot and poured hot water on top of them. She gave it a stir, replaced the lid, then slid her nan's favourite floral tea cosy over the top as she waited for it to brew, holding on to the cosy for a second longer than necessary as a new surge of grief took her breath away. Why *didn't* Nan call for help?

'I should've gone round to see her when I got back from bingo on Monday night,' said Audrey.

'The police told me she didn't go with you. I had no idea she was being interviewed about the Churchill desk. She never mentioned it.'

'She was very cagey about it with me as well. I think she only told me because she had to, because it meant she was missing bingo.'

Della got two mugs out of the cupboard and poured tea into them. 'Milk and sugar?'

'Yes please, dear. Better make it two spoons. Sweet tea's always best when you're upset.'

'The police still haven't been able to find out who the reporter was. Nan didn't make a note of it,' said Della, gesturing to the calendar hanging on the back of the kitchen door. The only entry for Monday was *Bingo with A* and it hadn't been crossed out.

'Did the police tell you I saw her? She was leaving as my friend dropped me off outside. Gave me the shock of my life.'

'Why's that?'

'Didn't they say? The reporter looked like your mum.'

Grains of sugar scattered across the counter and onto the floor where Della dropped the ceramic sugar bowl. It had broken into three pieces but she was oblivious. She stared at Audrey in shock.

'She looked like Helen?'

'Oh, let me help you with that mess,' said Audrey, clambering to her feet.

'No! Tell me what you saw.'

Audrey recoiled in surprise. Della had never shouted at her before.

'I saw a woman who looked a lot like Helen. She had the same long dark hair.'

'Where did you see her?'

'Outside. I was in the car being dropped off across the road and she was coming down the path from your nan's house.'

'How close were you to her?'

'I was across the road. She came out, went down the path and got into a car.'

'So you saw her face and thought it was Helen?'

'I didn't think it *was* her. Similar, that's all.'

Della gripped Audrey by the shoulders.

'How can you be so sure it wasn't her? Please, it's really important.'

The elderly woman floundered under Della's grasp. 'Well, I think . . . she seemed a bit younger.'

'But you can't say for sure? I mean, when was the last time you saw Helen?'

'Not since she left. But as I said, I didn't actually think it *was* her.'

Della let go of her shoulders and took a step back.

'Were you wearing your glasses?' she asked bluntly.

'My glasses? No, I only need those for reading.'

'But your eyesight isn't great, is it? I remember hearing

336

you say to Nan that things were sometimes blurry from a distance.'

Audrey looked offended. 'It's not that bad.'

'Yet you can't say for certain the person you saw leaving here on Monday *wasn't* Helen,' said Della triumphantly, her eyes shining. 'I think it was.'

'Oh my dear, I really don't . . .'

But Della wasn't listening; she was already reaching for her phone to call Maggie. In her mind there was no doubt.

Helen was back.

60

Bea took a sip of the tomato soup her mum had prepared for her, acutely aware of the three sets of eyes watching her keenly as she did. She was sitting up in bed, a wooden tray balanced on top of her duvet, while her mum sat next to her, Esme kneeled on the floor and their dad propped up the door frame across the room. They all wore the same worried look.

'I'm feeling much better now,' Bea reassured them again. 'I just felt a bit dizzy. I'm sorry you had to come home early, Dad.'

Chris Dennison shrugged. 'I wanted to make sure you were okay. You gave your sister quite a scare.'

'I know, and I'm sorry.'

Esme had become hysterical when Bea fainted outside the school. She thought her sister had dropped dead, even though the teachers who'd run over to help quickly reassured her Bea was still breathing. When Bea came round a few moments later, she could hear Esme sobbing to one of the staff that she always feared her sister's heart might give out because it had been weakened by the bulimia, which made Bea feel even more wretched for inflicting such a grievous worry on her.

Bea's form tutor then drove the girls home after the school had first called Caroline. Their mum arrived back at the house just as they did, full of anxiety and recriminations, which she aimed, somewhat unfairly, at the teacher. Bea suspected it was because Caroline couldn't do what she really wanted, which was to yell at her.

'Haven't you been keeping an eye on what she's eating?' Caroline admonished the teacher, who remained unruffled. Years of dealing with haranguing parents had honed an outer calmness.

'The lunchtime supervisors are well aware of Beatrice's issues and they always report back to me if they have any concerns about her eating. They haven't done that for many months because there's been no need to.'

'Well, it's the menu then,' said Caroline angrily. 'I'm surprised any of them want to eat the rubbish that's served up.'

'The food at school is healthy and nutritionally balanced,' the teacher had replied reasonably. 'Why don't we ask Beatrice what she ate today?'

Caroline paused then, knowing full well it went against Dr Reynold's advice to badger Bea about her food intake. So Bea stepped in to save her mum having to disobey him.

'I had a jacket potato with cheese and beans and salad, and an apple. I wasn't sick afterwards, I went straight back to class. It's my time of the month and I think that's what made me dizzy.'

The bit about her period was true, but not the bit about it making her dizzy. Finding out Sadie Cardle was dead was what made her faint, but no way could she tell her mum or teacher that.

She took another sip of soup, then another, until eventually the bowl was empty. Then, to prove she really was fine, she took the buttered slice of ciabatta her mum had also put on the tray and used it to mop the bowl clean.

'Good girl,' said her mum, taking the tray. 'You get some rest now. Come on, Esme, let's leave your sister alone.'

'No, she can stay,' said Bea. 'Want to watch TV with me?'

'There isn't time,' Caroline directed at Esme. 'It's gone six and I need to drop you off.'

'Okay,' said Esme, getting to her feet. Her little face was wan and her eyes rimmed with red where she'd been crying. It was only when Bea was safely home and tucked up in bed that her tears had stopped.

'Drop you off where?' asked Bea worriedly.

'I've got a sleepover at Amelia's, with her, Chloe and Daisy. We're going to watch *Pitch Perfect 2* and Amelia's mum's making us hot dogs,' said Esme, sounding more cheerful. 'She's also bought gallons of ice cream for afters.'

Bea felt light-headed again as she began to panic. 'No, you can't go. I want you to stay with me.' She wanted Esme where she could see her and where Sean couldn't get near her. She knew exactly what sleepovers were like, texting and chatting to boys online to all hours. What if Sean managed to worm his way into Amelia's house somehow? 'Please, stay with me. I don't want you to go.'

Esme looked torn for a moment, until their dad intervened.

'No, Esme's had this planned for weeks and she's going,'

he said firmly. 'She needs some fun with her friends after what she's been through. She was really worried about you.'

It sounded like an accusation and Bea was stung. 'I didn't mean to frighten her.'

'I know you didn't,' said their dad, sounding less harsh this time. 'I'm just saying that it's hard for Esme too, sometimes. Besides, you need to rest, so even if she did stay, you'll probably be asleep.'

Bea was beaten and she knew it. Her dad was right: it wasn't fair on Esme to expect her to give up her sleepover with her friends.

While her family left her alone, Bea sank back onto her pillow. The worry of what Sean might do was never going to leave her unless she took matters into her own hands and got rid of him from their lives once and for all. She couldn't go to the police because he'd already warned her what he'd do if she did. But there was another way . . .

61

Maggie saw the call was from Della but had to let it go unanswered. She'd left in such a rush to get to Trenton on DI Green's orders that she'd forgotten to get her hands-free earpiece out of the glove compartment and she wasn't going to retrieve it now, doing eighty miles an hour in the fast lane on the M40. Whatever Della needed to talk to her about, it would have to wait.

A white transit van shot up behind her and flashed its lights impatiently. She moved across into the middle lane and the driver glared at her as he went past, as though she was in the wrong for not driving at a more reckless speed. She resisted the urge to stick two fingers up.

A more direct route would've been to drive via Aylesbury, meandering past Buckinghamshire villages with idyllic sounding names like Bryants Bottom, Quainton and Padbury. But with traffic likely to be heavy at this time of night, zipping up the motorway from Mansell in the direction of Oxford, then cutting cross-country, was quicker, if far less scenic.

Half a mile later a road sign loomed into view on her left, announcing only two miles to go until the turn-off for Trenton. Maggie's pulse quickened and she suddenly felt more alert than she had in hours. It was six thirty now – what were the chances Umpire was still knocking around the station when she arrived? When he worked Major Crime cases he would sometimes sleep overnight in his office to get the job done, but maybe his hours were more regular with HMET. Or maybe he'd clocked off already to meet Renshaw.

The thought dismayed her. Fine if he didn't want to take things further with her, but why start seeing someone he knew Maggie couldn't stand? All those conversations they'd had about Renshaw, when Maggie had solicited his advice on how to deal with her unpleasantness and backbiting. Had he been attracted to her all along? Had it started at the benefit evening for the officer who was killed, or was it even earlier than that? Who made the first move, him or her? *Does he kiss her like he kissed me?*

'Oh God, stop this now. You'll drive yourself mad,' Maggie said loudly to herself. She switched on the radio and let Taylor Swift drown out her thoughts as she continued her journey.

Trenton police station was far flashier than Mansell in appearance and in function too, as the divisional head-quarters for the force's northern reaches. With a sweeping glass and steel facade fitted with photovoltaic panels to generate its own power, the station was both envied and derided, its critics claiming it looked more like the head-quarters of a corporation than a working police station.

The front-desk reception area was in the hollow of an atrium rising three floors above. The front-desk clerk was friendly and efficient and told Maggie in a brisk voice to take a seat in the tastefully decorated waiting area while she made DI Green aware of her arrival. Sitting down, Maggie wondered if the serene surroundings tempered how people behaved, knowing the front desk at Mansell could be a volatile place to work with frequent outbursts from members of the public. Here, she couldn't imagine anyone daring to speak above a whisper.

She gazed up at the atrium, curious as to which floor HMET were based on, and toyed with the idea of sending Belmar a text to see if he was around to meet afterwards. He and Allie had a spare room at their flat in the centre of Trenton and staying over at theirs would be infinitely preferable to the drive back and a night squashed on the sofa again. Her parents might be staying at the Premier Inn in the centre of Mansell but her flat was still overcrowded. A night at the Small–Fontaine residence would mean clean sheets, no early wake-up from the kids and seriously good coffee served with breakfast.

She decided to wait though, knowing there was little point making plans until she knew the outcome of the briefing and what DI Green expected of her over the weekend. Maggie needed a clear head for that and she knew the downside of staying at Belmar and Allie's would be the skull-crushing hangover she always woke up with the next day.

A few minutes later the front-desk clerk called Maggie over and handed her a security pass.

'DI Green's told me to send you up to the first floor and someone will meet you there.'

Maggie said thanks and made her way over to the bank of lifts. On the first floor the lift opened onto a balcony foyer that looked out over the atrium. The grim-faced officer waiting to collect her didn't bother to introduce himself.

'The briefing's already started. You're late,' he said.

'I've been kept waiting downstairs for ten minutes,' she shot back.

She followed him through two sets of security doors – each time he slapped his security pass against the sensor and fidgeted with obvious annoyance as the doors ponderously opened – until they reached the briefing room. It was packed and from her position by the back wall Maggie struggled to see over the heads of those in front of her despite her height.

DI Green was in full flow at the front.

'I'll be the first to admit we've been well and truly kippered by Eleanor Bramwell,' she was saying, her voice loud and rich as it carried across the room.

'Not us, HMET were dealing first,' said a male voice near the front. A murmur of approval rippled round the room.

Green shook her head.

'We haven't got time to sit here apportioning blame and telling tales. Our focus needs to be finding and arresting Eleanor Bramwell. She might look like butter won't melt but her husband says she's nothing of the sort.'

Green's gaze fell upon Maggie at the back of the room and she gave her a fleeting nod.

'Simon Bramwell is contesting his wife's version of events and compellingly so. He says that when he returned home from work on Monday evening at six p.m. Eleanor had prepared a meal for them both. Spag bol, washed down with a bottle of Cabernet Sauvignon. The food was fine but he remembers questioning the taste of the wine with her, said it was a bit bitter. She told him it was probably corked but as it was the only bottle of red left in the house it would have to do. So he carries on drinking and very quickly he starts feeling nauseous, so Eleanor tells him to lie down on their bed. The next thing he knows, he wakes up in hospital four days later with my ugly mug looming over him.' Green crossed her arms. 'He's categorically denying that he stabbed his wife, left her to die in the bathroom, then crushed up a ton of pills and washed them down with vodka to top himself. I think he's telling the truth, which means Eleanor staged the whole thing to make him the guilty party. She was probably banking on him dying so her story couldn't be contradicted.'

'We're supposed to believe she stabbed herself?' a female officer sitting at the front of the room scoffed sceptically.

'I've sent the medical report on her wounds to a consultant forensic physician to see if he thinks they could be self-inflicted,' Green clarified. 'We already know the wounds were shallow and don't exactly tally with her account of being frenziedly attacked by her husband. If he'd really gone at her like the Yorkshire Ripper, her injuries should've been far worse.'

Maggie could see she wasn't the only one in the room baulking at the idea of stabbing his or herself. A person would surely have to be utterly desperate to do that – or crazy.

Green pointed to a Perspex display board behind her, but the heads of those standing in front of her obscured Maggie's view of it.

'After myself and DC Neville here –' Green gestured at Maggie, who tried not to blush as the same heads swivelled round to scope her out – 'had our run-in with Eleanor at the Langston Hotel in Mansell, she went to the train station.

CCTV cameras picked her up on platform three, the London-bound platform, but she didn't get on to a train.' Green pointed again to the display board out of Maggie's eyeline. 'This shows Eleanor coming back out of the station about ten minutes later. She's hidden her hair under a bobble hat and has changed her clothes – presumably in the waiting room on the platform – which shows she was pre-pared, and probably why she risked going back to her hotel room to grab her suitcase after she knocked me out.'

'So she's still in Mansell?' asked the officer who had col-lected Maggie.

'Our colleagues down there are checking CCTV around the town centre as we speak but for all we know she could've nicked another vehicle and gone anywhere. We're talking needle-in-a-sodding-haystack.'

'If she did stage the murder-suicide attempt, does her husband have any idea why?' asked the same female officer who'd spoken up earlier.

'Well, my first thought was she'd done it because he was a nasty shit who liked to knock seven bells out of her and it was her way of escaping. But it looks like everything she told us about being abused by him was bollocks too. We've checked her medical records and there haven't been any hospital admissions in the past ten years for broken limbs,' said Green, catching Maggie's eye again. 'He's claiming he has no idea why she's flipped.'

Maggie wanted to kick herself for falling for Eleanor's lies. It was no excuse that she was being pulled two ways by the cases she was juggling: as Eleanor's FLO she should've spent more time poking holes in her story to make sure it was watertight and passed on her suspicions the moment she realized it wasn't. She should've seen through the fabrications.

'All of us believed her,' said Green, eyeballing Maggie as though she could tell she was mentally berating herself. 'She's a bloody good actress. Even her own husband had no idea what she was capable of and they've been married for nine years.'

'So what's the link to the attack in Mansell?' someone else piped up.

Green grimaced. 'At approximately one p.m. on Tuesday, a pensioner called Sadie Cardle was found severely injured at home. At first the police in Mansell thought it was a distraction burglary gone wrong, as there has been a spate of them across the town in recent weeks. However, on Monday evening Mrs Cardle had a visitor and we now believe that visitor was Eleanor Bramwell,' said Green, explaining the photographs and rings found in the second hotel room that had gone missing from Frobisher Road.

'What we don't know is why Eleanor went to see Mrs Cardle and whether it was her intention to hurt her. There must be a connection between them but so far we haven't found it. Eleanor appears to have disguised herself in a long black wig to visit Mrs Cardle, so be aware, folks, that she may have changed her appearance again as we look for her now.'

Maggie spoke up. 'Does Simon Bramwell know Sadie Cardle or her family?'

'He's saying he doesn't and is baffled as to why his wife would attack an elderly woman he's never heard of.'

As the group pondered a possible link, Green clapped her hands together loudly.

'Right, we need to find Eleanor Bramwell before she does something silly to either herself or someone else. I want every family member, friend, associate and casual acquaintance mined for information. Someone must know where she is. I know it's a big ask, but I want everyone working the weekend.'

There were no dissenting voices as heads bobbed in acknowledgement of Green's request, Maggie's included. Eleanor had duped her and she would work round the clock until her arrest.

Green issued a few more instructions then dismissed everyone with the order to 'crack on'. As the group dispersed, a path was cleared to the front of the room and she beckoned Maggie forward.

'Let's have a quick chat.'

Reaching the front of the room, Maggie finally had a clear view of the display board. She jerked to a halt as if she'd run headlong into a brick wall.

'Oh my God,' she breathed. 'It can't be.'

'What is it?'

At the centre of the board was a blown-up image of the Bramwells on their wedding day. Eleanor was resplendent in strapless ivory lace, her long blonde hair set in gentle waves and crowned by a diamante tiara, while her handsome husband beside her beamed into the camera. Maggie studied the picture for a few moments, drinking in every feature of the happy couple's smiling faces, until she was certain.

She turned to DI Green, her expression set like granite.

'That man isn't Simon Bramwell.'

62

Audrey didn't stay to drink her tea. Visibly shaken by Della's outburst, she went through a pantomime of pretending she could hear her phone ringing through the thin walls and scuttled out of the house before Della could dispute it.

Any guilt Della felt for manhandling the old woman was overridden by her growing excitement. It all made sense now, she thought, as she tidied away the mugs and rinsed out the teapot before returning it to the cupboard as well. After seventeen years away, Helen had finally returned to the family home – presumably for her inheritance, as that's what Maggie seemed to think her only motive would be. Nan kicked up a fuss – well, she was hardly going to hand the money over without an explanation of where Helen had been all this time – and a struggle ensued. Della didn't believe Helen meant to hurt Sadie and the police would take that into account.

'I know it was an accident,' Della mused out loud as if Helen was right there in the kitchen with her. 'Once the police know that we can give Nan a proper farewell and then you and I can get to know each other.' Her expression darkened for a moment. 'That doesn't mean you can replace

Nan. She's the one who raised me and loved me when you went off. But we can get to know each other as friends.'

Putting the chairs back in the dining room, Della tried to imagine what Helen's reaction would be to seeing her. Would her mum be proud of the person she'd become? Her face clouded again. What if Helen thought her job was rubbish, or she didn't like the way she dressed? What if she didn't approve of Alex? Troubled by her thoughts, Della wound her way down the hall and into the sitting room to put the television on. She needed a distraction until Maggie called her back. But when she spied the stain on the carpet where Sadie had fallen she felt sick. She backed out of the room and returned to the kitchen, listlessly opening the fridge to see if there was anything to eat. Everything was out of date and needed chucking.

She was hungry though, so she decided to order a pizza. She couldn't bear to get her usual Hawaiian – it had been Sadie's favourite too – so she called up for a margarita with a side order of coleslaw instead. The man who took her order said it would take up to an hour because it was Friday night, their busiest time, yet less than fifteen minutes later there was a knock on the door.

Della leapt to her feet, surprised. She grabbed her purse from the side and rushed down the narrow hallway. Flinging the door open, she was about to launch into a polite exchange with the delivery boy when the sight of a woman on the doorstep silenced her. Della assumed she was one of those annoying charity chuggers soliciting for money and was about to shut the door, but then she noticed the woman was holding a Lidl carrier bag full of shopping in one hand and some flowers that had seen better days in the other.

'Are you Della?' the woman asked brightly.

'Yes,' she answered warily.

'I know I should've called ahead to say I was coming,' the woman's words tumbled out in a rush, 'but after we spoke on the phone this morning I couldn't stop thinking about you and your nan and everything that's happened, so I jumped in my car and drove down. I'm Gillian Smith.'

For a moment Della couldn't speak. 'You're Gillian? You've come all this way to see me? Oh, how lovely of you, please come in.'

Thrilled, Della stepped aside to let her enter. Inside the hallway Gillian handed her the flowers.

'These are for you. I'm afraid they're all that was left in the shop. If I'd planned this properly I would've got you a decent bunch.'

Della accepted them gratefully. 'They're lovely. You really didn't have to.'

Gillian stared at the dusty surfaces.

'Is this the police's doing?'

'Yes, when they were looking for fingerprints. Let's go through to the kitchen, it's not so messy in there.'

'The place has hardly changed since the last time I was here,' Gillian remarked as she followed Della. 'Your nan always did like her knick-knacks.'

Della smiled. 'It's so nice to be able to talk to someone who knew her well.'

As she turned her back on Gillian to search in the cupboards for a vase for the flowers, a sharp bang reverberated around the kitchen. She spun round to see what had made the noise and stopped. Gillian had plonked a bottle of

Bombay Sapphire gin on the counter. Della trembled at the sight of it.

'I brought this for you too.'

'That's very kind of you, but I don't like gin.'

Gillian sighed. 'That's funny, your nan didn't either.'

'No, she didn't. She never drank, not even at Christmas.'

'That's not what I meant,' said Gillian evenly.

Della stared at her, confused.

'Did it take the police long to find the bottle?'

'How do you know about that?' whispered Della.

'How do you think, silly girl?'

Everything fell into place in one horrible swoop. Petrified, Della let the flowers drop to the floor and backed away. Gillian idly rubbed her fingertips on top of the counter next to the bottle.

'I came to say sorry but Sadie wouldn't accept my apology. I didn't mean to hit her that hard but it was the only way to get her to stop shouting.'

'Apology for what?' Della croaked.

Gillian blinked at her as though she'd asked another stupid question.

'For what happened to Helen, of course.'

Della gripped the edge of the cooker for support. She felt dizzy and light-headed. She needed air. She glanced to her right and saw the key was still in the lock of the back door. If she could just . . .

'Oh no you don't,' said Gillian, putting herself between Della and the door.

'What do you want?' said Della, panting now as she struggled to catch her breath. 'Why are you here?'

'You said you wanted to know about your mum, so here I

am. I was her best friend. I looked out for her, I was always there when she needed me.' Gillian's expression darkened. 'Well, almost.'

'You hurt my nan because of her?'

Gillian had a thin, narrow face – when she grinned and her skin pulled tight across her cheekbones she looked almost ghoulish.

'I told you, I didn't mean to.'

'What do you want with me?' said Della, quaking.

'I could tell you, but it would make far more sense to show you. You're coming with me.'

Gillian grabbed the bottle and hit Della square in the chest, sending her crashing to the floor. Crying with pain, Della rolled onto her front and tried to crawl towards the hallway door but Gillian stood over her and hit her again, this time across the shoulders. For a moment she floundered face down on the floor, her voice strangled by fear, until Gillian pulled her over so her back was against the lino again.

Gillian straddled Della's body and pinned her arms down with her knees so she couldn't move. Then she grabbed Della's chin and squeezed it tightly with her right hand so Della's mouth was forced wide open. With her left hand Gillian unscrewed the cap from the gin bottle and began to pour. Della tried to scream as the alcohol burned a path down her throat but the rapid flow of liquid rendered her speechless and within seconds she had started to choke.

She coughed and spluttered and her face turned puce but the gin continued to flow until, with one last futile gulp for air, everything went black.

63

Lou sat on the edge of Maggie's double bed and reread the text her sister had moments ago sent to say she was stuck in Trenton with work and hadn't had a chance to ring Craig yet but would later. Lou felt a stab of annoyance that Maggie hadn't made the call a priority. She wouldn't be able to relax until she knew exactly what she was up against and she didn't want to have to wait all weekend to find out.

If she had Craig's number she could call him herself. They'd met when he was dating Maggie and had got on well, and Lou was fairly confident he'd be fine with her approaching him. She'd always thought it was such a shame Maggie had dumped him and secretly believed her sister's ridiculously high standards when it came to relationships meant she was probably doomed to be single for a long time. Lou hated being on her own and could never fathom why Maggie seemed to prefer it. Her sister's rule of not allowing herself to fancy anyone who was already attached was especially mystifying; most of Lou's relationships had begun with an overlap and she never felt guilty about it. It was just one of those things.

She still hadn't heard from Arturs since the fire and knew

she wouldn't unless she called him first. Part of her wanted to speak to him to make sure he kept quiet about her being in the pub when the fire broke out, yet she also knew his silence was already assured because he wouldn't want to be dragged into any police investigation. His actions on the night of the fire proved that, when he did a runner and left her and the kids to it, the coward.

She flopped back against the pillows on Maggie's bed. If she could only unscramble her thoughts long enough to think straight, she'd find a way out of this mess. Between the fire investigation and the contents insurance not paying out, her life was in the shittiest state it had ever been and that was saying something considering what she went through after Jerome was killed. Back then though she only had Jude to think about; now there were three children counting on her to put things right and make life easy again. She hadn't a fucking clue where to start.

There was a tap at the door and her mum entered with a cup of tea and a plate of biscuits. Lou suppressed a smile. Jeanette Neville was never very vocal in a crisis, always leaving the talking to their dad; instead she showed she cared by keeping up a steady stream of refreshments. For Jerome's wake she had personally baked all the quiches and sausage rolls and buttered and assembled every single sandwich to feed the 200 mourners, even though Jerome's parents were happy to pay for a caterer to save them all the effort. Jeanette wouldn't hear of it though – those sandwiches were as meaningful to her as the wreaths that covered Jerome's coffin in the back of the hearse.

'I thought you might like a brew,' Jeanette said, putting

the cup and plate down on the bedside cabinet. 'Dad's bathing Mae while the boys do a bit of homework.'

'But their teachers haven't given them any. When I spoke to both their schools this morning to tell them what happened neither mentioned it.'

'I know, but your dad thought they should do something so he's making them write a short story based on football.'

'I'm glad he's taking an interest at last.'

Jeanette sank down on the bed next to Lou with a sigh.

'Don't be too hard on him. He knows he's been silly.'

'But why did he treat them differently for so long? Was it because their dads were both black?'

'I don't think it's that,' said Jeanette carefully. 'I just think your dad had your life planned out in his head to be very different to how it's turned out. It's what parents do. You have expectations.'

'That's not the boys' fault though,' said Lou hotly. 'My life is down to my choices, not theirs. They didn't deserve to be ignored.'

'I know that, and your dad realizes that now, and I'm sorry it's taken him so long. I can't tell you how overjoyed I am. It's been very hard for me not being more involved in their lives. I can't wait for them to come and stay with us in the holidays. We could even take them away ourselves.' Her mum paused. 'In fact, your dad and I have been talking and we thought you might want to consider moving closer to us, so we can help out more. I know Maggie does what she can, but she's always so busy with work.'

'Hang on, one minute Dad can't bear to be in the same room as my kids and the next he wants us to live next door?'

'It's only an idea,' said Jeanette hurriedly. 'But one you should think about. After all, you don't know when you'll get the house sorted and it's very cramped here for you all. You could come and stay with us for a bit, get a feel for the area.'

'But what about the boys' schools?'

Jeanette chuckled. 'We have schools where we live too you know, very good ones in fact. Look, we're halfway through November and the boys will be breaking up for Christmas in a few weeks. We might be able to get them places in new schools for the start of the January term.'

'Whoa, slow down, Mum! Leaving Mansell is a massive decision to make. I don't know how the boys would feel about leaving their schools and their friends. There's Maggie to consider too. How is she going to feel if we move away?'

An odd look flitted across Jeanette's face. 'It might be a good thing for her too.'

'Meaning?'

'Maggie doesn't have much of a life beyond you and the children and her work.'

Lou rippled with anger. 'That's my fault, is it?'

'Of course not, but I worry the reason she hasn't settled down is because it would mean cutting back on time she could spend with you and she won't do that. A bit of distance between you might force her to get out a bit more.'

Lou shook her head despairingly. 'This is too much to land on me now, Mum. I've got enough on my plate as it is.'

Jeanette got to her feet and smoothed down her grey woollen skirt, which she wore with a navy jumper, flesh-coloured tights and the fluffy blue slippers she'd grabbed at the last minute when she and her husband rushed from their home in the middle of the night. She looked a bit put out, but tried to hide it with a smile.

'Let's leave it for now then. I'll go and see how your dad is getting on with Mae's bath. We don't want him flooding the flat downstairs.'

Lou's mind whirled as her mum left the room. Moving closer to her parents would make her life easier with all the practical help they could give her and a fresh start was very appealing right now. With Mae's dad, Rob, moving to Majorca, they might even be able to help her financially when his maintenance payments inevitably dried up. But could she really pack up and leave Mansell? She shook her head to answer her own question. It was ridiculous for her to even consider it with the investigation into the fire hanging over her. If social services got involved, she and the kids wouldn't be going anywhere.

She swung her legs off the bed and perched on the edge of it next to the bedside cabinet. All she needed was Craig's number or even an address. Luckily for her, Maggie was a hoarder so there was a good chance that somewhere she'd find either of them written down. She didn't think her sister would mind her searching through her things because she never put anything away in the first place.

Lou pulled open the door to the cabinet and began rummaging through the contents, which included ear plugs, some ornate necklaces she'd never seen Maggie wear, a pack of playing cards out of their box and discarded chocolate bar wrappers. God, her sister was slovenly.

She reached her hand towards the back and pulled out an

envelope with her sister's name on. As she held it in her hands, her face curled into a frown. The handwriting was very, very familiar. Inside the envelope was a greeting card; when Lou carefully eased it out she saw it was in fact a Valentine's card.

On the front were two teddy bears embracing and one was holding a heart-shaped balloon. The words printed on the balloon said, 'To the One I Love', but someone had added in the word 'Really' between 'I' and 'Love' and underlined it five times.

Before she could open the card a photograph tucked inside it fell into her lap. Lou picked it up, her heart racing. It was a picture she had a copy of herself at home, of her, Maggie and Jerome, taken a few months before he died. The three of them were in the back garden of her parents' old house in Mansell, Jerome standing in the middle with his arms slung round each sister. Lou sat still for a few moments, trying to rationalize why Maggie had a copy of it. Had she given it to her? She couldn't remember. So much of that time after Jerome's death was a blur.

Lou put the photograph to one side and held the card in her trembling hands. The teddy bears no longer seemed cute – it was like they were mocking her. *Go on, we dare you to read what's written inside.*

For a second she thought she shouldn't open the card, that she should just shove it back in the cabinet and pretend she hadn't seen it. But it was too late for that: even if she didn't read it, there was no forgetting that it existed.

Slowly Lou opened the card and read the message phrased in a text speak she was painfully familiar with. A split second later she began to sob, her hand clamped to her mouth to stifle the noise.

To my sexy Maggie!
I want to be with u (and in u! ha ha!) all the time.
Soon it'll just be u and me. Promise!
It's u I want, nobody else.
I luv u
Jerome xxxxx

64

The confirmation came as DI Green swung into the car park at Trenton's Princess Alexandra hospital. She made a beeline for the space reserved for police vehicles as Maggie read out the email she'd just received that proved she was correct about Simon Bramwell.

'It checks out? Jesus. I feel like we found a loose thread on a jumper, gave it a tug and now we've got a whole crap bag of wool to unravel,' said Green.

'Do you think Eleanor Bramwell knows?'

'It's not really a secret you can keep from the person you're married to, is it?'

Green sheered into the parking space and yanked on the handbrake.

'I want you to do the talking. You know more about this than I do and it was you who got us this breakthrough. Don't go hard on him though – he's not done anything illegal and I don't want him running screaming to the Chief Constable that we're unduly harassing him.'

'I'll tread carefully.'

'Like I said, it's like a sodding big mess of wool and I don't know about you but I hate knitting.'

They climbed out of the car and walked briskly towards the hospital entrance. Maggie glanced across at Green and saw the determination blazing in her eyes. She was flattered the DI trusted her enough to let her lead the questioning but she knew she needed to stay focused. It didn't matter that she had a million questions for Simon Bramwell about his past; this wasn't the time to ask them.

What mattered most was what happened next. What mattered was finding his wife before it was too late.

65

The rain was coming down at an angle now, vast sheets of water that soaked through Bea's coat no matter how hard she pressed herself into the hedge outside Sadie Cardle's house to shelter herself from it. Rivulets of rainwater dripped from her nose and chin and her muscles ached from the effort of trying to stop shivering.

It hadn't been too difficult for her to sneak out once she'd looked up the name of Sadie's road on the *Mansell Echo* website, where it had been mentioned in numerous reports about the break-in. Bea had waited until it was nearly 8 p.m. then climbed out of bed, pulled on some clothes and crept downstairs. Her parents had shut themselves in the lounge to eat a takeaway in front of the television and share a bottle of wine and as they laughed loudly at whatever they were viewing, Bea snuck into the kitchen and let herself out of the back door, taking the spare key with her in case it was locked when she returned.

It hadn't taken her long to work out which house was Sadie's. She'd been walking slowly along Frobisher Road, trying to peer in windows, when she saw a woman holding a bunch of flowers knock on a door, only for Della to open it and let her in. Whoever the woman was, Della looked pleased to see her. Grateful for the stroke of luck, Bea then tucked herself behind the hedge at the bottom of the garden and waited for the right moment to knock on the door herself.

Twenty minutes later she was growing agitated. She bounced on the balls of her feet and the rubber soles of her trainers squelched against the wet concrete. How much longer should she give it?

In her head she rehearsed what she planned to say to Della about the break-ins. She understood Della might feel obliged to report her to the police anyway, but hoped that if she explained what Sean was like and how he'd threatened her into going along with his plan, she might think twice about it, especially as Bea was going to promise that she would never do anything so awful again. Then she could tell Sean he had nothing to worry about and he would finally leave her and Esme alone.

The front door of the neighbouring house opened and two elderly women came down the path, both sheltering under umbrellas. Bea moved again so she was concealed from view behind the hedge.

'I really think I should tell Della that I'm going to stay at your house for a day or two,' said the shorter of the women.

'After what she said to you? No, you shouldn't. She was very rude by the sounds of it.'

'She's having a terrible time of it, Sheila. I don't think you should be so hard on her.'

Bea realized it was the Sheila who worked at the charity shop with her mum. The other woman must be her sister, Audrey.

'Call her later if you're that bothered. Now come on, I'm getting soaked.'

The two women climbed into a car parked on the road-side and drove off. Sheila was driving while Audrey sat in the passenger seat with an overnight bag resting on her lap.

The street suddenly felt very empty without them, Bea's only company now being the lampposts emitting a weak orange glow blurred around the edges by the driving rain. As she pulled the hood of her coat further down her fore-head to keep her face dry, she didn't blame everyone else for staying indoors on such a dismal night. It had to be the reason why there had been no sign of Sean so far, despite how closely he'd been watching her that week. She'd been braced for him to sneak up on her as she left home but she hadn't spotted him lurking in her street and nor had he popped up as she walked the forty-minute route to Frobisher Road. Or rather she hoped the rain had kept him indoors like everyone else – because the alternative was that he had followed Esme to Amelia's and was outside there.

The thought made Bea quiver with fear. She had to end this before Sean got his hands on her sister. She sent Esme a text to check she was okay and having a good time at Amelia's and Esme pinged back a message within seconds confirming she was, on both counts. She'd signed it off with four heart emojis, which made Bea even more determined.

But before she could make a move, the front door to Sadie's house slowly opened and a blonde-haired woman, presumably the friend who had knocked for Della earlier, peered out into the gloom.

The woman didn't notice Bea pressed into the hedge as she slipped down the path and unlocked the boot of a red car parked nearest to the gate. It was only when the woman turned to go back up the path to the house that her face was illuminated under the lamppost and Bea got a clear look at her. She frowned. The woman looked weirdly familiar. Where had she seen her before?

She thought the woman was getting ready to leave and the coast would be clear for her to speak to Della, so Bea followed her up the gravel-pitted path to the house, ready to say hello. When she reached the front door, which was ajar, she realized the house was shrouded in darkness – the living-room light had been switched off but the curtains were still open. It was the same upstairs: curtains open, the rooms in darkness. Even if Della and her friend were at the back of the house, Bea would still expect to see a bit of light shining through from somewhere. Why were they sitting in the dark, she wondered?

'Hello?' she called out, pushing the door open further. 'Della?'

She was inside the hallway now but it was as black as ink and her eyes struggled to focus.

How strange. She'd been outside the whole time, so there was no way the woman and Della could've gone out without her noticing, unless they'd gone out the back door. But why would they leave the front one unlocked and open?

'Are you in here, Della?' she called out.

The tremor in her voice betrayed how frightened she was becoming. The two women must be in the house still but why were they being so quiet?

Every fibre of Bea's being screamed at her to leave but she couldn't go without knowing Della was okay. She had a really bad feeling about this.

Trembling from head to foot, she tiptoed along the hallway until she reached another door. The handle turned easily and she eased the door open to step inside the kitchen. It appeared empty, but as she fumbled her way in the darkness she suddenly sensed someone behind her.

Bea went to turn round but she was too slow. Something hard and heavy crashed into the back of her head and the pain was so agonizing that in the seconds before she collapsed she couldn't muster even the smallest of screams.

66

Simon Bramwell was far more amenable to a visit from the police than his wife had been. He looked weak and washed-out but that did not diminish his obvious attractiveness. It was his eyes that drew Maggie in first, framed by long lashes that would've looked effeminate on other men but on him were alluring. He was broad in build, the arms exposed by his short-sleeved hospital gown impressively muscular, and he had the robust look of someone who regularly worked out and ate well.

'Mind if we sit down?' Green asked, dragging a bright orange plastic chair right up to the bedside. Maggie followed.

'Of course. I want to help in any way I can,' said Bramwell with a weak smile.

Maggie felt uncharacteristically nervous as Green nodded at her to begin. With only the three of them in the small private room it wasn't as though she had an audience, but there was a lot riding on what happened in the coming minutes and she wanted to make a good impression on Green, who she'd come to admire and respect.

'We still haven't located your wife, Mr Bramwell,' Maggie

began. 'We're following up every possible lead but we want to ask you again if you can think of anywhere she might be.' Start softly, then hit him with it, were Green's final instructions before they entered Bramwell's room.

'I honestly can't,' he replied, fixing his dark brown eyes on her. There was something unsettling about the way he was appraising her.

'We believe she could still be in the Mansell area as she was last spotted at the train station but didn't board a train. Do you know why she would want to stay in Mansell?'

Maggie clocked the split-second flinch that Bramwell quickly segued into a shrug.

'I don't.'

Green nudged her foot against Maggie's. That was her cue.

'Isn't it because you're both from the town originally?'

'I'm afraid you're mistaken,' he said evenly. 'We're from Coventry originally, but now we live in Trenton.'

'Mr Bramwell, we know who you are. Or rather, who you were.'

His eyes bore into Maggie's for what felt like ages. Then he dropped his head and shut them as he exhaled. It was a long, sad sigh. Maggie and DI Green waited in silence until he raised his head again.

'How did you find out?'

'DC Neville is with Mansell CID and came across a picture of you from back in the day while working on another case, then she recognized you from the wedding portrait we have of you and your wife,' said Green. 'You should've told us you were from Mansell when I interviewed you earlier. I told you your wife had gone missing from a hotel in the town.'

'What was I supposed to say?' he protested. 'I wake up in hospital and you tell me Eleanor's tried to kill me and frame me and that she's attacked some old lady in Mansell and I haven't got a clue why.'

'You told DI Green that you'd never heard of Sadie Cardle, but you have, haven't you?' said Maggie.

Bramwell closed his eyes again.

'You also knew Helen Cardle, didn't you?'

When he didn't answer, Green nudged Maggie's foot again.

'Why did you change your name from Niall Hargreaves to Simon Bramwell?'

Bramwell gave a sharp intake of breath at hearing the name he hadn't used since 2004. The email Maggie had read out in the car to DI Green was from The National Archives in Kew, confirming that Niall Hargreaves had registered a change of name five years after the accident which killed three of his friends and resulted in a conviction for dangerous driving and four years in prison.

'Why do you think? I wanted to put the past behind me and start again. I couldn't be that person any more.' Bramwell's voice cracked and he appeared on the verge of breaking down. 'I live every day with what I did and I make no complaint about that, it's what I deserve. But changing my name has allowed me to build a different life from the one I would've had if I stayed as Niall.'

'Does your wife know you changed your name?'

A moment's hesitation, then, 'No.'

'Not when you got married?' asked Green. 'Wouldn't you

have had to present your original birth certificate to obtain a marriage licence?'

'I took care of all the paperwork, so Eleanor never knew I had to show my Deed Poll documents with my birth certificate.'

'Why didn't you tell her?' Maggie wanted to know. 'It's a pretty big secret to keep from someone you love.'

'I was ashamed. I didn't want her to know that my actions had caused the deaths of three people and that I'd been in prison. If I'd told her that when we met, she probably would've run a mile.' He looked beseechingly at Maggie. 'I thought I deserved a second chance. I did my time. I was young and stupid and I wanted to start again.'

'Is there any way she could've found out and that's what's sparked her behaviour?'

'There's no possible way she could have.'

It was Maggie's turn to appraise Bramwell and she quickly decided he wasn't as convincing as he thought he was. The dip at the base of his throat had reddened and his eye movements were now rapid and unfocused.

'If she has found out, it does give us a motive,' said Green to Maggie. 'Finding out her husband's lied to her all these years, it must've sent her nuts. There she is, desperately trying for a baby, and she finds out the man she married is not only an imposter but a killer too. She doesn't know anything about him! Can you imagine the shock? I'm not sure I'd want a complete stranger knocking me up.'

Maggie knew what Green was doing. She was trying to rile Bramwell in the hope he'd lose his temper and spill his guts as he defended himself. As she watched him glare at Green, she wondered what Della's reaction would be to them finding Niall Hargreaves. She had so many questions for him about Helen, but Green had made it clear that finding Eleanor was their priority. The mystery of Helen would have to wait.

Bramwell clammed up and folded his arms defensively across his chest.

'Your wife accused you of abusing her, which we know isn't true. But you are guilty of abusing her trust,' said Green sternly. 'She's got a very persuasive mitigating argument to throw at you in court about why she attempted to kill you, so you might want to have a think about the moment she found out you used to be Niall Hargreaves and share it with us. Because I don't believe you for a second when you say she doesn't know and neither does DC Neville here. Come on, Maggie, let's take a break.' Green got to her feet. 'We'll be outside waiting for you to remember. There's no rush, we've got all evening.'

67

Della regained consciousness not gradually but with a bang. She awoke, startled, as she was rolled out of a blanket into the boot of a car. She fell awkwardly on her right shoulder but there was nothing she could do to break her fall as her wrists were bound behind her back with some kind of plastic restraint that scraped viciously against her skin when she tried to pull her hands free. Her ankles were also tethered.

Her panic accelerating with every passing second, she tried to scream but her mouth was sealed shut with tape. Her throat still burned from the gin. Fearing she might pass out again, she made herself stop and take a few raggedy breaths through her nose and as she did she saw the boot lid had been left open a few inches. Squinting through the gap and the driving rain she spotted the rear of a car that belonged to one of the homeowners who lived opposite Sadie: there was a yellow 'Grandchild on Board' sign fixed inside the back window.

Della's heart leapt – she was still in Frobisher Road. Surely someone must've seen her being put in the car? Audrey never missed a trick – had she not seen?

Making as much noise as the tape across her mouth

would allow, Della tried to roll herself up into a sitting position, using her elbow as a prop, but as she raised her head it hit the inside of the boot lid. Her skull throbbed painfully, like she'd been struck down by the worst migraine imaginable.

Trying to ignore the pain, she raised her head again, slowly this time, to see if she could lift the boot lid open. She was almost there when it was yanked up and something soft but heavy landed on top of her, sending her crashing backwards and covering her face so she couldn't see.

'You need to budge over, Della. Make room for another one,' hissed Gillian, glancing over her shoulder as she pulled another blanket out of the boot. 'It's a good job you're both so small and skinny. It's like carrying children.'

Before Della could react, whatever was pinning her to the floor was rolled off her. She managed to turn her head far enough around to see a young girl squashed into the boot next to her. She was stunned to see it was the *Mockingbird* girl from the hospital. The girl's skin was ashen and her lips tinged blue.

Oh God, she's dead.

Della tried to scream but it was too late: Gillian had slammed the boot lid shut. Moments later the engine started and the car pulled away from the kerb. At first she could track their journey, sensing the left turn out of Frobisher Road towards Hampden Way, the right swing onto the London Road towards the town centre. Then they were traversing roundabouts and the momentum of being swung around made her lose her bearings completely.

She could feel the girl's body rammed in next to her but it was too dark to see her. Della tried to wipe her mouth on the side of the boot next to her, hoping that a corner of the tape might catch and lift so she could work it off. But two minutes of wiping her head from side to side told her it wasn't going to budge. As terror clawed at her insides, she began to cry. What did Gillian want from them?

The car veered round a corner then gained speed. Suddenly Della heard a moan, small, low and pitiful. The girl was alive. Della tried to call out to her but her voice was muffled by the masking tape and she could only make a moaning noise too. But there was another moan in response and Della bumped her body against the girl's to indicate she was awake. Then she heard a voice.

'Help me.'

Della cried with relief as she frantically butted against the girl again. She felt fingers claw their way up her front, groping across her face until they reached her mouth. Then, in the darkness, the girl picked at the tape until it came loose. With one yank she pulled it off and Della ignored the smarting pain as she gratefully gulped in mouthfuls of air.

'Are you okay?' she managed to say.

'My head hurts,' the girl sobbed.

'You're the girl from the hospital. What's your name?'

'It's Bea. I'm so sorry, this is all my fault.' She rested her head against Della's shoulder.

'Bea, you need to stay awake,' shouted Della, fearing she was unconscious again. The girl's hair felt matted and wet against her face. 'Bea! Wake up,' she ordered.

To her relief Bea spoke again, but her voice was almost inaudible. 'I'm awake,' she whispered.

'I know you're scared, Bea. I am too. But we have to be brave, okay?'

She felt Bea nod.

'Can you untie my wrists?' She heaved herself onto her side to give Bea access to her hands behind her back but it was impossible. They were secured with plastic cable ties and scissors or a knife was needed to cut through them. Bea soon complained her fingers were red raw from trying to pull them apart.

'Stop now, you're hurting yourself,' said Della. 'We'll find another way to undo them. It's going to be okay.' She tried to sound reassuring but she was both terrified and certain they were going to die.

'I want to go home,' Bea cried.

Della wriggled back round so she was facing Bea, who leaned against her. As they lay like that for a few moments Della could make out the sound of rain pelting against the boot over the noise of the engine.

'I'm sorry. I'm so sorry,' said Bea.

'Look, I don't know who that woman is or why she's taken us but this isn't your fault or mine.'

'I've seen her before, at—'

The rest of Bea's sentence dissolved into a scream as the car shot off the road and the terrain changed from smooth to uneven. The car pitched and skidded and Bea cried as she clung to Della. Then, with no warning, the vehicle screeched to a halt. The abrupt braking caused the muscles in Della's neck to pull violently.

Quivering with fear, they heard a door open and close, then shuffling footsteps. The boot lid was raised and a torch beam shone directly into their faces, dazzling them both.

'You're both awake? Oh good. That makes it easier. It's time to go for a walk.'

68

'I need a fag break,' said DI Green once they were outside Bramwell's room. 'Do you smoke?'

'No I don't.'

'Can you wait here while I nip outside then? If he asks for us before I get back, text me.'

Maggie was doubtful he was going to tell them the truth and said so.

'I understand why he wanted to change his name after coming out of prison, but if he really hasn't told Eleanor it makes him a seasoned liar,' she said. 'He'll have spent years pretending to her that he's someone he's not, which means he would've had to lie about his background, where he went to school, even his parents. You can only keep up that kind of pretence if you're good at fabricating the truth.'

'I think she does know and it's us he's lying to. Let's be patient and we'll get it out of him. Right, I'll be back in a mo.'

As Green disappeared out of the ward, Maggie checked her phone for messages. She had a missed call from Renshaw and a voicemail message, which she played back. Sounding upbeat, Renshaw had rung to say the fourth victim of the

Con Couple, the one attacked before Sadie, had come forward to say a detail had come back to her. When the male accomplice had slapped her and pushed her to the ground, causing her to fracture her wrist, the girl had got upset and told him not to hurt her. The victim was now convinced the girl had said his name and that it was something like Sam or possibly Sean. She was adamant it definitely began with an S. It wasn't a huge amount to go on but it was the biggest breakthrough they'd had so far. They were going to release the detail to the media in the morning in the hope someone would come forward with his full name.

'But I've got even better news than that,' Renshaw's message continued. 'The hospital has checked the CCTV from HDU and they've got footage of a woman who very much resembles Eleanor Bramwell ducking in and out of Sadie's ward prior to her death. The images are being enhanced to ensure a proper identification and forensics should be comparing fingerprints lifted from her house in Trenton to those found on the syringe used to administer Sadie's pain relief. They're also going to crossmatch it with the handprint found on the hallway wall at Sadie's house. Good call, Maggie. That nurse and doctor almost certainly owe you their jobs.'

Maggie was thrilled. When the voicemail ended, she decided to call Renshaw back and tell her about Bramwell being Niall Hargreaves. After that she might just have time to call Craig like she'd promised Lou she would. She didn't want to go home without some kind of update for her sister.

She was still thinking about Lou as she dialled Renshaw's number and it didn't register at first that a man had answered.

'Anna's phone.'

For a second Maggie was rendered speechless.

'Can I speak to DS Renshaw please,' she managed to ask.

There was a lengthy pause.

'Is this to do with work?'

'Yes, I'm a colleague, DC Neville. I need to speak to her urgently.'

The man's voice became muted, as though he'd put his hand over the receiver, but Maggie still heard him say, 'Darling, it's a work call.'

She didn't know whether to laugh or cry. The man who had just called Renshaw 'darling' was categorically not Will Umpire.

Renshaw came on the line. 'This had better be good. We were about to have dinner.'

'Sorry, you're going to have to stick it back in the oven,' said Maggie, grinning with relief.

'Shit. What is it?'

'There's been a development. Remember the picture I told you about, the photo of Della's mum, Helen, at the Mansell Show, the one of her sitting with all those people who were in that accident?'

'What about it?'

'The bloke sitting next to her in the picture is Eleanor Bramwell's husband, only back then he was called Niall Hargreaves.'

Renshaw let out a bark of astonishment.

'Are you winding me up?'

'No. He changed his name to Simon Bramwell five years after the crash.'

'Bloody hell. How did you work out it was him?'

'DI Green asked me up to Trenton and I saw Bramwell's picture in the briefing room and realized he and Niall were the same person. I hadn't actually seen a picture of Bramwell until then.'

'Did he have something to do with Helen leaving town? Is that why his wife went after Sadie?'

'He clammed up when we started asking about them, but he did claim Eleanor doesn't know about his name change or about him being in prison. He says he's been lying to her all this time. As far as motives go, he could be Della's dad and Helen lied to her family about having a one-night stand with another bloke called Andy. Or maybe she slept with both Niall and Andy and didn't know which one the dad was. Eleanor might've been upset to discover Della existed and took it out on Sadie.'

'What, she rowed with her and lost control?'

'No, I think the attack was premeditated. I mean, she drugged her husband, pretended to be a reporter to gain access to Sadie's house, wore a wig to disguise herself – her actions weren't spur-of-the-moment.'

'You have to get Bramwell to talk,' Renshaw urged. 'He must know exactly why Eleanor wanted to silence Sadie. Have you spoken to Della?'

'I've tried calling her but her phone's switched off. I think she's at Sadie's, sorting out the house.'

'I'll send a car round to pick her up. With Eleanor still unaccounted for, we need to make sure she's safe. Update me when you've spoken to Bramwell again.'

Renshaw said goodbye and hung up. Maggie sent Green a text to say it looked like Eleanor was also behind Sadie's overdose in HDU and they needed to resume questioning Bramwell immediately, then bowled back into his room.

'I've got nothing to say to you,' he said.

'I think you do.'

'I want my solicitor present.'

'By all means call them. But while we're waiting for them to arrive, I'm going to ask you a question anyway. Are you Della Cardle's father?'

69

Bramwell tried to hide his shock but failed miserably. His mouth went slack and he clamped his right hand to his chest, as though he couldn't breathe.

'You do remember Helen Cardle, don't you?' said Maggie measuredly as she sat down again at his bedside. He watched her keenly, his eyes filled with apprehension.

'Is Della your daughter?' she asked again. Bramwell had already proved how good he was at masking the truth: if she let him have too long to think he could concoct even more lies. 'You knew her mother well, didn't you? Were you the one-night stand she had that resulted in Della?'

Bramwell shook his head. 'I don't know what you mean.'

'Yes you do.' She changed tack for a moment. 'Did you know your wife secretly booked a hotel room two weeks ago in Mansell? At the Langston Hotel on Bishop's Hill. You might remember it from when you lived in the town as Niall Hargreaves; it's been there for decades.'

'I know the hotel, but I don't know why Eleanor would've booked a room there.'

'She paid for it in cash and the name she used when she registered was Helen Cardle. Bit of a coincidence, isn't it?'

Bramwell didn't respond.

'What's really ironic is that Helen's daughter, Della, actually works in the very same hotel. You know Della, don't you? She was just three when Helen walked out on her. The date was August twenty-first 1999 – the same day you killed your friends in that crash and also the same day you and Helen were pictured together at the Mansell Show. The *Echo* ran the photo in its coverage. I found it in their archives: that's how I recognized you.'

The door opened and Maggie looked round as DI Green entered the room. Their eyes locked and a look of understanding passed between them. Green said nothing as she leaned against the wall by the door, arms folded, face impassive.

'So we know you've met Helen Cardle at least once,' Maggie continued. 'Although judging by the way your hand was groping her thigh, I'd say it was probably more than that.'

Finally Bramwell spoke. His voice was raspy and thin.

'That photograph doesn't prove anything.'

'No, it doesn't. So I'll ask you again: are you Della's biological father?'

Bramwell clamped his hand tighter to his chest.

'I know Della is very keen to find out more about her parents. It's been very hard for her growing up without a mum and dad,' said Maggie. 'I don't think she'll ever get over the loss she feels.'

His eyes flickered shut. When he opened them again, they brimmed with unshed tears.

'How is her grandmother?'

'I'm afraid Sadie Cardle died on Wednesday.'

His hand moved from his chest to his mouth.

'You need to tell us everything,' said Maggie firmly. 'What is your relationship to Helen and her family and why did Eleanor attack Sadie?'

Bramwell shook his head.

'Please, for Della's sake.' Maggie held his gaze. 'She lost her mum when she was just a kid, she doesn't know who her dad is and the only family she had left was her nan and now she's dead. At the very least, she deserves to know why Sadie was targeted by your wife.'

He finally broke down.

'I didn't mean for any of this to happen,' he sobbed.

DI Green moved from the doorway and sat down quietly beside Maggie. Surreptitiously she took out her notebook and began to write.

'I never thought Eleanor would find out. I don't know how she did.'

'Are you Della's father?' Maggie asked again.

He shook his head.

'No. I never slept with Helen.'

'So you do admit to knowing her?'

'We were friends. Fleur introduced us. Fleur was seeing my best mate, Ross.'

'We know you and Eleanor are struggling to have children. Perhaps *she* believes you're Della's father and that's why she went to Sadie's house? We think she stole dozens of photographs of Della as a child from some albums Sadie had. They've been found in the hotel room she booked in Helen's name, along with Sadie's wedding and engagement rings.'

'Eleanor doesn't think I'm Della's father,' said Bramwell flatly.

'Okay, you need to help me out here, because I'm confused,' said Maggie. 'So why go after Sadie?'

Bramwell's shoulders slumped and he slowly exhaled. The fight had gone out of him. DI Green said quietly, 'It's time to tell us the truth, Mr Bramwell.'

He gazed off into the distance as he began to talk, eyes unfocused as his memory transported him right back to that day in August 1999, as real as if he was sitting there again on the grass with his friends.

'I fancied Helen, I had done for ages. She was beautiful. Not just to look at, but as a person too. She was funny and intelligent and we would talk for hours. But every time I asked her out she said no and she always used the baby as an excuse, saying she didn't have time to get involved with anyone. But I knew that was rubbish because she wasn't exactly the model mum. She hardly spent any time with the kid.' He swallowed hard. 'She didn't like me like that. She only saw me as a friend.'

'Tell us about the day of the crash,' said Maggie. 'Did Helen arrange to meet you at the Mansell Show?'

'Yes, in the afternoon. We hung out there for a bit and then sat in the park, drinking and talking.'

'Was she with you all day?'

'By late afternoon she said she wanted to go home in time for Della's bedtime. Her parents were giving her grief and threatening to chuck her out if she didn't get her act together. But I talked her out of going. I thought that if I got her to stay, something might finally happen.'

'Such as?' said Green, clearly wanting him to spell it out.

'I thought I could get her drunk enough to sleep with me.'

There was no shame in his voice as he said it. Maggie guessed it was because it wasn't the worst thing he did that evening.

'Did she?' asked Green.

'No.'

'What happened then?'

'Someone, I don't remember who, suggested we all go for a drive in my van, which was nuts because I'd been drinking all afternoon. But in those days you didn't care about drink driving like you do now. I think it was Ross who said we should go up to Barnes Wood to check out the disused chalk mines. They'd been boarded up for years but he reckoned he knew a way to get in. It took us a while to find them though; we had to leave the van in a lay-by and walk through the woods.'

'How did you get into the mine? A lot of the tunnels have collapsed,' said Maggie. 'The entrance was closed up and grassed over once the mines were shut down in the 1950s.'

'Not everything was covered over – there are the air vent shafts. Some of them weren't filled in and Ross knew where to find one. There was a grille over the vent that was padlocked shut but Kelvin managed to pick it open. We had to climb down this ladder inside the vent to get to the bottom but it was amazing once we got inside. All these little tunnels and caves to explore.'

'What happened once you were down there?' asked Maggie.

'We had more booze with us and carried on drinking. But then Fleur started to freak out about feeling claustrophobic and that's when someone suggested we play a joke on her by locking her in. But I thought that wouldn't be fair if she didn't like confined spaces, so then we decided to pretend to lock someone else in just to see how Fleur would react. It was a stupid, stupid joke.'

He suddenly turned to them.

'It wasn't my idea but all of us were in on it, including Helen. The plan was to drive round the block then go straight back. I even dragged Fleur to the van to make it look more convincing but she became hysterical and went for me as I was driving and I swerved into the path of the other car. I couldn't get out of the way in time.' He cried out in anguish. 'I killed my friends.'

They waited for a few moments to allow him to compose himself. Eventually Bramwell wiped his eyes roughly with his fingertips.

'You have to believe me,' he said. 'We always intended to go back and open the grille. We never meant to leave her down there.'

Maggie was confused. 'You mean Fleur? I thought she was in the van?'

'No, he means Helen,' said DI Green softly.

Maggie reeled back in shock.

'It was Helen you left down in the chalk mine, wasn't it?' said Green.

Bramwell couldn't stop the tears falling again. 'It was only meant to be a joke.'

'You left her there to die,' said Green matter-of-factly.

'Why didn't you tell anyone about her being down there when you came round in hospital after the crash?' Maggie butted in.

'It was nearly a month later by then. I didn't think she'd

be alive without any food or water and I thought I'd be done for leaving her. I freaked out. I was already facing prison for the crash – it would've been a whole lot worse if the police knew about Helen as well.'

'You didn't think she might've managed to get out?' asked Green.

'I really hoped she had, but we'd padlocked the grille shut again and I didn't see how she could've opened it on her own. So I called her parents from the hospital. Her mum answered and said Helen hadn't been home for weeks and they didn't know where she was or when she'd be back. That's when I knew for sure that she was still down there.'

'You let them and Della think she walked out on them?' said Maggie sharply.

Bramwell moaned, clasping his hands to his cheeks. 'There isn't a day that goes by when I don't think about what we did. But I would never have hurt Helen on purpose,' he cried. 'I mean, she was in on it – there's no way we would've locked her up and left her if she hadn't been. She thought it would be funny to see Fleur's reaction when we went back and Fleur found out it was all a wind-up.'

'But you said she had wanted to go home to see her daughter. Why would she agree to being locked up if she wanted to go home?' said Maggie.

'We were so drunk by that point I doubt Helen remembered she had a kid.'

Maggie battled not to show how upset she felt. All those years Della spent thinking Helen didn't love her and had abandoned her and all that time she was rotting away a few miles down the road.

'Does Eleanor know what you did?' she asked.

Bramwell rested his head back on his pillow and closed his eyes. 'I don't want to talk about this any more now. I want a solicitor present.'

'I could probably charge you with murder, you know,' said DI Green as amiably as if she was discussing the weather with him. 'How do I really know you didn't kill Helen on purpose?'

His eyes flew open.

'What? But I didn't kill Helen! It wasn't my idea to lock her up and leave her down there. Someone else suggested it, not me.'

'It all leads back to you though. The others are all dead. There's no one who can corroborate your story. You left Helen Cardle locked up down a mine to die and seventeen years later your wife attacks her mother.'

Bramwell paled. 'What I did then has nothing to do with Eleanor now.'

'The evidence stacked up against her suggests otherwise,' said Green, sitting back in her chair and hooking one leg over the other knee. 'Best you start telling us the truth.'

'I can't go back to prison,' said Bramwell, clearly terrified.

Green turned to Maggie. 'I bet it'll be a lot less cushy than the one he was in last time. And his stay will be a lot longer . . .'

'All right! But before I tell you, I want you to know I love my wife. When you find her, please tell her that. Tell her I love her.'

Maggie and DI Green both nodded.

He wiped his eyes again and took a deep breath.

'I was telling the truth when I said it wasn't my idea to leave Helen down there that day.'

'So who's was it?' asked Maggie.

'Eleanor's.'

70

Green pitched forward and placed her clenched fist on the edge of Bramwell's bed before Maggie could react.

'Repeat that,' said the DI sternly.

'I said it was Eleanor who suggested we leave Helen locked up for a joke.'

Bramwell sagged against his pillows and closed his eyes. He seemed to have aged twenty years before their eyes.

'You're telling us Eleanor was with you that day?' said Green, still leaning on the bed. She was as tense as a coiled spring.

His eyes flickered open. 'Not Eleanor . . . Gillian.'

Maggie gasped. 'Of course,' she breathed. 'Gillian Smith.'

'Who?' Green demanded.

'Gillian Smith was Helen's best friend. She was there that day too, wasn't she, at the Mansell Show?' said Maggie, talking directly to Bramwell. He nodded slowly, as though it hurt to move his head. 'Her picture was in the *Echo* as well, but when I saw her I thought she was Eleanor and I couldn't work out what her connection was to Mansell. But now it makes sense. Eleanor was Gillian Smith back then.'

Green turned and gaped at Maggie. 'You're telling me

Eleanor's changed her name too? How the hell did we not know that?'

'Because we weren't looking for it,' said Maggie. 'Eleanor was the victim when all this started and we had no reason to suspect her of anything.' She refocused her attention on Bramwell. 'There was no mention in the newspaper report of her being in the crash on the night you left Helen down the mine.'

'It was my side of the van that bore the brunt of the impact. Eleanor was in the passenger seat and had a few stitches but that's all. Maybe that's why it didn't mention her.'

'If she was only walking wounded, why didn't *she* tell everyone about Helen straight away?'

Bramwell's voice cracked. 'She said she wanted to protect me. She knew I'd be in trouble for drink-driving and didn't want to make it worse for me.'

'But Helen would've been alive to confirm she was in on the joke,' said Green.

'I know. I didn't really understand why Eleanor kept quiet but by then it was too late.'

Maggie thought back to the statement Gillian Smith gave the police investigating Helen's disappearance, when she revealed they'd rowed on the day of the Mansell Show after Helen brought up a boyfriend who'd mistreated her.

'Did you go out with Eleanor back when she was Gillian?' she asked.

'Yes, for a couple of months,' said Bramwell. 'But then I started to like Helen more and after that I didn't think it was fair to carry on.'

'No wonder she wasn't eager to tell anyone about Helen's

whereabouts. She had you all to herself, didn't she?' said Green. 'How long after the crash was it before you two were a couple again?'

'Not long,' Bramwell admitted. 'Eleanor came to see me every day and was there for me throughout the trial. She waited for me while I was in prison.'

'So you changed your names together to start afresh? You lied to us about her not knowing you were once called Niall,' Green sniped.

'I love my wife. It's my turn to protect her now.'

'Too late for that,' said Green. 'Why did she attack Sadie Cardle? What sparked all this?'

Bramwell looked completely broken, his face ashen as he pulled at the final thread of the story to unravel it.

'It started about eighteen months ago, after our first round of IVF failed. I don't know if it was down to all the hormones she was taking, because she's always been a bit overanxious, but Eleanor became paranoid and suspicious about everyone she came into contact with. She got it into her head that one of the nurses at the IVF clinic was really Helen.'

'Even though she knew Helen was almost certainly dead?' queried Green.

'I kept telling her that but she wouldn't have it. Eleanor was convinced it was the real Helen and that she was tampering with our embryos as some kind of revenge and that's why they weren't implanting. I really tried, but I couldn't make Eleanor see how crazy it sounded.'

Maggie thought about Belmar's wife, Allie, and the emotional rollercoaster she was on. Perhaps it wasn't so crazy.

'By the time our third try had failed Eleanor was delusional,' Bramwell continued. 'She got it into her head that this nurse, this so-called Helen, must be living back in Mansell and that Sadie would know where. She wanted to confront the nurse, to tell her to leave us alone. When she started talking about going to see Sadie I put my foot down and said that was it, no more IVF. It was sending her mad, and after all these years, the last thing we needed was for anyone to find out what really happened to Helen. I was so relieved when Eleanor agreed with me, but all the time she must've been planning to visit Sadie anyway and drugged me so she could.'

'Why do you think she disguised herself with a wig to visit Sadie and pretended to be a reporter?' said Green. 'Why not simply say she was Gillian coming back to visit?'

'Why has she done any of this? Booking the other hotel room, stealing the rings, stabbing herself to frame me? None of this is rational behaviour.' Bramwell began to cry again. 'I love my wife. I just want her found.'

'So do we, Mr Bramwell,' said Maggie gently. 'Do you honestly have no idea where she might be? Does she have any family remaining in Mansell?'

'No. Both our parents moved to Trenton when I came out of prison and Eleanor and I got a house there. It was easier that way: no difficult questions from neighbours about me being inside, no one referring to us by our old names. My parents had been under a huge strain too so it was a fresh start for all of us. I honestly don't know where Eleanor could be now.'

Green stood up and Maggie took that as her cue to follow.

'We will be back to interview you again once we've recovered Helen's body from the mine so you should call that solicitor now,' said Green. 'Oh, and there's an officer posted outside your door, so don't get any ideas about making a run for it.' She handed Bramwell her card. 'In the meantime, if you have a sudden flash of inspiration as to your wife's whereabouts, you call me immediately. If you love your wife as much as you say you do, you'll help us find her before she hurts anyone else.'

It wasn't until Maggie and Green were outside the hospital, enveloped by the cold night air, that either of them spoke. They sheltered under the glass porch that ran the length of the hospital entrance; it was raining so hard now that water flowed like a stream along the pavement gutter.

Green went first, as she fumbled in her bag for her cigarettes. Maggie saw the slight tremble in her hand as she lit one up.

'Tomorrow we'll recover Helen's remains. It's too dark to start anything now, but we can instigate a search first thing.'

'What about Eleanor?' said Maggie.

'We'll keep looking.'

'Do you believe Bramwell doesn't know where she is, after so many years of lying?'

'I don't know. But his breakdown just then was convincing enough.'

'So you're buying the rest of his story, about why Eleanor went to see Sadie?'

'You don't have kids, do you?'

'No.'

'I've got two boys: one of fourteen, the other eleven. Love the bones of them, can't imagine life without them. Yet I was never one of those women who thought that if I didn't have kids my life wouldn't be worth living. I wanted children, but I think I would've been all right if it never happened.' She took another drag of her cigarette. 'I guess what I'm trying to say is that I personally wouldn't have let it consume me, but some women do and it sounds like Eleanor's one of them.'

Green ground the butt of her cigarette under the heel of her boot.

'Right, we'll go back to the station, start widening the net.' She raised her face to the sky. 'One more night, Helen,' she said softly. 'One more night.'

'I'd better ring my DS,' said Maggie. 'Let her know what's going on.'

Renshaw picked up after one ring. 'I was about to call you.' Her voice was strained and she sounded upset. 'We sent a car round to Sadie's house but Della's not there. There are signs of a struggle.'

'She's gone?'

'Yes. Della's missing.'

71

They raced to the car park, feet slamming into puddles, Maggie the faster. She knew exactly where Eleanor was – where Della might be too – and Green needed no convincing otherwise. They were going back to the start.

It took them forty minutes to reach the outskirts of Barnes Wood, the blue light on the dash of Green's car clearing a path for her to floor it down the M40. Simon Bramwell might not have thought of it, but Helen's last resting place suddenly seemed the most obvious place to search for his wife.

By the time they reached the disused mines, Renshaw had corralled a response unit and Maggie and Green were both taken aback to discover Assistant Chief Constable Bailey was already at the scene. They didn't question it though. There wasn't time.

'We've found the entrance to the ventilation shaft and the grille was already opened,' said Renshaw. Maggie, wearing only an overcoat and her leather ankle boots as protection against the driving rain and muddy ground, envied her colleague's waterproofs and wellingtons. 'They're definitely down there,' Renshaw added. 'We've heard voices. But it's not just the two of them. There's a young girl with them and we think her name is Beatrice Dennison, Bea for short. Her parents reported her missing an hour ago. They've got one of those GPS tracker apps on her phone and her last location was Frobisher Road, right outside Sadie's house.'

'What the hell has she got to do with this?' said Green, flashing a surprised look at Maggie, who returned it with one of her own.

'Her mum volunteers in a charity shop on the High Street with Audrey Allen's sister. But she says Bea's never met the sister, or Audrey. The mum also says they rarely use the GPS app but did so tonight because they thought Bea had run away. She was supposed to be ill in bed but when they checked on her she'd vanished.'

Green interrupted. 'Okay, let's worry about how she's involved once we've got her out. Show us where this vent is.'

With Renshaw leading the way, the three of them carried torches as they traipsed along the densely covered, mossy path, Maggie struggling to keep her footing. Eventually they rounded a corner to reach a large clearing. In the middle was a square hole set into the ground and the grille that covered it had been flipped open on its hinges. The hole appeared to be sizeable enough to fit two people comfortably at the same time. Lights on tripods had been rigged up around the entrance and a couple of Maggie's CID colleagues, including Nathan, stood guard.

'Eleanor knows we're here,' said Nathan as they reached him. 'She's saying she'll only speak to Maggie, no one else.'

'Makes sense: you're her FLO and Della's too. Look at it as two for the price of one,' said Green drily.

Maggie peered down the hole. Even with the lights it was too dark to see where the shaft ended.

'Shall I go down now?'

'Try talking to her first,' said Renshaw. 'Here, use this.'

Maggie took the loudspeaker megaphone from her colleague. With everyone watching her, she spoke into the hand-held microphone. Her voice boomed across the clearing.

'Eleanor, it's DC Neville. I'd like to talk to you, please.'

She waited, eyes fixed on the hole. Renshaw timed the seconds slipping by on her wristwatch. 'Again,' she whispered, after thirty seconds had passed.

'Eleanor, it's me, Maggie. I want to know that you're okay. I know you've got Della with you, and Beatrice. Can you tell me if they're okay too?'

Della's voice rose from the hole. She sounded tearful and exhausted.

'We're okay. She wants you to come down to talk to her.'

Maggie looked to Green and Renshaw, but it was ACC Bailey who gave the order.

'Keep your radio open, we need to hear what's going on,' he said. 'She may be armed so you must hang as far back as possible and if there's any obvious risk you withdraw immediately. Are you wearing your vest?'

Maggie tapped her chest to indicate the stab vest she had on under her coat. 'Yes, sir.'

'Go on then. But be careful.'

She tucked her torch under her arm as she eased herself down the ladder. Rust had splintered the rungs and made them rough to the touch. Nathan and Renshaw aimed their torches down the shaft so she could see where to put her hands and feet.

The bottom four rungs were missing so Maggie let go and dropped down onto the ground. The heels of her boots sank into the soft, chalk floor, which was slick and wet, lending it a pearlescent sheen. She swung her torch round and ducked cautiously through a crudely fashioned chalk doorway into a small, cave-like room. Della was sitting on the ground trussed up; a young girl lay next to her, unconscious. Eleanor wasn't with them.

'Are you injured?' said Maggie, but she didn't go over to them. She needed to establish it wasn't a trap first. She swung the torch around but couldn't see Eleanor anywhere.

'I'm worried about Bea. She's been hit on the head. She keeps passing out,' said Della.

'There are paramedics above ground who will help her when we get you out of here,' said Maggie. 'Do you know why she's here?'

'She was trying to help but she got in the way.'

Maggie spun round at the sound of Eleanor's voice, aiming her torch in the direction it came from. The beam landed on Eleanor like a spotlight as she sat slumped against the far wall, her face so washed out it almost matched the pale chalky surface she was leaning against. Her right arm was no longer in a sling and rested limply against her body. Next to her on the floor was a blanket covering something and a quarter-full bottle of Bombay Sapphire gin. Shards of bright blue light bounced off the walls and ceilings, like water rippling against the surface. Resting in her lap were long-handled bolt cutters, which Maggie guessed she'd used to get through the padlock and chain securing the grille above.

'She's the girl you've been looking for,' said Eleanor dully. 'It was her and her boyfriend who robbed all those old people in their homes. She told us a minute ago, before she passed out again.'

Maggie stared down at the girl. She was one half of the Con Couple? She was just a kid.

'It's true,' said Della. 'Bea said she and her boyfriend did the other burglaries but they didn't break into Nan's house. She's been blaming herself for Nan dying though because she thinks whoever attacked her had copied them.' Della pressed her bound legs against Bea's back. 'She came to see me tonight to tell me the truth. She was trying to make amends.'

'I saw her at the hospital the other day, at Sadie's bedside,' said Eleanor. 'I thought she was Della because they look so alike. I'm sorry she's hurt.'

Was that remorse? Maggie seized on it.

'Then let her go. She needs to see a doctor.'

Eleanor shook her head. 'No, she has to stay here now. We all do.'

Maggie tensed as Eleanor reached for the bottle of gin and took a long swig.

'Why are you doing this?' she asked.

'I thought it was Helen's fault, that she'd come back to ruin everything, and if I could stop her we'd get our baby. But it wasn't her. Turns out she was where we left her all along.' She gulped down more gin then waved the bottle in Della's direction. 'Do you want to know what happened to her? Tell her, DC Neville. Tell her.' Set against her pale skin, Eleanor's irises appeared almost entirely black.

'What's she talking about, Maggie?' said Della, bewildered.

'*Just tell her.* I know you know. I know Simon's told you. Otherwise you wouldn't be here. You knew exactly where to find us. All of us.'

Eleanor's eyes strayed to the blanket-covered mound next to her – and instantly Maggie knew.

Helen.

72

'What's going on?' Della stuttered. Maggie could see she was frantically trying to pull her hands out of their plastic restraint and knew she had to act fast. She had to make sure Della didn't see what was under that blanket. With one eye on Eleanor, Maggie made a move towards Della and Bea, who was still lying prone on the floor.

'I'll tell you when we're out of here,' she said firmly. 'Eleanor, I'm going to take Bea now. Then I'm coming back for Della.'

'No!' Eleanor clambered to her feet, brandishing the bolt cutters. 'I told you, no one's leaving.'

'Why are you keeping us here?' Della wailed. 'What have I ever done to you? Why did you call her Eleanor? She said she was my mum's best friend, Gillian.'

When Maggie gave no reaction whatsoever, Eleanor gave a short, brittle laugh.

'So much for a husband protecting his wife. How long did it take for Simon to crack and spill his guts? Ten minutes? Five? Or was it even less than that? You know what,' said Eleanor, waving the gin bottle around, 'I think I preferred him when he was Niall.'

Maggie stared her down. 'What about you? Was life better when you were Gillian Smith?'

Eleanor staggered over to Maggie and swung the bolt cutters in her face, forcing her to snap her head back to avoid being hit.

'You think you're so clever, don't you? You think that if you get me talking about who I used to be I'll get distracted and you can arrest me for murdering Sadie and everyone can go home and live happily ever after.'

'Happily ever after?' Della was on her feet now, tilting as the restraints impeded her balance. 'You killed my nan, the only family I had. What have I got to be happy about?'

Eleanor twisted round angrily. 'She wouldn't tell me where Helen was and she started shouting. I didn't hit her that hard.'

'No, but you finished her off in the hospital,' said Maggie. 'We've seen the CCTV.'

Della began sobbing. 'She was all I had.'

'At least you had a family,' Eleanor shouted. 'I'm cursed!'

'Your inability to have children has nothing to do with what happened to Helen,' said Maggie.

Eleanor flew at her again. The bolt cutters missed Maggie's cheek by millimetres.

'It's my punishment for what I did! I did a bad thing and now I can't have babies because of it.'

'I don't understand what's going on,' Della implored Maggie. 'She killed my nan because she can't have children? What is she talking about?'

'I told you I never meant to hurt her!' said Eleanor, now pointing the bolt cutters in Della's direction. 'I adored Sadie. I used to go round every day after school with your mum and she was always so nice to me. When Helen was being horrible to me, which was all the fucking time, Sadie would defend me and tell her off.' Eleanor grimaced. 'I only wanted to know if Helen had come back. I didn't go to see her with the intention of hurting her.'

'I know. You thought the nurse at the IVF centre was Helen. You thought Sadie would know where she was.'

Eleanor looked startled for a moment.

'Your husband told us everything. You could've saved Helen,' said Maggie. 'You had the chance, right after the crash.'

The statement stopped Eleanor and she sank to the floor.

Maggie surreptitiously reached round her waist beneath her coat to unfasten her baton from her belt.

'Simon was in hospital and everyone else was dead. What was I meant to do? I loved him so much, I wanted to help him.'

'When did you stop loving him? I assume you must have, because why else would you try to kill him by putting the diazepam in his wine?'

Eleanor shook her head sadly. 'Of course I still love him. But I knew if he found out what I'd done to Sadie, he'd make me confess, so I panicked. I'd already drugged him so I could go to Mansell to see her – when I got back and saw he was still unconscious, I forced more tablets and vodka down his throat.'

'Did you mean to kill yourself?'

Eleanor gave a horrible rictus grin. 'No. If I can't have a family with Simon, I'll find someone else. Don't you get it? Everything I've done is for my babies.'

'There are a few things I still don't understand.' Maggie

needed to keep Eleanor talking while she figured out a way to get them all out of there. 'Why did you disguise yourself to visit Sadie? And why did you book that second hotel room?'

Eleanor smirked. 'The wig? I grew up in the next street and I didn't want anyone to recognize me, like Sadie's nosy next-door neighbour. Audrey would've had a field day if she saw it was me and been straight on the phone to the police once Sadie was found.'

'And the hotel room?'

'So I could keep an eye on her,' said Eleanor, pointing at Della. 'I thought if Helen was back, she might visit her daughter. I drove down every day after Simon went to work and hung around.'

'Why did you steal the framed photograph and Sadie's rings?'

'When I realized Sadie was hurt I thought I'd better make it look like a break-in. I'd picked up copies of the local rag while I was hanging around the Langston and knew there'd been others involving old ladies.'

'What about the album pictures of Della? Why take those?'

Eleanor seemed surprised by the question. 'They were lovely pictures. Della was such a cute baby.'

'Will someone please tell me what's going on?' cried Della. 'What happened to my mum?'

Maggie moved the torch beam away from Eleanor a fraction so she could see Della's face. Looking down, she realized Bea was awake. She went to say something but Bea shook her head slightly then closed her eyes again.

'Maggie?' Della prompted.

'This woman used be called Gillian Smith. She was your mum's best friend and she married Niall Hargreaves after the accident I told you about, the one that killed his friends. Niall was sent to prison for dangerous driving and after his release he changed his name too, to Simon Bramwell.'

'What did they do to my mum?' said Della, her voice barely a whisper.

Eleanor staggered to her feet again. She was incredibly drunk now, which put Maggie at an advantage. But she didn't want to make a move until she'd got Bea and Della out of there. She couldn't be sure that Eleanor wasn't armed with something other than the bolt cutters.

'Where are you going? Tell me what you did to my mum,' Della screamed at Eleanor as tears streamed down her face.

'Della, don't—' cautioned Maggie.

But it was too late. Before Maggie could stop her, Eleanor was across the room and pulled back the blanket. There was no mistaking the bones she exposed for being anything other than human.

As Della's anguished screams echoed around the chamber, Maggie saw a flash of movement to her right, then splinters of blue light danced across the ceiling as Beatrice, with all the might she could muster and using both hands, slammed the bottle of gin across the back of Eleanor's neck, sending her flying forward onto the ground. Maggie sprang across the room and slapped her handcuffs on Eleanor before she could move.

Bea dropped to her knees next to them, breathing hoarsely. Maggie could see blood dripping from a wound at the back of her head.

'I'm going to get you out of here,' she said, trying to make herself heard above Della's screaming. She spoke directly into her radio, her voice rapid and high-pitched.

'All clear. Suspect detained. Require urgent medical assistance.' Immediately she heard the clamour of shoes hitting the metal rungs on the ladder above.

Leaving Bea for a moment, she scrabbled across the floor to Della, chalk smearing on her trousers and coat. Della's screams were subsiding to wracking sobs as she dropped to the floor.

'I'm so sorry,' she said, placing her hand gently on Della's arm. Della looked up at Maggie, wide-eyed and bereft.

'She never left me on purpose,' she cried. 'She didn't walk out. My mum didn't mean to leave me.'

'No, she didn't.'

73

The decision was taken for Eleanor Bramwell to be questioned at Mansell station, but with DI Green as the lead officer and DS Renshaw second chair. Maggie didn't mind being kept out of the interview room – she knew her evidence would help convict both Bramwells and she was content with that.

Renshaw was also surprisingly accepting of the decision to let Green lead and was currently discussing their interview strategy with ACC Bailey as they stood by the roadside at the edge of Barnes Wood. As Maggie hovered close by, she saw Bailey furtively stroke Renshaw's hand and she allowed herself a grin. So that's who had answered the phone earlier, the man Renshaw had been reluctant to admit she was dating. That day in the car park, Renshaw must've thought Maggie had guessed it was ACC Bailey and that's why she was flustered. Hotshot indeed.

Maggie tried to slink away before they saw her but she was too slow.

'Ah, DC Neville,' said Bailey gruffly as he sprang apart from Renshaw. 'You dealt with that situation fantastically. It could've ended a lot worse if you hadn't remained so level-headed. I shall be putting you forward for a commendation.'

'Thank you, sir.'

With a brief glance at Renshaw, he walked away.

Maggie couldn't help herself. 'Really? You and the ACC?' She winked at Renshaw, who blushed.

'Oh, shut up,' Renshaw barked back, but she smiled broadly as she said it. 'He's right though: you did a great job. Eleanor had clearly lost the plot.'

'I don't think her psychosis is down to the hormones she's been taking. What she did required meticulous forethought, from booking the hotel room to crushing up the pills to drug her husband. Her actions were nowhere near as knee-jerk as Simon Bramwell wants us to believe and whatever either of them protests to the contrary, Eleanor wanted Helen to stay locked up in the mine to keep her out of the picture. I think her sociopathic tendencies surfaced long before she began fertility treatment.'

'I think you're right,' said Renshaw. 'Listen, you'll need to come in tomorrow to write up your statement and for a briefing. I'll be in too, so I'll see you then. Well done, Maggie.' She walked off to rejoin ACC Bailey.

The sight of them together made Maggie suddenly long for Umpire. She wished they were talking so she could tell him everything that had happened. It was one of the things she had loved most about spending time with him, the way they could spend hours poring over a case together, arguing points and tossing around theories. He would be thrilled for her to receive a commendation, her first.

Finding it too painful to think about, Maggie said goodbye to Renshaw and navigated her way past the dozen or so vehicles now parked along the grass verge, including the dark blue van belonging to the Forensic Investigation Unit. Chief Crime Scene Examiner Mal Matheson was already hard at work below ground to secure evidence and a forensic anthropologist was on her way from Surrey to help him take care of Helen Cardle.

Della was waiting above ground while Mal and his team beavered below. She was refusing to leave the scene because she didn't want to leave her mum. Maggie could find no words adequate enough to comfort her but she had let her know that she would continue to be her FLO throughout the coming months as the trial processes for both Eleanor and Simon Bramwell got underway. Della still didn't know the full story of how Helen came to be locked up in the chalk mine and it would be Maggie's job to tell her in the coming days.

Bea Dennison was also likely to be charged for her involvement in the first four burglaries but right now she was on her way to hospital. The wound to her skull was severe and she'd lost a lot of blood; as she was loaded into the ambulance she had suffered a fit and was unconscious again. Her parents and sister were on their way to meet her at the hospital. The police still didn't know the identity of her boyfriend.

As she walked around the side of the FIU's van, Maggie was almost sent flying by a patrol car screeching to a halt. Ready to swear at the driver for his haphazard parking, she stopped in her tracks when the back passenger door opened and Alex leapt out. He looked angry and upset until his eyes lit upon Della, who was being led by a paramedic towards an ambulance. Suddenly his face softened and his eyes filled with tears as he ran over and hugged his girlfriend.

'I thought I'd lost you,' he cried.

'I'm not hurt,' Della reassured him.

As he held her tight, Alex told her over and over again that he loved her.

Maggie's throat clenched with emotion as she watched them. Alex might not be her idea of a great partner but he was Della's. Maybe, she told herself, some relationships are worth fighting for.

Before she could talk herself out of it, she pulled her phone from her pocket and called Umpire's number. She wasn't expecting him to answer – not simply because it was gone midnight but because she thought he probably wouldn't want to. She was readying herself to leave a voice-mail message when his voice was suddenly in her ear.

'Maggie, are you okay? I've just heard about the Bramwell arrest.'

'I'm fine. I . . . I wanted—' She stopped. What *did* she want to say to him?

'Where are you?'

'Barnes Woods. We're wrapping up here and then I'll be going home.'

They both fell silent. Maggie began to feel foolish for ringing.

'I should go,' she said.

'Don't. Wait.' He seemed as unsure of what to say as she did. 'I'm sorry.'

'Sorry for what?'

'Ignoring your messages. For not talking to you when you

tried to talk to me. For coming round to your flat uninvited and behaving like an idiot. I overstepped the mark.'

Suddenly she knew what to say. She turned away from Della and Alex and the officers and paramedics milling around them so she couldn't be overheard.

'If I'm so bloody amazing like you said I am, why aren't we together?'

The line went so quiet that for one horrible, drawn-out moment she thought he'd hung up on her.

'I slept with Gill on Monday evening after the Rosie Kinnock sentencing, when I went back to hers so I could have breakfast with the kids. I was drunk and pissed off with you for shouting at me, and it just happened. The next morning I felt so bad it seemed easier to keep my distance than to have to tell you what I did.'

Maggie was almost giddy with relief.

'I don't care, Will. I don't care you slept with your ex-wife. I thought you and . . . well, it doesn't matter.'

'It was a one-off, I swear. Both Gill and I agreed the next day it was a mistake. Nothing's changed: we're still divorcing.'

'It's okay. You and I, we aren't even a couple.'

He paused. 'Yet?'

'I want to give it a go. But do you?'

She held her breath, expecting him to hesitate, but he answered immediately.

'I'm getting in my car. I'll be in Mansell in half an hour.'

Maggie could almost hear him grinning down the phone and laughed.

'I wish, but you can't come to mine tonight. I've got Lou and the kids staying.'

In a rush she told him about the fire, omitting the part about Lou not being there when it started.

'Tomorrow then.'

'Actually, I know this great hotel in Mansell. The manager, Mr Kendrick, might give us a deal . . .'

'I'll bring my toothbrush,' Umpire growled wolfishly.

She laughed again, then remembered something. 'That saying you told me, the one about a wise man getting more use from his enemies? Where did you hear that?'

Umpire thought for a moment. 'I think it was on some leadership seminar at HQ, with ACC Bailey. Why do you ask?'

Maggie smiled. 'No reason.'

A minute or so later they hung up, after agreeing he would come to Mansell the next day, once she'd been into work to write up her statements. Not even the fresh deluge of rain that had begun to fall could dampen her spirits now.

74

Caroline Dennison knew she should be worried – panicked even – but as she stared down at her eldest daughter's unconscious form, to her distress she found her overriding emotion was that of shame: deep, unrelenting, all-consuming shame.

How had it come to this? In a matter of a few hours her evening had spiralled from drinking wine with her husband in front of the TV to sitting in the paediatric ward at Stoke Mandeville hospital while the police waited to question their injured daughter about her involvement in a series of burglaries across their hometown, during which elderly women had been terrorized.

The shame burned harder, filling Caroline's throat with bile. This wasn't her family. This wasn't what they did. They didn't lie, they didn't break the law and they didn't hurt innocent people. The police said Bea had admitted to carrying out the burglaries, but Caroline didn't believe it. There was no way her child had brought violence and cruelty into the homes of those poor women. It had to be a mistake.

Medicated against the pain, Bea hovered somewhere between sleep and unconsciousness, that no man's land of dreamless rest. The fit she'd had in the ambulance was hopefully a one-off, the doctors told them. Her injury was serious, but not life-threatening. Time would heal it.

Caroline glanced over her shoulder to the far corner of the cubicle where Esme was curled up asleep in an armchair that had seen better days. A nurse had crept in a few minutes earlier with a spare blanket and had cast Caroline a look of sympathy she hadn't welcomed as she draped it over her youngest daughter. It was for sweet, considerate Esme that Caroline felt the most outrage. How could they even begin to explain to her what Bea stood accused of? Esme idolized her sister and would be devastated to think that others viewed her as some kind of criminal.

As soon as Bea woke up they could get to the bottom of what happened. She'd already put them through so much with her illness – it was unthinkable that she would put them through the anguish of something like this as well. The boy the police had asked them about, this accomplice of Bea's they were trying to trace, he was to blame for it all. He had to be.

Caroline heard footsteps behind her and turned to see her husband approaching.

'Can you come outside for a minute?' he whispered. 'There's a detective here who wants to talk to us.'

She concurred, rising quickly to her feet. In the corridor the detective introduced himself as DC Nathan Thomas and said he was stationed in Mansell, with CID. Caroline was struck by how young he was; he looked more like a university undergraduate than a seasoned police officer.

'I'm here to collect Beatrice's phone. It wasn't with the rest of her clothing,' he said.

The nurses who'd attended to Bea in A&E had bagged her clothes and taken them away to give to the police. Caroline cringed at the memory.

'I also want to ask you a few questions about Beatrice,' the officer added.

'Bea. We call her Bea,' said Chris, like that made a difference. 'Ask away.'

'Do you know anything, any little detail, about this boyfriend of hers? We know Bea wasn't acting alone and we need to find him.'

'Do you honestly think we would be standing here if we knew who he was?' Caroline flared up. 'If we'd known she was seeing someone and all this was going on, don't you think we'd have put a stop to it?'

'Caroline, please,' said Chris pleadingly. 'Don't make this worse.'

'Worse? How can this get any worse?' she said shrilly. 'Our daughter has been accused of something so horrible I can't even begin to get my head round it.'

'Mrs Dennison, I need you to stay calm,' said the officer firmly.

Caroline took a deep breath to quell the screaming fit that was building just below the surface, waiting for a signal to blow.

'I'll get her phone for you,' Chris told the detective. 'One of the ambulance crew who brought her in gave it to me when it fell out of her pocket.'

He scuttled off, leaving Caroline and DC Thomas in an awkward tête-à-tête.

'What will happen to her?' she asked him.

The detective frowned. 'I wouldn't want to speculate.

The outcome can depend on lots of things: evidence, expert reports, that kind of thing. Don't worry, your daughter will be given the opportunity to present her side.'

Caroline felt the ground shift beneath her feet. This couldn't be happening to them. They were a *nice* family. Things like this didn't happen to people like them.

Chris returned, clutching Bea's phone.

'You were lucky to have installed the GPS tracker,' DC Thomas remarked, holding out a clear plastic bag for Chris to drop it into. 'It was helpful for us, knowing she'd been in Frobisher Road.'

'We haven't accessed the app for about a year until tonight,' said Chris. 'We installed it when Bea first got the phone, but then she got ill . . .' He hesitated and looked to his wife for encouragement to continue. She nodded.

'Bea is a recovering bulimic. Part of her treatment has been working to re-establish trust between her and us, so we don't feel like we have to watch her every move to make sure she's eating properly and she doesn't feel like she's being spied on. We haven't accessed the app because of that.'

DC Thomas's brow knitted as he cradled the phone in both hands.

'But the app's still been running on Bea's phone this whole time?' he asked.

'Yes, we didn't uninstall it, just in case,' said Chris.

Through the plastic bag DC Thomas managed to scroll through the icons on the home page of Bea's phone until he found the app.

'What are you looking for?' asked Caroline, curiosity quelling her distress for a moment.

'I want to see if the app has a history, so we can see any

locations Bea's visited regularly.' And put her at the scene of every break-in, thought Caroline sourly.

'I imagine it's mostly school or home,' said Chris.

'Here we go,' said DC Thomas. 'It looks like there's at least a month's data saved.' He thumbed down the screen. 'There's an address that keeps cropping up: Colby Road. According to this, Bea was there all day on Tuesday.'

'She wasn't at school?' said Chris, shocked.

'Do you know anyone who lives on Colby Road?'

'Hardly,' Caroline blurted out. 'Isn't that one of those roads with those awful high-rise blocks of flats? It's a horrible area.'

DC Thomas appeared unimpressed by her critique and Chris shot her a glare.

'Do you think that's where he lives, the person who got Bea involved in all this?' her husband asked the officer.

'We'll look into it,' said DC Thomas.

'If I could get my hands on him . . .' Chris snarled.

'Mr Dennison, if you want to help your daughter you'll leave it to us,' DC Thomas warned. 'This is a police matter now.'

They lingered in the corridor as the officer departed. He was on his phone before he reached the exit. Straining to listen, Caroline heard him ask for an address to be checked: Flat 2, 43 Colby Road. Whoever lived there was about to get an unscheduled visit; Caroline hoped it was as unpleasant for them as this evening had been for her.

'Once Bea's awake, she can set them straight,' she said resolutely. 'The burglaries . . .' she winced as she said it. 'They weren't her idea. This person, this boyfriend, he made her do them – he must've threatened her or worse. She's a good kid, there's no way she would have willingly gone along with it.'

There was a sudden interruption, a nurse calling their names. Caroline and Chris rushed back into the ward. 'Your daughter's awake,' the nurse told them. 'You sit with her while I fetch the doctor.'

Caroline reached the bedside first. Her eyes locked on Bea's as she took her daughter's hand in hers.

'Mum, I'm so sorry . . . Please forgive me.'

75

Maggie crept up the stairs to her flat, mindfully avoiding the steps she knew creaked the loudest. She'd driven Alex and Della back to his place and it was now nearly 3 a.m. Yet when she let herself into her flat, she was taken aback to see that all the lights were still on.

She went to hang her coat up and stopped. The rest of the hooks were empty. Where were the kids' jackets? She looked up and down the hall, as though they might suddenly materialize. The pile of small shoes and boots that had accumulated by the front mat had also vanished.

Her pulse quickening, Maggie went into the lounge. Her duvet was folded up on the sofa as she expected to find it, pillow balanced on top, but the toys that had earlier littered the carpet were gone. Perhaps her mum had tidied up, she reasoned, yet she could see no sign of them tucked away. She started to sense that something wasn't quite right: the flat felt too empty, too quiet.

The two bedrooms were off a small hallway on the other side of the lounge. She opened the door to the spare bedroom first to check on the boys, just by a crack so as not to disturb them. But when she saw the double bed was empty she flung it wide open in alarm. Where the hell were they?

She took less caution opening the door to her own bedroom, pushing it fully open. Her bed was empty too and all the baby paraphernalia her dad had picked up at the supermarket for Mae had also gone.

Maggie shot back into the living room and grabbed her phone from her handbag. Maybe Lou and the kids had gone to the Premier Inn with her parents? But why wouldn't they text or call her to let her know? Was it something to do with the fire? Her anxiety growing, she called Lou's phone but it went straight to voicemail. Next she tried her mum. After a few moments Jeanette answered. She sounded sleepy at first but then her voice hardened.

'It's the middle of the night, Maggie,' she snapped.

'Where are they? I've just got home and the place is empty.'

She heard her dad's voice in the background but couldn't make out what he was saying.

'They've come to stay with us.'

'What? They've gone back with you? Why?'

'We drove back this evening while you were working. It was your sister's decision. We didn't force her.'

Maggie's mind fogged with confusion. No way would Lou take off to their parents' house with no word to her. What the hell was going on?

'Where is she? I want to talk to her.'

'She's asleep, as are the children. I'm certainly not disturbing them for you.'

The way Jeanette spat out her words made Maggie even more frightened.

'What is going on, Mum? Why are you being horrible?'

'Me being horrible?' Jeanette scoffed and her dad made a similar noise in the background. 'I don't think you're in a position to accuse anyone else of behaving like that.'

Maggie began to tremble. She'd had enough rows with her mum throughout the years to know that this one was serious.

'Mum, please. Tell me what's going on.'

'If you really want to know, perhaps you should have another look in your bedroom. I think you'll find the answer you're looking for in there.'

'Why can't you tell me?' Maggie pleaded. 'I don't have the energy for guessing games. I've just got back from work and I'm exhausted.'

'That's hardly our fault.'

'Mum! Why are you being like this?'

Jeanette lost her temper.

'I don't know how you can live with yourself for what you did. All these years you've lied to us. I'm ashamed of you, Maggie, and so is your father.'

Maggie spluttered down the phone.

'Ashamed? For what?'

But her mum didn't answer. Instead, as Maggie listened in disbelief, Jeanette Neville hung up. When she tried to call her back, her mum's phone was switched off.

Confused and panicky, Maggie retraced her steps back to her bedroom. She hovered on the threshold, trying to work out what her mum meant.

Then she saw it. Propped up on her pillow.

A Valentine's card.

Two teddy bears in an embrace and above them a balloon in the shape of a heart.

Acknowledgements

Once again I want to thank my editor Catherine Richards and the rest of the Pan Mac 'family' for their unending support and for all their hard work on my behalf, especially Francesca Pearce for her unwavering calmness and can-do attitude. Likewise huge thanks to my agent Jane Gregory and everyone at Gregory & Co for always having my back. Special mention must go to Duncan McGarry MBE, co-author of *Police Family Liaison* (Blackstone's Practical Policing), for being such an inspiration when I was writing this book – I sincerely hope I've done justice to family liaison again; any mistakes in procedure are down to me alone! I also want to thank the *Police Oracle* for being a great source of information, Sally Hinchcliffe for answering all my hospital-related questions and Dawn Spears and the children at the Disraeli School & Children's Centre for providing Esme's shopping list! Heartfelt thanks also go to Allie, Miriam, Petra and Alison for the much-needed brouhaha re-fuelling sessions while I was battling to get the book finished, to Hari, Aaron, Austin, Verity, Vickie, Lynne, Erin and all the LVHS girls for their endless support, and to my sister Sharon and parents Elaine and Mick for always believing. Finally, a special, love-filled thank you to Sophie and Rory. I couldn't do it without you.

Keep reading for an exclusive extract
from the enthralling new book featuring
DC Maggie Neville, publishing in 2018

FALSE WITNESS

It began with a lie . . .

Two children are seen on top of a wall in a school.
Shortly later one of them lies fatally injured at
the bottom. Did the boy fall or was he pushed?

1

Alan Donnelly's first thought on spotting the children on the ladder was to wonder whether it constituted a sacking offence under the terms of his contract.

His second was that he'd strangle the little sods when he got his hands on them.

One of them was already at the ladder's brow, the other not far behind. He couldn't see their faces clearly from that distance, but the girl in the lead had long blonde hair worn loose and wavy and was in a red gingham dress. From the size of her she looked like she might be in Year 5, possibly 6. The boy in her wake had cropped dark hair and was wearing smart grey shorts and a white polo top. He looked physically younger, a skinny little runt.

Alan threw down his shovel on the soil he'd been using to fill in the cracks in the turf. It was Sports Day next week and the playing field was uneven underfoot, a potential safety hazard for egg-and-spoon and sack race competitors, according to the head. Smacking his palms together to clean them, Alan set off across the grass towards the playground, angry at being pulled away from an important task to sort out misbehavers.

He'd warned Mrs Pullman something like this would happen if they didn't delay building work until the holidays started. During a tetchy meeting with her and the governors to discuss the plans, he'd likened cordoning off the playground while the kids were still at school to waving a bottle of vodka under the nose of an alcoholic. Far too tempting. They hadn't taken kindly to his metaphor and decided it would be far worse if they waited until the summer holidays and the work overran and the classes weren't finished for the new intake come September. Prepare for an early June start, he was told in no uncertain terms.

Yet here they were a week into the project and he was already being proved right. There wasn't time to be smug though, because unless he got those kids down off that ladder before anyone else saw them he'd be right in the shit. It wouldn't matter how they'd broken into the school or got onto the building site, it was the fact that they had, and security was his responsibility as caretaker.

There were three new classrooms being built, in a single-storey, L-shaped annexe. An outer wall of the first one was already completed – about seven metres high, it was what the children were standing on now. They appeared to be alone, no sign of any others egging them on. He checked his watch quickly. It was ten past seven – he had about twenty minutes before the first members of staff would start arriving.

His breaths grew shorter as he picked up his pace, and he reached into his pocket for his inhaler. He'd been using it a lot these past four days, since the heatwave baking Mansell and the rest of Buckinghamshire, and much of the southeast, had begun. He hated it, couldn't breathe it was

428

so hot. Yesterday the temperature had hit twenty-eight degrees and today was meant to be even higher.

The building site was separated from the playground by two-metre high interlocking panels, but the door cut into the centre panel was ajar, its padlock swinging loose. Alan couldn't remember seeing it fastened when he did his rounds the previous evening, but if anyone asked he'd say it was and the kids must've forced it open.

He stepped through the doorway and his heart skipped a beat. Both children were on the top of the wall, backs to him. The girl was staring down into the hollowed guts of the new classroom but the boy was crouched low with his arms splayed out, as if struggling to keep his balance. Alan guessed the breeze blocks could take their weight but it wasn't a wide wall, not even for feet as small as theirs. One misstep was all it would take.

'What do you think you're doing up there?' he called up, loudly enough for them to hear but not so loud it would give them a fright and make them stumble.

The boy rose slowly to his feet, then reached out and grabbed the girl's hand. He whispered something and she angled her head towards him just enough for Alan to see her face. He didn't know her name but she was in Miss Felix's class, Year 6. Had a bit of a gob on her, like most girls her age seemed to these days, but she wasn't one of the kids who usually warmed the row of chairs outside the head's office as they waited for a telling off.

'You need to get down now,' he said.

The boy's shoulders began to heave as though he was laughing and that made Alan see red. If there was one thing guaranteed to wind him up it was being mocked by cocky little shits. He gripped the ladder and dragged it along the wall so it was closer to where they were.

'You first,' he said firmly to the girl. 'Take it steady though.'

'I can't,' she said, her voice cracking. 'He won't let me.'

The boy's head whipped round. It was the new kid, the one who, a week earlier, Alan had caught skulking in the cupboard where they stored the art supplies. He'd read him the riot act, told him it was out of bounds to pupils, but he didn't report it because the cupboard shouldn't have been unlocked in the first place. He was still trying to get to the bottom of whose fault that was.

The girl said something but Alan didn't catch it because his focus was on the boy who had started moving away from the ladder, pulling her with him.

'Come back here,' he shouted, too pissed off now to mind his volume. 'I'll have you excluded for this.'

They both ignored him.

Alan knew he had to act, and fast. The teachers who liked to start early would be arriving soon, not to mention the construction workers. He had to get the kids down from that wall.

He started to climb the ladder, muttering all the swear words he wished he could say out loud but would get him sacked if he did.

A noise from above made him stop. The children were lurching ominously from side to side, holding hands, like they were performing a dance.

'Stop that now!' he hollered. 'You'll fall if you're not careful.'

They stopped. The girl panted, her cheeks inflamed, but

the boy was calm, his mouth curled into a lopsided grin.

'Right, let's stop this nonsense,' said Alan croakily as he scaled the rest of the ladder until his feet were only a few rungs from the top. He grabbed the rough-hewn ridge of the wall, hands shaking and legs like jelly.

'Walk towards me and I'll help you down,' he ordered. 'You'll have to let go of each other first.'

'Don't do that!' the girl suddenly screamed at the boy.

Alan shot out his right arm, stretching as far as he could, but his fingertips grasped only thin air and the ladder tilted violently under his shifting weight. Sights and sounds came at him like rapid gunfire and he cried out.

A lopsided grin . . . a blur of red gingham . . . a hand reaching out . . . streaming blonde hair . . . a high-pitched scream . . . a thud.

Then, silence.

Don't miss the first
DC Maggie Neville novel

GONE ASTRAY

It's your life. But he wants it.

When Lesley Kinnock buys a lottery ticket
on a whim, it changes her life more than she
ever could have imagined . . .

The captivating first chapter follows here

1

Tuesday

Lesley Kinnock dumped the six shopping bags just inside the front door and lunged at the alarm keypad on the wall to her left, finger poised to punch in the code that would silence its shrill cry. Halfway through inputting the number she realized with a start the alarm was already switched off. She tapped the digital display as it blinked intermittently at her, baffled as to why it wasn't set as it should be. The system was supposed to be infallible, able to outsmart power failures and the most adept of intruders, which was why they'd paid so much to have it installed in the first place. In a house as big and as rambling as theirs was, there were too many corners a person could hide around, too many nooks to steal themselves within. Without the invisible protection of motion sensors and CCTV, she'd never relax.

Punching the code in again made no difference and her anxiety was raised a notch. What if someone *had* managed to bypass it? Her husband Mack insisted any burglar worthy of his profession would find it easier to break into a prison than they would their fortressed home, but what if

433

he was wrong? What if someone was prowling around at that very moment?

Lesley peered cautiously into the entrance hall. Brightly lit by the daylight flooding through the opaque glass panels either side of the front door, she could see, to her relief, the space was empty. But while her body unclenched, her imagination had other ideas, drawing her attention to the five doors leading off the hall and whispering to her that behind one of them was someone just waiting to be disturbed.

Hardly daring to breathe, she fumbled in her bag for her mobile phone. As she pulled it out, the screen lit up to reveal a picture of her daughter, Rosie. It took less than a second for her brain to make the connection and, as it did, a wave of relief crashed over her. Of course! That was why the alarm was switched off – Rosie was at home today too. In her panic she had completely forgotten.

'Rosie?' she shouted shakily, her anxiety abating far slower than it had taken hold. 'Are you upstairs?'

There was no answer from the floor above. Wincing, Lesley picked up the bags weighed down with groceries and heaved them across the entrance hall, her flip-flops slapping noisily against the parquet floor. The thin plastic handles of the bags cut into her palms like cheese wire, but she kept her grip until she reached the kitchen and could set them down on the floor next to the fridge, a huge, double-door, American-style appliance that could hold more than a month's worth of food.

'Rosie?' she called out again.

As she flexed her sore and trembling hands, she realized the house was far too quiet for Rosie to be anywhere indoors and she must still be in the garden. At fifteen, her and Mack's only child viewed peace and quiet with the same disdain people reserved for traffic wardens and footballers with inflated salaries, and Lesley had grown so accustomed to music thumping through the ceiling and the TV blaring out from the lounge that the lack of noise jarred as much as the usual cacophony.

She kicked off her flip-flops, sending them skidding across the kitchen floor, knowing Mack wouldn't be impressed if he saw them sullying the natural slate tiles. He nagged her to chuck them away, complaining they looked cheap and she could afford better, but what was the point of her dressing up when he was away and she had no job to go to, no friends to see? The rest of her outfit also reflected the apathy that was her default setting of late: a knee-length denim skirt more than five years old that gaped at the waist because it was too big for her now, paired with a navy T-shirt faded from being washed too often. Her face was devoid of what little make-up she usually wore and her fine blonde hair was scraped off her face into a messy ponytail because she hadn't bothered to wash it since Saturday, the day Mack had left for his latest golfing trip.

The tiles felt chilly beneath the sweat-slicked soles of her feet but she welcomed the sensation. It was a hot day and the shopping had taken longer than she planned, but at least it was done now. In one of the carrier bags was a bottle of South African Chenin Blanc she planned to open that evening while catching up on the soaps. With Mack away she could watch them in peace without his sarcastic commentary running in the background. So what if Albert Square was nothing like real life? As she often retaliated, this new life of theirs wasn't that far removed from fiction either.

She wouldn't tell him about her reaction to finding the alarm switched off, she decided, in case he thought she was just being silly again. He accepted her neuroses regarding how secure the house was, but only up to a point; today's incident would most likely provoke more eye-rolls and sighs than sympathy.

A glance at the clock on the range cooker told her it was 1.13 p.m. If Rosie hadn't eaten yet – and the tidy state of the kitchen suggested she hadn't – they could have lunch together on the terrace. It was one of those rare, cloudless days in late May when it was so balmy it felt more like high summer. Having a break might take Rosie's mind off her next exam for an hour or so and draw her out of the shell she'd retreated into as her GCSE revision consumed her.

Glancing over, Lesley saw the back door was shut but she reckoned her daughter was probably still out in the garden. When she'd left to go shopping just before 10 a.m., Rosie was already sprawled on a blanket on the lawn, reading through a textbook. Her next GCSE exam was two days away on Thursday, and it was science, the subject she struggled most with and had done least preparation for. The school she went to permitted pupils to revise at home on certain days around their exams, but Lesley had doubts about the effectiveness of the policy as Rosie could be easily distracted. But it was the kind of 'progressive education' the private, all-girls school had built its reputation on and why it ranked as one of the best in the south of England.

The school, like their house, was in the village of Haxton

in Buckinghamshire, a county to the west of London known for being home to the Prime Minister's country residence, Chequers, Pinewood Film Studios, a moribund furniture industry and a belt of homes owned by once-famous television stars of the seventies and eighties. With a population of 8,318, Haxton was one of the smaller villages in the area, but what it lacked in size it made up for in affluence. Homes there rarely sold for less than a million and every year it featured in the *Telegraph*'s top-ten most desirable places to live in Britain. It was worlds away from Mansell, the town five miles down the road where the Kinnocks had lived before their £15-million win on the EuroMillions lottery had upgraded their existence to include gated communities and schools that cost £4,000 a term.

Lesley headed over to the back door but gave the solid oak island counter in the middle of the room a wide berth as she went past, as though it had more right to be there than she did. It was too big, too imposing, and in the fourteen months they'd lived at Angel's Reach – the name given to their house long before they bought it and which she would change in a heartbeat if only Mack would let her – had come to represent everything she loathed about their new wealth. It was all about show.

The presence of the island counter also embarrassed her, reminding her as it did of the first time they viewed the house and she'd asked the estate agent to explain what it was for, because she'd never set foot in a kitchen that had one before. The young woman, all glossy hair and glossed lips, had looked at Lesley more with pity than surprise.

'You want to know what the point of it is?'

More than a year on, Lesley's cheeks still grew hot at the memory.

'There are all these worktops already,' she had eventually replied, stumbling over her words. 'I just don't see why we'd need this great big thing in the middle of the room as well.'

Then, just to complete her mortification, Mack had burst out laughing, grabbed her by the hands and swung her in a circle, boyish excitement melting a decade off his forty-six-year-old face.

'Oh love, does it matter what it's for?' he crowed. 'With what we've got in the bank we can buy a thousand of the bloody things and keep them in a field if we want!'

The estate agent had echoed his laughter – no doubt cheered by the belief she was about to make a sale. But Lesley couldn't bring herself to join in and squirmed self-consciously as Mack danced her around the kitchen, her movements as jerky as a marionette's. In the end she was so desperate to leave she'd let him make an offer of the full asking price on the spot, even though it was the first house they'd looked at and she wasn't convinced it was worth the money. Still wasn't.

The flagstone terrace running along the back of the house was bathed in sunshine and Lesley raised her hand to shield her eyes against the brightness. White spots fluttered across her vision like tiny butterflies and she blinked hard to vanquish them.

'Rosie, I'm back. Are you hungry?'

When there was no answer she walked to the edge of the terrace and scanned the lawn, an immaculate carpet of jewel-green turf that stretched forward for 200 feet and was half as wide across. A red and green tartan picnic blanket was laid out on the grass, but her daughter wasn't on it. All Lesley could see was a textbook and Rosie's headphones coiled beside it like a thin white snake.

Her insides balled instantly into a knot, a familiar, corporeal reaction to not seeing her child when she expected to. Frowning against the sun, Lesley scanned the lawn again. Where the hell was she? Then common sense gave her a nudge: if the back door was shut, then Rosie had to be inside. She'll be upstairs and didn't hear you the first time you called out.

As the knot in her stomach loosened, Lesley went back through the kitchen, into the entrance hall and took the stairs two at a time. The door to Rosie's bedroom was ajar. She hesitated for a moment, knowing how Rosie felt about her poking around her room, but something caught her eye that propelled her inside. There was a bright yellow Selfridges box open on the bed, empty apart from some scrunched-up yellow-and-white-patterned tissue paper. Next to the box was a delivery note with the previous day's date and a receipt. Lesley snatched the receipt up. It was for a pair of ballet pump-style shoes in gunmetal grey with silver, crescent-shaped toecaps.

'You are bloody well kidding me,' she snorted.

Lesley couldn't see the shoes anywhere in the room but recognized them from the receipt's description. A fortnight previously, Rosie had begged her to order them online but Lesley refused, saying the £320 price tag was far too extravagant for herself, let alone a fifteen-year-old. Despite Rosie whining that all her friends had a pair, Lesley stuck to her guns and assumed that was the end of it. Clutching the receipt, anger displaced her anxiety for a moment. Rosie must've persuaded Mack to buy the shoes instead and either thought Lesley wouldn't notice or didn't care if she did.

Annoyed at being undermined again, she barged into Rosie's en suite bathroom without knocking. It was empty, but the shower had recently been used judging by the droplets of water still clinging determinedly to the glass door. She could also detect the rich, sweet, coconut scent of Rosie's shampoo. The aroma, along with the sight of her daughter's hairbrush left on top of the sink unit, long dark hairs trapped in its metal bristles, prompted a fresh wave of anxiety and the knot in her stomach squeezed tighter.

Anger forgotten, she ran to the top of the stairs.

'ROSIE!' she screamed as loudly as her voice would allow. Then she waited, ears straining for the slightest sound. Nothing. The house remained cloaked in silence.

Her heart beat wildly as fear overwhelmed her. Rosie knew better than to go out without letting her know first. She bolted back downstairs, pulse racing. In the kitchen she checked the marble-topped units but there was no note from Rosie saying where she'd gone on any of them. On the island counter she found a small pile of letters that must have been delivered while she was out. Lesley tore through the envelopes in case a message from Rosie had got muddled up with them. Usually she steered clear of any post they received, scared of what she might find. While bills held no fear for her these days, it was a new kind of demand that gave her sleepless nights: begging letters from strangers wanting a slice of their fortune. Mack usually dealt with them so she didn't have to read the threats and the pleas from people she didn't know and didn't want to.

There was no note from Rosie in the pile, so she dropped the letters back onto the counter and checked the corkboard on the wall next to the fridge, in case Rosie had pinned a note over the photos, cards and slips of paper listing the phone numbers of her school, their GP, dentist, the golf club. The corkboard stuck out like a sore thumb against all the marble, but it was the one concession she'd wrestled out of Mack when she argued the kitchen would be too sterile if they stuck to his plan of keeping every utensil and container out of sight, and every wall bare, so as not to spoil the sleek lines of its design. It was the same corkboard from their old kitchen in Mansell and gave Lesley a sense of home in a house she otherwise hated.

There was no message awaiting her attention. Her eyes strayed to the centre of the board, to a photograph of Rosie hugging Mickey Mouse, taken when she was nine and they'd scraped together enough money to go to Disney World in Florida. Rosie's hair was shorter then, cut into a neat bob that fell just below her ears, and had yet to darken to the brunette it was now. It was one of Lesley's favourite pictures, which was why it had pride of place in the centre, with everything else orbiting it like planets around the sun. As nine-year-old Rosie beamed out at her, she began to shake. She had to be somewhere. She wouldn't just go off . . .

Then it hit her. Kathryn. Rosie's best friend, who lived next door and was in the same year at her school. What was the betting she had the day off too? Rosie had probably gone round to see her and lost track of the time.

Buoyed by the certainty that's where Rosie was, Lesley

fetched her phone from her bag, which was on the floor next to the shopping. She'd call Rosie first and if she didn't pick up, she'd try Kathryn next. She pressed her thumb down on the 'R' key, which was programmed to speed-dial her daughter's number.

Walking back out onto the terrace, she lifted her face to greet the sun as she waited for Rosie to pick up, luxuriating in the warmth on her skin. It took a few moments before she became aware of the faint echo of a phone ringing. Puzzled, she followed the noise down the terrace steps and onto the lawn. Reaching the picnic blanket, she saw Rosie's iPhone lying on top of it, the word 'Mum' and a picture of Lesley illuminated as it rang. She hung up, trembling.

Rosie never went anywhere without her phone, the thing was practically glued to her hand. She'd never leave it behind unless forced to. Lesley looked wildly up and down the garden.

'ROSIE!'

There was a rustle in the line of fir trees that stood sentry along the bottom of the garden.

'Rosie, is that you?'

As she took off towards the trees, the grass suddenly felt sticky beneath her bare feet. She stopped, surprised, and looked down. There was a dark, damp patch on the grass, like something had been spilled. She reached down and grazed the blades of grass with her fingers and, as she drew her hand back, she let out a strangled cry. The tips of her fingers were stained red and when she lifted them to her nose and inhaled, she could detect a strong metallic scent, like the smell of pennies.

Or blood.